GIRRRL FIGHT!

Milhauser reopened the paperback and resumed reading aloud. We were well into the first dumb fight scene, where Gort skewers a couple of city guards through the heart, when a glimmering of an idea came to me.

"Mr. Milhauser, that's not such a great technique. You know, the heart is an awfully small target. Also you've got to get through the rib cage. Me, I prefer to take them in the abdomen. It's a nice big soft target. Or if your employer wants them brought back alive, go after the legs and try to cripple them."

That point was engraved on my memory; I'd once had a very embarrassing discussion with Duke Zolkir after a call. Trans-Forwarded from the P.T.A. had distracted me in the middle of a swordfight so that I forgot to keep any of the thieves I was after alive long enough to stand trial.

Milhauser gave me a cold, reptilian glance. "Gort," he said, "is the world's greatest swordsman. For him to pierce an opponent through the heart is child's play."

"Oh, yeah? You just don't know how hard it is. I bet you've never tried."

"I've done my research!" he snapped.

"And I've lived *mine*. Also, it's not that easy to pierce chain mail."

"Lady, will you *stop interrupting*? I've studied the matter in great detail, and . . ."

"Let's have a demonstration, then." I stood up, wriggling slightly so as to get maximum jingle from my chain-mail corselet and divided skirt. "I'm willing to let you try and skewer me. Or are you scared to fight a girrrl?" I added with a teasing pout and another strategic wriggle.

—from "Tales from the Slushpile" by Margaret Ball

DID YOU SAY Chicks?!

EDITED BY

Esther Friesner

DID YOU SAY *CHICKS*?!

This is a work of fiction. All the characters and events portrayed in this book are fictional, and any resemblance to real people or incidents is purely coincidental.

A Baen Books Original

Baen Publishing Enterprises
P.O. Box 1403
Riverdale, NY 10471

ISBN: 1-56865-688-2

Cover art by Larry Elmore

Distributed by Simon & Schuster
1230 Avenue of the Americas
New York, NY 10020

Typeset by Windhaven Press, Auburn, NH
Printed in the United States of America

Dedication

Of course by rights this work must be dedicated to:

Melanie Marttila

without whose efforts the book you now hold in your hands would be called *The Sequel Formerly Known As Prince* or some such.

However, it has come to this humble editor, as it must to all humble editors (the three of us get together for drinks sometimes down at Binky's Oyster Bar) that there is room in a really spiffy Dedication for more than one round of thanks and acknowledgment. Therefore, in this late hour of soft purple twilight and not enough gin, I would like to append the following tribute to a woman who is perhaps this work's chief Muse and guiding light, whether she likes it or not.

Also, Binky promised the Humble Editors' Club a round of free drinks if this Dedication caused the lady in question to send him an autographed photo.

Ahem:

> Hail to thee, O Lucy Lawless,
> *Xena* actress great and flawless!
> Beacon by whom we all steer
> In this book. Wish you were here.
> Thou who art a constant charmer,

Thou who wearest way cool armor,
Thou who provest, day by day,
Women have a lot to say
Whether sword or child in hand,
Spread our message through the land!
Say to every mother's son:
"We are strong, but we're still fun.
"Do not fear us, do not hate us,
"Never, never underrate us.
"We are Women, aye, you betcha.
"Want to rile us? We won't letcha.
"Whether what we choose to don
"From Frederick's comes or Pentagon,
What we wear don't signify
"Diddlysquat, for by and by
"You will learn (as most men do)
"We're your equals. Whoop-de-doo."
So once more, thee do we hail,
Lucy Lawless, and the Grail
Of full-fledged equality
Which we hope we'll live to see.
Thou who art, in syndication,
Hope of all the female nation,
Thou whom sponsors court and coddle,
Thou, our daughters' chief role model,
Thou who play'st no girlie games
But kickest butt and takest names,
Please accept this book, with thanks
From thy sisters in the ranks.

"Bad doggerel. No biscuit!"
—Dr. Samuel Johnson (attrib.)

Contents

Introduction, Esther Friesner 1

No Pain, No Gain, Elizabeth Moon 4

Slue-Foot Sue and the Witch in the Woods,
Laura Frankos 24

A Young Swordswoman's Garden Primer,
Sarah Zettel 32

The Old Fire, Jody Lynn Nye 48

Like No Business I Know, Mark Bourne 65

A Bone to Pick, Marina Frants &
Keith R.A. DeCandido 92

The Attack of the Avenging Virgins,
Elizabeth Ann Scarborough 109

Oh, Sweet Goodnight! Christina Briley &
Walter Vance Awsten 129

A Bitch in Time, Doranna Durgin 145

Don't You Want to Be Beautiful?
Laura Anne Gilman 162

A Night with the Girls, Barbara Hambly 171

A Quiet Knight's Reading, Steven Piziks........... 196

Armor Propre, Jan Stirling & S.M. Stirling 204

A Big Hand for the Little Lady,
Esther M. Friesner 222

Blade Runner, K.D. Wentworth 237

Keeping Up Appearances,
Lawrence Watt-Evans 253

La Différence, Harry Turtledove 268

Tales from the Slushpile, Margaret Ball 279

Yes, We Did Say Chicks!
Adam-Troy Castro 302

About the Authors 303

Did You Say "Chicks"?!

Introduction

Back for more, eh?

I'm assuming you're a repeat offender, having already purchased and read numerous copies of *Chicks in Chainmail*. (Well, they *do* make excellent gifts for birthdays, anniversaries, and most major holidays.) You're certainly not a repeat offen*dee*. Despite fears and collywobbles to the contrary, *Chicks in Chainmail* did not generate a firestorm of feminist outrage, thereby proving the point I made in my previous introduction: We *can* take a joke.

Well, duh.

What *Chicks in Chainmail* did generate was a landslide of questions. These fell into two simple, easy-to-digest categories, the first being:

"How come you didn't have more stories by men?"

Well, duh *redux*, babycakes. Ye Olde Editor solicited stories from the gents, but a whole lot of the gents demurred, citing fear of being chopped up into little bitty sticky bits by the ladies. (See above: Firestorm of Feminist Outrage! Film at eleven!)

The second line of inquiry was of the sort that does an editorial body's heart a power of good, namely:

"So? Where's the sequel? When's it coming out? Real soon now? Can't you make it sooner? Would *now* be too soon? Pleeease?" This question was inevitably followed by a slew of suggestions for the sequel's title, one or two of which zeroed in on the word "broadsword." (You'll have to excuse me from making the obvious rejoinder, but I've taken a mighty and sacred oath not the use the phrase *Well, duh* again in this introduction.)

Now I'm sure you'll all recall the tasteful disclaimer concerning the title of *Chicks in Chainmail*. It was, after all, printed right on the back cover of said book. It was furthermore backed up by my own ready admission that the title was mine-all-mine, please direct any enusing feminist outrage to my doorstep. If anyone asked, I would admit with all alacrity that the title in question was strictly *Mea Culpa* City.

No one *did* ask. Fancy that. We did get a number of compliments on the title, though, and whole lot of giggling. But I digress.

As the public clamor for a sequel mounted, the good folk at Baen (Purveyors of Really Cool Books to the Gentry) had a neat idea: A Name That Sequel contest! And so, via the Internet, on the Baen Web page, all interested competitors could submit their ideas for what to name *Chicks 2*, the prize being a generous selection of Baen books. My sources inform me that Baen had been running monthly contests for a while, but when this one hit, they got *thousands* of entries. Jim Baen himself came up with the idea for the contest, and judged same. (No, he did not do it because he was afraid of what I'd come up with for a *Chicks 2* title if left to my own devices.)

I have here in my hand certain documents which reveal that the winning entry, as posted by Melanie Marttila of our good neighbor to the north (*Canada*, okay? Do I have to do everything for you?), reads in part as follows:

Comments: Ok. I'm willing to bet that Babes with Broadswords has come up about a thousand times already. I want to be a little original so here are my best three:

Hot Leather Hauberks
PMS in Plate-Mail
Did You Say CHICKS?

Thus a star was born. Our thanks to Ms. Marttila and to all who entered the contest.

We think that *Did You Say "Chicks"?!* does its sister-volume proud. You'll recognize some of our authors from *Chicks in Chainmail*, back with new tales of Women Who Slay Too Much (And the Men Who Prudently Get Out of the Way), but you'll also encounter plenty of stories from some new contributors. We hope you'll enjoy them all.

The woman warrior in fantasy fiction is no longer merely a stereotyped barbarian tough who just happens to wear a skirt instead of a loincloth. Has humor humanized a formerly two-dimensional character? I like to think so. There are still all sorts of battles for us to fight, and many different kinds of armor for us to wear.

And we're still strong enough to keep on laughing.

No Pain, No Gain

Elizabeth Moon

Meryl the shepherdess woke from nightmares in which she waded through glue on grotesquely swollen legs. She opened her eyes to the smoky rafters of her mother's little hut, and stretched luxuriously. Bad dreams make good days, Gran always said. Flinging back the covers, she rolled out of bed and burst into screams. There they were, attached to her own wiry body—the plump soft legs of her dream, and when she took a step, it felt as if she were wading through glue. She didn't stop screaming until her mother slapped her smartly across the mouth. Gran said it was the Evil Eye, and probably the fault of Jamis the cowherd's second wife, no better than she should be, jealous because *her* girl had a mole on her nose, for which she had blamed everyone but herself. Everyone knew that the Evil Eye didn't cause moles on the nose: those came from poking and prying.

Meryl's new flabby legs ached abominably for days, but eventually she was able to keep up with her flock without too much trouble. Gran had a quiet word with The Kind One, and the cowherd's step-daughter broke out in disgusting pustules very like cowpox next market-day. Meryl figured it was all over, but she still wished for her own legs back.

❖   ❖   ❖

4

Dorcas Doublejoints, justly famed dancer at The Scarlet Veil, could do things with her abdominal musculature which fascinated the most discerning clients, and resulted in a steady growth in her bank account. She had trained since childhood, when her Aunt Semele had noticed the anatomical marks of potential greatness. So now, in the lovely space between her ribs and her pubic bone, all was perfectly harmonious, muscle and a delicately calculated amount of "smoothing," and unblemished skin with one artfully placed mole—the only plastic wizardry in which Dorcas had ever had to indulge, since by nature she had no marks there at all.

She woke near noon, after an unpleasant dream she attributed to that new shipment of wine . . . until she rolled on her side and felt . . . different. Where her slender supple belly had been, capable of all those enticing ripples hither and yon, she now had . . . She prodded the soft, bulging mass and essayed a ripple. Nothing happened. Dorcas thought of her burgeoning bank balance—not nearly as much as she wanted to retire on—and groaned.

Then she wrapped herself in an uncharacteristic garment—opaque and voluminous—and sought the advice of her plastic wizard.

Mirabel Stonefist had done her best to avoid it, but she'd been snagged by the Finance Committee of the Ladies Aid & Armor Society. Instead of a pleasant morning in her sister-in-law's garden, watching the younglings at play, she was spending her off-duty day at the Ladies' Hall, peering at the unpromising figures on a parchment roll.

"And just after we ordered the new steps the court ladies wanted, they all quit coming," Blanche-the-Blade said. "I haven't seen hide nor hair of them for weeks—"

"They'll be back," Krystal said, buffing her fingernails on her fringed doeskin vest. "They still want to look good, and without our help, they'll soon return to the shapes they had before."

The court ladies, in the fitness craze that followed the repeal of the tax on bronze bras, had asked the women of the King's Guard how they stayed so trim. In anticipation of a profitable side-line, the Ladies Aid & Armor Society had fitted up a couple of rooms at the Hall for exercise classes. But unlike the younger girls, who seemed to like all the bouncing around, the married women complained that sweating was unseemly.

"What annoys me," Blanche said, "is the way they moan and groan as if it's our fault that they're not in shape. I personally don't care if every court lady is shaped like a sofa pillow and about as firm—*I* never made fun of them—" She gave Mirabel a hard look. Mirabel, a few years before, had been caught with pillows stuffed under her gown, mimicking the Most Noble Gracious Lady Vermania, wife of the then Chancellor, in her attempt to line-dance at the Harvest Ball. That story, when it got back to the Most Noble Gracious Lady and her husband, had done nothing for the reputation of the Ladies Aid & Armor Society as a serious organization.

"I was only nineteen at the time," Mirabel said. "And I've already done all the apologizing I'm going to do." She unrolled another parchment. "Besides, that's not the point. The point is—our fitness program is losing money. We're not going to have enough for the annual Iron Jill retreat sacrifice unless we get some customers. And we're stuck with all those flower-painted step-stools and those beastly mirrors which have to be polished . . ."

"Recruits' work," Blanche said.

"Yes, but not exactly military training. As for the ladies themselves—they looked pretty good at the dance two days ago," Mirabel had been on what the Guard called "drunk duty" that night, and had attributed certain ladies' newly slender limbs to her sisters' efforts in the Ladies Aid and Armor Society Shape-up Classes.

"Who looked good?" asked Krystal. No one would trust Krystal for drunk duty at a royal ball; she was entirely too likely to disappear down dark corridors with one of the drunks she was supposed to sober up. She claimed her methods worked as well as the time-honored bucket of water from the stable-yard well, but the sergeants didn't agree. Mirabel, like most of the guards, thoroughly enjoyed sousing the high-born with a bucket of cold water.

"Well—the queen, for one, and the Capitola girls. You know how thick their ankles were, and how they complained about exercising . . ." The Capitola girls had taken their complaint to the queen, who hated the women soldiers.

"Yes . . . ?"

"They were wearing those new gowns slit up to here, that float out on the fast turns, and their legs were incredible."

"I can imagine," Krystal sniffed. "People with thighs like oxen shouldn't wear that style—"

"No—I mean long, slender, graceful. Even their ankles. I wondered what the Shape-Up classes had been doing."

"But—" Blanche frowned. "The last time they were in our classes, they had taken perhaps a tailor's tuck off those thighs, but their ankles were still thick."

"They must've found someone who knows more about exercise than we do," Mirabel said. "And that's why they're not coming to our classes any more."

"Nobody knows more about exercise than soldiers," Blanche said. "There's no way to change flab to muscle that our sergeants haven't put us through."

"There must be something," Mirabel said, "and we had better find it."

They were interrupted by the doorward, who ushered in a handsome woman muffled in a cloak far too warm for the day. Mirabel perked up; anything was better than staring at those figures another moment. She had the feeling that staring at them would never change red ink to black.

"Ladies," the woman said, in a voice meant to carry only from pillow to pillow, not across a drillfield. "I understand that you have a . . . an exercise program?"

"Why yes," Blanche said, before Mirabel could speak. "We specialize in promoting fitness for women . . ."

"I have a problem," the woman said, and put back the hood of her cloak. Mirabel gaped. She knew Dorcas by sight, of course, because she had often been the official escort for visiting dignitaries when they went out on the town. She had watched the more public parts of Dorcas's performance, and had thought to herself that if the dancer were instead a fighter, she would already be in condition.

"You?" got out before Mirabel could repress it.

"Someone stole my belly," the woman said. She stood up, and unwrapped the cloak. Under it she wore a sheer, loose, nightshift . . . and under the nightshift was a soft, billowy expanse of crepey skin. "My plastic wizard," Dorcas went on, "tells me that this belly belongs to someone else, but he cannot tell whose it is—only that it's very likely she—whoever she is—has mine. He can't get mine back, until he knows where it is, and whether this was a simple exchange or something more complicated. Even then he's not sure . . . he says he's never seen a case like this before." She glared at her belly, and then at them. "This one must be over forty years old—just look at this skin!—and it has all the muscle tone of mud. How am I supposed to earn a living with this? I can't even do my usual warm-up exercises. Do you have something—*anything*—which will tone me up?"

Mirabel felt a twinge of sympathy. This was no spoiled court lady, but a hard-working woman. "I'm sure we can help," she said. "But I don't know about the age part . . ."

"I don't expect miracles," Dorcas said. "I just want something to work with, so I don't lose money while I'm hunting for the trollop who did this to me."

"You have no idea?"

"No . . . I thought of that red-headed slut down at the Brass Bottom Cafe . . . you know, the one who thinks she can dance . . ." Mirabel nodded; she didn't feel it was the time to mention that the lissome redhead was reputed to perform the famous Gypsy dance "In Your Hat" even better than Dorcas. "But," Dorcas went on, with an air of someone being fairer than necessary, "she's in better shape than this." She patted the offending belly. "If anything, she's too thin. No, I'll be looking for someone whose skirts are too loose." She sighed. "So—when's class? And is there any possibility of getting private lessons. I hate to advertise my problem . . ."

"Private lessons?—" Mirabel was about to explain that since their classes had disappeared, all lessons were private, when Blanche interrupted.

"There's a ten percent surcharge for private lessons, Dorcas . . ."

"That's all right," Dorcas said.

"But I was going to say, since you're a working woman, like us, we'll waive that fee. It's mostly for the rich ladies who are looking for a way out of the work. And we could schedule you—" She made a pretense of going through the scrolls. "Well, as a matter of fact, I could just fit you in now, if that's convenient. Or two hours after first bell tomorrow, if not."

"Thanks, ladies," Dorcas said. "Soon begun, soon done."

At the end of the table, Krystal stirred. "Mirabel, you don't suppose—?"

"Those court ladies!" Mirabel said, slamming her fist on the table. "That would be just like them!" Lazy, hated sweating and grunting for it, but wanted svelte bodies anyway. They would think of stealing, and if they had found a black plastic wizard. . . .

"I wonder if it's happened to anyone else," Krystal said. "There aren't enough exotic dancers to supply flat tummies and perky breasts and slender thighs and smooth haunches and . . ."

"All *right*, Krystal. I get the point." Mirabel closed her eyes, trying to think how many court ladies she'd seen at the dance with markedly better figures. Had any of the other dancers been robbed? "I'm going to check on some things," she said. "You stay here and let Blanche know what we came up with."

Out on the street, she headed for the Brass Bottom Cafe, and stopped short outside. For the past half-year, a poster advertising the red-haired Eulalia's charms had been displayed . . . but it wasn't here any more.

"Painting a new poster?" she asked, as she came through the door.

"She's not here," said the landlady. "But we've got Gerynis and Mythlia and . . ."

"When did she leave?" Mirabel asked.

"Are you on official business?" asked the landlady. "Or just snooping?"

"Official as in King's Guard, no. Official as in Ladies Aid & Armor Society, yes."

The landlady sniffed. "So what does the Ladies Aid & Armor Society have to do with exotic dancers? Going to learn to be graceful in armor? Or sleep your way to promotions?"

Mirabel remembered why she never came here. The landlady cooed over male soldiers, and had a rough tongue for the women. "Ma'am," she said, trying to sound both pleasant and businesslike, "information from another exotic dancer suggests that all of them may be at risk. If so, the LA & AS wants to offer protection—"

"And make a tidy profit, no doubt." The landlady glared. "Well, you're too late for Eulalia, I can tell you

that. What's been done to her is nothing short of blas-
phemy, and now you come along with your story about
protection. It wouldn't surprise me a bit if you didn't have
something to do with her troubles, just trying to scare
all the girls into buying into your protections—" She
advanced from behind the counter, and Mirabel saw that
she held an iron skillet almost as broad as her hips.
Mirabel beat a hasty retreat. So much for that . . . but
if she could find Eulalia, the redhead might have more
sense.

Back at the Hall, Eulalia was slumped at the table with
a bright-eyed Krystal. Eulalia's midsection had gone the
way of Dorcas's, although the replacement wasn't quite
as big. Krystal had already signed her up for classes.

Eulalia knew of two other dancers so afflicted. "And
my cousin, who just came to the city last week, told me
about a plague among shepherd girls out in the Stormy
Hills. Only with them it's not bellies—it's legs. Those
girls do have gorgeous legs, from all that running and
climbing."

Mirabel looked at the map on the wall. "Umm." She
remembered that the court ladies had made a Progress
into the Stormy Hills a few weeks before. Or so they'd
said. She had thought at the time it was an odd place
to go for a Progress in late winter—or at any time, really.
There was nothing up in the Stormy Hills but bad
weather and sheep . . . and of course the herding
families that tended them.

They had insisted on being escorted by male soldiers,
too. At the time, Mirabel had thought that was just
another of their ladyish attitudes, of which they had
many. Most likely, they were still in a snit about the
exercise classes, and thought that the women soldiers
would make them walk too fast. They had refused to
go on hill walks as part of their fitness program.

"Something is definitely going on here," Mirabel said.
"We'd better have a word with our favorite plastic

wizard." He was still on retainer for the Society. And much as she sympathized with the dancers, if even half of them suddenly needed fitness classes, it would help make up the deficit from the court ladies' defection. They might come up with enough for the Iron Jill retreat sacrifice after all.

The first break in the case came from one of the girls who was in the pre-recruit class. She arrived full of giggles, and Blanche had to speak quite sharply to her.

"Sorry, ma'am," she said, her shoulders still shaking. "It's the older ladies—my aunt Sapphire and her bunch. You know they didn't like coming down here to your fitness classes—"

"I know," Blanche said.

"Well, they've got a dancing master now, calls himself Gilfort the Great, who claims that the female body is especially suited to fitness by dancing. They wear these little silk tunics—some of them even wear just a bandeau on top—and carry long scarves and ribbons and things, and while the court string quartet plays in the corner, they hop about—but never enough to sweat."

"But surely they're . . . er . . . losing condition?" Blanche asked.

"Terribly, at first," the girl said. "Then—overnight, almost—the dance began to work, and they were gorgeous. If I didn't want to learn swordplay, I'd go there myself." She caught the look on Blanche's face and stepped back. "Not really, of course, ma'am, but—it is kind of pretty. In its own way."

"But what were you laughing at, then?"

"Well . . . on my way here, I passed behind the potted palms, and the dancing master was telling them all they had the bellies of belly dancers, and the legs of shepherdesses, and the arms of apple-pickers. And I just couldn't help thinking, 'and the brains of boiled cabbages' . . ." Her voice trailed off, with the quick mood change of adolescence. "I don't know why I thought it was so funny, really, just—most of the time they'd be horrified if anyone called them dancers or shepherdesses, and they were lapping it up, giving him these soppy grins."

"Apple pickers," Blanche said. "I never thought of apple pickers."

"If they're wearing those two piece outfits, we can certainly recognize our bellies," Dorcas said. Eulalia nodded. "But we don't want them to see *us*."

"That's what potted palms are for," Mirabel said. "Those giggling girls are always hiding behind the potted palms; you can wrap up to look like chaperones."

She herself looked like nothing but what she was, one of the Royal Guard. She took up her stance at the door of the third-best ballroom, sent Dorcas and Eulalia behind the potted palms, and waited.

The queen glared at her when the ladies arrived. "Where's Justin? He's our regular guard!"

"Justin's sick this morning, your majesty," Mirabel said. Justin knew when it was healthier to be sick; he'd said he was tired of watching them fancy ladies misbehave in front of a foreigner anyway.

"Well . . . I certainly hope he gets well soon."

The queen's body looked, Mirabel had to admit, about half the age it had at Prince Nigel's wedding. Trim waist, slender taut legs. Too bad nothing had improved her sour face. The other ladies twittered and cooed as the dancing master appeared, leading the musicians.

He was a handsome fellow, in his way. He had broad manly shoulders, a deep chest, a light step, and white teeth in a flashing smile. In fact, if not for his thick gray hair, he would have seemed the picture of handsome, rugged, young manhood.

Gray hair? She looked again. Smooth-skinned, no wrinkles; hands of a man no more than thirty, if that. Some people grayed early, but their hair usually came in white, and his was the plain gray of stone. Wasn't there something about gray hair on a young face, some jingle? She was trying to remember it when she noticed that the fronds of one potted palm were shaking as if in a windstorm, and strolled casually over.

"Be still," she said as softly as possible. With the wailing of the dance music, she didn't think they'd hear.

"That—!" Whatever Dorcas had been about to say, Eulalia smothered successfully with a scarf.

"Get her out of here," Mirabel said. "We'll sort this out later."

What Dorcas had seen, it transpired, was her belly— unmistakeable not only for its singular beauty and talents, but for its mole.

"But she's letting it go," Dorcas wailed. "It's been two weeks, and I can tell she hasn't done a full set of ab crunches yet."

"I saw mine, too," Eulalia said. "And that woman must eat eight meals a day. The hipbones are already covered."

"You *could* use a little more contouring, dear," Dorcas said to her, too sweetly.

"*You* could use a little *less*," Eulalia said, not sweetly at all. They looked like two cats hissing; Mirabel slapped the table between them.

"Ladies. This is more important. Can you identify your bellies well enough for a court?"

"I'm sure," Dorcas said, eyes narrowed.

"And I," Eulalia agreed.

The judge, however, insisted that they had no proof. "A belly," he said firmly, "is just a belly. There is no evidence that it can be moved from one person to another."

"But that's *my* belly!" Dorcas said.

"Prove it," the judge said.

"That mole—"

"According to expert testimony, that mole was so placed by plastic wizardry, and Lady Cholerine has a receipt from a plastic wizard to show that she paid to have it put there. You, madam, do not have a mole . . . or a receipt."

"Of course *this* belly doesn't have a mole," Dorcas said. "It's not mine. *You* should know—"

"Keep her quiet," the judge said icily, "Or I'll have her in contempt!"

Dorcas glared at the judge, but said no more.

Afterwards she exploded to Mirabel. "He knows perfectly well that's my belly—he's had his tongue on that mole, when it was where it should be, on me. He just doesn't want everyone to know it."

Feristax, the LA&AS wizard, smiled when Mirabel told him about that fiasco. "If we can get them into court again, I think I may have something."

"What?" asked Mirabel crossly. She was not about to humiliate herself again in court.

"It's a new concept." She had heard that before. "After that problem with the random access storage device—"

"When you got our tits mixed up," Mirabel said. "I remember perfectly. Go on."

"Well . . . there's always been exchange, you know. Someone with red hair wants yellow hair; they get the red hair spelled off, and yellow hair spelled on. That puts red hair into the universe, and removes yellow hair. So if someone else wants red hair, there it is—it's an exchange, not a creation. But it's not a theft or anything."

"Like money," Mirabel said.

"Exactly." The wizard beamed at her. He had found the right level to communicate. "But, as with money, there are thieves. If there's no red hair—just for an example—"

"YES!" said Mirabel, stroking the haft of her knife; the wizard blenched and went on hurriedly.

"If there's no red hair, then they'll do a universal search for an individual with red hair. And contact a local practictioner—sometimes not even a licensed wizard!— to spell-steal it away, where it becomes available to the person who wanted red hair."

"What color hair does the victim get?" Mirabel asked. "Or do they just snatch them bald-headed?"

"Gray, usually," the wizard said. "Very few people ask for gray, except of course wizards." He patted his own storm-colored hair, so incongruous with his youthful unlined face.

"Aha!" That was the thing about gray hair. *Gray hair on young visage, might be a wizard.* "He had gray hair, that dancing master. And he was young."

"Did he have a badge of license?" asked Feristax, touching his.

"Not that I saw," Mirabel said.

"Then, if he *is* a wizard, I'll bet he's a renegade. Do you know his name?"

"Gilfort the Great," Mirabel said.

"Sounds like somebody's apprentice pretending," Feristax said.

"Dorcas's belly isn't pretending," Mirabel pointed out. "So—what is this new technique that might get everyone's legs and bellies back where they belong?"

"Ah. That. Well, the incidence of what we call 'prosthetic theft' has been rising in Technolalia, and they've developed a way to trace the origin of exchanges through something known as a virtual watermark."

"Watermark? Like on silk?"

The wizard laughed deprecatingly, but with a nervous look at the dagger in Mirabel's hand. "In the . . . er . . . flesh. Another possibility is a transunion connectivity spell, which allows the individual who originally inhabited the body part to control it while under the spell."

"Huh?"

"You mean," Dorcas said slowly, "that if we used this spell, and I wanted to, I could make my belly dance on someone else's body?"

"Precisely," the wizard said.

"I like it," Dorcas said, with a dangerous smile.

Half a dozen shepherd girls and apple-pickers, plus Dorcas and Eulalia, stood in a row on one side of the courtyard, and the court ladies they accused stood on the other.

"You can't make us undress in public!" the queen's first lady-in-waiting said, her cheeks mottled red.

"That isn't necessary at all," Sophora Segundiflora said. "All you have to do is stand there and watch." She had been invaluable in getting the court ladies there; they were no more inclined to disobey the new chancellor than the women soldiers had been when she was the senior member of the LA&AS.

"Watch what?"

Sophora said nothing, but waved to the musicians.

At the wailing of the pipes minor and the nose-flutes, Dorcas and Eulalie began to dance "In Your Hat," their limbs describing fluid arcs and volutes, though their still-reluctant substitute bellies came nowhere near the movements required.

"This is disgusting," the queen said. "In *our* court—!"

"Well, it's not up to standard," the king said, without taking his eyes off the dancers, "but worth watching nonetheless . . ." The queen glared.

The observers gasped suddenly. Two of the court ladies were jerking spasmodically, clutching at themselves with both arms.

"What's wrong with them?" the king asked. "Are they sick?"

"They're trying to dance," Dorcas said, without missing a beat of the dance. "That's my belly—"

"No, that one's mine," Eulalia said. "It's got that little extra spiralling wiggle . . ."

Some of the guards had begun to make enthusiastic noises, and now they burst into cheers: "Eulalia! Eulalia!" and "Dorcas! Dorcas!" as they pointed at their candidates for those respective abs among the court ladies twitching and writhing.

Sophora held up one massive hand, and the courtyard fell silent.

"It's clear," she said, "that terrible things have been done to your people, your majesty, but I don't believe that these ladies had evil intent."

"Ha!" muttered Mirabel.

"I believe they were deluded by the enchantments of a black plastic wizard—" A gasp of horror swept the yard. "—who posed as a dancing master." She pointed.

The dancing master attempted a fast reverse shuffle, but found himself up against the bronze breastplates of a half-dozen Royal Guard, several of them women.

"See his gray hair!" Sophora thundered. Several small bits of masonry fell from the castle walls and shattered on the pavement. "That is no natural hair—that is a wizard's choice." She waved, and Feristax came forward. "You all know this wizard, long a respected practitioner in our fair city. Let him now examine this imposter."

"He's not even a licensed wizard," Feristax said confidently. A night's work on the informational plane of the multiverse had located the man's own identity codes. "He's a supplier of magical components for *real* wizards . . . In fact, he is the fellow who shipped me that very imperfect random access storage device which caused so much trouble last year. I've been told that he lost his franchise with several reputable manufacturers recently, that he has been suspected of tampering with network traces and virtual watermarks."

"It's all a stupid conspiracy!" the man—dancing master or black plastic wizard—yelled. "It's just a way to keep down the talented and let lazy fools like you—" He stopped, a dagger at his throat.

"Gilfort, he calls himself," Feristax said. "If it please your majesty, I can reverse his iniquitous and illegal spells."

"Perhaps in a more private place," Sophora murmured in the king's other ear. "These ladies have been foolish and gullible, but you would not want to humiliate them . . ."

"Oh . . . no . . ." the king looked bewildered, his habitual expression. The queen glared at Sophora, who smiled back.

"For your own benefit, your majesty," Sophora said.

At the end of the speedy trial—the judge, with Sophora leaning over his shoulder, did not delay proceedings in any way—all body parts were restored to their original owners, except for one: a shepherd girl in the Stormy Hills, slowed by Lady Alicia's flabby legs, had not outrun a wolf. Alicia got to keep the girl's legs, but had to send 20 gold crowns in compensation . . . or choose to spend the summer herding sheep for the girl's family. She sent the money.

Because the Ladies Aid & Armor Society had incurred unreasonable expense in acquiring exercise equipment for the court ladies to use, the ladies had to agree to three classes a week for the next year, by which time the step stools, mirrors, and showers would be paid off.

And, as a special reward for their discovery and solution of the problem, the Ladies Aid and Armor Society received a unique contribution to their annual Iron Jill retreat.

Thirty sulky ladies in silk tunics stepped smartly up and down the flower-painted stools to the rhythm of mallet on shield, and the brusque commands of the LA&AS top instructors.

"Aaaall right, ladies . . . and FIVE and FOUR and THREE and TWO and ONE . . . now the other foot and EIGHT and SEVEN and SIX and FIVE . . ."

"Let's see those smiles, ladies! A proper court lady always smiles!"

"More GLOW, ladies! Let's see some GLOW!"

Gilfort the Great, Dancing Master to the Royal Court and (privy) black plastic wizard, sat on the rock in the middle of the clearing, hands bound to the ring thereon, and wished he had never left Technolalia. Twenty-seven of the women of the Ladies Aid & Armor Society had shown up for the annual Iron Jill retreat, at which (so he had heard) terrible rituals were performed. No male had seen them and lived to tell about it.

The corresponding male-bonding ceremonies he knew about, having been taken to the fire-circle to drum and dance by his father and uncles. He had been forced to down raw fish and even a luckless mouse; he had run naked through the meadows and woods screaming the worst words he knew.

But this? Around the rock, the women swirled, seeming to ignore him, as they stripped off armor, kicked off heavy boots, and unpacked provisions for the first night's dinner.

"Hunting tomorrow," said the tall muscley one who had prodded him in the back most of the way here. "Tonight's the last night for this boughten stuff."

"Yeah . . ." breathed the others, and then they did look at him, and he wished they hadn't.

"By the time we find and kill, we'll be ravenous," a perky blonde said, growling a little. "If the Mother sent us off as usual, we won't really have much of a supper tonight . . ."

He could see that they didn't. Bread, cheese—not much of it—some pickles. To his surprise, they brought him a pot of stew, and urged him to eat his fill.

"It's all right for *you*," they said. He wasn't hungry, but the menace of their swords suggested he had better obey, and he forced the stew into a reluctant belly. Later, he hardly slept—it was amazingly difficult to sleep on a hard rock, with his hands tied, and the knowledge that twenty-seven hungry women had plans for him the next day.

Just as the first gray light seeped into the clearing, the women began to wake. First one then another stopped snoring, rolled to her feet, spat, and let out a loud yell. Birds took off, wings clapping, in all directions. Twenty-seven yells, in everything from lyric soprano (with a fine vibrato) to tenor, and afterwards they all looked at him again.

"Now didn't that feel *good*?" asked the brown-haired brawny one. "Let's do it again, and this time let *all* the tension out. Iron . . . JILLLL!"

Twenty-seven women yelling Iron Jill at the tops of their lungs sent all remaining birds thrashing out of the trees at high speed, and in the echoing silence afterwards he could hear distant hoofbeats becoming ever more distant.

"Ahhh," said the brawny one, stretching. "Usually we can't do that right away, not if we want any breakfast, because it scares the game, but this time . . ." She smiled. Gilfort the Great fainted.

When he woke up, he was being slapped gently enough by several of the women.

"Oh goodie! He's awake," said the perky blonde.

"Now, what you have to do," said another, "is this: we point you away from the castle and city, and then you run. And then we chase you."

"Such fun," said the blonde one. "You've had more food and a good night's sleep." He tried to protest, but his mouth was dry. "We give you a flagon of water and some sandwiches; we have nothing. You might well outrun us; we might have to subsist on nuts and berries. Even beetle grubs." She giggled.

They sounded so cheerful. They sounded so confident.

"It's just—" Strong fingers clamped his cheeks; bold eyes stared into his. "Don't come back this way, Gilfort. I shouldn't warn you, not really, but—the rules are, if you come back this way, we can do it all. Tear you. Slowly. Limb. From. Limb. We like it, but you probably wouldn't. So best to run *that* way, Gilfort. We do it quickly, when it's a running prey."

"Like a deer," one of the others said. "Prey, not sacrifice."

"Attaboy," said the brawny one, and they hauled him to his feet, attached the water flagon to his belt with care, tucked a packet of sandwiches in his pack, and unbound his hands. "That way," the brawny one said again. "We give you ten Iron Jills head start."

Gilfort staggered away, the stagger quickening to a run as his body found a use for all that adrenaline. Behind him, the first roar of the women: "Iron . . . JILL!" He leapt over a fallen log, raced down a little slope, splashed through the creek. "Iron JILL!" Up the slope on the far side, slipping in drifts of leaves, fingers desperate for a grip on branches, rocks, anything . . . on up, and up, a long gentle slope that offered his burning lungs no rest. "Iron JILL!" Down again at last, gasping, sweat burning his eyes, to another creek too wide to jump. He plunged into icy water, slipped on a rock and fell headlong. "Iron JILL!" came faintly from behind.

Hours later, sore, panting, blistered, stung, scraped, scratched, and very aware of his great good fortune, he emerged on the Hacksaw Pass road back to Technolalia. He had heard the strident call over and over, in those desperate hours, sometimes nearer, sometimes farther away, as the crazed pack of starving warrior women sought their lawful prey. But now he was at the road, and once over the pass he would be safe. Forever safe, because he certainly wasn't ever coming back.

✧   ✧   ✧

The crazed pack of starving warrior women, sprawled at ease on the soft spring turf of the clearing, burped in varying tones. A couple of hours after they'd sent Gilfort off, the supply cart arrived, complete with the festive foods appropriate to an Iron Jill retreat, including the molded chocolate statue of the Mother of All Women Warriors. It had taken the last coin in the treasury, but without the sacrificial chocolate, it just wasn't an Iron Jill retreat.

They were full now, overfull, and hardly able to sing along when Dorcas and Eulalie (honorary inductees to the rites this year) struck up the traditional Hymn to Iron Jill:

> "Women must cook, so women can eat
> Is mostly the rule,
> But *not* on retreat . . .
> Too much fat, and too much sweet
> Should be avoided
> But *not* on retreat . . .
> An iron woman's no fun at all
> So eat your fill and have a ball.
> Food in the belly
> Love in the night
> Chocolate today
> Will make all right."

When night fell, the flames leaped high, and when the vision for which they had come, Iron Jill herself, walked among them . . . they rolled over and ate another piece of chocolate. Iron Jill smiled at her daughters, and her daughters smiled back.

Slue-Foot Sue and the Witch in the Woods

Laura Frankos

I reckon you all know the story of Pecos Bill, the greatest cowpuncher that ever lived. Most of those tales mention Bill's beautiful bride, Slue-foot Sue, and explain jest what happened on their wedding day, when Sue tried to ride Bill's horse, Widow Maker. Sue was a mighty fine rider, but Bill didn't want her riding that wild mustang. No one alive, 'ceptin' himself, could ride that cayuse. But Sue, being a woman, had made up her own mind. Not long after the preacher had read the vows, Sue grabbed Rat, Bill's pet rattlesnake which he used as a quirt. She packed Bill's bowie knife, then, still in her wedding dress, she ran to the corral and leaped into Widow Maker's saddle. Bill was right: he bucked Sue clear up into the sky. She ducked her head under the moon, came back to earth, where she bounced on her steel bustle and went back up again. She bounced and bounced for days.

Some folks say Bill had to shoot pore Sue, to keep her from starving. Others say he pulled her down with his lariat. But this here is what really happened:

Sue wasn't jest bouncing up and down in the same spot, she was bouncing in an easterly direction, and

24

a-goin' so fast, even Bill couldn't catch up. She bounced clear across the country, leaving big round circles in farmers' fields that shore puzzled the sod-busters. She left a big gaping hole, chockfull of nothin', smack in the middle of Washington, D.C., but that didn't faze the folks there much: they're used to that sort of thing. She flew clear across the Atlantic and Europe, too, afore she managed to stop in the middle of a dense birch forest, deep in the heart of Russia. She saw those thick tree branches and knew it might be her only chance, so she hauled out Rat. Gripping his tail, she flung his head towards the trees. "Bite, Rat, bite!" Sue shouted, and Rat bit. When Rat bit something, it stayed bit.

Sue swung gently to the ground and told Rat he could let go. She tied him around her waist and gazed at the silvery birches.

"Well, Rat, we are in a pickle," she said. "Better find out how to git home. My, but Bill is gonna be mad at me. And on our wedding day, too. I'll have to find some way to settle his fur when we git back. Trouble is, it's mighty dark."

Then Sue heard the sound of hoofbeats. A handsome man in fine, white clothes on a lovely white horse came into view. "Excuse me, pardner," Sue called, "but I'm a mite lost. Could you tell me . . ."

Without a glance at her, the white rider galloped past and into the sky. "Well! I never!" Sue exclaimed. "I'm not in Texas any more, that's for certain. These folks need a lesson in manners! Oh, well, here's the sun's coming up. Maybe I can find a road."

As Sue trudged along, she saw a small house in the distance. As she drew nearer, something peculiar flew overhead in the same direction. At first, Sue thought it was the biggest, blackest buzzard she'd ever seen. But it was an old lady, riding in a kind of pot, a-steering with a rounded stick.

It hovered above Sue and the woman looked down. "Are you a naughty Russian girl?" she croaked.

"No, ma'am. I'm a good, red-blooded Texan girl who's plumb lost. And on my wedding day, too."

The old woman shook her head, her matted hair flying. "Be off with you!"

"I'd like to be off, ma'am. But I haven't any notion which way's the Hell's Gate Gulch Ranch. That's my husband's outfit."

"I gain nothing by helping you."

Sue muttered. "Selfish, that's what these foreign types are. Any Texan would help a stranger in trouble with asking twice." She raised her voice. "What if I make it worth your while?"

"Eh? How can someone like you be of any use to me, Baba Yaga, queen of all witches?"

"I could do some chores, mebbe. If that's your place up ahead, it's a real sight. Clean the yard? Tend to your stock?"

"I make the wicked Russian children I find in the forest do such deeds before I pop them in my stewpot." Baba Yaga stared hard at Sue. "But you are full of spirit, and I have been sorely bored of late. We shall contest one another, you and I. Two out of three skirmishes. If you win, I shall show you the way home. If you lose, you shall give me all your valuables."

All Sue had was her wedding dress, the bowie knife, and Rat. Bill would be awfully steamed if she lost them, but she had to chance it if she was to git out of that woods. "Okay," she answered.

"Follow me," said Baba Yaga. She flew to the hut, which was the queerest place Sue ever did see. The fence was made of human bones and on every post was a skull, with eyes a-glowing red. The hut itself was standing on four giant chicken legs.

Baba Yaga called out, "Izbushka, izbushka, lower your door to me." Darned if the legs didn't squat so they could enter!

The inside of the hut was as cheery as the outside. There was more dust than on the Staked Plains. Human hands crawled around on the floor, but that didn't bother Sue none. She grew up among tarantulas.

"I shall test your skills at magic," said the witch. "Can you best this?" Baba Yaga reached in a cabinet for a bottle. She swigged it, and shrank to the size of a mouse.

Sue thought hard. "Here's the only way I can change my size." She unfastened that darn spring bustle that got her into this mess.

"Not good enough!" squeaked Baba Yaga. "I have won this contest." She zooped back to her proper size and examined the bustle. "Curious. Now, for the second skirmish, we shall fight, steel to steel!"

Sue gripped the bowie knife, which was the original knife old Jim Bowie gave to Bill's ma when Bill was a tyke. She watched the witch, who waved her hand at a cobwebby wall. Suddenly, a sword flew off a shelf and whizzed around Sue's hair, neatly slicing off one of her purty red locks.

"Behold my enchanted blade, which cuts of its own power," said Baba Yaga.

Sue was a mite surprised by the magic sword, but she figgered nothing could stand up to Bill's bowie knife. That knife was so sharp, its shadow could shave Bill's whiskers. As fast as the magic sword was, it wasn't a match for the bowie knife's shadow. The shadow sliced right through that sword, which fell to the ground with a clank, clobbering one of those little creepy hands.

Baba Yaga screeched.

"My round, fair and square," said Sue, sheathing the knife. "What's next?"

The old witch stomped to her cabinet and pulled out a wooden staff. Leastwise, Sue thought it was wooden until she thumped it on the floor. Then it turned into a wild, hissing snake with real nasty yeller eyes. "You are mine, Texassss girl," hissed the snake in a voice sort of like Baba Yaga's with a lisp. "There is no defensssse."

Well, Sue didn't even have to unhitch Rat. As soon as Rat saw that other snake, he unwound himself and slithered to battle. Of course, nothing packs stronger poison than a Texas rattlesnake, unless it's Pecos Bill's spit. Rat made quick work of Baba Yaga's magic snake. One bite and that Russian reptile was stiffer than he had been when he was impersonating a wooden staff. The old witch was so shocked, she couldn't say a word.

"Two out of three," said Sue. "Now show me the way home."

"It is too late," Baba Yaga grumped. "Wait until morning."

Sue helped fix supper and the witch gave her a blanket. Sue went to the barn, preferring the company of the goats to those crawly things in the house. She was sweeping the stalls when another rider, all in black and on a coal black stallion, trotted into the sky. He ignored Sue's calls, too. Darkness fell as Sue complained, "These are the rudest folks on earth!"

"Slue-foot Sue!" squeaked an animal at Sue's foot. Rat hissed at it, but Sue hushed him. The critter looked like a walking pincushion. "Baba Yaga means to kill you," it said. "Tonight she will fly to gather herbs for a potion to overcome your magic."

"That's downright dishonest. I won fairly. What can I do? Do you know how to get out of these woods?"

"Baba Yaga's hut will take you wherever you wish," said the animal. "If you can make it lower its doors after she leaves."

"I can do that. I'm much obliged to you, even if you are pricklier than most cactuses."

"I'm not really a hedgehog. I'm an enchanted prince named Dmitri."

"You're a kindly soul. That's good enough in my book."

"Actually, I'm a Romanov, not a Gudenov. Could you please drop me off at the Great Gate of Kiev when you escape?"

"I surely will."

At midnight, when Baba Yaga blasted out of her hut like a cyclone on the prairie, Sue and Dmitri crept past the nasty fence of bones. Sue remarked, "My Bill's come up with something called barb wire. Works much better than a bunch of shin bones."

Dmitri sniffed the air. "Hurry! Hurry!"

"Here goes: Izbushka, izbushka, please lower your door to me."

The chicken legs didn't budge for a second, then they slowly squatted. "Whew!" said Sue. "I didn't think that would work."

"You confused it when you said 'please,' " said Dmitri. "Baba Yaga never does."

"My mama raised me right," said Sue. "Okay, you old izbushka, please take us to Kiev and then straight to Hell's Gate Gulch." The hut began running, *thump-thump-thump*, through the woods. Sort of like a stage-coach with big feathered legs and ugly yeller feet where the wheels oughta be.

People in Russia say that when Baba Yaga found her house missing, you could hear her scream from Siberia to St. Petersburg. But Sue and Dmitri, bein' mighty tired, slept through her tantrum.

That hut could run, all right. Unlike a horse, it didn't need to stop to eat and rest. It wasn't long before they reached Kiev.

"Thanks for your help," said Sue. "I'll remember you every time I see a porky-pine."

"Thank you, Slue-foot Sue."

The only thing that slowed Sue down was the Atlantic Ocean. Being part chicken, that hut didn't want to go in the water at all! But it was trying to carry out Sue's orders. It was in a real fix, scraping and scratching at the edge of Norway. That's where those things they call *fjords* come from.

Sue figgered out what to do. Remember, she could ride any critter on earth, exceptin' Widow Maker. Why, Bill first saw her riding a catfish down the Rio Grande with jest a surcingle. So Sue made herself a lariat out of reindeer hide, there bein' no proper cowhide, and lassoed a whale, which wasn't any bigger than a Texas catfish. When it was nicely broken, she coaxed the hut up onto its back.

By and by, they reached the United States and the hut set off again, *thump-thump-thump*. It was almost dinner when they reached the ranch. Sue went to find the cook, Bean Hole.

"Miss Sue!" Bean Hole yelled. "Bill will be powerful happy to see you!"

"Oh, I don't doubt it, but oncet he's done kissing me hello, he's still gonna be mad because I rode Widow Maker. I gotta do something to settle him down and I know jest the thing, but I'll need your help."

A little later, Bean Hole rang the bell for chuck, and Bill and the boys filed in. Bill's hat near did fly off his head when he saw his Sue sitting there. Jest as Sue said: after that first joyful reunion, Bill started scolding.

She held up her hand. "Wait, honey. Tell me all that later. I don't want your supper gettin' cold." Before Bill could say anything, she disappeared and returned with Bean Hole, carrying a huge tray.

"That's the biggest durn drumstick I ever did see!" said Bill. "Where did you come by that?"

"I got it specially for you," Sue said, looking as sweet as molasses. "And there's three more waitin'."

"Mmmm," said Bill, munching away. "Nothing beats a Southern gal's fried chicken."

"And I brought back a nice new shed, but it will take a heap of cleaning."

"Um-hmm."

Bill et up those drumsticks and was in a mighty good mood. But how did Sue keep him that way? Well, remember, they never did get to celebrate their wedding night. Not that you'll read about *that* here. There are certain things that oughta remain private-like.

A Young Swordswoman's Garden Primer

Sarah Zettel

"Do you know who I am?" Allys pulled herself up to her full height. Her flaming, auburn curls brushed the shop's low ceiling.

The shopkeeper did not look impressed. "You are Allys the Bold, Swordswoman of the Mystic East, daughter of Ferra, daughter of Ganelle d'Rainier, or so you said. But I am Drethwain, Shopkeeper of the First Order and in the name of my family honor, I will not sell you a magic item for less than thrice what I paid for it!"

Allys sighed. She could, of course, kill him and take the rusty hauberk in the corner, but she was wearing her business clothes. When people hired a Genuine Barbarian Swordswoman, Deeply Versed in Secrets-of-the-Mystic-East, they wanted brass and jewels, jingly gold chains, flowing purple cloaks, gleaming headbands holding back flaming tresses, a sword that would split an elephant, and daggers tucked into all manner of exotic locales. This town was crowded, and after her personal business was concluded, she would almost certainly need to find work again. Allys saw no point in letting the paying customers, or even the potential customers, down.

"This world is all illusion anyway," Chi Xe, her surprisingly young Wise-Old-Master had told her. "Work with it."

The problem was, the outfit was an absolute bitch to try to fight in.

Allys sighed and gave the hauberk on its crooked stand an appraising look. It was almost solid rust. Cobwebs trailed off its short sleeves.

If that oracle was pulling a fast one, I'm going to drop her into that sacred well head first. She had paid the skinny, doe-eyed woman for three answers to three questions; Can I regain my ancestral castle? What aid do I need to accomplish this? Where do I find it? The answers: yes, wear the magic armor of the D'Rainiers, and the northwest corner of Drethwain's Shoppe of Ancient Mysteries, had led her here to confront this greasy man with definite feelings about his standing in the world.

She held up her hand. "Far be it from me, Sir, to seek to undo any man's honor." She planted her shiny, black boot on a creaking chair, and pulled out one of her daggers. With a grunt, she twisted the biggest scarlet "jewel" out of its pommel and tossed it to Drethwain.

"That is the ruby Tharyx, taken from the dagger that killed the dragon Quaraeth the Most Fell. Whosoever carries it cannot be deceived by any lie or illusion of man, monster or god."

"Is that true?" Drethwain squinted at the stone.

"As far as you know."

He gave her a gap-toothed smile. "The shirt's yours. As is."

She did manage to get him to wrap it up first. She had no intention of getting rust and cobwebs smeared all over her glittery work clothes. She slung the bundle across the rump of Grandiere, her huge, white (naturally), gelding (symbolism is important) and swung herself into the saddle. She cantered out of town, waving her sword and singing fierce-sounding nonsense she'd picked up from Chi Xe. You never knew who was watching.

Her camp was three leagues from town in a wooded dingle. She dismounted Grandiere, removed his tack, let him drink, wiped him down and tethered him where he could graze.

Her horse attended to, she took care of herself. She stripped off the gold-and-emerald headband, and the auburn wig underneath it, rolled the huge sword in the flashy cloak and disengaged the uncomfortably located daggers. In a few moments, she was her wilderness self; short black hair, leather travelling clothes, hunting dagger at waist and short sword in easy reach near the campfire.

Feeling relaxed and ready for real business, Allys unwrapped her purchase. She picked it up by the shoulders and shook it. The mail links rattled like a dry cough. Flakes of rust and dust showered down. It looked battered, decrepit, and decidedly unmagical. It also looked too damn small for her.

Gritting her teeth, Allys slid the hauberk over her head. To her surprise, it fit perfectly. She brushed the links down. They rattled.

Take it off.

Allys froze.

Take it off, now!

Allys laid her hand on her sword. The voice wasn't coming from any direction. It was just there.

Take this damn shirt off and go away, hear me? I don't need any cheapskate barbarian wannabe getting blood on me!

Allys's heart beat hard at the base of her throat.

No, I am not the shirt. Flaming fig-trees, you've got an untidy mind up here. Where'd you get all these . . . zenny? . . . ideas? Oh, the Mystic East. Foreign Parts, I should have known. No, I said that already. I am not the shirt. I am the woman stuck in the shirt. Damn family

*curse. Blessing Aunt Didi said, but she liked waving
swords around. Every woman of the d'Rainier line who
died in battle takes a turn in the shirt, giving her skills
to the current wearer. Well, I was battling the* mentha
veridis *in the kitchen garden when the lights went out,
and now there are no more women in the D'Rainier line
and I'm stuck in here!*

As quickly as she could, Allys yanked the hauberk off.
She dropped the shirt onto the ground. It rattled for
a moment, then lay still on the dirt and dead leaves.

Not good. Not good at all.

The prophecy said she needed to be wearing the
D'Rainier armor to retake the castle. Maybe that cranky
soul in there knew a secret entrance, or some special
weakness that belonged to the Evil Wizard who occupied
the place. Problem. Cranky obviously did not like being
stuck in the hauberk and needed the death of another
D'Rainier woman to get her out. There was one, too.
Whoever that was in there obviously didn't know that
Ganelle D'Rainier had escaped and fled the country
when the castle was taken over. Ganelle wandered with
the horse nomads of the Mystic East and had a daughter
who had a daughter, who had come back and bought
the armor from Drethwain. What if the spirit in the rusty
chain mail decided to get Allys into a battle so Allys
could die and take her place?

This was very, very not good. Especially since Cranky
in there could obviously read Allys's mind.

Allys did not believe in trying to outwit prophecies.
Wizards, daemons, Evil-Gods-from-the-Foulest-Regions-
of-the-Seven-Hells, yes, but, prophecies, no. They always
came back to bite you on your more intimate leathers.
She was told she needed to be wearing the D'Rainier
armor, so wear it she would. But how could she keep
Cranky from rummaging around in her head and getting . . . ideas?

Allys sat down cross-legged and regarded the hauberk.

She turned over every thing Cranky had "said" to her, trying to work out its implications.

Untidy mind you've got . . . Cranky'd complained. Did she have a tough time reading more than one thought at a time? Could be. Could Allys bury her identity and true purpose behind one of Chi Xe's interminable Mystic Philosophic Verses about about falling blossoms and the sound of silence? No, too complicated. She didn't know what else she'd have to be doing while Cranky was rummaging. Something simpler. An image. Flying monkeys, or green polar bears, something like that.

Allys closed her eyes. "D'Rainier," she said, and visualized flocks of monkeys with eagles wings swooping and swarming all over a noonday sky.

"Who are you?" Polar bears. Bright emerald ones sitting on ice floes.

She practiced calling up the crowded images with every variation of her ancestry she could think of until well after full dark. At last, she rolled the hauberk in its cloth wrappings and herself in her woolen traveling cloak.

It took forever to get the damn monkeys out of her head so she could sleep.

Allys woke up as soon as dawn's light squeezed through the trees. She breakfasted, and repacked her gear onto Grandiere's back. She picked up the roll she'd made of the hauberk and weighed it in her hands.

Put it on now? Or wait until I get closer to the castle? Allys chewed her lower lip. She had technically already begun her quest for the castle, so the prophecy was ticking. Besides, if Cranky knew anything, it'd be better to find out about it right away so she could formulate her plans.

She slipped the hauberk over her leather jerkin.

You again? I thought I'd had the last of you. Go away. Leave me alone.

"No," said Allys through clenched teeth. "I need your help."

Then you're sore out of luck you fool girl . . . What is your name anyway? Hi! Where'd all these monkeys come from?

Allys smiled softly.

Ragwort and jasmine, get these things away from me! I have never felt anybody with such a bizarre set of thoughts! Are you sure you're sane?

Allys shrugged.

You don't even know. Huh. Figures. The sane ones give the damn shirt back after the first night. Great. I am stuck in the mind of a crazy woman with a monkey fetish. And a thing for a tall man with a funny name.

Allys started. "How'd you know about Chi Xe?"

He's all over the place in here. You're fighting him, you're learning bad poetry from him, and there's some dreams over here, Missy, that I bet you'd never tell your mother about.

Allys felt her face begin to burn. She knew exactly which dreams Cranky had found. She'd had one just last night where . . .

Shame on you!

Allys clenched her teeth and concentrated.

Hi, there! Hey! Down! Watch it! What the hell are all these green things!

"Listen, I need your help . . ."

What now? Home? What are you doing going to my home? And where do you get off calling me Cranky? I am Lady Genevive D'Rainier!

"All right, Lady Genevive, I am going to take Castle D'Rainier from the Evil Wizard who's occupying it."

For a moment nothing but silence occupied Allys's head. *You are mad. That wizard killed my entire family while they were sleeping. I was the only one awake. I had a new formula I wanted to try out . . .* For the first time Allys felt something other than resentment flow from the presence of Lady Genevive, and that was fear.

"This is nothing," Allys told her mental passenger. "I've fought Evil-Gods-from-the-Foulest-Regions-of-the-Seven-Hells . . ."

Yuch! You fought those ugly . . . Green gods of morning, they do make a loud splat when they fall don't they?

"I can handle one wizard."

But why . . . GET THESE MONKEYS AWAY FROM ME!

Allys concentrated on monkeys in quiet groups of ones and twos, listening to what she was saying.

"Evil Wizard's encircled the castle with a forty foot tall wall of thorny hedges to keep back attack." She concentrated on her memory of the place. No guards, either human or monstrous, just these iron-colored branches twisted around each other as if a blacksmith had beaten them into shape. The wind that had ruffled Allys's hair and Grandiere's mane did not stir the branches at all, instead it whistled between the sword-sharp, foot-long thorns.

Datura Stamonium Grandiose. The thought sent a breath of awe through Allys's mind. *They aren't native to this area. What is it doing here?*

"Standing between us and the castle." Allys had already broken two swords and an axe trying to get through the thorns. She could have sworn the wind's whistling had turned to laughter as the axe handle splintered in her hands.

Are you out of your mind? An axe for a Stamonium Grandiose? *Why didn't you just gnaw on it?*

Allys raised her eyebrows. "So, what would you suggest?"

Salt. Lye. Dig down and seed the soil with it. If you want to kill the plant, kill the roots. You're just like Aunt Didi. The world begins and ends on the point of a sword. No idea what's important or beautiful.

Salt? Lye? "I was hoping there was a secret tunnel

used by some lord to sneak out to his paramour or other exploitable weakness."

What kind of books did your mother raise you on? You think you need something other than salt to break up a fairy charm? That there's a demon weed that can stand up to the rendered fat of an unbaptized baby cow?

"Well, when you put it that way . . ." Maybe she should have tipped the oracle a little better.

Prophecy? You went to an oracle to find me? Why . . . Oh, god, what are these green things you're so fond of? Can't you control them? They stink!

Her strategy was working well enough to rattle Cra . . . Lady Genevive, but, Allys still needed her help. Probably. A partial answer as a friendly gesture wouldn't hurt. Probably.

"I want to settle down and see if Chi Xe wants to get married . . ."

I should hope so after some of what you've . . .

Monkeys, monkeys, monkeys . . .

Back off you chittering ninnies . . .

"Good castles are expensive and hard to come by. I want to raise little barbarianettes without having to be pregnant on horseback. I want a home to come back to after a long, hard fight."

Allys waited for the snide commentary, but none came. *Someplace you can be yourself,* was all she heard.

"Yes," a sigh of relief at being understood escaped Allys.

My garden was a place like that. The yearning in the thought was so strong, Allys felt tears sting her eyes. Her mind filled with a picture of a serene place: beds of fragrant flowers separated by grassy paths and lovingly trimmed hedges, brilliantly colored rose trees, a carefully tended area for utilitarian vegetables and herbs. Allys had never longed for such a place before, but now a wave of need washed over her, a palpable desire to feel earth on her hands and smell green scents all around her.

Allys had been seeing the wizard as an impersonal

adversary, merely in the way. Now, she felt stirrings of very personal dislike inside her. How could anybody take all that from Lady Genevive? It wasn't as if she didn't have Aunt Didi hounding her all the time to put down that hoe and pick up a sword . . .

Allys sucked in a breath. "Lady Genevive, what are you doing to me?"

Not a thing. If my feelings are leaking over into yours, it's not my fault. You're the one who insisted on wearing the fool shirt.

Allys pulled the hauberk off, and held it tight in both hands for a moment. Having somebody separate sitting in her head and sniping at her was one thing, but feeling their feelings, that was something else again. That could get dangerous. What if this gardener's emotions effected her judgement in battle? What if she got sidetracked watching the daisies grow instead of battling the Evil Wizard who was unfairly holding onto her inheritance? What if she stopped being herself and let Genevive get her killed? Allys shuddered. She stowed the hauberk with the rest of her gear, embarassed to see her hands shake. Maybe it was already enough. Maybe she'd already gotten what she needed . . .

No, that was dangerous thinking. She'd probably get through the thorns and be strangled by some flesh-eating vine that Genevive knew how to dismember. No. She'd put the chain mail back on when she got closer to the castle.

Maybe I don't have to do this, whispered a treacherous voice from her heart. Unfortunately, it was entirely her own. *Maybe I can can just turn around and go home.*

No. Her hands curled into fists. *I promised.* What Allys had told Genevive was true, as far as it went. She'd left out how she'd sworn to her grandmother on her deathbed that she'd take the castle back and return their family to their native land. She couldn't go back on that. Not ever. No matter what.

I just have to trust the polar bears and monkeys to do their job. She mounted Grandiere. *After all, I was never fool enough to think this was going to be easy. Was I?*

By mid-afternoon, Allys and Grandiere trotted through the abandoned grasslands at the foot of the Twilight Mountains. A fat bag of salt and a clay jar of lye now hung beside Grandiere's saddle bags. Once, these meadows had been tended fields, but now the forest and bracken stretched out to reclaim them. If Allys squinted hard, she could see the remains of burned out cottages being overtaken by the weedy onslaught of nature. The only sounds were the wind through the grasses and the thump and jingle of Grandiere's passage.

I'm going to have to advertise for some Humble-but-Hardy-and-Picturesque-Rustics to come resettle this place once I'm done.

The mountains loomed closer and Castle D'Ranier's spires separated from their shadows, but the castle's walls did not. Twisted, needle-tipped fingers of darkness wound around them, obscuring them from sight.

The castle's appearance changed very little as she drew closer. The leafless, serpentine branches took on a glint in the fading sunlight and the background silence deepened, throwing the whistle of the wind around the foot-long thorns into sharp relief. Allys hated the fact that there were no guards. It smacked of overwhelming arrogance. Some swordswomen preferred their opponents that way, but not Allys. She liked them scared of the world. The scared ones didn't think as much.

Allys reined Grandiere to a halt and unloaded the salt, lye, spade and hauberk. She tethered the horse loosely to a thorn branch.

Allys picked up the hauberk and with a deep breath, slid it back on.

Oh, you're back. I thought you'd changed your mind.

"Not yet." She took up the spade, looked around for a likely spot at the base of the thorn hedge and shoved the blade into the ground.

Gods, you've got no idea how to dig, have you?

Allys's hands jerked. Her eyes bulged as she watched her hands take a fresh grip on the spade. Her leg raised and stepped her foot down on the blade, causing it to bite deep into the earth.

"What are you doing?" She demanded as her arms heaved the earth aside and bent to dig another spadeful free.

Getting this done before New Year's. Stop squirming.

"You can't just . . ." Allys clamped her jaw shut. Her hands and back worked the spade. The hole deepened as if by magic. Apparently Lady Genevive could, and was, and was doing a very good job. The earth melted from around roots that were even thicker and more twisted than the branches.

"So, there you are, you little daemons," Allys heard her voice say. "But not for long." Her body turned around and picked up the lye jar.

"You could at least leave me my voice," muttered Allys as her hands pried the lid open and dumped a healthy portion of the stinking, grey-white substance onto the exposed roots, following it up with a healthy shower of salt.

Fuss, fuss, fuss. Allys's boot stamped the mixture down into the soil around the roots. *But, have it your way.* Allys felt her withdraw to the back of her mind. *Now, this is going to take a week or three before results . . .*

A crackling noise drifted down overhead. Allys, in control of herself, jerked her head up. A sickly pallor spread over the iron colored thorns. One by one, they crumbled into fine ash and dissipate on the wind.

Or not.

The pallor spread to the tangled branches. Allys jumped backward just in time. A whole section of hedge crashed to the ground, revealing the ivy covered walls of Castle D'Ranier.

Allys grinned.

Home? What do you mean home?

Uh-oh.

What promise? Your grandmother? What is going on?! Allys swirled a flock of monkeys around the memory of her grandmother. But this time it did no good. Lady Genevive swore and swatted in the back of her mind, but she plowed straight through the fantastic animals.

Ganelle's granddaughter! she shrieked. *Why didn't you . . .You thought I'd . . . How COULD you!*

Genevive's shock was so cold and so bitter, Allys shivered.

"I'm sorry. I was afraid you'd . . ."

I know what you were afraid of! I'm sitting up here with it. If you think that little of me, you can just take this shirt off right now and send me back to my junk shop.

Allys laid her hand on her sword and concentrated on the way in front of her. She stepped through the hedge's ragged gap. "After I've taken the castle, I'll be glad to, Lady Cranky."

Ungrateful . . .

Allys called up the green polar bears and sent them after Genevive. Lady Genevive cursed and punched at them. *Ill-mannered, snippy, distrustful . . .*

Allys made the bears hold their ground so she could keep most of her concentration on the way in front of her. It was still quiet. The castle walls had been well maintained, leaving no chinks in the mortar, and all the windows were on the second storey. The ivy stems were only as thick as her index finger, no good for climbing. She'd have to find a door.

"Oh, do allow me to welcome you in." A man's voice spoke from thin air.

The ivy tendrils pulled away from the wall with a noise like someone tearing lettuce. They swooped down around her. Allys gripped her sword hilt but the vines yanked her hand away.

"Genevive!" she cried as the branches snaked around her neck and shoulders.

What am I? Your servant? You dragged me out here so you could use me and stick me in a closet somewhere and didn't even want to tell me what happened to my sister!

"I'm sorry!" The ivy spun Allys around, passing her from tendril to tendril. She dug her boot heels into the ground, but it did no good. The ivy just held her tighter and heaved her from one branch to the next.

Yes, I can tell.

Ahead of her, a mass of ivy thrust itself between the hinges of a side door and heaved it open. It hoisted Allys into the air and tossed her inside. She sprawled belly down on cold flagstones. The door slammed shut behind her.

Gasping, Allys hauled herself to her feet. She stood in a narrow hallway. Torches flickered in sconces on the wall, revealing bright tapestries and clean floors. The Evil Wizard obviously liked his comfort.

And if Lady Genevive was a crouching, sulky presence in the back of her mind . . .

Sulky! How dare you!

. . . At least she still had her sword. She drew her weapon smoothly.

"Now, now, we can't have any of that in here." Allys's limbs froze.

"Oh, not again."

Genevive's touch had been natural, like being a well-worn pair of gloves. This was a grip of iron squeezing each of her muscles in turn and forcing her to move. Her arm sheathed her sword and her legs walked, carrying her through the arched spaces of the great hall, up the sweeping staircase and into one of the tower rooms.

Wizardly chambers were pretty much all of a kind. Books, braziers of bright coals, glassware, unidentifiable lumps of vegetable, animal, and mineral all giving off smells that made you realize you didn't want to know what they were. The Evil Wizard stood in the center of the room where Allys couldn't help but get a good look at him. His black velvet robes were inscribed with silver Mystic and Mysterious symbols that gleamed in the sunlight streaming through the broad windows. He wore a matching black skull cap and his pointy beard reached almost to his waist.

Allys scanned the symbols and groaned. She'd thought he was just one of the Evil Wizards. His robe showed him to be one of the Truly-Mercilessly-Evil-Bretheren. She wished he'd give her back control of her body so she could kick herself.

"Ah-ha!" His eyes widened as he looked her up and down. "Allys the Bold! I am so glad you have come. Let me introduce myself. I am Ligera, Master of Wizardry and Master of Life Itself."

Her tongue, at least, seemed to be working. "Catchy title."

He ignored her. "And how nice of you to have brought your great-aunt."

???

"Lady Genevive. I am delighted to make your acquaintance." He bowed deeply. "It distressed me greatly to find the D'Rainier armor and your unfortunate soul had vanished from my castle. But now that Allys has so graciously returned you, it is my earnest wish that you be set free."

Free? He'll set me free?

"Lady Genevive, no, he's a liar . . ."

"Tush. Do not talk back to your elders." He flicked his long fingers. Allys's hand smacked her own cheek. "I shall set you free. Your niece shall die battling me and take your place in the hauberk. After which, I shall have her melted down and reformed into a shape more useful to me."

But . . .

"Raise your sword, Allys," the wizard's cold blue eyes glittered. "You shall fall on it before we're done."

"No!" Allys bent all her will to keeping her hands at her sides. "I am Allys the Bold! You cannot control me!"

"Nothing living escapes my control! Behold!" He swept his arm out. Allys had no choice but to look.

NO! screamed Lady Genevive

Outside the window lay a nightmare. Glowing fungi like pustules or corpse's hair covered the ground, overshadowed by mounds and masses of sick, waxy creepers. Shrubs with black stems and flapping red leaves writhed and squirmed in what had once been flower beds. Closest to the castle grew thick plants like corn, but under the leaves, Allys saw the snapping jaws of Great Danes and leopards.

"These are my creations! I control all life! All life!"

"But not the dead!" A wave of warmth surged through Allys's blood. Allys's sword was in her hand. Her legs moved, carrying her toward Ligera. Her mind was filled with Chi Xe's teachings. Never go straight for the wizard, go for his apparatus. Allys's foot kicked at the nearest table. It toppled over. Glass and paraphernalia smashed to the floor.

"No!" screamed Ligera. "You will halt! You will obey me!" A green-black aura of power glowed around his hands. A bolt shot out and caught Allys in the chest, slamming her against the wall. It hurt, but didn't bother her in the least. She pushed herself forward and caught the edge of a brazier filled with coals. She tipped it over onto the alchemical wreckage.

Any suggestions, niece? Fresh flames arose, green, purple, blue and black.

Oh, do continue on. You're doing just fine.

Thank you.

Ligera howled as if the flames licked at his flesh. His hands waved. A gigantic serpent, spitting fire and venom rose from the flames. Genevive gave the body a grin and Allys concurred. This was familiar territory. The serpent slithered forward.

Now, this looks particularly instructive. Genevive pointed to a particular set of memories and put the Bounding-Doe-of-Morning technique into play.

Oh yes, that's a good one. Allys landed behind the snake. The sword buried itself in the back of the snake's head with a satisfying, meaty thunk.

Genevive swung the body around and raise the gory sword high. *Does this really work?* She asked as Allys's mouth sang out the words to the Ancient Song of Self-Defense, which, Chi Xe said mainly translated into "Got'cha, got'cha, got'cha!"

Ligera fell back. He was beginning to blister and pant a little.

Probably had his life force stowed in a box somewhere among all that junk. Very common conceit among evil wizards.

Really? What interesting things you do learn in the Mystic East.

"Lady Genevive! Why do you attack me? I offer you freedom!"

Fury burned through Allys's blood. "You killed my garden! That *was* my freedom!"

Ligera laughed out loud. "Oh, is that all? I am Master of All Life! I will give you another garden! A better garden! Any garden in the world!"

"Really?" breathed Genevive. "You could do that?"

Genevive! No!

He waved his blistered hand "Any garden in the world! Indeed . . ."

He looked down at where Allys's sword had plunged into his chest up to its hilt, up along her arm and into her eyes.

Genevive smiled. "Any garden in the world needs fertilizer."

The Old Fire

Jody Lynn Nye

Mev clenched her hands together to keep from jumping into the arena after her daughter. At ten years of age, Kitra was so small, so delicate, Mev worried about her getting hurt. But this was the final examination. If Kitra was ever to prove herself, this was the time. The little girl stood at one side of the sandy expanse, taking big breaths that made her shoulders heave under the oversized leather tunic. Suddenly, she sprang into action.

"Eeee!" Kitra shrieked, bearing down on her opponent, her little sword raised in both hands above her head. "Take that! And that!"

The other child, taken by surprise, put up a poor fight. In no time at all, Kitra was holding the bigger boy down with her foot. She pointed the blunted sword at his throat and shrilled, "Surrender or die!"

"That's my girl," Mev said, brushing a tear from the corner of her eye. The child not only looked just like her, with her broad, pointed chin and eager black eyes, but she was a chip off the old tilting block. Mev was so proud she felt her heart would burst. From the hubbub coming from the judges' enclosure near the barrier, she thought it was a sure thing that Kitra would

48

be accepted for junior combat training. The other
parents, most of them farmers, millers, coopers and
shopkeepers, gathered up their disappointed young-
sters, and went back about their business. They
weren't really cut out for the warrior trade. Kitra, on
the other hand, had just proved she was fit to carry
on a proud family tradition. Mev might not be in the
adventuring business any more, but she was giving the
world its next heroine.

Something rapped Mev on the shoulder, and she
turned around, hand automatically reaching for the
sword at her belt. Secondary responses took hold in a
moment, telling her that there wasn't a sword there—
hadn't been for years—and that knocking the head off
one of her neighbors was frowned upon. Instead, she
folded her arms and stared balefully at the man who
had touched her. He was a stranger.

"And who the blazes are you?" Mev asked.

"You're Mev Grayshield?" The man asked, looking her
up and down. "I was expecting someone more . . ."

Mev put her hands on her hips. True, those hips were
somewhat more rounded than they'd been when she was
part of the attack force that brought down the Fendarian
citadel ten years before, but nevertheless, they were an
integral part of the same woman. True, her mass of
thick, frizzy dark hair pulled back with a leather thong
was shot with white, and her muscular arms were getting
a little flabby around the triceps, but how did anyone
dare to doubt her identity?

"More what?" she snarled, sticking out her jaw. It was
still an impressive jaw.

The skinny, bearded man backed up a hasty pace. He
wasn't so much to look at, himself. Probably fifty, ten
years older than Mev, a hand's-breadth shorter, and he
had the pathetic, pale complexion of a man who went
outside only when he had to. He blinked watery blue
eyes at her.

"I'm looking for you, because I need to hire a fearless adventurer."

"Still fearless," Mev said, with a shrug, "but I retired years ago."

The man pursed his lips in amusement, and looked past her at the arena, where Kitra was receiving the congratulations of her companions, the ones who could still walk.

"I see," he said, "but I need you. I am the Wizard Folminade. I serve the Duke of Kelevlund."

"Sorry, friend. There are other qualified warriors. I keep in touch with a number of my old colleagues. I'll give you their names. Ask around. Try the bars in any big city." She started away.

"No," the man insisted, hurrying after her. Mev sized him up with an eye. He was puny. If he got fresh, she could break him in two with one hand. "It's you I need. There's gold in the deal for you. Lots of gold. A lifetime's worth."

Mev eyed him with speculation. It was the first thing he'd said that had made any sense. "All right. Come back to my house and we'll talk."

While Kitra sat on the floor and played siege with her dolls, the stranger outlined his mission.

"Haste is an issue," he said. "You are familiar with the Amulet of Zgrumn?"

The very word hummed with power on the air in the little cottage. Mev felt the stirring of old campaigns in her memory. She nodded.

"I never came across it, but I've heard of it. It'll heal your ills if you can pronounce its name correctly. Changed hands a hundred thousand times. Is that the one?"

Folminade nodded his head. "The duchess is very ill. The healers can do nothing for her. I think it's a magical malady, but my degrees are in divination and strategic defense, not medicine." He looked around the cottage. It wasn't a half bad place, Mev had to admit, although she was a lot better at razing houses than building them. The door had a defensive barricade that barred it in three places when it was shut. The window shutters had spikes on the outside. Even the chimney had a steel grate seven feet from the top so an intruder could get partway in, but couldn't get out without giving her plenty of notice. Only twelve feet underground she could tap a hidden stream. The secret well head was concealed under the clothespress at the foot of her bed. The wizard's soggy gaze returned to her. "We need the amulet."

"Why come to me?" she asked.

"Litfusia has it."

Litfusia! The name sent a chill up Mev's back and down through her belly. She hadn't heard that name in years.

"You're the only person who's ever gone into the white dragon's cave and come out alive," Folminade said. "You can find your way quickly, more quickly than anyone else." Before she could protest, he grabbed for her wrist. "Please. There isn't time for anyone else. His Grace is counting on you. And there's the reward to think of."

Well, Mev could take or leave the nobility, but money was money. The gold from her first withdrawal from Litfusia's hoard was about gone, and there would be combat school fees to pay, not to mention the fact Kitra was growing out of her kiddy armor; and Mev's two older children, one in wizardry school, one in service to the local lord, always needed something. She hated above all things to tell them they couldn't have it. A ducat didn't go as far as it used to.

"All right," she said.

Folminade's eyes shone like torches under glass. "You won't regret it."

✧   ✧   ✧

Had it really been twenty years? she asked herself as she cleared away brush and fallen rocks from the mouth of the hidden tunnel that led to the maze of airways far below the dragon's eyrie. Folminade stood by with his arms crossed, watching. Useless bag of bones. The mountain, Litfusia's mountain, loomed above them, dark, rocky and barren, but it didn't seem as terrifyingly high as it had the first time. The paths she had thought as so dangerous and precipitous before were not especially perilous, in light of twenty years' experience. She welcomed the chance to put her first enterprise in perspective, to see if after all this time she really had deserved respect for it, or not.

"Hurry," Folminade said. "It'll see us."

"No," Mev said, calmly. "It'll see the lunch we left out, first. Two nice bullocks and a wild sheep bleating its head off should ring the dinner bell for any self-respecting firebreather."

With a lever formed from a fallen tree branch, Mev pulled away the last rock blocking the entrance. A foul, cold blast of air slapped her in the face. This was it, all right. She wished she could bottle *Eau de Dragon's Lair*. She'd make a fortune. Anyone who wanted to keep out intruders could spray it all over the outside of his or her house. Unfortunately, it wouldn't keep out tax collectors or beggars. Greed seemed to be the only thing that made you immune to it. Mev put her arms through the straps of her pack, and lit the first of the pitch-soaked torches she'd brought along. Rule two of the barbarian's handbook was that one never lasted long enough to get you out again. Rule one was never carry anything too heavy to keep you from running for your life.

Folminade watched her impatiently. The wind whipped his robe around his skinny legs.

"Well, get on with it," he said.

Mev took a deep breath and prepared herself to climb into the tunnel. Folminade sat down.

"Aren't you coming with me?" she asked.

"Heavens, no!" he said, peevishly. "I'm not an adventurer. I'm a scholar. I've told you what to look for. That's all you should need."

"Useless bag of bones," Mev repeated sourly to herself. She thrust the torch into the entrance.

The flames burned away the cold and with it, much of the rotten smell. Thick swags of spider web and ghostly white moss hung in her way. Mev chased them upward into thin black cinders with the torch. There was a temptation to clear the tunnel to the walls, but the housewife part of her retreated farther into her mind the higher she climbed.

The white dragon was an old adversary, almost the first one Mev had ever faced, as a young and foolish warrior maiden. Litfusia had been very young, too. In retrospect, Mev was grateful for the advantage. It had had very little experience in dealing with humans. Luckily for her, because she had been so green, she'd made all the mistakes the older warriors had warned her not to, which would have gotten her killed by an older and savvier dragon.

With the help of old charts and a guide, Mev had sneaked into the lair through the maze of twisting natural tunnels that served Litfusia as a cross-ventilation system. While it slept off a heavy meal (thoughtfully left out for it beforehand by Mev) she had gathered up a bag of treasure.

The white dragon had collected an astonishing assortment of valuables in a relatively short career. Mev had become so engrossed in picking out the best of the loot that she stopped listening to the dragon's breathing. The sudden silence was what had made Mev look up at last. Never let it see you, the others had said. But if you do, look hard. It'll be the last thing you'll ever see.

She would never forget as the two of them stood eye to eye, just for a split second. Sometimes she still saw it in her dreams: the white face, almost as tall as she, with its glowing red eyes, backswept fringed ears, and catfish whiskers around the toothy, pointed jaws. On her paws and on the joints of its huge white wings, Litfusia had red claws longer than Mev's hand, but it didn't need them as weapons. That image was burned into her memory forever, then the dragon's pupil slits narrowed, and it hauled back its big head to inhale. Mev ran for it. As the warrior maiden had fled the cavern, the dragon gave her a fire blast to remember her by, burning her leather tunic right off her skin. Mev hadn't been able to sit down for a month. She still had the scars.

Mev had also forgotten to arrange with her guide to stay long enough to guide her back. She had become damned sick of dragging the heavy bag after her by the time she found her way out, though the sum was worth the trouble. Her house, her clothes, and even the sword hanging against her spine had all been paid for by that one great adventure. The escapade gave her bragging rights among bigger, older, and more experienced warriors of both sexes, and made her reputation.

Dragons had long memories and short tempers. The fact that Litfusia would certainly try to kill her if it recognized her was all part of the game. Litfusia was older and wiser, but so was Mev. She meant to earn that reward, if she could. After all, it wasn't easy to reenter the workplace after taking off years to raise a family. She'd always meant to, once her last child was old enough to take care of itself. Mev never thought that the opportunity would be offered to her so soon.

With a good dollop of cash in hand, Mev could look forward to a very comfortable old age. She could be picky about her next mission, if she took any at all.

When she had been young, she had had to take what she could get. There'd been no thought of retirement benefits for old female warriors. There hadn't been any thought of retirement benefits for old *male* warriors, either. No one thought warriors could look forward to retiring at all. The job had a nearly 100% mortality rate, if you did it right. Few survived to grow old. Such a thing was considered to be a failure at one's profession. Fewer still thought of providing for their dotage. Mev herself hadn't ever considered the future.

She gained perspective entirely by accident, after she and the warrior general Ricasso had fallen into each others' arms after a long, hot battle in the fifth year of her career. Neither of them ever thought about the possibility of pregnancy. Swordfighting was generally considered to be effective as a means of contraception. Afterwards, it was too late for her to do anything but wear loose tunics. The Stork Goddess was on the way. At last, Mev had had no choice but to retire and go back to her village to await her offspring. Suddenly, she had to consider the needs of someone else, who had call on her services before kings or dukes or gods.

Motherhood was an unprecedented situation in her experience. Mev had to admit that even though she'd found adventuring hard, there was nothing harder than raising a family. Babies were helpless. They couldn't do anything for themselves. When you screamed at crying infants, they sobbed harder. They couldn't assist in a pitched battle. All of them spat out the healthy diet of hardtack and cabbage water she had lived on for years. They liked soft beds and little animals.

No invasion she had had to withstand, no siege she'd lifted, no monster she had battled, no forlorn hope she'd defended had ever pushed her so close to despair. She was ready to defend her children to the death. This was good when they needed her to dispatch nightmare monsters and wild animals, but she hadn't the slightest idea how to deal with back-yard spats between her little ones and the children who lived in the nearby cottages, or the parents of those children, who kept a healthy distance from the storied swordswoman who lived in their midst like a phoenix in a chicken coop. (She was pretty certain that was why her elder daughter had chosen to enter wizardry school in a village half a day's ride away; none of the boys there would ever have seen her mother bring down a running hare with an ax.) All that came with hard-won experience. She had a lot more respect and sympathy for other women, who hadn't an iota of defense training, yet still stood between their little ones and armed enemy soldiers.

Ricasso had come through her village a few times over the years on the way to a battle or a siege, his visits resulting in a couple more children, and further delays to Mev's return to work. The last time she'd seen him was nine months before Kitra's birth. She heard that he had died gloriously in battle, exactly the way he'd have wanted to go. Pity. He'd have enjoyed this mission, a straight grab-and-run, with the possibility of additional loot, plus a guaranteed reward for success. It was almost impossible to fail. She could almost picture herself as that fierce, young warrior maiden who had helped to overrun citadels, force city gates and kill a thousand enemies. Onward, she urged herself, climbing steadily up through the narrow tunnels toward the cave of the dragon.

Whew! The way hadn't been this tight when she was a lass. The gussets that her village blacksmith had had to put up each side of her chainmail jerkin were put to the test in the last few yards before she reached Litfusia's cave. No way to deny it: she wasn't the sylph she'd been. She had already had to abandon her bronze breastplate at the last turning. Mev tossed her torch out before her and left her pack behind in the last wide bend. With a mighty wriggle, she emerged in a low stone chamber like an anteroom. On the other side of a crack in the stone was the hoard, and somewhere in its midst, the amulet. She guessed it had taken her three or four hours to make the climb. She was out of breath. Her torch flared and guttered from the breeze coming in Litfusia's front door. Mev hid it on the inside wall so its flame couldn't be seen from the other room. She put her eye to the opening.

The air was warm, telling her the dragon was at home. Had Litfusia eaten up the bait she had left out on the path, and come back to sleep it off? Litfusia was there, all right, but not sleeping. Mev spotted it under the mouth of the cavern that led out into the upper air. The dragon was writhing around, bellowing and blowing streamers of flame from its sharp-toothed jaws. Litfusia seemed to be fighting with another, much smaller red dragon. The great white beast's rough hide glowed like a moonstone.

Good, Mev thought. It'll be too busy to deal with me. She crept through the crack, onto the heap of treasure. Mev looked around her in dismay. By the Raven God, why did tax collectors never visit beasts? At the current high rate of tax in the kingdom, this lot would have been reduced by 40% at least! It was going to take Mev forever to sort through it. Litfusia's fight couldn't last much longer. It seemed as though the white dragon was winning. The wee beast, less than a tenth her size, was on the ground, flopping around limply. Mev stared at it in disbelief. No! Litfusia wasn't fighting. She was giving birth.

Mev had never thought of the beast as having a gender, let alone that it was female. Dragons of both sexes were equally long-lived and greedy. Female, she mused, as she turned back to the heap of treasure. Think of that. Huh. Well, thank the gods for useful distractions.

While the dragon was busy, Mev set about looking for the amulet. Folminade had given her a full description. She wanted a six-foot staff with snakes wound around it and its name engraved on the collar of the big, round, blue gem that was set on the top. That was surely what had attracted the dragon's attention in the first place. Litfusia liked blue. No sapphire hoard or cobalt mine a thousand miles in any direction was safe from its—*her*—marauding. Staying in the shadows, Merv crept over piles of necklaces, goblets, heaps of gold and gems, jewel-encrusted weapons that shifted under her or poked her as she passed. What a load of garbage! Did the dragon collect just *anything* because it was gold? She slid down a dune of treasure with a noise like a thousand pans falling downhill. Thank gods the dragon was making too much noise to hear her. Mev tripped over a thin shape that for a moment filled her with hope. It turned out to be a herald's trumpet. Why had Litfusia stolen a herald's trumpet, of all stupid things? Not that Mev herself had any particular use for heralds; if people didn't know your name, having someone blather it all over the landscape wasn't really going to do much for your reputation. Maybe the poor bugger had looked tasty. Mev gulped, hoping Litfusia wouldn't fancy a middle-aged swordswoman.

In a low dip, she came across a full suit of blue armor for a very tall man. Mev was afraid to open the visor and see if the original owner was still inside. The quantity of bones and partial skeletons strewn about the cavern told her that plenty of unsuccessful adventurers had essayed Litfusia's hoard since she'd been there. Maybe she *had* had a run of beginner's luck the first time. Sweat ran under the bronze cap on her head and dripped into her eyes and down her neck. Her palms were wet and slippery under the heavy gloves. For the first time, she felt pulled down by the effects of age and a less energetic lifestyle than she'd led as a warrior. She must be careful.

Mev heard a change in the sounds behind her. The

dragon was crooning and keening horribly, flames licking about her head. Had it spotted her? She flung herself over the piles of treasure into a crevice of the rough stone wall, pulled her cloak over herself, and huddled down. Mev gasped for breath. She was more out of shape than she had thought. Merely pulling a plowshare, chopping wood, and hauling bags of grain was no substitute for real exercise. Mev vowed to start a toning regimen the moment she got out of here. Time was running away.

The noises got more desperate. Mev moved aside a fold of cloak to see what was happening.

Litfusia was going crazy. She was crooning, bending her long scaly neck down, then throwing it up in the air to keen. Her wings flapped aimlessly, driving dust and ashes around the cavern. Her pale hide had lost all its luster. Mev picked herself up just a little to see the dragonet. It wasn't moving. There was no flame coming out of its open mouth. It wasn't breathing. Litfusia was bending over it, emitting soft cries of distress. What would Ricasso do in a case like this? She could almost hear his voice saying, "Kill them both, while you have the chance." But Mev couldn't do it.

The red dragon chick lay still, and Litfusia was powerless to help it. Mev felt something she never thought in a thousand lifetimes she would feel for any dragon, and this one in particular: compassion. The baby's pilot light hadn't lit. Mev knew a lot about dragons, and had studied this species in particular before her first trip. Firebreathers were *born* breathing fire. If they didn't flame in the first few minutes after birth, they didn't make it.

Litfusia kept trying to breathe into its mouth, but her flame was too big. She'd toast the chick, it was so small. She was too panicky to control herself. Mev felt sorry for the little one, and, in a sense of perfectly reasonable self-preservation in a mind so clear it amazed her, decided the last thing the kingdom needed was an insanely bereaved mother dragon cannoning around the landscape. Mev wriggled over the treasure heap and made for the tunnel where she had left her torch.

She came back with it in her hand, walking openly into the center of the cavern. The noise alerted Litfusia, who was facing her way when she emerged. The dragon pulled her head back, eyes wide, the whiskers around its mouth standing out rigid. Mev's mouth dried with fear as she stuck her chin out defiantly at her old enemy.

"Yes, it's me, you old blowtorch," she croaked, her throat tight. All her muscles ached, and her hand trembled disgracefully. "I've got this. Your baby needs help." She tried to approach the unmoving infant, but Litfusia put her head between it and Mev. The dragon shot out a tongue of flame, and Mev jumped back. She glared.

"Time's a wasting, you stupid mobile furnace! Move aside!" Mev shouldered the huge head away, and jumped for the infant dragon before Litfusia could try to flame her again. She knelt beside the body and took the small head in her right hand, prying open the mouth with her thumb. Dammit, but those little teeth were sharp! The knuckle-long canine pricked right through her best gauntlet.

Mev brought the torch close and tried to get the flame into the small mouth. Even that weak fire was too big. She couldn't break the ember apart, and there was no useful fuel in the cavern; Litfusia had burned it all up over the years. Mev cast around for something smaller. The trumpet! Perfect! As the dragon's head followed her like a giant weathervane, she clambered back to get the long tube.

The trumpet was a yard too long, but it was soft gold. With her sword, she whacked off the bell and turned it up into the dragonet's mouth like a funnel. She shoved the torch ember into the bell and blew the flame down

the infant's throat. Mev felt ridiculous, breathing flame
to save the life of a dragon. The Spider God would have
loved the irony. There was a hiccup and a smell like
burning leather, then a blast of flame roared out the
trumpet's end. Hot! Mev dropped the tube and waved
her fingers to cool them. The infant dragon opened its
eyes. They were yellow-gold, like amber with the sun
behind it. They fixed on her, and the chick trilled
adoringly.

With an indignant howl that sounded like jealousy,
the big dragon pushed Mev away. Litfusia crooned over
the wriggling infant like any mother, picked up a clawful
of meat from somewhere and dropped it in front of the
infant. The baby fell to hungrily, gurgling fire as it
cooked and ate its first meal. Mev, remembering the
trumpet and the suit of armor, wondered what the meat
was, and felt a little sick.

Litfusia suddenly remembered she was being observed.
She reared her head back again and glared fully at Mev.
Nostrils steaming, she took in a big lungful of air. Mev
was outraged.

"Oh, this is the thanks you give me, huh?" she said,
planting her hands on the hips of her chainmail jerkin.
"I exposed myself, putting myself in peril to save your
baby. To hell with you, then." So it was to be a battle.
She reached for her sword hilt. Her skills were rusty.
She had no idea how she'd fare.

Litfusia stopped, letting the smoke trickle out of both
sides of her mouth. The fire in her red eyes abated, as
if she was taken aback. She cocked her head at Mev,
whimpering with frustration. She looked at the baby, and
back at the human female. Making a noise between a
gurgle and a roar, the dragonet had moved on to the
second pile of meat. It looked at Mev, too, its bright
eyes fearless, knowing that its mother would defend it
from every nightmare monster that moved. Chicks
weren't that different from babies, Mev realized. And

the dragon knew it, too. Litfusia felt *gratitude* towards
her, and had no notion of how to handle such a concept.
Mev wasn't certain, either. She'd never had a monster
in her debt before.

"Wizard's amulet," Mev said, letting her hand drop.
"Staff with round gem on top. That's what I came for.
I'll fight you for it if I have to, but frankly, we're too
old for that kind of thing, and you've got better things
to do."

The dragon appeared to agree. Grudgingly, she arched
her long, white neck right over Mev's head and pointed
into a corner the warrior had had no time yet to search.

"Thanks." Mev stood up, torch in hand. Something
touched her leg. The little red dragon was reaching for
the brand. "Oh, all right." Mev didn't need it. There was
plenty of light to see by from the cave mouth. She
offered the torch to the chick, who chewed happily on
the ember. Litfusia made a dangerous sound in her
throat. She *was* jealous of Mev, something that made
the human woman feel smug.

She picked her way over the ground, surveying the
treasure as she went. A big armring rolled in front of
her feet, and she reached down for it. It was solid gold,
studded with rubies. Not Litfusia's usual style. Bugger
Folminade's reward; she could get what she needed right
here. Mev started to put it in her pack. She heard a
warning growl from the dragon.

"All right, all right," Mev said, dropping it like a guilty
child. "Can't blame me for trying." In a heap against
the cavern wall, Mev saw a finger of gold and knew at
once she had found what she sought. The crowning blue
gem glittered as she took the staff. Mission accomplished.

"Thank you," Mev said, turning back to Litfusia.
"You've got a pretty chick, by the way."

The head cocked again, as if to thank her. Then, it
drew back on its great neck. Litfusia took a huge, deep

breath, and Mev knew the truce was over. They were back to business as usual. She wasn't about to argue. Flames were licking out of Litfusia's nostrils, and smoke was curling around her head. Mev didn't need it spelled out any more obviously. She ran for her life.

She turned and hurtled for the tunnel mouth. As she stumbled down the piles of golden treasure, she heard the roar of flame. Mev felt heat blast her from behind as she tumbled head first over the threshold. Ow! Not again! As Mev scrambled back through the narrow stone tube with the staff in her fist, she heard a deep, grunting sound. Litfusia was laughing. Then Mev heard scaly feet rustling away over the piles of coins, another mother going back to her baby.

"Why did you spare the dragon?" Folminade wailed, when Mev told him the story. He wrung his skinny hands together. "You could have killed both of them! They were vulnerable."

"You only hired me to get the staff," Mev pointed out, thrusting it into his arms. She stood over him with her arms folded, and waited. She couldn't have sat down if she'd wanted, not with the new burn on her bottom, but she felt energized by accomplishing a successful mission. "Dragons are extra. Lots extra."

It wasn't strictly true, and they both knew it. He was aware of her reputation, knew that the fierce Mev Grayshield had had no trouble executing extracurricular kills for free in the past, but he hadn't been up there. It had not been in her to attack the dragon or its chick. After all, Litfusia had been a fellow female in trouble. She was sure the dragon wouldn't have given her the same courtesy, but that was the difference between humans and dragons. Part of the game. "My reward, please."

The wizard, grumbling, reached for the heavy leather bag at his belt. He poured a small pile of coins onto a flat rock, less than a third of the contents. "There you are."

"Thank you," Mev said, and took the bag. Folminade started to snatch it back, but Mev cleared her throat meaningfully. With a wary look in her direction, he withdrew his hand. He'd be safer facing the dragon than to be cheap with Mev. People like him really burned her backside. Mev shifted, and the heavy chainmail jerkin rubbed uncomfortably over her new scorches. Even more than Litfusia.

"Quite," Folminade said, with resignation, picking up the remaining coins. "My lord and lady thank you for your service."

"Call me any time," Mev said, with an airy wave. "I'm back in business." The wizard started off down the path toward the valley with the precious amulet in his hands, shaking his head and muttering. She grinned after him.

Besides, she thought, as she tied the pouch to her pack, she could think of her act of mercy as job security. Now that she'd ensured the survival of the next generation of dragons, there would be a beast left for her daughter to challenge one day. But Mev would definitely have to warn Kitra to fireproof the backside of her armor.

Like No Business I Know

Mark Bourne

When the gateway from Faerie reopened into our world, it happened on a sunny Tuesday afternoon, in Los Angeles, three feet from a West Hollywood swimming pool.

Laura Lundy placed the twenty-pound dumbbell next to the patio chair and padded barefoot toward the swimming pool, the phone against her ear. "I'm sorry, Robert. I don't mean to bitch at you. You know I'm glad you're my agent—"

And that was true, too. The short, thin man on the other end of the phone had done more for Laura's career in just seven weeks than all her previous agents put together. Of course, the others hadn't seen much reason to put Robert's kind of effort into her career. (Well, except for poor Adam. She hoped Robert's predecessor was recovering okay in Miami.) "—I *know* there's nothing you can do about the strike—"

The voice on the other end interrupted her for the third time in two minutes. Laura clicked the phone back to the second line, where the reporter from *People* waited. "Sorry, Tony. What was the question? Oh, right. Sure, *Xora: Avenger Priestess* wasn't how I expected my ship to come in, but I was happy to hop on board when it pulled into port two years ago. My agent—I mean, my *previous* agent, Adam Duchowski, helped me land the role—" She didn't add that since then the syndicated TV series had moved her out of her tiny overpriced apartment and into this house in the Hollywood hills and this swimming pool she was pacing back and forth alongside. "Hold on another sec, Tony, sorry—"

Click. "Yes, Robert, I'm listening. Sure, you know I appreciate you. Hell, you're a miracle-worker— Yeah, I saw it. Came today." She edged her toes beneath a poolside *TV Guide* and with a deft kick somersaulted it into her waiting hand. Its cover displayed Laura's (rather, Xora: Avenger Priestess's) thick night-black hair, toned sword-wielding arms, and photogenic devil-may-care smile.

"Says here I'm 'at 29, the hottest, buffest new star since Linda Hamilton' and that I've been invited to a half-dozen *Xora* conventions across the U.S. and England. Seems that thousands of total strangers on Web sites and something called alt.fan.xora know more about each episode than I do." She read dramatically: " 'Her just-revealing-enough-for-primetime costume has becoming a fashion fad at clubs and so-called scene parties where leather and chainmail are worn by people who don't necessarily slay semi-convincing monsters and defeat tyrannical overlords on a weekly basis—' "

Good thing Terry wasn't into that kinky stuff, much. Dear Terry. Laura enjoyed the parts of their life together that were plain old "vanilla." Well, vanilla with nuts and strawberry syrup, perhaps. Lately, though . . . (*Heart to brain: new subject, pronto!*) "You're my agent, Robert, so how come you never tell me about those conventions?"

Click. "Hi, Tony, you still there? Overnight success? Well, yeah, if you consider overnight being six years of cattle-call auditions, TV movie bit parts, and one year as the 'official spokesmodel' for ExerTan—the only

aerobics workout machine and tanning booth in one!—
infomercials. Adam saved my life by getting me out of
that one—"

Funny thing about Adam, his having that breakdown
and quitting the business so suddenly. That was less than
two months ago. Good thing Robert Goldfarb had
appeared out of nowhere to pick up the pieces and take
her on. The wiry ball of energy in the loud suit, gaudy
jewelry, and slicked-back hair had been on the sound-
stage when word about Adam arrived. He handed her
his card, took her to lunch, and displayed a persuasive
Type-A personality. Before she knew it she had signed
a bottom line with R. P. Goldfarb Talent Agency. Poor,
stressed-out Adam. She hoped he was okay in his Florida
condo. How come bad things happened in groups?

Click. "What? Yes, Rob, I know the writers have joined
the other unions and you can't do a thing about that—"

Heart to mouth: bad move. Terry was a writer hoping
to make that One Big Score. With talent to spare, but
too damn stubborn to play the Hollywood game. Terry
had, instead, that One Big Weakness that could keep
a writer waiting tables at Sunset and Crescent for the
past two years: integrity. Integrity to a vision. Integrity
to self. Hardly cardinal virtues oft rewarded by
Hollywood success. With the frustration that caused on
top of everything else in their lives— How long had it
been since they'd *really* made love, vanilla or any other
flavor? *Heart to chest muscles: squeeze!* She scrunched
her eyes shut at the still-fresh memory of Terry stepping
out the door and saying softly, sadly, "I'll call you later."
During the past three days, every time Laura's phone
rang, it had been Robert on the other end. *Brain to
heart: knock it off, you jerk!*

"—Yeah, the trades are printing as many rumors as
they are union proposals. Christ, what if SAG really does
pull the plug too? That's the last thing this town needs:
more out-of-work actors, with me along with them. Hell,

Rob—" *Click*. "—After a month of no shooting, the whole season's schedule is shot to hell, the execs are panicking, negotiations are stalled, and the sponsors are pulling out faster than a teenage boy without a condom. I hate not knowing when I'll be working again. No, wait—Tony? Jesus, you weren't supposed to hear all that—" *Click*. "No, Rob, I know you didn't call just to hear me complain. It's these damn strikes, that's all—" *Click*. "—Plus after a year and a half, Terry just up and decides that I'm more involved with my career than my personal life or anyone in it. Says I get distracted from the important details. Wha—? Tony? Aah! I'm sorry. You didn't hear that. *Don't write it down!*"

Click. "You've been saying you're going to do something about it for four weeks! What can you do? You're just an agent, for Chrissakes! No, I'm sorry, I didn't mean it like that. Stop it, Rob. It's just that . . . Oh, come on! You know I— Yeah, well, fine. Call me later. I've certainly got nothing better to wait for!"

Click.

"Goddammit shit bastard hell! No, not you, Tony, sorry. Look, I've got to go. My jujitsu coach just arrived with my monogrammed hari kari knives. Bye."

She wanted to slam the receiver into its cradle—hard. But the goddamn cell phone made a most unsatisfying *snick* as she closed it. So she threw the phone across the pool. It struck the marble wall on the far side and exploded into a spray of plastic and metal pieces. Some landed in the pool. L.A.'s eternally clear, blue, afternoon sky reflected peacefully in the little ripples that spread across the water's surface.

Laura screeched between clenched teeth, collapsed into a deck chair, and cried. What she wanted more than anything else in the world—more than an end to the sudden chain of strikes that was crippling her work, more than her hope that *Xora* would be a stepping stone to even better roles and career peaks, more than even her life-long dream of making it big, really big—was to feel Terry's soothing, steady hands rubbing her shoulders. Their own familiar rhythm: first the left shoulder, then the right, then both, then down . . .

"Shake it off, toots! We got work to do!"

She leaped to her feet, spun toward the voice, and prepared to kick a groin or sprint toward safety.

No one was there. No intruder. No one who could have produced that gravelly, gruff male voice. Maybe he was hiding behind that mirror.

Where had that full-length, oval mirror come from? And why was it floating unsupported above the tiles near the exercycle?

"Hello?" she called.

"Wait just an orc-schtupping minute," replied the sandpaper voice.

Laura stepped cautiously toward the mirror, keeping the door to the house accessible on her right. She had another phone just inside, with 911 set on the autodialer.

The mirror was as tall as she was and defied gravity above the deck tiles in exactly the same way her bathroom mirror couldn't. She positioned herself so she could see her reflection in its perfectly flat, clean surface. She'd gained a bit in the waist lately. . . .

"Oh, do let's get on with it," complained another voice from the mirror. This one was high and clipped. "We haven't much time. You're holding it upside down!" With an accent like Cary Grant's.

"I'm doing the best I can," bellowed the first. "So shut your gob, ya green pointy-eared fruit!"

"Enough!" a third demanded—a woman's voice, strong and clear. "I gave *you* the stone, goblin, because *you* insisted on being be the first through the worldveil. Quickly, fool! One stone cannot part the veil for long!"

"Yes, forgive me, Mistress," acquiesced Voice #1. "I forget how you told me to hold it. Oh. My thanks, kind Mistress."

From the reflection of Laura's bare belly, a curly-haired head poked out of the mirror and into the Hollywood sunshine. The head was attached to a squat, business-suited man who stepped out of the mirror and approached her. His bare, hairy feet slapped the tiles like hams. Though no more than three feet tall, the muscular form beneath his rumpled brown suit suggested he could easily bench-press as much as she did.

L.A. does things to a person. After eight years here, Laura had become immune to certain types of shocks.

His swarthy hands clasped a crystal as big as his potato-shaped nose. It (the crystal) glowed with a fiery blue aura. He slipped it into a jacket pocket, stepped forward, and sandwiched Laura's right hand between both of his, shaking it roughly.

"Gurack Thornhollow's the name," he said. "Glad to finally meet you." With a silvery sparkle, a lit cigar appeared in his hand. It smelled imported. The little exec-thing began pacing the swimming pool and gesturing emphatically.

"I'll get right to the point, sweetheart. You're marvelous, kid, simply marvelous! Obviously a newbie, but still the best thing this show has going for it." He stepped out over the pool, hovered above the water for a beat, then pivoted and marched back toward her. "With me as producer and director, we're gonna take this series right to the top, straight to Number One! Y'know what I'm saying? I've got the best writers and the best talent working for me. Y'know why? Because I'm the best—and I only work with the best! You and me, kid, we're goin' places! *Xora*'s already the hottest ratings smash between Tir na n-Og and Avalon, and now with pan-dominion cablespells we can finally crack that rural orcish market! I tell ya, baby, we're goin' to the top! First, though, we need to make a few changes—"

"Oh, do not bore her to death before we've even made our proposal," exclaimed the Cary Grantesque

voice. Its owner stepped (or floated?) out of the mirror—
a body lithe, ethereal, and clearly belonging to a world
other than Poolside L.A.

"You're an elf," Laura exclaimed, her hands rushing
to her mouth in reflex astonishment. Delicate and
elegant, its presence made her think of green sun-
dappled glades and rings of courtly spirits gathering by
moonlight. Things she had never seen before. "How—
how do I know that?"

" 'Elf' is a better word than many," sniffed the being.
He stepped hautily past the first visitor—a goblin, she
suddenly knew—and appraised his new surroundings
disapprovingly. "I prefer 'Elder People of Faerie' myself,"
he said, curling his lip exactly like the snooty maître d'
at Andrico's. "Though I am aware that I am in the
minority on the issue. As to how you know that, I gave
you the knowledge beforehand, immediately before
stepping through the veil. I also soothed the fear that
was building within you. You will find that it speeds
communication. And we have much to discuss with
precious little time."

"Cut to the chase, leaves-for-brains," barked the
goblin. He took Laura's hand and tried to pull her aside.
She pulled back, hard, causing the little grotesque to
stumble. "Hey, nice grip there, sweets," he said, letting
go. "I like that." Then sotto voce: "Don't let greenie
there bother you. He's been pissed at this world ever
since he saw those Keebler commercials. Ha!"

The elf crossed his arms and rolled his eyes blueward.
"Oh, please!"

"Cease the prattle, underlings!" thundered the
woman's voice. "Speak to our good lady with respect and
deference. She is an artist and a professional, not a
servant pixie. And we need her willing services."

The source of the voice stepped out of the mirror.
A woman, all right. But Laura couldn't imagine even
Joan of Arc radiating the powerful presence this woman

exuded. She was, in a word, striking. Six feet tall. Lean yet powerfully muscled. Her bronze skin all but shimmered with inner vitality. The only marks on otherwise smooth, tanned flesh were a few pale scars branding her forearms and left thigh. A mane of auburn hair cascaded about her shoulders, encircled on her forehead by a jeweled coronet. One hand was wrapped around the hilt of a polished sword hanging on her hip. If her gleaming leather-and-metal outfit, particularly those rune-embossed gold hemispheres cupping her impressive breasts, was as heavy as it looked, she didn't betray any sign of it.

For the first time in her career, Laura felt flabby and puny by comparison. Still, there was something . . . soft about this woman. *Good* soft. Maternal perhaps. Aged. Experienced. Though she wore a body that looked little older than Laura's, her clear green eyes and wise face betrayed a maturity that Laura only hoped to one day achieve. She was who Xora wanted to grow up to be.

"I am Nnagartha of the Golden Strength," the woman proclaimed. "Favored sword of Finvarra, King of Eirinn Faerie. It was I who defeated the dragon Ruadherra and the Black Wizard Tyrkobal; who led the centaur armies and won the heart of the mighty Ton n'Uthara during battles against the Dark Hordes—" Laura squinted in the sunlight glinting off those breasts. "—Who led the Daoine Sidhe against the Fir Bolg on the Plain of Pillars, and who instructs the young ones of Faerie in stories of the stars and the quiet power of the cool, watchful moon."

Everyone in this town has a résumé. "Okay. Assuming you're not a delayed hallucination triggered by something slipped to me at Jay Leno's party last week, why are you—" Laura spread her arms to include the space from pool to exercycle to towel rack. "—here?"

"Because, Lady, our long quest led us to you." Something in her voice darkened. Her hands clenched into fists that would probably pulp Brazil nuts. "From

the Fortress of Power beneath King Finvarra's palace,
one of our kind stole the sacred veilstone, a crystal from
the Mountains of Darkness. It has the power to part
the veil between worlds, to open a . . . a passage twixt
realms." She indicated the mirror. "The stone was used
to enter this world. It has taken us a long journey to
find another. Now we must entreat your help to finally
capture the thief."

Or was it Letterman's bash? That Barrymore chick
was awfully chummy that night. "Why me?"

"The trickster who eludes us has targeted you, and
through you he seeks his revenge against what you have
done for the folk of Faerie. So through you we shall
find him."

"Who's 'targeted' me? And for what? What have I
done to . . . to . . ."

"The folk of Faerie."

"Whoever!"

"You have, in fact, done a great deal for the many
who populate the world that split from this earthly realm
so many centuries ago." Leather creaked and metal
flashed as the woman circled Laura like a teacher sizing
up a potential pupil. "You have brought them pleasure,
excitement, and a new thirst for adventures and legend-
spinning. Many of our realm, particularly the young ones,
have not experienced such things for a long time. Not
since the last of the Dark Hordes were vanquished, and
the final Black Wizard dissolved into misty eternity. You,
Xora, have renewed the memories of our glorious former
days!"

"Xora? I'm not Xora. That's just a part I play!"

"We know that, of course. Yet it is a part we love
in a drama that captures—albeit crudely and imper-
fectly—the spirit of our kingdom."

"You mean you watch *Xora* in . . . wherever you come
from?"

The goblin tossed his cigar into the pool, where it

sizzled and vanished. "Listen, babe. *Xora: Avenger Priestess* is the hottest thing to hit the Golden Realm since the bards' festival allowed the rude limerick contest. You're a hit, and everyone wants more of it!"

Nnagartha raised a finger. The goblin shut up. "You see," she said, "I am not unacquainted with this world, and the energies that carry your staged enactments through the ether can pierce the veil between this world and ours. With some difficulty, and after much debate, I convinced the Mages Guild to conjure receiving boxes so that we too might see and hear the images that freely flow through the veil."

"You watch TV in Fairyland?"

Nnagartha looked pained. "Simply Faerie, Lady. And it *has* been a long time of peace." She gazed wistfully into the pool, lost in memories Laura could never imagine.

"Your little play-acting," said the elf, "is the most popular such. . . program in our realm. Though, I must say, I rather prefer more substantial fare. Travel documentaries, for example. But the common folk clamber for more *Xora: Avenger Priestess*, and no new tales have been forthcoming for more than a lunar cycle. All we—they—receive are . . . oh, what is that word you have?"

"Reruns," Nnagartha said.

"Thank you, my Mistress. Lady Laura, we are here to help you create more of these adventure tales, though this time we shall help you do them with greater, shall we say, accuracy."

"Greater *accuracy*?"

"More realistic. Truer to life." The elf's posture stiffened even more—exactly like that maître d' at Andrico's. "Really, Lady, even you must admit that the centaurs in that one episode looked rather, to put it delicately, unconvincing. Our own centaur forces are presently awaiting their first cue. And your roc! Oh, dear . . . if I had a sense of humor I would have doubled over laughing at its clearly artificial claws. And all the magic-users thus far portrayed obviously know nothing of a real mage's art. That's not to mention the shoddy dragons—"

"Enough, my assistant," admonished Nnagartha. The elf bit his lower lip, silently.

"Flowerhead's right," exclaimed the goblin. He adjusted his tie into an even less attractive position. "There's been no *Xora* for weeks now, and we're here to help out."

"Well, of course there's been no *Xora*," Laura countered. "Everyone's on strike!"

"Not a prob, babe. I got writers, crews, and supporting cast waiting to jump in and save the show and your shapely ass."

Laura pivoted and stamped away. "No way! This is too unbelievable. I half-expect Kathy Lee Gifford to jump out of the bushes and tell me I'm on *America's Weirdest Home Videos*."

"But you must." Nnagartha was now insistent. "The veilstone is gone and the thief has escaped to this world. You have no idea of the danger the two together represent. There are reasons why the realms were separated and the stones kept carefully guarded."

"Yeah, right! Your security system was clearly burglar-proof. Why drag me into your little snatch-and-run?"

"He did it *because* of you! He hates *Xora*. He hates you! With the power remaining within the stone, he has the ability to shape the wills of others. There's a reason why the strikes are happening all at the same time. His next plan is to spread scandalous stories about you to sabotage your career."

Laura spun to face her. "*What?* How do you know that?"

"We know this malfeasant. It is his way. Also, he boasted of his plans to drinking companions. No one took him seriously until we discovered the veilstone missing and read the taunting note he left behind. He has done this sort of thing before. You, unfortunately, are his latest victim. So you *must* help us capture him." She waved her hand in an odd pattern. The mirror changed. It was now a window open onto a vast meadow. In the distance, gentle green hills became immense mountains laced with waterfalls. Between the window and the mountains, perhaps ten miles away or a hundred, a shimmering city of golden domes and jewel-hued spires reflected the same sun that shone on Laura's bare back in L.A. Like Judy Garland's Oz, complete with Technicolor.

Nnagartha gave Laura a generous moment to take in the view. "We ask you to follow us through the veil and—"

"What? Me step through there?"

"There, in Oberon's Green, we shall create a new episode of *Xora*. My people will provide all that is needed to perform, record, and broadcast the story throughout Faerie. The magic released during this will attract the malefactor, bring him out of hiding. Then we shall capture him. Afterward you may return here with all the afflictions he has brought upon you undone and gone."

Laura eyed the window warily. "And what will happen to my career if I don't help you?"

The demi-amazon shrugged. "Nothing."

"Nothing? Really?"

"Absolutely nothing. Ever." Nnagartha's eyes were as cold and hard as her swordblade.

"I see." Well, what else did she have planned before she hit the unemployment lines? "So, what do I do?"

"I will tell all presently. We must hurry. No doubt our thief's veilstone has already alerted him to our presence. We must capture him unawares, or he can use his stone to lock us all on the other side—permanently."

A dragon's snout poked through the window, followed by the head and the beginnings of a long neck. Covered with irridescent green and gold scales, its Spielbergish head could barely squeeze through the opening. Softball-sized eyes blinked and cavernous nostrils twitched in the SoCal air. "So will she do it?" it said. "When do we start? I have some suggestions for the script. First, I think the dragon should get lots more lines—"

Nnagartha thwacked the snout with her fist. "Silence, Ruadherra!"

"Well, pardon *me!*" huffed the beast. Sulfurous smoke roiled from its nostrils as it retreated back into the opening.

"Actors!" grumped Nnagartha.

"Tell me about it," Laura replied.

Following Nnagartha, Laura stepped through the not-window onto a meadow of lush, green grass and wild-flowers. Nearby, a brook gurgled serenely, and the air smelled of sweet berries and honey. A pair of unicorns gazed at her with intelligent eyes, then turned and galloped over a hill. The sharp, shocking contrast with the world she knew—with the smog and the traffic noise and the subconscious spoor of thousands of stressed-out people—knocked Laura off balance. Collapsing into a soft copse of foxglove or bluebell wouldn't be a bad thing.

"Here it is, babe," said Gurack as he stepped out of the view of Laura's backyard pool. "Here's our set. And your script." He handed her a stack of vellum sheets stitched with gold twine. "It's called 'Dragon's Wrath,' based on a real event that happened, oh, a hell of a long time ago. You'll love it. 'Course, we put some spice in it. Y'know, added a few characters, made it one big battle in act four rather than the series of small ones. Gave you—I mean, Xora—some good scenes with our local talent. It'll be a hit. Love ya, babe." He looked around the meadow. "Where the hell are the others? Where'd that troll-calloopin' dragon go? Goddammit, I told them to be here on time—" The director stomped grumbling off toward the sparkling city.

"How do you feel?" asked Nnagartha. She placed a firm yet gentle hand on Laura's shoulder.

"A bit wobbly, I guess. This isn't how I expected my day to go."

"You will be at ease soon, I promise. This land can have an effect on people. I remember my first time back—"

"What do you mean?"

Nnagartha pulled back her gorgeous auburn hair, more out of distraction than necessity. "Oh, nothing, my girl. Your script is ready, and all the cast and crew have been rehearsing their respective parts. They will be pleased that you agreed to join us. Before the others return, though, I must fight you." With a quick gesture, she withdrew her sword and flowed into an attacker's stance.

"Excuse me?" Laura said. She backed up a step and almost tripped over a massive sword on the ground behind her.

"Take the blade," Nnagartha demanded.

Laura did. It was a *lot* heavier than the props she was used to.

"Attack me," the other woman ordered.

"Why?" Laura swung the sword in her warm-up pattern, gauging its heft and size.

"Because I desire it!" And Nnagartha arced her blade in a killing swing.

Laura blocked it, but the blow forced her to her knees. Nnagartha stood over her, sword already sheathed and fists on hips.

"What the hell what that for?" Laura shouted. "You tried to kill me!"

"Not at all." The warrior offered Laura a hand. Laura refused, standing and brushing herself off on her own. Pleased, Nnagartha added, "I apologize, Lady. It was just a test. Xora brandishes her blade with ease and grace, though I suspect that that has more due to editing than actual warrior's skill."

"My swordplay coach says I'm the best student he's ever had."

"I don't doubt that, Lady. You are good—in your world. Here, though, we have set different standards. You must look as though your can fight with Xora's skill, or else your fans here will be sorely disappointed. Would you like a few pointers?"

Sparring with a pro far better even than her coach? She *did* have a lot of stress to work out, and Terry didn't like her practicing at home. . . .

Laura smiled. "Can't let down the fans."

Shiiinng! "Then attack me."

Laura did. It felt good.

An hour later, the meadow was a stage set populated by assorted gnomes, sprites, goblins, faeries, and warriors. Swords and shields clanged together like thunder as the centaur army practiced the climactic assault from act four. Nnagartha was off somewhere searching for something. . . or someone.

Feeling strong and more than a little sexy in the authentic costume Nnagartha had provided for her, Laura sat studying her script on an Alice-sized mushroom that seemed to have appeared for just that purpose. A quick study, she had already memorized her lines and was rereading goggle-eyed the outrageous scenes coming up. Who was playing this "Bran" character, the capital-H Hero who enters after the first few scenes? Probably another over-inflated, self-loving, brainless beefcake like all the others the writers kept sticking her with.

Footsteps behind her. Furtive and hesitant. She turned. A young elf boy, shy and awkward in his leaves and pointed ears, stood gazing up at her raptly.

"Hello," she said. She hopped off the mushroom.

The boy elf wore a moss-green tunic, on the breast of which was pinned a large, round button. The button bore words written in red script. Laura leaned close to read:

I *do* have a life!
It's *Xora: Avenger Priestess*!

From her experience, that wasn't a good sign.

"Excuse me, um, Laura. . . Miss Lundy?" the elfling stammered. "I'm your biggest fan. I know you're busy, but, um, I was wondering if I could ask you a few questions? Only for a minute?"

The centaurs were arguing loudly about who was most photogenic and therefore should lead the attack on the dragon's lair. There was time. "Sure."

He rushed to her side. "Okay. In episode 12, 'Lettuce Prey,' when you battled the enchanted plant creatures of the evil Lord D'spair, how come you controlled the ivy monsters with D'spair's Sword of Power but you had to chop up the wolfweed beasts to stop *them*? Did the ivy monsters have more lifeforce than the wolfweed beasts? Or were the wolfweed beasts enchanted by a different level of magic?"

Oh, to be able to conjure up the idiot writer who came up with that one. She smiled politely. "I don't know."

"Why didn't Lord D'spair hide the Sword of Power in a secret place instead of displaying it in the center of his trophy room with bright lights shining on it?"

"I don't know."

"When you were captured by Lord Kandor in episode 31, 'Dirge for a Scourge,' and he had you chained to that wall above the Pit of Eternity, and you asked him, 'Before you kill me, will you at least tell me what this is all about?' why didn't he just say no and drop you instead of telling you his plan and giving you time to escape?"

"I don't know."

"How come in episode—"

With a quick motion, she jutted her elbow into the side of his head—hard. "I don't know."

"Lady Laura," called Nnagartha's voice. Pleased by the distraction of the approaching warrior, Laura was startled to see striding confidently alongside Nnagartha the most handsome man she had ever beheld. Square-jawed and Adonis-featured beneath a leonine head of hair that would make Fabio consider implants, he was the type of man for whom the term "mighty-thewed" was invented. Wearing an animal hide draped about his stunning shoulders, a leather breech cloth that bulged with robust good health, and leather leggings up his solid calves, he could make a fortune smoldering those soulful blue-green eyes on the covers of romance novels.

"Lady Laura, this is your leading man. His name is Bran—"

"—Son of Tur Gwynthorn, mightiest of the Northern Kings!" he said, bowing. "My Lady, it is a privilege to serve at your side. Pray, be patient with me, for I am new at this 'acting' art that Mistress Nnagartha asks of me, and you are even more beautiful standing before me than you are in the mages' vision boxes."

Nnagartha gave Laura a wink. "I'll leave you two to get acquainted. Perhaps you should go over your lines together. I see that Gurack is almost done rehearsing the dwarfs."

When they were alone, Bran took Laura's hand and held it as if it were a sacred relic. "My Lady," he said with a voice like Brad Pitt massaging her feet with aromatic oils. "Long have I admired you from afar, and worshipped you as a goddess. When told that I, of all the men of our kingdom, had been chosen to play he who captures your heart, my own heart nigh burst with song."

In any other case, Laura would have spoiled the moment by trying to stifle a giggle. Yet unlike the typical muscleman from Central Casting, this handsome specimen wore—if little else—an honest reality that was refreshing. Clearly he didn't just play at being a Hero. The firm, sculpted-by-Michelangelo face betrayed a boyish earnestness that softened his aura of strength and rugged nobility.

The goblin approached and jabbed Bran in a thigh bigger than the goblin's head. "Okay, hunkazoid, save the fan mail until the wrap party." An old-fashioned megaphone sparkled into the director's hand. "Listen up, everybody! Let's start with scene four, in which Bran—that's you, buddy—first encounters Xora after the unsuccessful battle against the Black Dragon of Doomlair. Elven Sages, you be ready for your entrance. Pixies, check your scripts; take your positions and be ready to fly in and beg Xora and Bran to attempt another raid on the dragon's cave. And Ruadherra, this time don't keep ad-libbing the way you did in rehearsal. We don't need a prima-fucking-donna. There were other dragons at the audition, you know."

At Gurack's direction, will-o'-the-wisps rose from the ground to light the scene effectively. Something flitted near Laura's face. She resisted the urge to swat it. When it stopped in mid-air at her eye level, it looked like a Hummingbird Barbie wearing night-goggles. Nnagartha had explained that these small faeries with the "mage-cams" were the audio-visual crews for their production.

After a few moments, Gurack stood on Nnagartha's shoulders and surveyed the set. At last he brought the megaphone back to his lips. "Act one, scene four. And *action!*"

It was a good shoot.

After Gurack again praised her performance, touching her often enough to discover that his nose was an easy target, he hurried away to warn the dragon against continued unnecessary improvisation. Where was Nnagartha? Her mentor had spent the hours looking nervously about, studying people and objects with intense scrutiny. At last, Laura saw her on the far side of the meadow, speaking to the regiment of goblin balloon bombers. Nnagartha was frowning. Laura had decided to check up on her when—

"Lady, may I speak with you?" Bran had stepped alongside her. She shot a glance at Nnagartha, who was examining a goblin balloonist by holding him at eye-level with one hand.

"Sure, Bran. For a minute."

"Lady, where I am from, a man shouts his love for his woman to the trees and the hills and the stars."

"What about to the woman?"

Bran blinked, then smiled. His white teeth glistened. "To her he entreats more softly. I wish to ride into battle if only to be your champion and win for you a lover's victory. In longing desire for you to stay here with us and let me woo you with courtly reverence, I have composed a song. Would you like to hear it?"

Flattered. Flustered. Part of her wanted to giggle, another to cry. He was probably a good hugger. "Oh, God. I'm sorry, Bran. That's sweet, really. It's just that—" She waved her hands about vaguely. "I already have someone in my life, and we're—"

"Another man, a mighty warrior true and virtuous, has earned your affections, my Lady?"

She looked him squarely in those gorgeous aqua-blues and nodded. "Something like that."

Bran gazed into the distance. Emotion threatened to crack his proud visage. "Then he is a worthy man indeed to have captured your love so fully. I may be a mere prince and a warrior, yet I can feel your love for this man, and the pain it has recently caused you." He inhaled deeply, held the breath a moment, then exhaled a slow sigh that conveyed sadness and resignation. "I would like to meet him, and pay him the honor and respect I feel for the one worthy of your love, my Lady."

"I'd love to introduce you. You two'd get along well, I think."

"Warrior to warrior then! We three shall drink from shared flagons and toast the memories of loves lost and finer loves gained!"

"Right." He *was* cute. Buns of steel, oh lordy.

Striding her way was Nnagartha, Gurack struggling to keep up with her.

"You're worried," Laura said.

"Observant as well, I see," Nagartha declared without sarcasm. "Yes, I am concerned. I had hoped that our activities would attract our prey, but I cannot sense his presence. He is a master of stealth and disguise, and I trusted my hunter's experience to make uncovering him easy work. I was mistaken. My fear now is that this was all in vain, that he has chosen to stay permanently in your world. The damage he could do there. . . I do not like to think about it."

Gurack coughed. "Look, pardon me, Mistress, but we still got a hell of an episode of *Xora* in the works here. Wouldn't it be worth it just for that? I mean, I know it ain't like the old days and all, but hey, you gotta admit the people are gonna love 'Dragon's Wrath.' They'll pay more attention to it than anything else. Even the Jesters Guild has tossed in the towel and contacted me about producing a comedy series. It's just too bad we can't make more than one new *Xora*. Oh, I can see it now! A whole 'nuther series shot on location! With the best director—that's me—and the best—"

"That's enough," said Laura. She was deep in thought, an idea dancing just out of grasping range. "Something Gurack said just now," she whispered. "I believe I now understand why he took the veilstone, why he wishes to see *Xora* canceled." She raised her voice. "Give me the veilstone!"

Gurack looked stunned. "Say again, Lady?"

"Give. Me. The veilstone." Her best Xora intonation.

"I'm sure it's here somewhere. Just a minute." While the goblin searched his pockets, Nnagartha fixed Laura with a questioning look.

Just play along with me. Let me be the pro here.

"Fraggin' pockets! Here it is!" Gurack handed the blue crystal to Laura.

She held it in her palms. It was heavier than she expected, and warm, and began glowing with auroral colors. "Is it true, Nnagartha, that with this stone I could close the veil between this world and mine forever?"

The warrior was silent for a moment. Then a shade of a smile twitched the corners of her lips. *Bingo!* "Why, yes, Lady. If that is your wish."

"So I could conceivably keep on playing Xora here, without the troubles of strikes and studio executives and shifting time-slots."

Laura heard the soft sound of Nnagartha's foot pressing down—hard—on Gurack's. The goblin yelped. "Why, um, yes, of course, Lady!" he bleated. "Absolutely! Why, any, er, thing you want, you just ask me." Then he followed Laura's directing eyes to the left. His own eyes met hers, then widened appreciably. *Bingo 2!* "As a matter of fact, you're great! Marvelous! A sure-fire smash! The best entertainer this land has ever seen. And I do mean *ever*! You can write your own ticket, with total control of your career. I'll get a small percentage, of course, a finder's fee, but you'll be the top of the heap, let there be no mistake about that!"

A sheet of rough paper materialized in his hand. In ornate script at the top was the word *Contract*. "By signing here with one hand while holding the stone in the other, you will be granted an exclusive and binding contract to be Faerie's most favored actor. You'll be the toast of the entire Kingdom. Finvarra himself is eager to get your autograph. Here's a pen." He gave her a colorful quill. The veilstone glowed even more brightly. The window behind them wavered and fluttered like a bad transmission.

What if it didn't work? She didn't like the way the window flickered now. Her backyard was difficult to see, going dark and fading to static snow. Laura gripped the quill tightly.

Nnagartha took the contract from Gurack, looked around for a suitable writing desk, then walked ten paces to the left, placing it on the giant mushroom. Laura followed. "Here's a good place to sign," she said. "When you do, the veil will be closed forever, the veilstone powerless, and you will be our land's most favored performer. With no turning back." The last sentence held a barely shaded hint of warning.

"I know," Laura said firmly. She placed the pen to the paper. The stone was a tiny sun now. She didn't want to look back and see what was happening to the only passageway home.

"Here goes," she said quietly and began to sign.

The surface of the mushroom bucked, knocking the pen from her hand. Laura jumped back as the mushroom shifted and melted and folded in on itself like origami. Within seconds, her agent stood where it had been. "No! Stop!" he yelled.

"Robert!" Laura cried. Though she had been expecting it—rather, she'd prayed that she hadn't screwed up big time—the sight of the wiry little man startled her.

"You sign anything and I'll—" He lunged at Laura. She, in perfect form, shrieked her trademark Xora battle yell, subconsciously evaluated weight, strength, positioning, and anatomy, and shot a *mae geri kekomi* front thrust kick that caught Robert in the chest. Three point two seconds after launch, her agent plopped to the ground like a goblin balloon bomb.

The snooty elf, apparently waiting invisibly for such a moment, formed out of the air and waved his hands. A translucent bubble of green light englobed Robert. Or whoever he was. Whoever he was stood groggily and pounded on the inside of the bubble.

"You'll never work in this dominion again! You hear me?" He kicked the bubble and shouted and cursed some more, all to no avail. At last he gave up, sat, and sulked, looking more like a pouty child than a . . . than a slick-talking, career-sabotaging asshole.

The goblin director approached the bubble. He raised a palm, where an official-looking badge appeared. "Gurack Thornhollow, FBI. You, Puck, alias Robin Goodfellow, alias Robert Goldfarb, are hereby charged with grand theft, use of a veilstone without authorization, breaking and entering into a forbidden reality, and behavior unbecoming the Designated Shrewd and Knavish Sprite of Faerie. You will be detained until you stand trial before your peers and the High Court." A pair of little gold handcuffs manifested in his hands. With a twinkle they vanished and reappeared clasped around Robert's—Puck's wrists.

Laura felt her eyebrows arch up to her hairline. She gawped at the ugly little goblin. "You're a *cop*?"

"Faerie Bureau of Intervention, ma'am. Undercover specialist."

"But I thought you were just another jerk director."

The goblin waved a hand through the air with a flourish. "Acting!"

"Brilliant!"

"*Thank* you!" He bowed from the waist.

Nnagartha crossed her arms sternly. Her face was distressed, but not angry. Like a mother scolding a troublesome child, she said, "Puck. Why?"

The being in the bubble was no longer disguised as

Robert Goldfarb. Instead, his naked green-gold skin, pointed ears, and wide comical face made him look less arrogant, almost. . . puckish.

"You stopped paying attention to *me*," he said. "I was the King's and the land's most favored entertainer!" He pointed a long finger at Laura. "Until *she* came into our homes on the mages' boxes. It was I the people wanted, who played tricks and japes, then sang songs and made the people laugh even in the darkest times. Until Xora, until *her*."

Laura nodded. "That merry wanderer of the night. You jest to Oberon and make him smile, when you a fat and bean-fed horse beguile. And then the whole quire hold their hips and loff, and waxen in their mirth, and swear a merrier hour was never wasted there."

"Aye," said the prisoner softly.

"Lady?" Nnagartha said.

"Titania, summer stock."

"Ah. You realize, Lady, the risk you undertook? The magic was real, otherwise it would not have convinced him of your sincerity. If you had actually signed the contract, the veil would have closed and the stone used to create it would have been spent. There are no more veilstones known. You would have been trapped here. Very likely forever."

"That's what I figured."

The director-*cum*-detective puffed on an elaborate curved pipe. "What I don't understand is how you knew?"

"Easy. You gave me the clue. 'They'll pay more attention to it than anything else,' you said. 'Even the Jesters Guild has tossed in the towel.' I know what it's like to be a replaced performer, to be out on the streets two minutes after that final curtain drops. Let me tell you, it never gets easy and you never get used to it. I realized that with *Xora* at the top of the ratings around here, there was someone else who *had been* number one for a long time beforehand. If I were that someone, I would be more than a little pissed. Maybe pissed enough to be tempted to do something about it. I gambled that the last thing he would want was *me* getting his permanent four-star engagement with all the frills."

"I am a fool," Nnagartha said. "This is largely of my own making. Mine and the other peoples of the land. We should not have been so . . . distracted. That will carry weight in his favor with the High Court."

Laura squatted to look at Puck eye to eye. "After that, it was easy to figure out that the only new person in my life, beginning the same time as the strikes and the production shut-down and my problems with Terry, was my new agent—the miracle worker, as I called him."

"Hey!" R. Goodfellow managed to look indignant. "I had nothing to do with your piddling relationship problems. That's all *your* doing, and I'm not the least bit surprised about it. Criminy, if I were your mate I would have packed my bags long before Terry did. It doesn't take magic stones to see that you're more career-centered than people-centered!" He'd done a good job picking up earthly jargon. How much of that came from our TV shows, she wondered. Still, if he had meant to sting her, it worked. Hard.

Gurack paced the area authoritatively. "And you deduced that he was disguised as the mushroom because the mushroom hadn't been here when we arrived."

"Actually, 'guess' is a more accurate word than 'deduce.' But yes."

"You realize, I trust, that sudden manifestations of giant mushrooms and similar flora are no surprise around here."

"It was to me!"

Gurack nodded thoughtfully, cogitating on this new deductive approach.

Nnagartha said, "The trickster now owes you a boon. He must grant you one wish, whatever it may be. And

I assure you, he will do it well and willingly." Her voice carried a threat, and Puck nodded vigorously. "You were the victim of his ability to shape the wills of others. If you like, you may use that ability to your own advantage. It is only fair."

She indicated the window. It was steady now. The image of her backyard pool was crisp and clear and inviting. A familiar person—a beautifully, lovingly familiar person—sat on the edge of the pool.

"Jesus! What's Terry doing there?" It *was* Terry! Back at home. Talking with someone else—

"Jesus! What's *Bran* doing there!"

Bran's voice resonated from the window as he stroked Terry's blonde hair. "Lady," he was saying to the lovely woman, the most important writer in Laura's life, "Where I am from, a man shouts his love for his woman to the trees and the hills and the stars. . . ."

"Christ!" Laura shot to her feet. "How am I going to explain that?"

"You could use the boon," Nnagartha said, sounding all the world like a butch Glinda the Good. "You could make sure that she came back to you and stayed with you."

It was tempting.

"No," Laura said. "This one is my problem. I want Terry to want to come back on her own. We have a lot of talking to do." *Heart to itself: nice work, kiddo.*

"As you wish, Lady. Is there any other boon you desire instead?"

She wanted to sprint through the veil, usher Bran back through it, and watch it vanish. But not yet. "There is one." She cocked her head at the sulking figure in the bubble. "He knows what it is. I need a good agent again. I suspect he had a hand in getting rid of my former agent. He can help Adam and fix that particular problem, if you please."

"As you say, Lady."

Ruby slippers? Cut that crap. Laura stepped toward the window. The sun was setting on the meadow, the glittering city, and the cast and crew of *Xora: Avenger Priestess—Special Edition*. Maybe they had enough material for a travel documentary.

The window wavered and dimmed as she crossed through it. Bran passed her going the other way, looking puzzled. The last thing Laura heard was the dragon chatting with someone near the brook.

"Acting's fine for a start," the beast exclaimed. "But what I really want to do is direct."

A Bone to Pick

*Marina Frants &
Keith R.A. DeCandido*

"They're having another council," Matrena whispered, leaning over the fence into Vassilisa's garden. Neither the whispering nor the leaning was necessary—besides Vassilisa, the only living creatures within earshot were the half-dozen chickens milling aimlessly outside their coop, and Vassilisa's cat asleep in a sunny spot on the windowsill. But Matrena liked nothing better than telling a secret, so when no secret was available she made do by delivering ordinary pronouncements in a conspiratorial whisper. "They've been in there since sunrise!"

Vassilisa looked up at the sky. It was almost noon. "And they say we talk a lot. What are they waiting for, a message from Heaven?" She scooped a handful of seed from her apron pocket and tossed it to the chickens, who immediately began fighting over it.

The town's men had spent most of the week trying to decide what to do about the Tatars, who had sacked five nearby villages in the past month, and who were now rumored to be less than three days south of Voronye. The town elders had sent messengers to Kiev, asking for soldiers to protect them. The messengers came back with notes saying that "the request from the noble township of Voronye is being taken under advisement by the Tsar." Whoever did the Tsar's advising must not have considered Voronye all that noble, though, since no soldiers were forthcoming.

So the men held councils, the women whispered across fences, and no one actually did anything.

"It's a hard thing to decide—" Matrena began, but Vassilisa interrupted.

"There's nothing hard about it! The soldiers aren't coming. We have to protect ourselves."

"We can leave."

"The Tatars are nomads. They're used to traveling all the time. Most of us have never even left this town. While we stumble around trying to get our horses to do something other than pull a plow, the Tatars will catch up and pillage us on the road instead of here."

"Heaven forbid," Matrena made a quick warding sign. "Must you always believe the worst, Vaska?" Vassilisa winced. She hated being called Vaska, but she had long ago given up complaining about it. Besides, Matrena wouldn't let her get a word in as she barrelled onward: "That's what comes of living all alone for too long, with only chickens for company. You need a husband, a few little ones to cheer you up. You know my sister's boy, Danillo, is looking for a wife."

Vassilisa suppressed a sigh. Only Matrena would think of matchmaking with the Tatars knocking at the door. *When they come, she'll probably ask them to marry her nieces*, she thought.

Matrena seemed to be waiting for a response, so Vassilisa said, "I'm sure Danillo can find someone pretti—someone more suitable than me."

Matrena was not to be dissuaded. "He's not looking for a beauty, you know." Vassilisa bit her tongue. "You cook well, and keep a clean house. That makes up for a lot."

Even for freckles and hair the color of carrots? Just what I've always wanted, to be courted for my borscht recipe. Vassilisa searched for a politely neutral response, but before she could think of one, the subject of the conversation came walking up the path toward Matrena's yard.

"Danillo!" Matrena ran to the gate to let him in. "Is the council over? Have they decided what we're going to do?"

"Yes, Auntie." Danillo kissed Matrena on the cheek and gave Vassilisa a polite nod. "We will leave tomorrow morning and head for Kiev. If the Tsar won't send soldiers to protect us, he can shelter us instead."

"Tomorrow morning!" Vassilissa shrieked in a voice that sent the chickens scurrying back into their coop. "How far do you think we'll get, with less than two days' start? The Tatars will ride us down before we're halfway there!"

"They'll kill us for sure if we stay here," Danillo said irritably. "What else can we do?"

"We can stay and fight," Vassilisa snapped. "If the Tsar won't help, we must ask elsewhere."

"Elsewhere?" Danillo repeated incredulously. "If not the Tsar, then where? Do you propose to climb to the sky and ask the Sun for help?"

"No. I propose to go into the forest, and ask Baba Yaga."

She knew as soon as she spoke that she made a mistake. Matrena and Danillo gaped at her. Then they both fell back a step, and made signs against the evil eye.

"Don't even joke about such things," Matrena gasped. "She's a witch, Vassilisa."

"I know she's a witch. That's why she can help. If we can find her—"

"Enough," Danillo interrupted. "This is hard for all of us, Vassilisa. I know you're frightened, and saying things you don't really mean. So I'll forget all this talk of seeking help from witches, and so will Matrena. Now you go start gathering your things, and stop talking nonsense." He folded his arms across his chest, and jutted his chin at Vassilisa. It wasn't much of a chin, but Vassilisa pretended to be impressed.

"I'm sorry, Danillo. You're right—it's only my fear talking. I will see you later." And she fled into the house, before she could say anything else to shock the neighbors.

"Stop talking nonsense, he says." Vassilissa paced the length of her house, muttering to herself and kicking the furniture. "They're planning to try and *outwalk* a Tatar horde, and he tells *me* to stop talking nonsense?" She kicked the wall this time. The shelves rattled. She had already overturned one chair, and sent a jug full of cream crashing to the floor, much to the delight of the cat. Vassilisa considered cleaning it up, then decided not to bother. The whole house would be ashes in three days' time, anyway, unless someone did something.

Unless you do something. The thought kept popping up again and again over the past hour. Vassilisa stopped her pacing, and looked around her home. It didn't take long—she had just the one small room, dimly lit by the early afternoon sunlight filtering in through the two windows. There wasn't much furniture, and the only spot of color was a woven rug patterned with white and yellow roses that Vassilisa made the year before. Not exactly the Tsar's palace in Kiev, but it was hers, and she had no wish to lose it.

Vassilisa made up her mind all at once. She *would* go into the forest and look for Baba Yaga. Let Matrena and Danillo quake in their shoes and make warding signs. As far as Vassilisa was concerned, a choice between witchcraft and dying was no choice at all.

There was no point in lengthy preparations—she planned to be back by next morning or not at all. Vassilisa put out extra food for both the chickens and the cat, and wrapped up half a loaf of bread to take with her. The other half she put on a saucer together with a small bowl of salt, and placed the saucer by the oven in the hope that it would bribe the *domovoi* to guard the house from mishap while whe was gone. A pair of sturdy shoes, a red shawl to keep her shoulders warm, and she was ready to go.

She didn't see a soul on her way out of town. Presumably, everyone was at home, packing up their possessions for the journey. *Just as well*, Vassilisa thought. Given the mood she was in, if someone asked where she was going, she would probably tell them. She had a bad moment as she walked past the church, imagining Father Pyotr's reaction to her plan, but the church doors were shut, and the priest was nowhere in sight. Vassilisa breathed a deep sigh of relief, and sped up her steps.

Three hours later, she was beginning to wish that Father Pyotr had been there to stop her. She had never gone this far into the forest before. It was much larger, and darker, than she expected. There were no paths, no clearings, no sign of human life at all. The trees grew so close together that their roots intertwined. It seemed to Vassilisa that she had tripped over every single one of these roots in the course of one afternoon's walk. All she had to show for her grand quest were a torn dress, scraped knees, aching feet, and twigs festooned about her hair.

"The Devil take this forest, and every tree in it," she muttered as she picked herself up off the ground for the thousandth time. Was it her imagination, or did that last withered root actually move to snag her ankle as she tried to step over it? "How hard can it be to find a hut that walks on giant chicken legs? You'd think a witch that likes to eat human flesh would make herself easier to find when human flesh actually came looking for her." She brushed the dirt off her skirt, and resumed walking.

Ten paces later, she was flat on the ground again. This time she knew the bare, dead-looking oak tree in her path had tripped her on purpose. She actually saw the root moving just before she fell. Vassilisa sat up, rubbed her elbow where she bruised it in the fall, and tried to think. She was not going to get anywhere if she had to fight the forest every step of the way. Already, the shadows grew long. It would be dark soon. Vassilisa didn't relish the thought of spending the night outside, but she was not turning back. If nothing else, she wasn't sure she'd find the way. She hadn't expected to be out this long, and the bits of string she'd left to mark her path would be invisible in the dark. Baba Yaga was her only chance, not only of saving the town, but of ever seeing the wretched place again.

"I'm not leaving," she announced to the forest at large. "Do you hear me, Yaga? I'm not leaving! You might as well show yourself, because I'm staying in this forest until I either find you or drop dead!"

Her only answer was the rustle of leaves, and the call of wild geese somewhere in the distance. Vassilisa abruptly realized how foolish she must sound, sitting there covered in dirt and twigs, yelling at the trees. She stifled a laugh, and climbed to her feet again, resolved to keep walking until dark.

As soon as she stood up, she saw something that she could swear hadn't been there before her last fall: a narrow path weaving through the trees. Vassilisa stared at it suspiciously. Had she missed it before, or had it just appeared? Was it an invitation from Yaga, or a trick? Would lead her in circles until she was hopelessly lost?

It didn't matter, she decided. The only way to be sure was to go ahead. Vassilisa straightened her shoulders and tried to look brave as she stepped onto the path.

The route it led her on was so twisted and round-about, she almost concluded that it was a trick. But no root tripped her as she walked, no dead branch tore at her clothes or snagged her hair. And while he wood grew darker and darker around her, the path was lit as clearly as if it were midday. Vassilisa tried to take comfort in these things, and pressed on.

The path came to an end at a place that was lit as bright as the candles in Father Pyotr's church. But the light did not flicker, not even when a light breeze rustled the branches and blew a twig out of Vassilisa's hair.

Vassilisa hiked up her skirt and ran toward the light. The trees parted before her, and she stumbled out into a large clearing. The light was so bright now, it dazzled her for a moment, and she stood blinking away tears until she could see again.

In front of her was a waist-high picket fence made entirely of bones. White, gleaming bones, neatly held together with twine. Vassilisa gave a little scream, quickly stifled as she realized that the bones were much too large to be human. She couldn't imagine what they might be. Even bears didn't grow this large. The gate was made of smaller bones tied to form a grid. Bird skulls the size of large cabbages were set at even intervals all along the fence. The light came from their eyes.

Past the fence, just as the stories told, stood a hut on chicken legs. The legs were taller than Vassilisa, yellow and wrinkled, with claws buried deep in the ground for anchorage. Behind them, she could make out what looked like a vegetable garden, and a small chicken coop.

But for its support, the hut itself looked perfectly ordinary with its wooden walls, thatched roof, and two small windows with brightly painted yellow shutters. Vassilisa wondered how Baba Yaga got in and out, with her front door six feet above the ground. Did she fly? And how was Vassilisa going to get up there?

"Hello?" she called out. "Is anyone home? I am—"

"I know who you are!" The door flew open with a bang. A wooden ladder slid out and hit the ground with a thud. A pair of skinny legs appeared, clad in sagging woolen stockings and shod in woven bast slippers. The legs found purchase on the ladder, and a moment later the rest of Baba Yaga came into view.

She was obviously ancient, but she clambered down the ladder with no apparent difficulty. Having reached the bottom, she clapped her hands twice, and the ladder scooted back into the house by itself. Yaga turned, placed her hands on her hips, and glared at Vassilisa across the yard.

"There," she announced. "I've shown myself. Are you happy now?"

She clutched a wooden spoon in one hand, and wore a stained white apron over her dress. Vassilisa wondered what she might be cooking, then decided she didn't really want to know.

Vassilisa made a respectful bow. "I'm sorry to disturb you, grandmother, but this is important. I need to talk to you."

Yaga sneered, baring uneven yellow teeth. "Talk to me? Aren't you afraid I'll put the evil eye on you? Make you ugly? Make your cow's milk go dry?"

No, I'm afraid you'll decide that my bones are just the thing to mend that gap on the other side of the fence. Vassilisa's mouth felt dry. She told herself that if Yaga wanted to eat her, she would've tried to lure her inside, not scare her away, but the thought didn't provide much comfort. Well, if she couldn't feel brave, at least she could act it.

"I'm already ugly, and I haven't got a cow. May I come into the yard? I hate talking over a fence, it makes feel like I'm gossiping."

"Too bad," Yaga shook her spoon at Vassilisa. "You think I let just anybody into my yard? You tell me what you want, and I'll think about it."

"Very well." Vassilisa moved to lean on the fence, then remembered what it was made of and hastily straightened up again. "I want you to help me save Voronye from the

Tatars. You're a witch, there must be something you can do."

"Must there? I doubt the Tatars will come into the forest to bother me. And what do I care for Voronye? There's nothing there except mud and stink and stupid people who blame me every time a cup breaks or a pot overboils. If I went into your marketplace, people would spit and throw turnips at me. If I went into your church, the priest would drive me out. Why should I help you?"

Vassilisa wanted to point out that she would not spit and throw turnips, but she doubted it would make much difference to Yaga. She tried frantically to think of something that would make a difference, but she was too tired to match wits with Baba Yaga the way heroines in stories did. All she could think of was how much she wanted to sit down and take her shoes off.

"I don't know," she admitted. "But there must be something you want, something that would convince you. Tell me what it is, and you can have it." In truth, she couldn't imagine anything she might have that a witch could want, but there had to be something. There just *had* to be.

Baba Yaga stared at Vassilisa with an amazed expression. After a few moments, her eyes squeezed tightly shut, and her head shook. She made a noise like a creaky hinge. It took Vassilisa a moment to realize she was laughing.

"Anything I want?" Yaga wheezed between laughs. "What a generous town! And what if I want a mountain of gold, or the palace in Kiev, or the moon?"

Vassilisa sighed. "Then Voronye will die, and you'll get nothing. But I don't believe you want the moon. Tell me your price, and I'll meet it if I can."

Yaga stopped laughing, but a grin still crinkled her face. "You? Or the town?"

"Me. No one in Voronye knows I'm here. They didn't want to ask you. So whatever bargain you make, it will be with me only."

Yaga stepped closer to peer into Vassilisa's face. Up close, she smelled of mushrooms and herbs and freshly cut onions. Vassilisa had expected the whiff of human flesh, though of course she had no idea what cooked human flesh smelled like. *Maybe it smells like mushrooms*, she mused, then quickly pushed the thought away.

Baba Yaga tapped her spoon against the fence absent-mindedly. The wood made a little clicking noise against the bone.

"You're a brave girl," she finally said, "but not very smart."

Vassilisa was stung. "That's not what they say in Voronye."

"Oh, really? And what do they say?"

"They say I'm a smart girl, but not very pretty."

"Do they?" Baba Yaga gave another creaky laugh. "Well, they may be right. After all, they've known you longer. Why don't you come in, so I can get to know you too?"

She gestured with the spoon, and the gate swung open of its own accord. Vassilisa pretended not to be impressed as she walked through. But once inside the yard, she could no longer restrain her curiosity.

"What kind of bones are those?" She pointed at the fence. "I've never seen any that big."

Yaga patted the fence fondly, as if it were alive. "Chicken bones."

Vassilissa didn't know whether to laugh or be scared. "Chickens? They must grow taller than the trees! What do you feed them, and where can I get some of it?"

Yaga looked highly pleased with herself. "The chickens are ordinary size. It's the bones that are large."

"I don't understand."

"Of course you don't."

They walked into the back garden, stepping carefully between the neat rows of turnips and cabbages. When they reached the chicken coop, Baba Yaga took some seed from her apron pocket, and scattered it on the ground. The chickens promptly scurried out, clucking self-importantly at each other, and began pecking at their dinner.

"See?" Yaga said. "Ordinary chickens. And as long as they live, I can't make them anything else. It's only the dead things that do my bidding." She bent down and plucked a weed that had insinuated itself among the carrots. "This is dead," she said, "but it hasn't realized it yet. I'll tell it now." She held the weed close to her face and murmured at it in a voice so soft, Vassilisa couldn't make out a single word. As she spoke, the weed began to shudder and writhe in her hand. The leaves curled and the stalk shriveled. Its color changed from green to yellow to brown. By the time Yaga finished speaking, only a withered husk was left. She breathed on it, and it crumpled to dust and blew away.

"I can help you," Yaga said. "But there will be a price."

"Name it."

"Oh, no. It's not for me to name. I will give you a spell to drive away the Tatars. Go home. Use it. And wait. When you know what the price is, come back here."

"How will I know?"

"You'll know." Baba Yaga grabbed Vassilisa's arm, and hustled her back toward the hut. "Come along now. The spell will take most of the night. We must prepare."

"We?" Vassilisa squeaked. "I don't know how to prepare any spells!"

Yaga only laughed again.

The sun was just rising over the treetops when Vassilisa staggered into Voronye, dusty and disheveled, and lugging an extremely heavy and awkwardly shaped sack over one shoulder. She found most of the town's population gathered in the marketplace. Those who owned horses had harnessed them to carts loaded with all their worldly possessions. Those who didn't, carried bundles stuffed with as much as they could lift without toppling over. Vassilisa quickly spotted Matrena—her cart was larger than anyone else's, and piled twice as high.

"Vaska! Here you are. I've been looking for you all morning." She poked Vassilisa's sack, which rattled in response. "You won't get very far carrying that. My cart is too full, but I'm sure Danillo will find a spot on his, if you ask him nicely."

Vassilisa was too tired to deal politely with Matrena's matchmaking. "I'm not going anywhere," she snapped. "And don't call me Vaska. I hate that." She dropped the sack into the dirt with a groan of relief, untied the twine that held it shut, and turned it upside down. A pile of white bones came spilling out into the dirt, followed by a grinning human skull that bounced twice before landing with a thud at Matrena's feet.

Matrena shrieked. Some of the people standing within earshot turned, saw the bones, and also shrieked. The noise spread like ripples through a lake until Father Pyotr elbowed his way through the crowd to see what the commotion was about. He did not shriek at the sight of the bones, but placed his hands on his hips and glared at Vassilisa.

"Where did these come from?" he demanded.

"I should think that would be obvious," Vassilisa said.

Father Pyotr simply glowered in response. Once, that glower would have sent Vassilisa meekly to her knees in apology, but after spending an evening with Baba Yaga, she was not so easily intimidated.

Still, she supposed she'd have to tell them sooner or later. "Baba Yaga gave them to me," she said. There was a collective gasp, and everyone except Father Pyotr fell back a step. The priest stood his ground, though he did cross himself somewhat more emphatically than usual.

"Are you insane?" he hissed. "You think we don't have enough trouble, without you bringing unclean magic among us? You'll bring bad luck to the journey, we'll be lost—"

"We don't have to go anywhere," Vassilisa interrupted. "Yaga's put a spell on these bones to drive away the Tatars. We'll be safe now."

"Safe!" Father Pyotr's voice rose so much that he started to sound like Matrena. It was all Vassilisa could do to keep from snickering. "And who will keep us safe from Yaga, when she comes to demand her price? When she wants our blood for her potions, or our bones for her next spell?"

"She won't. I came to her alone, so I pay alone. She swore on it."

"And you believed her?" Father Pyotr grabbed Vassilisa by the shoulders, and gave her a vigorous shake. "What's wrong with you, girl? Are you bewitched, or just stupid? An oath means nothing to a witch, she'll—"

"They're coming!" someone screamed. Vassilsa turned, and saw a rising cloud of dust in the distance on the other side of the wheat fields.

"That's impossible." Father Pyotr let go of Vassilisa's shoulders and took a shaky step back. "They—they weren't supposed to get here for another two days."

Vassilisa rolled her eyes. "Why don't you go tell them that?" she suggested. "I'm sure if you explain politely that they are ahead of schedule, they'll go away and come back on Sunday."

No one responded to this. People were too busy grabbing their bundles and running, or jumping on their carts and riding, or rushing about in circles and screaming that they were going to die. Vassilisa put her hands over her ears to help shut out the noise, stood over the bone pile, and recited the spell Yaga had taught her the night before.

As she spoke the last word, the bones began to move. At first, they crawled along the ground, spreading themselves in a circle around Vassilisa's feet. Then they floated into the air, spinning as they rose. A few seconds later, Vassilisa stood at the center of a rattling whirlwind of bones.

The ground beneath her feet trembled slightly. She couldn't tell if it was a side effect of the spell, or just the sign of a Tatar army approaching at full gallop. All she could see was a blurred wall of white. And dust. The carts, the ground, and the marketplace stalls were all covered with generous portions of dust, and the bones kicked up all of it. Vassilisa sneezed. *Maybe I should've done this in a cleaner place. Like the church. Father Pyotr would love that. . . .*

Something detached itself from the whirlwind. It looked like several human ribcages fused together into a solid mass. It struck Vassilisa's chest and stayed there, forming a breastplate. Other bones, equally misshapen or restructured, attached themselves to her sides, her shoulders, her back. She barely had time to gather her skirt up around her hips before the bones surrounded her legs. She lifted her arms, and bony sleeves encased them. As a finishing touch, the skull grew as big as a bucket, and landed on her head with one final clunk.

The whirlwind ceased. In its place was an armor made of bones. A heavy, stuffy, and extremely uncomfortable armor, with some of the dust still trapped inside it. Vassilisa sneezed again, banging her head against the back of the helmet, and looked around. She couldn't see very well through the eye holes, but it seemed to her that about half the town's population had fled the square. The rest were watching her from a distance, muttering softly among themselves. Father Pyotr was still there, clutching the crucifix around his neck and praying under his breath.

"It's all right," Vassilisa told them. Her voice echoed hollowly inside the skull helmet. The ground was shaking harder now—the riders must be getting closer. Unfortunately, she could not turn her head inside the helmet to look at them. *So what do I do now?* she thought.

Then the armor began to walk.

Vassilisa yelped and flailed her arms. Or rather, she tried to flail them, but could only rattle them about inside the sleeves. The armor moved with a will of its own, and all Vassilisa could do was ride along.

It turned to the right, then walked her out into the middle of the field and stopped. Now she could see the approaching riders—the small, dirt-spattered horses, and the wiry leather-clad men. There weren't as many of them as Vassilisa expected, but there were certainly more than enough to trample Voronye into the ground. They came closer and closer, but once again the armor would not move.

Sweat poured down Vassilisa's face. She started to panic. The entire army was going to ride right over her without breaking stride while she stood there trapped in a pile of bones. *Why did it form around me if I can't control it? What kind of magic is this, anyhow?*

Then the first line of horses came to a dead stop. Vassilisa could hear shouting, and clanging, and stomping hooves, as the riders in the back tried to avoid collision. Some failed, and the horses went down screaming, taking their riders with them. Vassilisa mentally braced herself. *Surely the armor will move now.*

It didn't.

Maybe now it will let me *move it.* She tried to take a step forward, and succeeded only in banging her knee. *And maybe not.*

The Tatars regrouped much faster than Vassilisa expected, but nothing they could do would make their horses move any closer.

Finally, Vassilisa realized what was happening. The armor didn't need to move as long as the riders stayed mounted—the horses knew death magic when they smelled it, even if their riders didn't. They trembled, they whinnied, they pawed the ground, but they wouldn't move an inch. One of the riders fired an arrow, which struck the armor in the chest. Vassilisa felt no impact, but heard the crack of broken wood as the arrow snapped in two and fell to the ground. More arrows came, with similar results.

The armor, apparently realizing that it now had to deal with humans, chose this moment to take a step forward and raise its arms—which almost yanked Vassilisa's arms out of their sockets. The armor clawed at the air like an angry bear.

Deciding to participate in the only way left her, Vassilisa shouted, "Boo!" It came out sounding like the howl of a demon.

That finally did it. The horses broke and ran, and the riders made only a token effort to stop them. Within minutes, only a trampled wheat field remained to show that an army had ever come anywhere near Voronye.

When the Tatars were out of sight, the bone armor fell from around Vassilisa, hit the ground with a dull thud, then crumbled to dust.

It wasn't until the next morning that Vassilisa realized that something was wrong. The previous day was filled with activity as the people of Voronye returned to their homes, unpacked their belongings, and gathered in their back yards to gossip about what had happened. Vassilisa herself had been too tired to do anything more than stagger to her own house, collapse on the bed, and sleep. But early next morning, as she went out to feed the chickens, she called her usual greeting to Matrena, and Matrena crossed herself and backed away.

It got worse from there. She went to market, and the women spat and threw turnips at her. She tried to go to church, and Father Pyotr wouldn't let her in. Children pointed at her and screamed "witch" until their mothers dragged them away.

After two days of this harassment, Vassilisa realized she could not live like this. Leaving aside any other considerations, she really hated turnips.

Well, she thought, *at least now I know what price to name to Baba Yaga.*

On her second trip into the forest, this time carrying her few belongings and her cat, Vassilisa spotted the path immediately. The forest seemed less tangled, less dark, almost welcoming. Baba Yaga waited for her outside the hut, looking much the same as she had before, except her apron was cleaner. She still smelled of mushrooms and onions, as well as a spice Vassilisa couldn't identify.

Without preamble, Vassilisa said, "You knew this would happen, didn't you? You could've told me."

"Would you have listened?" Yaga replied.

Vassilisa thought about it, then shook her head. "I suppose not. They didn't deserve to die, and I'm glad I could help them. But I can't live with them anymore. They all think I'm a witch."

"Of course they do. They may be stupid, but they're not that stupid. You are a witch."

Vassilisa blinked. "What?"

Yaga opened the gate, and led a stunned Vassilisa into the yard. "You think that spell works for just anyone?" She patted Vassilisa's arm. Her hand felt warm and friendly. "I think you'll like being a witch. I'll teach you while I can, and when I'm gone you'll have the hut and the chickens."

Vassilisa stopped before stepping onto the ladder that led into the hut. "Tell me one thing, though—you don't have a nephew looking for a wife who can cook, do you?"

Yaga glared at her. "Don't be ridiculous."

"Good." Vassilisa relaxed. "I'll stay, then."

The Attack
of the Avenging Virgins
(as told by one of the
Valiant Vanquished)

Elizabeth Ann Scarborough

Southern Campaign,

Dear Mum,

I hope this finds you in good health and spirits. Me?
I am too hot, otherwise fine. This country is not what
you'd call healthy, being full of little insects that bite
and suck your blood and make you swell and itch. Also
full of swampland and jungle, with large toothy reptiles
and asps. Which would not be so bad, except that most
of the asps are officers. (Heh heh. Little joke, Mum.
See? I have not lost my wacky sense of humor.)

I thought I should send this off before we leave
Sooltri, which as you know is the capital city of Ecotri,
our immediate neighbor to the south (see crude map
enclosed).

I enclose for you this very nice pair of gilt embroidered lacy knickers I found lying around here. They
looked to be about your size. The former occupant
wasn't wearing them at the time, being otherwise

109

engaged with several of the fellows from my unit. But don't worry, Mum, it's not like they're *nice* girls around here. Foreigners, you know. Funny looking, filthy habits, just heathens, really. Still, the knickers were rather fetching and I thought you might fancy them.

Captain Burden says that taking the capitol was only the beginning. To truly conquer these barbarians, we have to wipe out their outlandish religion at its roots— the sacred temple of their goddess, whose name starts with an A, it seems to me. Amy? Annie? Agatha? No, none of those seem right. It was longer than that. The temple is supposedly guarded by hundreds or maybe even thousands of beautiful virgins, cruelly kept by these misguided souls from fulfilling their true nature as mothers, wives, sweethearts, or dinar-a-dance girls by the head virgin, known as the Virago, the high priestess of their outlandish goddess, whatsername-that-starts-with-an-A. They also guard the true objective of our mission, the fabled Sacred Assets, said to be even more wondrous and valuable than the considerable booty we've gathered thus far.

Anyway, we must cut our way through many miles of jungle to get to the temple, which is hidden in the mountains.

If you wonder how I've become such an expert on this mysterious country, I'll tell you. Sgt. Swinborne briefed us on it earlier today.

It took Sgt. Swinborne a couple of days to get this information from the locals—but once we took the palace and he was able to use the facilities at the royal dungeon on the royal family, it was amazing how cooperative and eager to please everyone was. Like little children, in a way. Normally they don't seem to value life the same way we do, perhaps it's the heat? But people are sentimental about the nobility, if you can call them that. The queen, who is the sectoolar, sekyouler? Non-religious, anyway, ruler, because she obviously got married and had children, which our Sarge found helpful, anyway, she was particularly anxious to please once the sergeant began chatting up the little crown princess.

Sarge said her former majesty couldn't talk fast enough, actually. Says she told him the temple is actually inside the mountains, in this great maze of caves—the mountains here being made of some unsuitable porous rock. She said we'd never find it because it was miles and miles away and the jungle was full of man-eating animals and the aforementioned asps and large toothy reptiles and such. He pointed out to her former majesty very reasonably, he said, that there surely must be a nice path back there, since it *is* the seat of their religion and they must go out that way for ceremonies and such and she said, no, that the temple virgins periodically come into the city to bless everyone and that otherwise they seclude themselves and do sacred stuff, like making sacrifices and polishing collection bowls and guarding the Sacred Assets and such. This generally keeps them busy enough to keep them from being seen by men. When we troops talked it over among ourselves after Sarge told us this, we figured they had to be kept away from the lads because they were very beautiful and unlikely to remain qualified for their jobs as temple virgins if they got out much.

Well, we're just mopping up on the raping, killing, looting and pillaging now. We are rather undermanned to hold the city, such as it is. A shame we had to do the looting before we make the trek to the temple. Now we have to carry it all with us, as there is no one here to guard it. No place really, once we finished using the cannon on all those buildings. They were rather flimsy things, with spires and curlicues and onion domes and such, and fell apart immediately. Hard to imagine it ever amounting to anything, now, though it looked ever so grand and full of itself when we first arrived.

Must rush now. Time to put one foot in front of the other, as it were. I'm glad I mostly got a bit of jewelry for you and Sarah and Gisela. A few loose gems to turn a profit on, maybe. Pried 'em out of the eyes of the heathen idols. Things were thick with these jewels and not just the eyes, if you know what I mean. Lucky for me that A goddess likes her baubles. They'll be lighter to carry than what some of the other fellows have. Sarge was just dying to bring a lot of the tools he found in the dungeon. Said he wanted to speak to the temple virgins and do a bit of anthropological study on the local religion with the aim of discrediting it and converting the populace. Religious fellow, our Sarge. He brought along her former Majesty, thinking she might enjoy the pilgrimage, though she's a bit long in the tooth and rather too tattered from the initial persuasive tactics of our Sarge to be of much interest to the lads at the moment. But Captain Burden said that ours is not the first invasion force of our folk to come down and decimate the capital city. Sid Smythers, who is a curious one, raised his hand and wanted to know if we weren't the first, how did we know there would still be virgins and Sacred Assets left. Captain said we didn't, exactly, but after the reports came home that the troops had taken the city and were on their way to the sinister temple, the invasion forces inconveniently disappeared *completely* and *forever* into the unknown. He says at least fifteen other attempts have been made and not one man has ever returned. Just so you'll understand if you don't hear from me very often for awhile.

From Deep in the Jungle
Night Watch
Dear Mum,
Hi? How are you doing? I am fine though hot and wet and have a bit of foot rot from walking on the

squishy jungle floor. I wouldn't want to worry you, but I must say that there is something very strange indeed about this jungle. This afternoon Corporal Peabody was eaten by a very pretty flower and Symington lost half his right hand and the fingers to the first knuckles on the left trying to drag poor Peabody, who was making an awful ruckus, out of the blasted posy. Swinborn had to speak quite harshly to the old queen about failing to warn us of this particular danger. He said the next time something of the sort happened, he would see to it that she came out no better than the lad caught unawares by the indigenous flora, as the brothers at our school would call it.

The queen apologized, weeping with sincerity and also because of her split lip, and said that the flower was not known to her but must be one of the magical traps laid by the temple guardians along the trail. As they changed from time to time, she could hardly be held responsible, could she? Sarge growled but don't worry, Mum. I know how tender hearted you are but, actually, it's unlikely he'll feed the queen to the blossom because we do rather need her to guide the way. He's got a collar fixed round her neck and a bit of rope to pull her back in if she looks like she's going too far into the jungle. I must say, Mum, these people have their pride. She wears the bloody thing as if it was made of diamonds and golden chain.

LATER

Well, that was rather interesting. I was just sitting here writing to you when the queen drags herself over and says to me, in quite the sort of cute accent these people have because they can't speak properly like we can. "So, you are mercenary, yes?"

"Oh no. No indeed," I said. "I am a patriot, fighting for—er—you know? King. Country. The right way of life and all that."

She gave a sigh every bit as great as the one you do when Sister soiled the frock you'd spent all day washing and ironing. In fact, under the old shiner she'd got back in the city and the newly split lip, now that I saw her close up, she looked not too different from Mrs. Benshoof down the block. You know, dark and exotic and yet as common as anything, in a regal sort of way, of course. But not a bit hoity-toity, as you might think.

I mean, there she was, a queen, talking to me as if we were on guard duty together. I hadn't seen her close up or heard her speak until then. Well, you could tell she was a fine educated lady by how she knew our language, couldn't you? Even if it was a little hard to understand her. I wondered if I ought to bow or something. She didn't seem to care one way or the other, so I skipped it.

"What is that you're working on?" she asked in a chatty fashion.

"Just a letter to me Mum," I told her. Well, of course she was the enemy and all that but it wasn't as if I was telling her how many reinforcements we were expecting or which men were our best marksmen.

"You have a mother?" she asked, sounding surprised.

"Of course I do! Everyone has a mother—Ma'am," I said, remembering her queenship just in time.

"You'd never think it, the way your men treat our women," she said—well, ruefully, of course. She naturally would rue what had gone on and what had become of her. No help for that, was there?

"Oh that," I said, glad it was dark because I felt the heat rising in my face. "That's just war, you know. Spoils and tactics and such. Nothing personal."

She laughed a rather unpleasant laugh. "I hardly see how it could have been more personal, but never mind. How does your mother take the news you send of your exploits here against my people?"

"Dunno, really," I admitted.

"You don't?"

"Well, can't really post letters until someone is sent home and right now nobody is going, so I just keep track, like. I did send one out of the city, but there's been no time for a reply. Sent some lovely souvenirs to Mum and Sarah and Gisela. That's my sisters, Sarah and Gisela."

"*Did* you?" she asked. "What are they like, Sarah and Gisela? Do they grovel at your feet?"

She had a bit of trouble pronouncing their names but the girls would've liked how their names sounded in her mouth, split lip and all. Sort of softer and furry and with longer hisses on the s's. Very foreign. Classy, I rather thought. But then, you'd expect that of a queen. Even a heathen one.

"Oh, my goodness no. They're both on the bossy side, actually. Sarah's tall and plump and blond and Gisela is short and skinny and redheaded," I said. "Sarah's good at games and is ever so fond of animals and Gisela wants to be a queen herself when she grows up. That's what Mum says. Leastways, Gisela is always managing others and only does as she likes. Say, I don't suppose you'd care to tell me a few things about the queening business I might pass on, would you?"

She sighed. "I'm not a particularly shining example at the moment, I fear. But I'll tell you what. If you will allow me to attend to my personal needs in private, just there, beyond that bush, so I need not be humiliated further in front of your—comrades—I will write to your sister myself."

"You write in our language?" I asked.

"Why not? I'm speaking to you in it, am I not?"

"Oh, I beg your pardon, Ma'am, that you are. I—uh—I think I should probably take charge of the end of your rope, just so Sarge doesn't have my skin off. I won't look, I promise, but it's as much as my job is worth if you escape."

"I wouldn't dream of it," she said, and smiled at me. Somehow I didn't get the impression she liked me at all, though. She took the end of the rope, like she was going to help me, and held it up so the end dangled by my nose. She swung it back and forth, all the time smiling.

I didn't think anything of it, at the time, except that she was an odd one. Don't recall her spewing forth foreign enchantments or any of that sort of thing. Just swung the rope, back and forth, back and forth, while I watched it like a great ninny.

Then she strolled over to the bush, the rope trailing her like you always hear of the trains of court gowns doing, elegant like. She just twitched it a bit as she went round the corner and lady, rope and all disappeared behind the bush . . . how curious. (ZZZZZZ)

LATER

Dear Brother St. Elmo of the Martyred Albatross,

I am writing to you from this place to ask you for spiritual guidance and counsel. You're the only one I can talk to about this because Mum would not understand if I had the bollocks to tell her. But it's been said around the school that you were in the Navy before you took your vows and became sainted and all, so between your being a saint and a sailor, I figured you'd know what's what.

The thing is, we're on campaign see, you probably heard about it. And there's this ex-queen prisoner our Sarge made to guide us. You can go see my letters to Mum (enclosed—be so good of you to deliver them) if you need more background. She'll be glad for your visit, I'm sure.

The thing is, while I was on guard duty, this queen comes up to me and asks if she can take a whiz in private like, away from the lads, and I saw no harm to it as Mum always taught me to respect the ladies—well,

Mum and my sister Sarah's good right hook. This queen
was pretty friendly, for an enemy. And from how long
it took her, I figure it must have been a long time since
she went.

But while I was waiting there, eyes and ears open,
as I thought, still thinking myself as alert a sentry as
ever hoped to skewer an officer for not identifying
himself as friend or foe, peculiar things began to happen.

First thing I heard, over the sound of the royal
waterfall over behind the bush, was this funny-sounding
bird flying over. I couldn't see it, of course. The trees
in this jungle are thick as the warts on Brother St. Maisie
the Maladjusted's nose and even though you feel the
sun hot as anything, you never see daylight and it drips
steaming raindrops all day long and all night as well.

Back to the bird, it was making a cry that could have
curdled milk to cheese while it was still inside the cow.
Very upsetting sort of thing to hear that time of the night.
None of our boys woke up though and I decided it was
just me, being jumpy. Pretty soon this bird got answered
by another bird, and then another one. I got a bit worried. If these were songbirds, their taste in music was
somewhat unusual, to say the least. I wondered how large
they were. They certainly were loud enough.

Then the queen, or at least somebody who looked
just like her, comes back around the bush. Her smile
was much nicer than when she left, I supposed because
of the relief and all.

I changed my mind when she was followed by
another woman, and another and another, all nearly
naked except for frocks of some linked metal overlaying
matching metal unmentionables. They were tittering and
squealing like schoolgirls but they were very large and
mature schoolgirls indeed.

They made the queen and me look like dwarves, but
they didn't stoop, the way some tall girls do.

The queen spoke to a lady much taller than the

others, who wore her hair pulled back and had magnifying glasses surrounded by studded bronze over each eye. She looked much like Sarah's hockey mistress. I heard her say "Virago" but couldn't make out the rest.

The Virago nodded to one who wore her curly pale hair in a tail down her back. Made her look a bit like an oversized duckling. The two of them looked at me and jabbered.

"Wha—what are they *on* about?" I asked the Queen.

She stooped down and whispered, "I told the Virago to give you to Melisel to take first. And to be gentle because you write to your mother and didn't peek. Perhaps, if you are able, you will thank me for my mercy later."

I wish I could say, sir, that the rest of it was all a blur but actually I remember it quite well. The girl Melisel stretched like a cat getting ready for a meal, then did a couple of handsprings, causing her metal frock to rise well above her shapely thighs, and did cartwheels so that I became aware that my first impression of her attire was erroneous—of course, metal knickers would chafe something terrible so she had dispensed with them—or any other kind. Well, I thought to myself, and as it turned out I was quite right, as I often am, (Mum says it's second sight but just good sense is what I think) whatever else may be said about nubile maidens, a girl who would do such tricks in such lack of attire was capable of anything. And though everything was atttractively covered with soft and rounded skin, she was, as I said, a very large girl. Also very athletic. Also very very strong, as I was soon to discover.

I supposed she was doing this to convince me that resistance was futile, which I had already decided, as she displayed her mighty, albeit extremely attractive, thews and sinews and such.

Meanwhile, all the other women also were taking full advantage of the element of surprise. Though I can't say I was able to pay a great deal of attention to much of anything else, I did notice that, judging from the flash of smoothly muscled limbs gleaming in the moonlight, the other girls were cavorting about in the same acrobatic way and with the same lack of decency. It occured to me that either these ladies were professional trollops, if you don't mind my using such a blunt word, or that they were very naïve and would shortly be taught a lesson by our lads, who had been awakened by the girlish giggling and squealing and perfumery and the thumping and bumping of feet and hands, backsides and bellies hitting the ground in the course of various tricks.

I suppose we should have each reached for our weapons but the truth was, the only weapons any of us apparently felt the need for were the ones fully alerted by the antics of our attackers. It was only crossing my mind that another sort of dagger might also be useful in this case when I saw that the ladies seemed to be into their grand finale, where they landed, each astraddle one of our lads. One, in fact, Melisel of the pale gold horsetail, was astride me. My weapon—the metal one— was out of reach before the thought had quite finished forming.

Melisel's pale hair hung over me like a ghost, her bared teeth and eyes twinkled in the shadow of it, as did the tiny brass things that protected a very insignificant portion of her voluminous upper anatomy. Not that she was fat at all. Not a bit of it. Well, some bits.

I hardly know how to tell you this, Brother. She— uh—had her way with me. Wicked way, of course. Ravished me, that is. Up to a point, beyond which I was not able to go. I thought it might be from inexperience. I thought the other fellows were no doubt making a more thorough job of it, but as for myself I fear that I let the—er—side—down.

Even worse, the queen looked on the whole time, her expression not changing no matter what happened.

"Who *are* you?" I cried, in something somewhat like, but not quite the same as, agony.

The queen obligingly repeated my question in her own heathen tongue and the girl laughed merrily and licked my face impertinently . . . All while holding her dagger at my throat.

"She's one of the temple virgins, of course," the queen pointed out. "All of these women are."

"Hardly," I pointed out. "If this is any example of their military tactics, they can hardly be virgins."

"Oh, you mean *this*? *This* doesn't count," the queen said with a dismissive wave of her hand. That hurt.

"Does so!" I protested with some difficulty, the dagger pressing into my adam's apple.

The queen smirked and shook her head. "Does not. The Holy Virgins are now performing the Coup of Conquest, which is completely different from the deflowering you seem to think you're close to affecting. It is very much an opposite sort of thing."

I was too distracted to ask why that was, unfortunately, for I was desperately trying to bring matters with Melisel to a more satisfactory conclusion. I hope you won't repeat it to any of the other brothers or mates of mine that instead I simply ended up exhausted, deflated, defeated and desperately craving a smoke and a nap.

Oddly enough, that was exactly the point at which I became once more alert to reality—which, of course, I hadn't realized I wasn't before.

But all at once the girl's weight no longer pressed me to the ground, the moldy air hit my open eyes, and I sat up, fully clothed. My steel weapon was in the hands of Melisel, who seemed to be real enough, but the queen was standing far off, over by where Sarge had laid his bedroll. He was making an awful groaning sound and holding his goolies. In and among my fellows stood these big buxom girls, looking very stern indeed.

And despite my former observations on the ladies' fashions, they wore full metal jackets *and* knickers with their chain mail frocks—a powerful suit of armor indeed. They were obviously well able for us and resistance at this point didn't seem a very good idea. Especially since each girl held one or more of our weapons in a business-like manner.

Melisel jerked me to my feet and we joined a procession of my fellows, each of whom was now in the grip of one of the temple "virgins," who were disappearing into the woods. As we passed a pair of the girls, they clamped leg irons and chains upon our wrists that bound us all together in a way that wasn't a bit jolly.

We trudged on into the night until, at dawn, the girls removed a bit of shrubbery from the mountainside and revealed a very narrow opening in a mountain face that otherwise looked absolutely solid. We entered into a kind of open air grotto. It was an amazing site, a temple carved from the stone the mountains all around it. Caves forming windows and doors all the way up. Would have made a lovely market, and was, despite being made out of free stuff already on hand, quite as impressive as any of our churches. They must be tax exempt here too. Long flights of steps led halfway up one of the mountains to the main entrance. This was great fun in our chains, as you may imagine.

The ladies abandoned us in a long barracks-like chamber, without food or water. I have no idea what's to become of us but in case we're to be put to death I was just wondering if fornicating with a heathen priestess was a sin if one doesn't fully, shall we say, achieve the goal? I do hope you will send up a prayer for yours truly in the event this reaches you.

Yr. Former student

❖   ❖   ❖

Dear Mum and Our Ambassador,

I am training a pigeon in my spare time, which I don't have much of, to carry my messages to you. Unfortunately, the bird is a bit thick when it comes to maps and street numbers and such but I trust sooner or later he'll get the hang of it. Or perhaps some other bird will be flying toward the embassy.

I had hoped I might manage to make contact myself, since the queen and her large lady friends immediately packed us all back to the city. This time, however, we traveled by way of quite a good road Her Majesty had not remembered to tell us about before.

Under the gentle (hardly) direction of our recent enemies, we've all been given jobs at hard labor rebuilding the city, mending broken idols and replacing the jeweled bits, building shelters and so forth while we are left to sleep in the mud and fed the same thing for weeks and months at a time.

Very much like boot camp, actually.

Our chow comes from a soup line run by Local Temple 303, where the girls are not especially virgins and are a bit smaller than the mountain lasses. The food is cold but it tastes well enough except that it makes your belly ache all night until you spew it all up in the morning. The bad conditions haven't done much for anyone's temper. In fact, the men are behaving in rather strange ways. I saw Captain Burden hurl his soup at the wall and declare that he simply *had* to have pickled cod and clotted cream that day or he wouldn't be able to go on. At that Sarge (poor soul) started weeping and said that it was simply too much to expect him to carry on as he had been when the officers who were paid ever so much more behaved like spoiled children.

The rest of us have had the cravings and the vomiting too, though that finally mostly went away after the initial endless weeks of work. They switched our diet to some sort of gruel then. This wasn't as tasty as the soup and is for some reason bloats a fellow something fierce. My ankles are so swollen some days I can barely walk and my feet look like oars. And my—er—chest hurts, around the tender bits.

While we are working, a lot of people line up to throw things at us and jeer.

Through it all the temple virgins pretend not to notice. I tried winking bravely at Melisel when I saw her but she just stared straight ahead and pretended not to notice. Fickle wench.

Some of the women just smirk at us, though they talk nicely enough with the temple virgins. My belly is as big as a hay bale and I've gas something awful and feel as if I'm going to have to get rid of it somehow or die, quite frankly.

A couple of days ago, just when it seemed our conditions were improving, as we were given a sort of sweet with our gruel, some of the men began screaming and falling down, grabbing themselves and crying and grunting. I found out first hand last night that it was because they were in a lot of pain—I know I certainly was. I thought I'd split wide open with the agony of it all. The pains were an hour apart to begin with, then every fifteen minutes or so and every ten and so forth until at last it was just one long unbearable century or so of anguish while the thing that seemed to fill me from gullet to goolies, a thing with sharp hooves and needles like a porcupine, was being pried out by some invisible force using a battering ram and a fireplace poker.

It finally ended but I am still very tender and well and truly knackered.

Fortunately, this morning for the first time, though the work is not done, we have been ordered to stand in a line and face our accusers. We have been here, and I know as the Virago makes a point of telling us how long we've been in captivity every day, as it it has some meaning we don't understand, some three months shy of a year, but it's been like forever. Please send troops or money or whatever they ask and get us out of here.

Sacred Secret Temple—The Creche
Dear Mum,
    Hello. It's me again. Your son. At least, I started out that way.
    Wish you were here, and I mean that more than you may realize.
    You see, the vengeance of the virgins upon us was a terrible and subtle one indeed. While we stood at attention beside our work stations, the Virago, with the Queen at her side to translate, read out a list of our crimes.
    "Now," the Virago said sternly, looking over her magnifying glasses at us, her chain mail frock jingling like a jailer's keys in the high wind that swept sodden debris up and swirled and smacked it against the various onlookers as well as us accused. On the other side of the Virago stood Melisel, her curly horse tail fanned out and spread like a cobra's hood around her head. "You the war criminals will be faced by your victims and your punishment will be meted out as is appropriate."
    A troop of city women, some of them young, some older, some barely more than children, and all somewhat familiar, trooped forward. Each carried a bundle, some carried more than one.
    The Virago's magnified eyes were the blue of glaciers as they met the gaze of each man.
    The Queen translated. "What is it with you guys? Your country never seems to learn! We are just sitting down here minding our own business, worshipping Our Goddess, sculpting beautiful images of Her, eating, drinking, trading, our citizens falling passionately in love with each other and carrying on blissful consensual sexual relations in order to have happy, healthy children who will carry on our chosen lifestyle

while respecting that of others, when here you come
again. Once was not enough for you. You come over
and over, never letting us alone nor taking no for an
answer. In the olden days, our foremothers would
simply impale any of you who sacked our city, making the punishment fit the crime against our women
under the protection of our Great Goddess, the Divinity whose name is Diversity, Affirmaterra." (That's
it. Not Amy after all, but Affirmaterra. I'd heard them
jabbering it, of course, but until the queen translated,
I didn't know.) As soon as the name was uttered, all
the women stamped the ground and raised their fists
in salute while shouting, "Yes!" or so near as to make
no difference in their own tongue. "However, we have
since gained enlightenment. Impaling was messy, noisy,
smelly, and generally icky. It was also a waste of re-
sources—trees *died* to make the stakes that impaled
your countrymen. So over the years, we have come to
rely on our Sacred Assets instead (at this the women
did a stomp-stomp, slap right mailed hip with right
metal gauntleted hand, left with left, and each fist is
socked into the air so that the whole salute has six
counts to it—stomp stomp, slap slap, sock sock, sort
of thing), the life-giving force of our Womanhood which
we conserve and dedicate to Affirmaterra, the Divinity of Diversity (the goddess's salute, described above)
to neutralize and nullify you, to punish you."

We lads looked at one another in dismay. The Sacred
Assets weren't golden treasure at all then? Oh dear. We
could have dispensed with the temple all together then,
saved ourselves the trouble and gone home with the
booty we just finished rebuilding into the temples and
idols and such. Hindsight is better than foresight, I
suppose, particularly in this case, if you'll pardon me
for being a bit crude, Mum.

"Through the use of the Assets we made you helpless.
And in administering the goddess's Nectar of Natality,

we have transferred to you the pains and bodily indig-
nities endured by your female victims in the aftermath
of your cruel misuse of their Goddess Given bodies."

"That's what it was all about?" muttered Symington.
"Well, it was worse than kidney stones just like me wife
always said it was. Don't suppose they'd let me go to
tell her so, do you?"

He got smote just then and only the Virago and the
Queen could be heard after that.

"During the Gestation we have made use of your
formerly misspent strength to repair some of the damage
done to our buildings.

"But at last, the time has come to see to it that you
reap the harvest of your crimes. Extend your arms in
front of you, *now.*" Since we were all chained together
still most of us had little choice but to obey and held
out our arms. Whereupon each of the townswomen, with
the nastiest possible expression on her face, handed each
of us one or more bundles. Which promptly began
howling and wetting and crapping and demanding to be
burped and cuddled.

After that, chain-mail skirts swinging, the Virgins
force-marched us back out of the city and to the
mountain temple, up to our old room. The creche, as
they call it.

It has no windows, only one door, and accoustics that
echo each whimper, whine, and squall into a din—and
that's before all the others join in.

None of us have slept for months. My guts and
backside and chests have been aching me something
terrible. See, the nectar makes us able to feed the little
dears from our own manly breasts but all the tots seem
to have come born with teeth.

Moreover, the virgins are always on hand to scold us
and tell us we are cocking up everything and how their
mothers raised children and how you can't fold a nappie
that way and what are we thinking, letting the child cry

for two seconds before we pick it up once more to pet
it?

Symington says it is like having a battalion of mothers-
in-law. And the other day, the Virago caught Sarge, as
she said, trying to abuse one of the triplets he is charged
with the care of. After she gave him a sound thrashing
in front of us all (and he never stood a chance, believe
me. That woman is at least ten feet tall and her arms
are bigger around than most of the babies), she assigned
him latrine duty in perpetuity, using only a thimble and
a toothbrush to clean the area, plus he must wash all
of the nappies by hand forever after.

I hate to say it, but I'm glad not to have to do it
myself any more and it serves him right. I felt sorry for
the poor little triplets though, and said so. Melisel
overheard me and I thought perhaps she might be
pleased and like me again, but instead she smiled in a
very roguish way and spoke to the Virago. Now I have
four tots to tend. They're all very good, really, but it's
a lot of work and very tedious. We lads never have time
to speak of manly things among ourselves and there are
no campfires, just the large fireplace at the end of the
hall where we take turns sitting to nurse the kiddies,
too exhausted to speak.

MUCH LATER
Dear Mum,

I hope this finds you and my sisters alive and well
because the thing is, it looks as if I may be coming
home. This may even reach you before I do.

A lot has happened since I last wrote, when was that,
almost 20 years ago? I have tried to sketch the children
for you at various stages but unfortunately, the only
things I could find to draw with were bits of charcoal
and the wall and the Virgins are not likely to let me
bring that along (ha ha).

Oh, we've kept very busy. Although the Virgins

themselves have taken care of schooling and training our little ones into the bright and attractive young people they are today, they have also been schooling some of us. I have learned a great deal about Affirmaterra, the Divinity of Diversity, and have for the last five years made offerings for all of you in Her Name. I have been at the head of all my classes, thanks to special tutoring from Melisel, my dear mentor.

It's because I've done so well that I'm to be allowed to come home. I won't be alone. In fact, I'll have about three or four hundred young people with me, so I do hope the crops have been good. After all, the children ARE sired by the lads of our country but with their proper Ecotrian upbringing, the Virgins feel it would be a civilizing influence to return them to the land of their fathers. I am coming along as Guardian, under the protection of Melisel, who was appointed Virago upon the death of the old one.

So, I'm afraid you'll need to set a few extra places at the table but don't worry. I've grown very handy with both the cooking and the washing up.

See you soon!
Yr. Returning Son

Oh, Sweet Goodnight!

Christina Briley & Walter Vance Awsten

Fern let the gentle rocking motion of the horse between her legs soothe her anger as she rode along—but still, how dare that farmer say such a thing? What did *he* know?

He probably didn't even think she'd heard him, but she had, clear as a bell. There was nothing wrong with her ears, and she'd had years of practice listening to the world through the padded steel of her helmet. When she had the helmet off, as she did now, she could hear a roadside conversation perfectly from a dozen yards away.

"You wouldn't get *me* in bed with a bitch like that," that farmer had said to his son as the two of them watched her ride past. "She'd probably break your ribs with those arms of hers. And think what she'd do with her legs!"

"It might be worth it," the son had replied, and the farmer had punched him on the shoulder, and they'd both laughed like fools, not realizing she'd heard every word.

"Idiots," she muttered. "I do my best to keep them safe, and this is the respect they show me? Don't they know how much padding there is in this armor? They think I'm some sort of musclebound freak?"

The farmer's comments were bad enough, but the son's reply bothered her more than she cared to admit; it was a bit too familiar. He *liked* the thought of broken ribs in the bedroom?

Her mount shook his head and snorted, and she reached forward to pat his neck. "At least *you* have the sense not to beg for the whip," she said to the ebony stallion.

There was no question that the casual exchange of remarks had touched a nerve, and brought up a well-spring of accumulated unhappiness. "How did my life get to be such a mess?" she mumbled to no one in particular as she straightened in the saddle. "I love my work, and I'm damned good at it, but my love life . . . ugh!" She grimaced.

Of course, she knew the two were connected. She was a respected guardswoman, the only such woman in Lord Worsley's employ, feared by every bandit in the North Riding, known for both her incorruptibility and her superb swordsmanship—both traits she had worked hard at for more than a decade. That was fine for her professionally, but when the time came for sweet and gentle romancing, most men saved it for something a bit more feminine.

Fern hadn't *intended* to become a guardswoman. She had merely wanted to learn the art of the blade.

She remembered well when the desire to do so had first gripped her. She had been fifteen, standing in the street with her friend Antonia, and struggling to see over the crowd that had gathered to watch two swordsmen spar outside The Fine Companion, the local tavern.

"Look at them move—it's as if they dance!" Fern had exclaimed. "Oh, Antonia, don't you wish you could move like that? And the swords sweeping and flashing in the air—isn't it beautiful?"

"A pox on being so short!" Antonia had said. "Fern, it's not fair! You can see and I can't!"

Just then the crowd in front of the girls had parted as the action moved toward them, and those most in danger of catching a stray swordstroke stepped back out of the way.

Fern didn't move.

"Fern, get back, you'll be hurt!" Antonia shrieked. Then she snapped, "And no, I don't see any beauty in a sword. It's but a weapon. If you're a man you use it to kill someone for some foolish reason or another, or to show off, and if you're a woman you use it because you have to, to defend yourself. Now Fern, please, get back!"

But Fern hadn't stepped back. She'd stood there, swaying to some unheard rhythm of which only she and the swordsmen were aware. It wasn't until Fern suddenly realized that she had become as much a part of the show as the fighters that she had reacted to Antonia's entreaties by looking around.

Not only had the crowd been watching to see if Fern would move out of harm's way, but the two soldiers had begun playing their act to this tall, budding young woman who gazed at them so intensely. When Fern had blushed and finally stepped back the two men had abruptly stopped their sparring and sheathed their swords. Then, each draping an arm over the other's shoulders, they had turned towards her, chuckling.

"Fern," Antonia had whispered desperately, tugging at her friend's arm, "they're coming over here. Let's hurry away!"

Fern had hesitated, torn between a desire to learn more about these men's sword skills and the wish to avoid any further embarrassment for both herself and her friend. The decision was out of her hands, though, for when she had glanced over her shoulder she saw that the crowd had not yet dispersed enough for them to make a quick getaway.

"Shhh," Fern had hissed. "We'll have to make the best

of it. Anyway, they're not bad looking—better than the boys our age you go on about."

"Hallo there, girls," one of the approaching men had called out. "'Tisn't polite to stare, you know."

"Pardon us, sir," Fern had replied, essaying a quick curtsey. "I was, perhaps, too fascinated with your skill with a blade to remember my manners."

The man who had spoken had grinned at her. "Well, in that case, we'll forgive you. My name's Ridley, and this sorry gent is Willem," he had said, indicating his comrade. "We're just passing through on our way home from Lord Balarin's war, but we'd be pleased if we might share your company for a bit."

"Sir!" Fern had drawn herself up to her full height and, with much more confidence than she felt in the situation, had replied firmly, "You are strangers to us and we're far too young to consort with men your age!"

"Our age!" Ridley had laughed. "Such fossils are we, eh, Willem? All right, then. But I saw how you watched us earlier—would you have a lesson in the sword, perhaps?"

Fern had caught her breath. She knew she should be wary—should just go home, should keep safe. But to learn the art of the blade! To feel for herself the flow and power of sword and body working together that she had so admired earlier! Fern had not been able to bring herself to pass up such a chance.

That first lesson, there in the street, with a bemused Willem and a horrified Antonia looking on, had merely whet her appetite. As an older and wiser Fern looked back now on the more private lessons that had followed, oh, so long ago, it was all too obvious just how right she had been to be wary. The soldier's motive for the offer had hardly been altruistic.

"Sly bastard," Fern mused to her horse. "He just wanted to teach me the use of his own 'little sword.' And what better excuse to wrap his arms around me than to guide my hands on a blade?" She shook her fist at the empty woods around her, "But, by the gods, I took to both skills like a fish to water, didn't I? Ha! There's a flow and beauty in each of them, eh?" Fern allowed herself a tight-lipped smile at the thought.

The mastery of the sword had started as simply a personal challenge, she remembered. Her smile widened—then vanished. "I should have made disembowelling that soldier a 'personal challenge,' " she told her mount, "to use me so and then go on his merry way!"

She hadn't, though. That wouldn't have been ladylike, and back then she had cared, at least a little, about what the neighbors thought of her behavior. She'd kept her sexual escapades to herself, and as for her fascination with the sword . . . ? Again her thoughts went back.

"Honestly, Antonia, how many times have I told you I have no desire to make trouble or spill anyone's blood?" They were out in back of the barn where Antonia, sick of Fern's fruitless efforts to turn her into a half-decent sparring partner, had thrown down her wooden practice sword in disgust and launched into another lecture about how Fern was going to be sorry about all this nonsense.

"I do it for the love of it," Fern insisted. "It's not as if I want to make a career out of swordfighting and run off to be a soldier! It's just a frivolous hobby I indulge in after all my chores are done. I want to marry someone nice, settle down, have children, just as you do. You know that."

"I still don't understand," Antonia sighed as she bent to pick up the discarded sword, "why you think all this dangerous, sweaty work is something to do for fun. But if I'm going to be your best friend I guess I'd better help, and try to protect you from yourself!"

"Think of it as exercise, and a way to work off foul tempers." Fern smiled. "Now again, like this . . ."

At the time, it had indeed been marriage and children Fern had wanted for a career. "I hadn't the backbone to be a professional fighter back then anyway," she explained to her ever-silent mount. "If I had, I'd have never let myself be bullied into marriage by that morose cobbler!"

The stallion's only response to Fern's words was to twitch his ear, dislodging a fly.

She had never really loved Durgan, although she had convinced herself that she did; she wasn't sure she'd even *liked* him very much. He had been insistent, though, and her parents had thought it was a decent match. She had finally given in and married him.

At the wedding Durgan and his friends were all drunk, shouting at one another about nothing and virtually ignoring her. She still remembered sitting there in her best gown, wondering what she had gotten herself into. She had looked across the room and noticed the village smith, a young man named Jacob who was the only sober male in the place, staring at her. She had forced herself to smile brightly at him when what she had really wanted to do was to stand up and call the whole thing off.

Jacob had walked out a moment later, apparently as disgusted by Durgan and his friends as Fern had been. She really wished that she, too, had walked out. But defying her family, telling Durgan to go to hell, finding herself work—she hadn't been capable of *any* of that back then. And she had been downright embarrassed about her love of swordsmanship. She had gone on practicing in secret with a few trusted friends she had found who could wield a sword better than dear, now-married Antonia; she had never mentioned it to her husband, and had only practiced when he worked elsewhere.

She hadn't had the courage to speak up about anything.

Once she actually had her own children, however, three children Durgan ignored as much as possible save to complain about the cost of feeding them, she began to take note of some of her own personal strengths, and to view her abilities with a sword in a new light. Where she had always tended to be the go-along-to-get-along type before, now she had something, or rather, three someones, to fight for, and with money tight some of the openings around town for guards or soldiers skilled with a sword looked pretty tempting.

When the famine came, and the war with Karnsland, Durgan didn't work much. Fern still remembered her first open confrontation with him.

"The children haven't eaten in two days!" she had shouted, when she found him sitting outside his shop with a stoop of ale in his hand, swapping lies with Armand the tailor.

"What do you want me to do about it?" he had asked, once he got over his initial astonishment at her unprecedented outburst. "Times are hard. No one's buying shoes. There's no money for food."

"You have money for drink for yourself!"

"I need to keep my strength up, for when the customers come back." He looked sincerely puzzled by her anger.

She hadn't known what to say to that, hadn't been able to think of any arguments that Durgan might listen to; she had fought her temper down and gone home.

Behind her she had heard Durgan chuckle to Armand, "Must be her time." Her anger had simmered anew to be dismissed so lightly, but she had held her tongue and walked away.

That night, though, she had suggested that he try to find some other source of income until business improved.

"What do you want me to do, go for a soldier?" he asked, slapping one hand onto his potbelly and holding the other arm out to display how bony and poorly-muscled it was.

"Soldiers wear boots, don't they?" Fern had asked.

"But they don't buy them here," Durgan had said.

"Couldn't you go where they *do* buy them?"

"Go? But this is *home*. The war won't last forever, and next year's crops will surely be better—just wait, Fern."

But she had looked at little Aelf's hungry, pinched face and decided that she and the children *couldn't* wait. If Durgan wouldn't do anything about it, she would.

She had sat down the next morning and carefully reviewed all her assets, and had come to the conclusion that applying her skill with a sword was her best chance at keeping the children fed.

She remembered wryly how frightened she had been when she walked up the hill to the manor house. She had thought that Lord Worsley might have her thrown into the dungeons for her impertinence, or might laugh at her.

Instead he had smiled wearily upon hearing her tale of woe, and had tossed her a small purse.

"The famine has been hard on us all," he had said—though he scarcely looked as if he had missed any meals. "This will feed your children for a time."

She had hesitated before picking up the purse—yes, it would feed Gord and Alis and Aelf for a time, but she wanted to be sure they would *always* be fed. Saying anything more, beyond a quick "thank you," had been one of the hardest things she had ever done, but she had said it all the same.

"When I said I was ready to fight for you, my lord, I meant it—have you no employment for someone skilled with a sword?"

That had startled him. He had stared at her for a moment, then sent for Ambrose, his master-at-arms, to test her. He hadn't said so, but Fern still suspected Lord

Worsley had thought she had no idea how difficult it was to use a sword, that she was bluffing and would make a fool of herself in short order once the practice blades were drawn.

She hadn't. Old Ambrose had been impressed, and Fern had been employed. She had gone home dreading Durgan's reaction—wouldn't he think it a blot on his manhood to have his wife working as a manor-house guard?

Durgan had frowned, then shrugged. "Make sure they pay you in advance," he had said. "After all, it won't last long—we want to get every penny we can."

She hadn't said anything. She had been afraid he was right. And she had been relieved that his response had been so calm, when she had expected anger. Let sleeping tempers lie.

That was hardly the last unexpected response she got out of Durgan, though. She still remembered every detail of her husband's astonishing response when she had brought home her first suit of armor, courtesy of her new employers, Lord and Lady Worsley. He had stared at her wide-eyed as she held up the bundle of steel and leather, and licked his lips.

"Oooooh," he said. "Get the children to bed and model it for me . . . but skip the undergarments!"

She remembered it all *too* well.

"I did as he asked, too, you know," Fern informed her four-legged companion. "First work, then dinner, dishes, diapers, and bedtime stories, and then went to take care of him too! Fastening that heavy, and blasted *cold*, steel breastplate over my poor, bare nipples was hardly on my list of things I really wanted to do right then! What he wanted to do right then was as clear as . . . well, it was obvious."

Then Durgan had added a new twist.

"Hit me! Make me touch you! Tell me what you're going to do to me!" he had pleaded.

"I thought I'd puke!" she told the horse. "Damn it, I was *exhausted*! Sleep was all I wanted, and now this rot! But I knew him, gods, did I know him!" She shook her head ruefully.

What Fern knew was that if her husband didn't get his way he would yell at her, or worse, sulk, and she'd never get her longed-for sleep. And eventually she'd have to clear the air by doing what he'd asked for originally, and then some.

"It tore me up, though," she sighed. "To twist the beauty and fire of the deed like that. But the genie was out of the bottle and 'darling dear' would never let me have him any other way after that."

Even while her home life deteriorated, though, her career had flourished. She gradually won respect among Worsley's other guards with her skill and her common-sense manner. Lady Worsley was particularly appreciative of Fern's tendency to talk first and only resort to the sword if absolutely necessary, whether handling an unwelcome intruder or a rowdy guest. "It's so much easier to keep the carpets clean with you around, Fern, dear!" she had remarked once, with her famous smile shining.

As for Fern's life outside of work, it just got more unbearable. Durgan had taken to wearing Fern's armor himself whenever he got the chance. The cold mail skirt slapping against his own maleness had given him some bizarre mix of pleasure and pain.

It wasn't long before Fern had had enough.

Her recollection of the night she'd told him to get out was crystal clear. In his typical mature fashion he'd angrily rammed his fist through a window and then screeched in pain.

"Do something! I'm bleeding to death!" he had shrieked.

Fern's thoughts had flashed to the men she had seen die stoically in the field as she glanced at the lily-white rag Durgan had wrapped around his wrist. She sighed inwardly. He was a baby or a liar to the end. Who knew which? And who *cared*?

When at last he had grabbed a few of his things and stormed out she had barred the door behind him and cleaned up the broken glass, noticing wryly that there was not a drop of blood visible among the shards. She had slept, exhausted, on the floor outside the children's rooms, with her sword beside her.

"Why are you sleeping on the floor? What happened to the window? Where's Daddy?" The children's voices had awakened her.

When Fern had answered their questions with some reassuring half-truths they had calmed down somewhat. They were upset to learn that their father was gone, but not too upset. Frankly, when your father has a rotten temper, and your mother carries a sword, and they're not getting along, well, better to have your father separated from your mother than from his head.

A sudden jolt flung her from her memories back to the present day. Fern struggled to keep herself from going over her horse's head as the beast stumbled and came to an abrupt halt. Dismounting, she was dismayed to see he had thrown a shoe.

"Damn!" she said. "So much for an quick ride home. I guess we'll have to stop by Jacob's smithy."

That was not entirely an unwelcome thought. Quiet and gracious, with a pervasive sense of humor, Jacob had always seemed a bit out of place as a blacksmith. His exaggerated manners never quite seemed to fit the coarseness of his surroundings.

"Oh, well," she said. "My errand for Lord Worsley went smoothly enough—that particular bunch of trouble-makers won't be back this way any time soon, so there's no great hurry about getting anywhere. And it's not as if I mind Jacob's company." She straightened up and looked thoughtfully down the trail toward the smithy.

"I can never read that man, you know." She smiled. "But it's an interesting challenge to try. All the same, I'd have preferred you'd kept on all your shoes, you dumb beast, so I could have gotten home to a hot bath and my children."

With a sigh she set off again, now on foot and leading her lame mount. Her thoughts drifted back to the path her life had taken over the years.

She'd been lucky in a lot of ways. With the end of her marriage and her fool husband gone who-knew-where, one would have expected balancing children and employment to be a problem, but Lady Worsley had leaped to her rescue.

"My dear, I have been agonizing for simply ages over how to find suitable playmates for my children and yours are such gems! I would be delighted to have them stay in the nursery with Nanny and my little ones whenever you are occupied elsewhere!"

The offer had been a godsend and Fern really did like both Nanny and Lady Worsley, if only Lady Worsley wouldn't gush quite so much.

Fern had suddenly been free to run her own life, with no short-tempered cloud sharing her bed and raining on her parade. And all those men! . . . Smiling, warm, appreciative men who'd been flirting with her for years. Surely one of them would give her the kind of affectionate, thoughtful, mature (but occasionally silly), relationship she craved! Perhaps that fellow guardsman, or maybe the grocer . . . ?

"Guess again." Fern growled, scuffing the dirt as she walked and wishing more than ever for that hot bath. Muscles stiff from the long ride now complained about walking so far, but she angrily ignored her aching thighs and strode along.

Some of the guardsmen had considered a female warrior to be an unnatural thing and had refused to associate with her when not on duty, but others had been eager to see more of her. A few townsmen had seen her in her armor and been openly admiring. She had never been left lacking male company.

Somehow, though, not one of the affairs had panned out.

"Oh, they had their moments," Fern recalled angrily, "But when the relationship made it to the bedroom every single one of the bastards was looking for this big, powerful knight-bitch to beat and humiliate him. And that last one! First the fool badgers me into fulfilling his stupid dominatrix fantasy, and then he has the gall to say he's entitled to extra kindnesses from me as I had abused him so!"

By the time Fern reached the blacksmith's place she was flushed, not only from the heat and exertion of the long walk but with anger and frustration as well. Jacob took one look at her and offered her a drink of water from the earthen jug he always kept tucked in the shade, well away from the heat of the forge.

She accepted it, still half-lost in memories, and as she drank she thought again how everyone simply assumed, because she used a sword for a living, that she wanted to spend her entire life dominating people. The men who wanted to be dominated swarmed to her, and the others, the ones who might have been worthwhile, stayed away.

"What makes men such idiots, anyway?" Fern burst out after wiping the water from the corners of her mouth with the back of her sleeve. She reached up again, this time to brush away a mix of sweat and tears from her eyes.

"Excuse me?" Jacob asked. "Is the water not to your liking, perhaps? Or perhaps you're miffed with the four-hoofed male behind you who has forced this detour?" He smiled at her, slightly bemused but with concern in his eyes all the same.

She blinked at him, then blushed. *He* hadn't done anything wrong. "By the gods, I'm sorry, Jacob," she said.

"Thank you for the drink. It's not you, and it's not the horse either. It's . . . well, it's a long story."

"Rest your feet while I take care of the beast's shoe, and if you care to complain to me about the gods' whims in the process, I've a sympathetic ear. I promise to 'tsk, tsk,' in all the right spots."

Much of Fern's anger had burnt itself out by now, and she'd no desire to rekindle it by another mental review of her personal life. Once in an afternoon was quite enough! But perhaps, she mused, she might share some of her problems and at the same time find that chink in Jacob's emotional armor that she sought.

"Do you find people mix up who you are with what you do?" she asked. "I may have a job as a knight, but that's not who I am! Or is this a man's way of thinking, that you are what you do?"

"I don't know about it being 'a man's way of thinking,' " Jacob said. "I've always seen a more vulnerable side to you than your armor would imply, but I'd say that many folks of either sex miss such things. After all, ask yourself, do you see me as just a smith?" He smiled at her briefly, but then turned his attention to the stallion's hoof.

She stared at him, caught off-guard by the question. Actually, up until that moment, she had indeed thought of him just as a smith—a rather unusual smith, but too aloof, too closed off, to think of in a more personal way. She suddenly found herself staring at the firm line of his shoulders and back at the same time she noticed how gently he handled her horse, running his hand tenderly down the leg.

"Well, I . . ." She hesitated, suddenly at a loss for words—facing down bandits and negotiating with brigands she could handle, but this sudden change in an old relationship had her baffled. She chose her words carefully.

"I've always thought you were a good looking man, Jacob, and polite, but well, distant." She tried to find some way to phrase what she wanted to say without admitting the truth, but then gave up.

"Gods, you're right, Jacob. I saw you as a smith and nothing more. I guess I've never thought of you outside your professional role because, in all the years that I've known you, you never seemed to invite any relationship beyond a professional one."

"I might point out that you were married for virtually all those years—happily married, I thought."

"Little did you know!" The barrier had broken, and she poured out her frustrations and fury over Durgan's failures as a husband.

After that the conversation drifted on to other matters—nothing of great moment, but an exchange of thoughts that left her feeling warm and satisfied. By the time Jacob was satisfied that the horse was fit to ride, Fern was grateful for that thrown shoe—and after the goodbye hug Jacob gave her she thought that perhaps he might need a cold shower even more that she had wanted a hot bath. They exchanged promises of dinner together two days hence, and Fern rode away from the smithy towards home in a markedly different humor from the one in which she'd arrived.

She found, at dinner and in the days that followed, that his graciousness was more than skin deep and his gentle touch was not reserved solely for his four-legged clients. Much to her delight, it seemed that Fern had finally found someone who believed in "Do unto others . . ." It amused her to describe to him some unreasonable, but all too common, bit of behavior that she had encountered from some man in the past and watch Jacob get this wonderful, genuinely bewildered expression on his face as he responded:

"Why? That doesn't make sense." Or, "That's ridiculous." Or, "Why would he expect that? That's not fair to you!"

"I know that, and you know that, but he did it just

the same," she'd reply with a chuckle, at last finding some humor in her previous misadventures.

Eventually, late one evening, when the children had decided to spend the night in the nursery, a long intimate talk with Jacob turned into long intimate caresses. The couple retired to Fern's room.

"You know," Jacob warned, "I'm really nothing special in bed. Open-minded about things, and affectionate, yes . . . but really, well, boring."

"Ye gods, man! I deal with crisis for a living!" she shouted. "I subdue giants, battle two, three men at a time! Hell, my contract includes fighting dragons if need be! Do you think I need high drama in the bedroom as well? Affection is wonderful! Boring is good! Bore me!"

They burst into laughter and he hugged her tightly. She reveled in the shared humor and in his touch. Finally she pulled back to gaze into his eyes; those deep, gorgeous, tender, blue eyes she had overlooked for so long. "And now sirrah," she sighed in a voice soft and husky, "Please, if thou wouldst . . ."

"Yes, darling?"

"Go you gently into this sweet, good knight!"

A Bitch in Time

Doranna Durgin

Shiba sat on the bare wood planks of the cabin porch, wiggling her bottom away from a persistent splinter. Mail hung heavily on her shoulders and across her back, and the leather-lined helmet chafed her ears despite its custom contours. Hot in the sun, it was. Across the tunic on her broad chest hung a short row of service pins and one smooth, polished medal. Shiba would have ripped it off if she'd been given the choice. What good was valor when it wasn't enough?

Good for a thorough rolling-on, that's what.

Beside her stood the Line Mate, the man in charge of the border cabins that represented the first line of defense against illegal magics. He wore his only everyday work clothes. Well, *he* wasn't waiting for his new partner.

"Patience," he said, resting his hand on the skirt of mail that hung over her long ears. "He'll be here. Naught for you to worry."

Shiba made a grumping noise and lifted her nose to the air, expertly sorting it for any taste of stranger-odor. There! Was that . . . ? She whined, licked her lips, and tried again. Definitely!

"Coming, is he?" the Line Mate asked, expectantly eyeing the path that led from the woods. His other name

145

was Eldon, though Shiba thought he ought to pick one name or the other and stick with it. "All right. Just you keep in mind that he's only recently lost his own partner. That does things to a lineman, you know."

Shiba's tail quivered, and her forehead furrowed into furry wrinkles. The scent of her new partner was strong in her nose, stronger than any words Eldon might say. People talked all the time anyway, whether they had something to say or not. She strained her eyes—not the strongest of her senses—and yes, there he was! Just visible through the trees at the edge of the cabin's small clearing, a tall walking stick in one hand and a full satchel slung over the other shoulder. Shiba whined as he emerged from the woods, and licked away the drool gathering on her lips.

"Easy," said Eldon, as Shiba's new partner approached. The man's easy stride seemed a tad too casual.

"Tallon," Eldon said. "Welcome. You made good time."

"Good enough," the man said. Shiba liked his voice. It had a roughly furry texture not unlike her own. He nodded at her. "See you musta spent some time getting ready for me. Wasn't necessary."

"I didn't do it for you," Eldon said. "I did it for her. She was strongly attached to the old man. It's good for her to have a little ceremony, something to mark your arrival as out of the ordinary. I can't help but worry about the way you two are going to mesh."

Tallon dropped the satchel and looked thoughtfully at his new linehound.

Shiba gave him her Noble Beauty pose. After all, she was of the best bloodlines and strikingly marked. The black of her back was glossy beneath her chain mail, and her chest, belly, and legs were white, so heavily ticked with black that from any distance they looked blue silver. The black of her head and ears was divided by a neat ticked blaze that spread out to take over her muzzle, and her eyebrows were punctuated by deep brown. Her body was sturdy, her tail strong and graceful, and her ears fell long and soft, the perfect complement to her hanging flews. Best of all, her legs—long, heavy-boned and angular—were up to the task of following her incomparable nose.

She knew all this because Jehn, her former partner, had told her so. She believed him utterly, just as she believed everything he said.

Tallon just shrugged. "We'll get along fine," he said. "Jehn'll have trained her right, and beyond that, a dog's a dog."

Shiba couldn't believe her ears. She looked at Eldon, who appeared to be speechless. *A dog's a dog*, ey? Her ears, previously cocked forward like big floppy wings at the side of her head, flattened. She rose and circled the man, eyeing him with cold brown eyes. *A dog's a dog?* Well, this dog was a *bitch*. Tallon would not only do well to keep that in mind, he was about to find out exactly what it could mean.

Shiba gave his satchel a sideways look. It *did* mean she couldn't lift her leg on the thing. But there were other ways . . . Shiba dropped shoulder-first on the satchel and rolled with the dramatic wiggles and flourishes commonly reserved for the rankest carrion.

Tallon seemed to have missed the point, for he never made the necessary apologies and overtures to earn Shiba's forgiveness. Of all the linemen on the border, why give her *this* one to break in? No matter how long he'd been a lineman elsewhere, Tallon was the green one here, for this was *her* territory. A lifetime—all three years of it—of protecting this section of the border from spellrunners meant that she knew all its hiding places, and all the tricky runners in the area.

For a while there, spellrunners had taken to disguising the smell of magic with the much stronger scent of *critter*. It'd worked, too, because Shiba, like any other linehound, had a passionate hate for the oily-furred, long-bodied, toothy-jawed, witless—and here she had to pause in her thoughts to get hold of herself—critters. Why, their true name was such an abomination that a proper bitch never even said it, not even to herself. *Critter*, that's all they were ever called by a linehound, all of whom were thoroughly trained from their natural inclination to hunt down and shred every critter whose scent trail they crossed.

But the spellrunner ploy only worked for a while, until Shiba caught the faint scent of magic beneath the critter/human trail, and learned that critter plus human smell was as good as smelling magic. Jehn had been so proud of her the day she'd treed those first two spell-runners. And how silly they'd looked, perched up in that small trembling tree. One limp, tubular critter body, tied to lay scent in their footsteps, dangled from each heel and spun slow lazy circles just at the height of Jehn's head.

Shiba's tongue lolled out in a laugh just thinking about it. For once, a memory of Jehn that didn't bring pain or guilt along with it. She'd done a good job that day, and Jehn had bragged of it amongst the linemen many a time.

Tallon's voice interrupted her morning bask in the sun. "Let's go," he said. "Time for rounds."

Shiba's jaw snapped shut as he moved out before her, his stupid walking stick at his side where he should have left space for her. He took to the woods, heading for the worn path that followed the line of the border. She followed in his footsteps, but clogged her nose with his dust and the scent of his old boots for only a few moments before breaking out ahead of him.

"With me!" he said sharply, letting her know she wasn't to stray far from him, that he didn't trust her. His pleasing voice had long since lost its charm. Shiba, moving right along in her leggy trot, was tempted to *not hear* him. But no, for the sake of Jehn's memory, she couldn't do that. She snorted a little sneeze of impatience and let him catch up. And then, when she glanced back, she saw he was fumbling at his waist for the leash he carried, like most linemen, simply wrapped around his body.

The *leash*! She stared at him in horror. She hadn't been on a leash since she was a yearling! How could he even think of—oh, the shame of it! Her body folded in on itself in mortification until she was all but cringing at his feet. Oh, what would Jehn say? Tallon must have seen how close she'd come to *not hearing* him, and now he didn't trust—

Smffle. Even in her mortification, Shiba had to breathe, and her nose was something she could never ignore. Tallon's hand hesitated over her neck. *Smmmmfle*!

Crittersmell Tallonsmell oldoldJehnsmell deersmell summerbellsinbloomsmell crittercrittercrittersmell and beneath it all, *magicsmell*. No magic made it past *her* border! Shiba barked, the short, choppy bark that signaled a magic trail, and looked up at Tallon, waiting his decision.

He didn't make one. He hovered over her, his hand clearly thinking *leash* while his mouth hesitated on the command to *find it*. Shiba's nose told her *crittersmell magicsmell* and she hunted the air, eyes on Tallon, until the odors resolved themselves. *Crittersmell magicsmell crittermagicsmell*! No hesitation this time, Shiba bawled full trail cry right in his face.

Tallon, so startled he tumbled back on his bottom, yelled, "Son of a *bitch*!" as Shiba surged to her feet, mastered by the smell of magic and no more by any lineman. Not even Jehn could have stopped her as she lunged into the trees and latched on to the trail. "Son of a bitch!"

Well, Shiba thought, at least he was getting closer

than plain old *dog*. She ran the trail full out, until the crittersmell overwhelmed the magicsmell altogether, so sharp it stung her nose and she ran with her head in the air, belling triumph to the trees as she raced past. She overshot the trail, and it took only seconds to backtrack the critter where it crouched in a tree. Treed, treed, *treed*! Her sweet, full trail cry changed to something choppier as she stood against the tree trunk, getting a face full of crittersmell from the scruffy specimen clinging to the lowest branch of the tree. Stupid critter, it ought to have climbed a little higher! Treed, treed! she barked joyfully, leaping up so far she fairly blew its fur back with the blast of sound. The less significant noise of Tallon's approach cornered very little of her attention. Bounding ever higher, she bellowed treed treed treed *critter*! and on her last bounce, leapt so high her head was level with the critter's.

With a squeak of mindless fear, it shot out off the branch like a sling-shot stone, landing squarely on Tallon's chest. His stupid walking stick flew into the air as he slapped frantically at his body, always one step behind the panicked critter. Finally the thing launched off his head, and as Tallon flung one last *grab* at it, he lost his balance and came down hard on his back.

The air whooped from his lungs, but that didn't stop him from snagging Shiba's collar as she bounded after the critter. She dragged him several feet, belling trail all the while, until his shoulder slammed up against a tree. *Magicsmell*! she cried woefully, and looked down at him from a vantage point of just over his face.

He still hadn't found his breath, though he seem to be trying to say something. His face red, his lips moving soundlessly, all he got out was, "—a *bitch*!"

He was learning! But was he all right? The noises that came from him still didn't sound normal. Shiba looked down the scant hand's breadth separating her nose from his face, and—

❖   ❖   ❖

Shiba stretched out full length on the shady side of the clearing, her ears mournfully long and her eyes accusing and wounded. Chained. Disgraced. Fastened to the cabin porch like any common hound mutt.

Maybe if she hadn't been so hot from the run . . . maybe if she'd had time to calm, to regain her composure, maybe if—

No, let's face it. She always drooled a lot. It was just Tallon's bad luck to have had his mouth open so wide.

Shiba wore her harness with ill grace, plodding along the border path with her ears hanging low and long. The harness, like her mail, was meant for combined operations with other linehounds and their Linemen. Not for daily work. Definitely not. Sullenly, she kept just enough tension on the leash to throw off Tallon's natural stride. The tip of that stupid walking stick stubbed against the ground in uneven intervals, providing Shiba with spiteful satisfaction.

At least she had Eldon's mild comments to salve her wounded pride. "Did you check your detector?" he'd asked Tallon, referring to the only magic allowed in the kingdom—a device that detected the same magic Shiba could sniff out so much more easily.

They'd spoken in the cabin, where they'd thought Shiba—chained to the porch—couldn't hear. And when Tallon admitted he didn't think to check, Eldon said, "Shiba's not a [critter]-chaser. Give her some room."

Except he hadn't said critter. He'd said the Awful Word instead. Even so, that hadn't stopped the little swell of appreciation in Shiba's hound heart.

Not that Eldon's words had done much good. "She isn't acting right," Tallon said. "I think the incident with Jehn broke her."

"That wasn't her fault," Eldon said. "The old man went too far over the border when she was on trail, and fell right into one of the spellrunner traps. It was just a scare-spell . . . if only his heart had withstood the shock, he'd be in retirement right now."

Thinking of that day, Shiba whined, right there in front of Tallon, in harness, on the leash. Jehn had winded the horn-recall with his last breath—the recall that meant break trail, and which any linehound, Shiba included, was liable to ignore. She hadn't, though, not on that day. She'd found Jehn just as the silver-chased horn fell from his limp hand to the mossy ground, and it'd taken three Linemen to haul her away from his body when her howls finally guided them to the spot.

"I didn't say it was her fault." Tallon's response to Eldon had been sharp enough to come clearly through the cabin walls. "I said I think it broke her. And I'm not about to chance losing another dog."

Shiba's whine turned into more of a grumble at *that* memory, and now she gave an extra jerk against the leash. Shiba, broken? Ready to farm out as someone's pet? Critter-crap!

Ah, yes, and there was some now. Shiba wrinkled her nose at the scent, but she recalled the magic-critter from the day before and let her nose do her thinking. *Crittersmell*, it told her, predictably enough. *Crittersmell . . . magicsmell*! She barked, and looked over her shoulder at Tallon.

"Uh-uh," he said. "You'll do this one in harness."

Magicsmell!! she told him, barking more demandingly the second time.

"Good girl. Find it, Shiba!"

Leashed? Why . . . he meant it! All right, then. Just see if he could keep up with her. Nose to the ground, she hauled him into the woods, and immediately hit trail so strongly she just couldn't help the bellow that escaped her. Ohhh, yes, *magicsmell*! Forgetting her resentment at the leash, Shiba hauled Tallon along behind her, racing along the mixed scents of critter and magic. The nasty

creature couldn't be too far ahead—here! Here, it had
treed, and in a silly little bush barely taller than Tallon.
Treed, treed! Shiba bounced into the air, joyfully inhaling
the magic and happy to be bawling treed in another
critter's pointy little face.

A jerk brought her down to earth, startled. Tallon's
firm hand on the harness kept her there. "Another
[*critter*]," he said, his voice strangely flat. "Shiba, Jehn
would be ashamed of you."

Magicsmell! she barked at him. If only humans had
something better than that puny little thing they somehow called a nose!

With jerky movements, he retrieved the magic detector from its belt pouch, aiming it at the critter. "Nothing.
I didn't think so."

The disappointment in his voice made her fold up upon
herself despite the insistent tickle in her nose that meant
magic. Jehn hadn't detected magic when she'd chased the
critter-enhanced spellrunners, either. But he'd always
trusted her nose. She was a linehound, *his* linehound, and
no detector would ever be as sensitive. Tallon, now . . .
Tallon was stroking her head in a sad way. "It's all right,
Shiba. We'll just start you over from the beginning, if we
have to. That's a girl, it's all—"

The cowardly critter could stand no more. It sailed
over Tallon's head, emitting a little warsqueak on the
way. Shiba answered it with a belling cry—*magicsmell*!
Slave to her nose's delight, she flung herself after it,
jerking Tallon off his feet and onto his face. The weight
meant nothing to her; she dug her feet in and dragged
him with her. And then the leash flopped loose behind
her, and in her freedom she thought nothing of Tallon
and everything of the *magicsmell*.

It was her job, after all.

She was barking treed when he caught up with her,
the critter cowering not far overhead.

"Shiba!" he bellowed, timing to catch her between barks. There was anger in that voice. Definite anger.

Suddenly, Shiba remembered the feel on the harness as she'd dragged him over roots, the sound as he broke through low-lying brush with his face, the ripping noise of good stout broadcloth as he hit the greenbriar she'd slicked right through . . .

Just as suddenly, she realized she was high off the ground, balanced on three different branches with one front foot clawing to find purchase in the bark . . . of the tree . . . she was in. Tallon looked up at her, and now she saw astonishment mixed in with the anger on his face. She could see the way his hair was thinning on top, too. She barked encouragingly at him.

He fisted his hands on his hips and said, "Shiba, *come down from that tree.*"

Come down? She didn't remember getting up here—how was she supposed to get down? Her front foot slipped again; bits of bark rained down on Tallon's head. Come down? Not a chance. Never.

Tallon looked at her, looked at the critter, looked at her, swore . . . and started to climb. That was more like it! Shiba wagged her tail. They'd get the *magicsmell* together!

But when Tallon came to a stop between Shiba and the critter, it was to reach for Shiba's harness. Ohhh, no. He wouldn't—he *couldn't*—

He tugged. Shiba's four legs turned to twenty, all clawing for purchase amidst the convoluted branches of the low-slung maple. One insistent man's arm was nothing against ninety pounds of determined hound.

Tallon muttered another curse, his gaze swiveling to the critter. Beady-eyed, it stared back, all four stubby little legs wrapped around its branch, its tail hanging down like something already dead, a naked scaly appendage no farther from Tallon than he was from Shiba.

In one quick, decisive movement, Tallon grabbed that tail, ripped the animal off the branch, and flung it at the ground. *Magicsmell* on the move! Shiba's nose-brain kicked in and she launched herself into the air, no more thinking about the long drop than she did about Tallon's precarious position—

Whump! They collided and fell together in a collection of flailing limbs. Tallon hit first, curling up to take it in a roll; Shiba bounced off him and careened off in the opposite direction, ending up on her back with all four legs in the air, askew and undignified.

She scrambled to her feet and located Tallon. He'd ended up on his back, too, his arms and legs looking as disorganized as Shiba felt. Shiba shook herself off, shedding leaves and twigs. She went to encourage Tallon to do the same, peering down into his open eyes from much the same vantage point she'd had the day before.

He scowled back up at her. His eyes grew less dazed and more angry. Uh-oh.

And then . . . then . . . Shiba smelled the smell. The *magicsmell*. Enthusiastically, she sniffed the air around Tallon, and the juncture of his body against the ground. Oh yes, oh joy, definitely, the *magicsmell* was *here*—

She couldn't help herself. She bawled the discovery to Tallon, whiskers brushing his face. His eyes squinted against the noise; his nose wrinkled against her breath.

But he kept his mouth closed.

Tallon's shirt flapped in the breeze, shifting another hand's breadth along the porch railing. Stark against the light wet cloth was a bloody, greasy stain in the approximate shape of flattened critter.

It didn't look like it had washed out very well.

Shiba skulked at the edge of the woods, a limp, flattened critter at her feet. She hesitated, knowing the words Tallon would use to greet her. He'd been angry enough *before* he'd fallen out of the tree. Now that she'd twice torn herself from his grasp to retrieve the critter he kept throwing away, there was no limit to what he might do.

Gingerly picking up the greasy blot of dead critter, Shiba slunk into the clearing. He must have been watching, because he came out to meet her at the top of the porch steps, his expression dark. Shiba all but crawled the last distance between them, gingerly placing the critter at his feet. Quietly, almost inaudibly, she whuffed—a doggy whisper. *Magicsmell*.

The anger melted from his face. "Poor Shiba," he murmured. He stroked the top of her head and down the length of her ears. Shiba pushed her head into his hand with some relief. Thank goodness, he was finally smelling the sense of her actions. "You've worked hard today," he told her. "Come in and get some supper."

Hers was not to question food. She followed him willingly, watched while he picked out some of the best bits from his meal, and gratefully shoved her nose in her bowl when he put it down.

While she ate, he threw the critter away. And then he chained her.

Shiba started the night locked in the cabin with him, but that hadn't lasted long. Fed up with her whining, Tallon chained her in the moonlit clearing. Nose to the sky, Shiba broke into howling. Halfway through the night, she stopped the howling and broke the chain instead. She greeted Tallon on the porch in the morning with the stiffened critter between her front paws.

He gravely thanked her, shut her in the cabin, and threw the critter away. Shiba spent the day with her head on her paws, wondering that any good lineman could be so dense. Tallon walked the border alone that day, using only his wits, the stupid walking stick, and his detector. When he returned, tired and cranky, Shiba blasted through the open door and into the woods.

Tallon had taken some care to secrete the critter away from the cabin, but it had taken on a distinct *deadcrittersmell* and wasn't at all hard to find. Carrying it was another matter. Shiba gingerly grasped the tip of its tail and dragged it home, leaving behind great patches of its fur.

Tallon sat on the front porch, his head in his hands. It didn't look like he'd ever made it inside after Shiba's escape. He looked too weary to hide the critter again; this time, maybe he'd take the time to look it over, to find whatever gave it *magicsmell*.

However, when she proudly presented him with her flat stiffened decaying bald critter, taking a closer look at it seemed to be the last thing on his mind.

The next day, Tallon buried the ragged little corpse. That made the job of finding it a little tougher, but Shiba persisted, and in the end she thought the encrusting dirt coat was a distinct improvement over the critter's splotchy baldness. Tallon, she thought, gently laying the prize in his lap, would surely agree.

Tallon didn't.

Dramatic over-reaction, she sniffed to herself, quietly curling up in the far end of the cabin to sulk herself to sleep—a task more easily accomplished once Tallon stopped making so much noise. Sooner or later, he'd understand. Shiba was a Linehound, and the boon and bane of a Linehound was its perseverance. Shiba would retrieve the critter corpse again and again, until Tallon finally got the message, and she would do it until she was presenting him with nothing more than greasy bones.

Some called it being stubborn, but then, they didn't know any better.

He'd fixed the chain—it was much shorter now, but that was her own fault—and wrapped the end around

the bottom of a porch railing post. But he'd unwittingly
made the job easier for her, by choosing the post that
she'd long ago marked with her milk teeth. Left behind
for the day, Shiba quite happily applied her strong adult
jaws to the same place.

She was taking a panting break when she smelled
magic, and she stopped spitting splinters to check the
air, licking the end of her nose to hike it to full power.
Ohh, yes, *magicsmell*, coming from a distance but still
thick with strength. She barked sharply, announcing her
find to no one at all, and sat up on tight alert. *Magicsmell*, and strong enough that Tallon's silly little detector
would find it.

The sight of Jehn's body flashed into her mind. Jehn
had gone over the border to follow magic scent without
her, and had died for it. What if Tallon had learned
nothing from the lesson and done the same, braving the
magic-infested woods of the Other Side without a
linehound?

"Ahhrrr-ahhhr-arrhhwoooo!" Shiba bark-howled,
demanding immediate freedom so she could go do her
job. The startled birds at the edge of the clearing
flittered away into the woods, and nothing else paid her
any attention at all. "Ahhrrr-arrrhhwoooo!!"

Nothing. No one swooped into the clearing to release
her *rightthisminute*. No one even told her to shut up.
All her patient chewing forgotten, Shiba lunged against
the pull of the chain, again and again and—

The chain gave. Yelping with surprise, Shiba rolled
head over heels in the dust of the clearing; behind her
came a great clattering noise. When she found right-
side-up again, she discovered she was free. Free, that
is, if you didn't count the post and several sections of
railing attached to the end of the chain but no longer
to the porch.

Paying it little heed, Shiba charged off into the trees,
following the *magicsmell* and leaving splintered wood and

mangled brush in her wake. At first she gave call, but
soon found herself working too hard to manage it. As
fast as the railing shed bits of itself, the post and chain
gathered greenbriars and branches and clumps of moss—
and one big poison ivy vine, roots and all. That particular
acquisition had slowed her a moment, but not for long.
She was well over the border, and by now had *tallonsmell* and *crittersmell* and *strangehumansmells* in her
nose and brain.

When she topped the little rise above Tallon, she'd
smelled enough so she wasn't surprised by what she saw
below her. Tallon sat against a tree, his expression
unhappy. Not too far away but definitely out of reach,
his stupid walking stick leaned against another tree.
There were several men standing around him, gesturing
angrily. A little donkey-drawn cart stood off to the side,
loaded with critter cages and reeking of magic.

She was here in time! Tallon was alive, the magicsmell
was hers to tree! Shiba didn't hesitate; she threw her
momentum into a headlong rush down the hill, baying
a wild challenge. The post, railing and debris combination gathered life of its own, and bounded wildly
along until it was beside—and then ahead of—her. The
ring of men around Tallon looked up with identical
incredulous expressions, a whole circle full of open
mouths and astonished eyes. Tallon's face went from
surprise to a fierce smile, and he hollered, "Atta girl,
Shiba!"

By the time the men thought to run, it was too late.
Shiba blasted through them, the juggernaut railing at
her side, and took down two men with her momentum
alone. The chain tangled the ankle of a third and her
teeth sunk firmly into the arm of the unfortunate who
grabbed her. No strange man was going to get between
her and the *magicsmell*, oh, no! With two mighty bounds
and a leap of prodigious proportions, Shiba landed on
top of the critter cages. A terrified chorus of warsqueaks

heralded her landing, and she responded with a mighty bellow of *treed*! *TreedtreedTREED*!!

The offended donkey commenced to kicking, battering the cart with its heels; Shiba did a jig to keep her balance as the whole contraption jerked and wavered, and then suddenly dissolved out from beneath her. She found herself sitting on the wreckage of cart and cages with critters squirting out in all directions. One quick snatch nabbed her a squirming critter, and she sat proudly in the midst of her chaos with her mouth full, stubby little critter legs sticking out on either side and frantically paddling the air. Now . . . where was her lineman?

Tallon, it seemed, had used the confusion of her entrance to snatch up his stupid walking stick and turn it into a whirling weapon unlike anything Shiba had ever seen. The strangemen had pulled long knives—at least, the three who'd been able to get out of the tangle of post and rail and chain and branches and roots and vines—but none of them even got near Tallon.

Her new lineman could take care of himself!

Tallon stood panting, leaning on the stick, ignoring the fallen men around him as he stared at Shiba. Suddenly he grinned, and just as suddenly Shiba found she again adored his furry voice. "Looks like my new linehound isn't crazy after all. Good girl, Shiba!"

Good Tallon! Shiba thought. She'd have told him so outright, but it wasn't polite to bark when your mouthful was squirming.

Eldon sat on the porch with Tallon, looking out through the wide gap of missing railing. Shiba had started the evening there—unharnessed, unchained—but the discussion had reminded her of a job left unfinished: the training of Tallon. She'd wandered off, and Tallon hadn't tried to stop her.

He and Eldon had finished talking about interesting things, anyway—the way the spellrunners were using critters to carry amulets and curses across the border, using simple geases to drive the creatures to their destinations—and had moved on to intense discussion about a new lineman down the border who was actually a linewoman. They talked about her legs the way Jehn had spoken of Shiba's.

Hmph. Shiba had never seen a human man or woman whose legs could cover ground like her own. Just look how quickly she'd accomplished this little task! She reentered the cabin clearing not long after she'd left it, moving in a loose, purposeful trot. She ignored the porch steps and leapt up through the railing gap, a jump that placed her precisely before Talon's lap. Just where she wanted to be.

She opened her jaws and dropped her burden into Tallon's hands. It hardly stunk like critter anymore, really—just the nice clean smell of decay.

"Yahhhhh!" Tallon yelped in surprise, flinging his hands up so the critter went flying. It landed on the other side of Eldon with a hollow thunking sound, losing bits of itself in the process. The tail landed separately.

Eldon had that helpless look of someone trying very hard not to laugh. Shiba's tongue lolled out; she laughed for him. And then Eldon did what she'd wanted Tallon to do all along. He picked up the stiff flat balding dirty decaying critter and looked it over. "Ah," he said, pointing at the encrusted little leather tube around the critter's ankle. "Here's something that doesn't belong on our side of the border."

"It's got one of the amulets," Tallon said, groaning. He threw up his hands. "I give up, Shiba. I'll never doubt you again."

Shiba opened her mouth wide in her best bitch-smile. Tallon, it seemed, was trained.

Don't You Want to Be Beautiful?

Laura Anne Gilman

Getting into the chair was the easy part. Getting out of it was proving to be more difficult. Annie shifted on the high-legged chair and felt—what was her name again? Monique? Angela? Hortense?—felt the harpy from cosmetics hell grab her chin in purple-painted talons.

"Hold your head like this, naturally."

Naturally for you, maybe, Annie sulked as the woman carefully stroked bronze powder onto eyelids already weighted down with chemical concoctions. Four layers, already, Annie counted back. And from the way that harpy had been eyeing that canister of "sealant" powder, it was likely to become five. Mummies had fewer layers than this.

All I wanted was a new mascara!

"Think of makeup as layers of protection," the harpy said, her red-lined, red-creamed lips barely moving. She blinked her heavily coated lashes once, then reached for the sealant. "When you wear it, you feel better. Stronger. More in control. And when you feel that way, you *are* that way. And with our special SPF moisturizer underneath, you never have to worry about your skin being attacked by the elements. Defense and offense in the

162

same wonderful package!" She beamed, as though she had said something wonderfully clever, and was waiting to be rewarded. Annie sat, silent, staring straight ahead. Even if she had wanted to say anything, she wasn't sure her jaw would move any more.

Eyes finally finished, skin tone evened, eyebrows darkened, cheeks burnished in two shades, lips penciled and blotted and creamed, Annie was presented with a mirror and the hard sell.

"The no-makeup look is still important, but with just the essential application of color . . ." the harpy rattled on, replacing the instruments of her trade with fresh, still-boxed versions laid out on the gleaming glass-and-chrome counter top like virgins awaiting their sacrifice. Annie flexed her face carefully, wondering if the layers would crack and fall away. She wondered if her cat would recognize her. Protection? More like armament, she thought. Bullets couldn't break through this.

"Now, you'll want the foundation, of course, and the oil-free concealer. And even if you don't take the moisturizer you'll need our nighttime rejuvinator for the under eye area to stop those wrinkles—"

"No."

The harpy went on, determined not to be stopped by such feeble protest.

"No," Annie said in a stronger voice. "No, I'm sorry, but I, um." Her resolve failed her and she jumbled the words in a shamed mumble. "NoI'msorryIhavetogo-Idon'twantanythingthankyouthanksanyway."

She slipped off the stool and reached for her pocketbook, determined not to reach for her wallet. But the harpy was not in a business for the easily dissuaded.

"But what about this lipcolor? Bronze apple is just *perfect* for you! And don't you want our special gift? It's a silver atomizer filled with our signature scent— here! Smell!" And she reached backwards for a cardboard scent sample.

Taking advantage of the harpy's distraction, Annie ran.

As she rode up the crowded elevator, Annie could swear that she heard the sound of gnashing teeth behind her. But when she risked a glance over her shoulder, just before the first floor disappeared out of sight, the tall, lab-coated form of the Makeup Warrior had latched on to some other hapless browser. Breathing a sigh of relief, she absently rubbed at her eyes, grimacing when she realized what she had done. Now she no doubt looked like a well made-up racoon. She felt even more depressed. So much for a shopping trip as a way to combat the seasonal blues. Maybe new clothes would be the ticket.

Getting off on the third floor, Annie headed for the table of cashmere sweaters, the red sign advertising a pre-holiday 25% off. Despite the resurgence of neon colors, she was certain there was a wearable sweater in the pile somewhere. Unfortunately, half the known shopping world had gotten there first. Summers of retail training took over, and she found herself refolding the sale-tossed mass of sweaters and stacking them neatly. After refusing to answer two different queries—I'm sorry, I don't work here—and not finding a single sweater in the colors she wanted, she gave up.

Hey.

"What?"

She spun around, convinced someone had called her name, but the shoppers pushed by with just the right amount of holiday-induced aggression. Nobody stopped, nobody was looking at her.

You know you want it.

"What?"

That was said too loudly, causing the young girl across the table to look up at her oddly. But only for a moment. There were more important things to be considered than one crazy woman shopper. Annie watched in disbelief as the girl held up a lime-green sweater and nodded in satisfaction. The girl was a redhead, the combination should have been a criminal offense.

Down here. Over here.

Annie looked down involuntarily. Her hand, resting palm-down on the table, jerked away in surprise, causing her to stumble slightly.

Just next to where her hand had been, there lay a small green-and-pink patterned box. Long, and narrow, and about the size of a lipstick.

Annie blinked, then shook her head quickly. "Someone must have left it there." That was it, someone had stopped to look at their purchases, maybe held the lipstick up to a sweater to see how they'd go together, and forgot about it. The voice, it must have been someone calling to a friend, two shoppers gotten lost in the herdlike huddle of bundled bodies. Acoustics in a store this large were always off-putting.

Turning to move away from the table—there wasn't anything here she'd want—Annie looked down at the tiled walkway and counted her footsteps as they clacked in her flat-heeled boots. Around the white-plastered corner, she let out her breath, then peeked back at the display space. Nothing on the table except sweaters.

Shaking her head again, she slung her pocketbook over one shoulder and went off in search of more color-friendly prey.

Half an hour later the soothing ritual of trying clothes on had wiped the incident from her mind. Dismissed as the combination of stress, guilt, and too much cappuccino after too much wine last night at dinner, her mind was more importantly occupied with the possible social repercussions of grey leggings and a red silk tunic shot with silver threads. Too much for the office, maybe, but not for the office party . . .

Tossing them into the "potential" pile, Annie reached

for the next item, a blue wool dress one shade lighter than her eyes. Pulling it over her head, she had a passing concern about getting makeup on the clothing. Wasn't there a shield or something you could get from the salesclerk, to protect your face? Stopping to check her face in the mirror, she saw that yes, indeed, she did look like a racoon, the eye shadow had already begun to fade, and her cheekbones had been denuded. *So much for that high-priced sealant,* she thought with not a little vindication. If it wasn't for those high-pressure tactics, nobody'd ever buy anything from those cosmetics counters at all. Stronger, hah! More in control. Double hah! The only thing that would make her life a little more in control would be two extra days each week.

Stepping backwards to view the effect of the dress in the full-length mirror, Annie felt her foot crunch down on something.

Ow!

Startled, she looked down to see another small pink-and-green box flip onto its side. This one was smaller, and flatter. *Like a powder compact,* she thought unwillingly.

You stepped on me! The voice was accusatory, and not a little indignant.

Backing away slowly, Annie kept her eye on the box on the floor. If it had moved, if the voice had spoken again, she wasn't sure what she would have done. But it wouldn't have been pretty.

"I'm losing it. I'm absolutely, positively losing it."

Biting the inside of her lower lip, she raised her right hand to chin level, then made a full body swoop to pick up the abandoned box, holding it in her open palm and raising it to eye level.

It sat there, innocuous. She didn't hear anything.

And then a pair of blue eyes opened on the edge of the box and stared directly into her own eyes.

Take me home? it asked wistfully.

Annie dropped the box, scuttling backwards until she hit the wall of the dressing room. She didn't scream, some small semirational part of her mind realizing that a nervous breakdown was not something you wanted witnesses to.

The box landed with a soft thump on the carpeting, and lay there for an endless moment.

This is a fine time for an acid flashback. Did I ever drop acid? She wasn't sure if shrooming counted. You weren't supposed to have flashbacks from mushrooms.

Her breathing had just gotten back into something approaching normal when the box shuddered, like a horse shaking off flies, and flipped over, eyes blinking reproachfully.

You dropped me. I could have broken.

Annie opened her mouth to scream, convinced now that a nervous breakdown would be something she would welcome.

I could help you. I *want* to help you. Why won't you let me?

Ah, she don't need us. She's good enough on her own. She don't need any help. Ain't that right, beautiful?

Annie turned her head slowly, sure before she'd looked what she would see. The closed door of the dressing room hadn't stopped the compact—why would she expect it to come alone?

Mascara leaned against the far corner of the dressing room, exuding gunslinger poise like Sharon Stone on her best day. Little Ms. Tough-it-Out thinks she's got goddess genes, thinks a little dimestore color'll get her through the day. Hah.

Stop it! the compact demanded, shuddering violently. Annie blinked, pretty sure that the comment was directed, not at her, but at the other box. Leave her alone. It's chemicals like you that always make people hate us. You're gloppy and sticky and I wouldn't want you either!

Blue eyes swiveled back to look up and up and up,

until Annie felt like Gulliver confronting the Lilliputians. Crouching, she went to her hands and knees, feeing silly but unable to resist.

I think it's that way the wand is shaped, all spiky and sharp, the compact confided in her. I know I'd be irritable if I were like that.

A rude noise was the mascara's only reply.

"I'm not hearing this. I'm not seeing this. I'm not doing this."

Ooo, someone's in a major state of denial . . . The mascara's comeback was cut short by a scraping noise, and both Annie and the compact swiveled to see two small boxes shove themselves under the door.

Omph. Did we miss the party? Oh good, she's not dressed yet. Dammit, where did that brush go? Always sneaking off somewhere just when you need it . . .

She doesn't want us. That was the compact again, sounding close to tears. So far, it was the only one that manifested features. Annie told her herself to be grateful for small favors.

"It's not that," she said, feeling an odd urge to reassure it. "It's just that I don't wear a lot of makeup . . ."

We're not a lot of makeup! the two newcomer boxes chorused together. We're not much makeup at all! They both giggled. You ditched that concealer back by the sweaters. Nice going. It always thinks it knows best, being the first one on all the time. We'll show it. Let us show you what we can do!

Weren't you two shade-heads listening? the mascara asked. She don't want *any* of us.

But, but . . . The two small boxes formed one eye each—brown, Annie noted—and peered at her. But we're neutral! We can go with anything, in the office or out on the town.

You sound like a commercial, the mascara sneered. And quit with the doublemint twins gig already.

The two eye shadows lapsed into hurt silence,

glaring backwards at the mascara box, then rolling their shared eyes forward to look at Annie as she knelt on the floor.

The powder compact lay inches from her face, blue eyes staring up at her hopefully. She hated to do it, she really did, but enough was enough. She'd been attacked, harassed, hard-sold, importuned, insulted . . . all right. That was her fault for going shopping during the Christmas season. But she *refused* to be guilted.

"I. Don't. Need. Makeup. Especially overpriced makeup. And especially especially not overpriced, chattering *pushy* makeup!"

And with that, she grabbed her own clothes and jammed herself into them, picked up her pocketbook, and swung open the dressing room door, sweeping all four boxes out of the way. A muffled jumble of complaints, punctuated by one fluent swearword floated up to her ears. Ignoring the odd look a woman standing before the three-way mirror gave her, she fled the hallway, leaving her try-ons in a desolate pile.

Not looking to the right or the left, she swung around display stands and threaded her way through the crowds, stopping only when she stepped onto the crowded down escalator. Holding on to the railing with both hands until her fingers cramped, she stared straight ahead, refusing to acknowledge the shoppers wanting to push by her. Something in her eye irritated her contact lens. "Damn flaking overpriced mascara," she muttered.

Please, ma'am?

The soft voice carried from somewhere off to her left side. She jolted, her right hand reflexively going to the strap of the pocketbook slung over her left shoulder. Her glance remained fixed straight ahead at the floor rising to meet the slow tread of the escalator.

Please? The voice was definitely coming from her pocketbook. A familiar voice.

I want to go home with you. I want to make things

better for you. I want everything to be perfect for you.
I'm only here to help you.

A pause.

I don't have any reason to exist, except you.

Annie stood in front of the gleaming silver-and-
chrome counter, not looking at anything in particular.

"Can I help you?" The saleswoman oozed charm and
a caring condescension.

"I want to take this powder compact."

"Of course. An excellent choice. Just that hint of
protection, to smooth out the skintone on days when
you're not at your best. Will there be anything else?"

A long, strained pause . . .

A Night with the Girls

Barbara Hambly

"What's the problem?" Starhawk of Wrynde swung down from her horse in front of Butcher's infirmary tent. Though she hadn't been in a mercenary camp in almost two years, she had a soul-deep sense of familiarity about the place, like the outhouse behind a familiar tavern: Are we back here *again*? Only the outhouse would have been quieter. Past the walls of Horran, the sun dipped toward the Inner Sea, red behind the squat black towers of siege engines. In front of tents the mercs sharpened swords and polished armor, repaired straps, chatted up the camp whores, or diced. Cook-fire smoke gritted in the eyes, profanity in the ears.

Be it ever so humble . . .

Butcher craned to look past Starhawk's shoulder. "Where's the Wolf?"

"And I'm so glad to see you, too," replied Starhawk.

The troop physician laughed, embarassed. "I'm sorry." She made a show of checking her breeches pockets and the leathern purse at her belt. "I must have left my manners in my other clothes. I'm damn glad to see you, Hawk, but I meant it in my letter when I said we needed Sun Wolf here."

"Sun Wolf's in the mountains, chasing down some

woman who's supposed to be teaching magic." Starhawk
ran the horse's reins through the ropes that wrapped
one of the barrels piled outside the hospital tent, and
pulled down her saddlebags. "Don't tell me you've got
another wizard in the city." Two years ago the troop,
of which Starhawk had once been second in command,
had the misfortune to have a curse placed on it during
a siege. The results had not been pleasant for anyone.

Butcher scratched her short-cropped graying hair, and
led the way into the tent. Inside, her two apprentices
were closing the flaps and lighting lamps. A slave came
past with dishes of porridge on a tray. A couple of mercs
from one of the smaller troops, as well as those of
Captain Ari's army, were sitting up in their cots; but
nobody who looked like soldiers of the Prince of Chare,
who'd hired them. Elsewhere a man muttered in
drugged pain. Here on the Gwarl Peninsula, where the
trade-routes ran from Ciselfarge and points east, there
was plenty of access to opium.

"I don't think it's a wizard." The physician led the
way through the aisle of cots to a curtained-off rear
corner of the tent. "But sure as pox there's something
going on. Take a look at this."

An enormous woman rose from beside the cot as
Butcher led the Hawk through the curtains. Starhawk
nodded a greeting.

"Battlesow here found him," explained Butcher. "They
were on watch together, night before last. They usually
watched together." She brought the hanging lamp down
close, and twitched the sheet back.

Starhawk said, "Mother Pusbucket!" and stepped
away.

"We don't know what did that." Battlesow had a small
girl's sweet, lisping voice, faintly absurd in most circumstances. It was hard with anger now. "He was lying with
his back against the roots of an oak-tree, with his sword
in one hand and his dagger in the other."

"I have them in the other room." Butcher stepped forward, covered over the scabbed and puckered horror again. "We cleaned him up—he was still breathing—" Starhawk shuddered at the thought. "—But there was blood all over the weapons, old blood, like you find in week-old corpses. You've seen some weird things, since you and Sun Wolf left the troop and started mucking around with wizardry. You ever seen anything like that?"

"Sure." The Hawk gazed down at the outline of the distorted face, the sticky rings of dabbled blood visible beneath the sheet. "Last time I saw the bottom of a boat that had been bored through by worms. But those holes were the size of my finger, not my wrist."

"I've been asking." Butcher led the way along what had probably been a farm-path. The sheathed glow of her lantern bobbed on charred tree-stumps, burned and ruined hedges, and here and there the smashed-in ruins of a house or a barn. Horran was a prosperous little trading port, Starhawk recalled from her own mercenary days, the major source of income for the Prince of Chare. She'd heard in Kedwyr that the Prince had recently hired Ari of Wrynde—Sun Wolf's successor to the command of the troop—to help convince the Horran town fathers not to declare independence. These, she guessed, would have been the garden farms that supplied the city dwellers with fresh vegetables and milk. The Mother only knew where their owners were. Probably sitting in the hills waiting to see who would win.

"According to latrine rumor, five outpost guards have disappeared in the past eight days," Butcher went on. "This morning I made a little tour of the perimeter—nearly getting shot by both sides for my trouble—and found three bodies in the cellar of a farmhouse. They were too chewed-up for me to tell much. Rats, mostly, but some of the wounds didn't look like rats, or like any animal I've ever seen. They were jammed up under the floor-joists."

"That where we're going now?" Starhawk had her sword in her hand, watching all around her, only half listening to what Butcher said, and to the heavy scrunch of Battlesow's boots on the path behind her. It would help a lot, she reflected, if she knew what she was listening for.

It would help even more if Sun Wolf hadn't gone off to look for that little old lady in the Kanwed Mountains who was supposed to braid love-charms out of moonlight. They were quite clearly up against magic here, and even Sun Wolf's unschooled powers would be of more use than the swords of the doughtiest mercenaries. Love-charms were easily manufactured anyway: you just wrapped a piece of paper bearing the words "I love you" around ten or twelve gold pieces, and there you were. In an emergency you could dispense with the paper.

"There's going to be a sortie through here tomorrow night," explained Battlesow's breathless little soprano. "There's a watchtower right over that way, guarding a postern. You're taking your life in your hands anywhere in here by daylight."

"If there's something hiding out in these ruins," said Butcher, "I for one don't want to see—" She stopped, holding up her hand for silence.

Starhawk smelled the thing before she saw it. The stench of old blood and maggots, of dust and burned hair; the stink of rat-piss and grimy beggar-rags. It seemed to come from everywhere, disorienting, drowning the night—if she hadn't been aware that the wind was onshore she would have thought it was only the stink of the city under siege. There was a sound, too, just briefly: a clicking, knocking clatter squishily muffled.

Then a whitish blur near a barn's broken wall.

Butcher brought her mouth almost to Starhawk's ear. "It's got someone."

Starhawk looked again, straining to see in the starlight. After a moment she signed the other two to stay close, and moved towards the place. Butcher generally didn't carry a sword but she could use one, and had strapped hers on for the occasion. Battlesow had, in addition to her four-foot broadsword Daffodil, a halberd with cross-guards on the blade like a boar-spear's, and an iron war-club that could have brained a horse. Before leaving Butcher's tent all three women had geared up with what mercs called dogfight leathers, armbands and collars bristling with spikes, mailed gloves and scouting-weight cuirasses of leather and plate. Starhawk reflected uneasily that the outpost guard she'd seen at the infirmary had almost certainly worn something similar. It was unlikely he'd taken it off for a scratch and been ambushed at just precisely the wrong moment, oh darn.

The barn had been burned during the initial fighting around the walls; roof and rafters had fallen in. In the Gwarl they ususally dug root cellars underneath the barns. If the thing was seeking a lair it—

They came around the corner of the wall and it was there.

It struck unbelievably fast, Starhawk slashing for the dripping pits where eyes had once been. It *was* worms, she thought: they burst through the curtain of filthy rags that covered the squirming globby flesh, huge as serpents, their round reddish heads groping blind. She pivoted sidelong—the thing faced around and as Battlesow rammed it back with the halberd, it opened its mouth and extruded something that looked like a maggot the size of a hosepipe, snapping and reaching. It had hands, though, human or once-human, like the head. They grabbed the halberd's shaft and wrenched it free of Battlesow's grip— Battlesow who could break a cow's neck with a punch— and lunged at the big woman. Nothing daunted, Battlesow waded in with a leather-wrapped and mail-shod right hook that sent the creature spinning into the night.

Starhawk and Butcher closed up on either side of their friend, fast, a triangle facing three ways out. Three swords, three daggers ready—not that swords or daggers had done the outpost guards a whole lot of good. Starhawk panted with shock and exertion, the adrenaline-rush of combat making her hands shake, but for a long time the dense blue-black shadows around them were still, chancy in the glimmer of the stars.

"Holy pox and cow-pies," said Battlesow, and leaned from the spiked defensive ring to pick up the lantern. Starhawk smelled the rank cheap oil and realized that the stench of the creature had faded.

"And Ari's still getting guys willing to stand perimeter guard out here?" Starhawk shook her head. "I underestimated his powers of persuasion—or overestimated the intelligence of some of the guys in the troop, I'm not sure which." She settled into flanking position behind Butcher as the physician followed the dribbled slime-trail the thing had left, back towards the barn. "Does Prince Chare know about this?"

"Ari brought him into the infirmary this morning, while the guy you saw was still alive. Chare kept talking about resistance fighters from the countryside and what horrible weapons they carried that could do that, and how we'll all just have to be more careful."

"Weapons my ass. Yike!" she added, as Battlesow slipped the lantern-slide and raised the lantern to throw yellow light into the root-cellar before them. "He can't be one of ours," she added, studying the youthful, snub-nosed face—what could be seen of it under the blood—and the expensive if tattered clothing.

Butcher shook her head. "Look at his hands. He was somebody's clerk, or a student. He isn't even wearing a sword, look. Poor sap must have just been walking home." She looked around her at the darkness. "What the hell *is* it, Hawk? Sun Wolf's been learning hoodoo for two years now, and that thing's hoodoo if I ever saw it."

"I'm guessing it's a wight of some sort," said Starhawk. "According to the books the Chief picked up in Vorsal they're usually hungry like that. When they meld into corpses they often have some kind of vague memories or thoughts picked up from the brain of the corpse, but they're not bright enough to take orders or anything. And if it *is* a wight, we'd better make ourselves scarce, because wights are—"

Her hand flipped up for silence and in the same instant, it seemed, Butcher rapped shut the lantern-slide. The three warriors pressed automatically back against the wall and slid along it, getting clear of the boy's corpse, swords held low in the shadows beside them but ready again.

The stink of the wight was like drowning in rotting glue.

White movement where the starlight struck, in front of the ruined barn. A vast obscene wriggling under the filthy shroud. Bony hands groping over the ground.

Battlesow leaned to breathe in Starhawk's ear, starlight slipping over the shaved curve of her head, the glister of the five-carat diamond in her ear-lobe. "What's it looking for?"

"Probably," breathed Starhawk back, "its teeth." She'd seen several go flying when Battlesow decked the wight.

The bony fingers fumbled something up from the mud, traveled to the slobbery mouth. Then back to the earth, picking at pebbles, old nails, miscellaneous animal-bones and snail-shells. Looking more closely, Starhawk saw how the thing's head was wrapped in a sort of dirty turban, beneath which wisps of hair hung down, faded in the blanched light like frost-painted grass. Butcher raised her sword a little—she could amputate a leg in fifteen seconds—and Starhawk touched her hand, and shook her head.

"Cutting it to pieces won't help," she breathed. "It'll still come after us."

"If this situation gets any better I'll burst into song. Where's Sun Wolf when you need him?"

"Where's any man when you need him?" muttered Battlesow.

The wight froze.

Pox rot it, thought Starhawk, *it heard us.*

It was on its feet then and turning, not towards them but in the direction of the black crumbled debris of what had been the main farm building, as two figures emerged from the darkness. One stepped forward, lifting a halberd—a woman, the Hawk identified it, by the movement more than by the dim glimpse of trailing braids—and the wight fell on the newcomer, knocking her down and aside with the force of its rush. The second figure, also female though both were clad as men in breeches, tunics, and boots, sprang to her companion's defense, slashing with another halberd, a weapon whose length and leverage were often chosen to compensate for a woman's lighter weight and shorter reach.

Drawn off its first victim, the wight whirled upon the second, and by that time Battlesow, Butcher, and Starhawk had reached the struggling group. Disregarding all Starhawk's warnings about dismemberment Battlesow plowed in like a demented woodchopper on hashish, Daffodil rising and falling in time to battle-cries like the shrill barking of a very small dog. Wriggling, serpent-sized maggots flew and splacked on the damp earth; one brown-gummed bony hand whirled away and crawled spider-wise into the ruins. Mewing and pawing, the wight backed off and fled; Starhawk and Butcher had to grab Battlesow to keep her from following it into the darkness.

"Stinking thing." Battlesow spit after it. "That'll teach it."

"It won't," pointed out Starhawk. "They don't learn. They just come back. Indefinitely. Whatever you do to them, they incorporate into themselves. Absorb it, and make it part of their attack."

"I was married to a man like that once," remarked Butcher.

They turned back. The tubulate, serpent-like growths had already crawled away from the ruined dooryard. One of the two newcomer women gave over trying to help her friend to her feet and sprang up herself, grabbing her halberd and bracing herself for another attack.

"Relax," said Starhawk, crossing to them and stopping just out of halberd-range, not that she thought either woman capable of doing much damage. She sheathed her sword and her dagger, and held up her hands to show them empty. "That thing yours?"

The two women—one standing, the other, whom the wight had first borne down, scrambling painfully to her feet—looked at one another, then at Starhawk and her friends. The older woman, scrawny as a cut-rate chicken a poor housewife would have to boil for most of a day, said at length, "In a manner of speaking. Are you all right, Elia?"

"More or less." Her friend brushed filth and soot from her sleeves, wiped the spattered slime of the wight's mouth off her face, to reveal a plain, square-jawed, motherly countenance. She leaned her halberd against the wall near her and held out her hand to Starhawk. "I am Elia, representative to the town council of Horran from the Seven Streets district. This is Teryne."

"Starhawk of Wrynde. Butcher," she nodded back at the others who still watched, weapons ready, for the return of the wight, "and Battlesow. Why 'in a manner of speaking'? Did you call it into being?"

Teryne spat, a crone's eloquence. Elia said, "No. I was not informed of the town council meeting at which the decision to—to create such a thing—was taken." She added drily, "From all I can learn, a number of us weren't."

"I could have told them," Teryne said in her harsh, surprisingly deep voice. "I did tell them, Brannis Cornmonger, and Mowyer Silks, and all their merchant friends. Told them old Aganna Givna was so angry and spiteful in her old age that if they opened up her tomb and let the charnal-wight claim her body, the way that book of theirs told them how, she'd turn on anyone she could get at, not just the troops of the Prince."

"Book?" Like Sun Wolf, Starhawk was always on the lookout for the ancient lore of the craft, the only remnant of teaching left. "They had a book of magic?"

The old woman gestured like one shooing flies. "Brannis Cornmonger, that's Mayor—though now he calls himself President of the Independent Polity, if you please." Her voice would have burned holes in a linen shirt. "Only it's not a proper book, not thick, that'll tell you the why and the wherefore. Like so be it's a cookbook, that'll just say how."

"Oh, great!" Starhawk rolled her eyes. Sun Wolf had a collection of such grimoires, picked up in his travels. He also had a collection of appalling stories about people who'd followed the recipes enclosed therein, without inquiring as to what spells of limitation or protection might have been left out of those terse instructions to mix sea salt with human blood, or to repeat certain words in certain places at the dark of the moon. "So these idiots just pulled the ward-spells off a tomb and set up a drawing-circle. . . ."

"To do Brannis Cornmonger justice," said Elia, wrapping her graying braids onto the back of her head and rearranging the pins that held them, "I personally would rather not have Prince Chare's forces take and sack the town. It isn't anything to me if Cornmonger gets fed hot coals by Chare's executioners, but having neighbors, and sisters, and nieces, and a mother who stand to be sold into slavery after being raped repeatedly, I do understand our mayor's—excuse me, *president's*—attitude." She folded her arms, and regarded the three mercenaries with accusing eyes. "The only problem is that wights apparently don't prey simply on one side, no matter what kind of instructions get written in the circle of their calling."

"*As* I told him," Teryne said again. She tilted her head a little to regard her friend, then the mercenaries before her. "Not that he'd listen to *me*. 'Old wives tales,' he said; as if reading that scrap of a cookbook made him a wizard instead of just a man who used to live next door to the grandson of one. I notice the man who wrote that book isn't around no more."

"Well, the Wizard-King pretty much took care of all competition, good and bad, before he was killed," said Starhawk. She scratched the sweat and gore from her loose soft tousle of pale hair, and turned back to consider the starlit glimmer of wet ground and mucky shadows where the wight had been. "You'd think he might have had the sense to ask, though."

"People often don't want to know," Elia said, "when they think they see a way out of their difficulties."

"Particularly not if there's talk in council of dumping those whose stubbornness and greed started the trouble with the Prince in the first place," put in Teryne.

Starhawk was silent for a time, thinking. Thinking about matters she had read in Sun Wolf's books of magic—proper books, Teryne would have called them, that *did* talk about the why and wherefore of such matters as wights. Thinking about the political situation in the Gwarl Peninsula, something she and Sun Wolf had kept up on through tavern gossip and merchants' reports with the professional curiosity of one-time mercenaries whose livelihood had once depended on knowing who was fighting whom and why. Thinking about the cities she had helped sack, back in her fighting days, and of why she had quit being a mercenary. Thinking about the men and women of those cities that she had met: who they were, and what they wanted out of life.

Thinking about the fact that the wight-stink was

growing stronger again, thick and rancid on the night air.

"—book of his said that if the names of his enemies were written on the walls of the tomb when it was opened, the wight would go after those enemies," Elia was explaining to Butcher. "I asked him—and I wasn't the only one—what would happen if the wight started hunting, started killing, inside the city as well as outside. Brannis said that wouldn't happen."

"Brannis didn't inquire," remarked old Teryne drily, "whether Aganna could *read* the names of Brannis' enemies or her own name, for that matter, which she couldn't."

"The council voted against Brannis' plan," Elia went on. "But two nights later the husband of one of my neighbors disappeared—the shutters of his room broken in, and the smell there . . ." She stopped and looked around her at the darkness, realizing that while she had been speaking, the smell had returned. Stronger, and growing stronger still.

"Give me that lantern, Butcher," said Starhawk. "And watch my back."

The four women formed up a perimeter around her, a moving circle that followed her out into the open patch of ground where the mud glistened with the foulness that had dripped from the wight's wounds. Starhawk slipped back the lantern slide and knelt, edging this way and that in the muck, searching.

"There's been three others taken so far, that I know about," Elia said. "That's just from my neighborhood, which is one of the poorest in the city."

"Your Mayor could have saved himself trouble," remarked Butcher. "I can't see Prince Chare turning loose one square foot of territory that belongs to him no matter how many soldiers get killed, his own or somebody else's. He's a stiff-necked bastard."

"Stiff-necked has nothing to do with it." Starhawk

pulled off her mail-backed glove to run her fingers over the greasy earth. "The council of Horran's got to be negotiating with the Lady Prince of Kwest Mralwe. Chare would be a fool to let Horran out of his— Ah!" She found what she sought and picked it up, crumbling, brown and slimed from the dirt. Deep in the darkness, beyond the orange-lit shoulders of Butcher's scouting-leathers, beyond Battlesow's thick tattooed neck and shaven head, a noise started, a low throaty growling, like a cat when cornered by a dog.

"Tell me this," she added, searching more quickly now—there had to be more of these. "Did somebody on the council come up with articles of compromise? Here—No, dammit, just a dog's foot-bone. Articles are pretty standard in fights like this and I heard something about it when the Chief and I were over in Ciselfarge last month. Here we go." She picked up a second hard little chunk, wiped it off and stowed it in her belt-pouch. The growling in the darkness grew louder.

"Coriador Toth." Elia's voice sounded strained, but she kept it steady and quiet. "He's one of the greatest merchants of the town, but a good man. Neither Chare nor Brannis would sign—Chare because he said it gave away too much to the Council, Brannis because it didn't give enough."

"Idiots, both of 'em," said Teryne.

"Can you get us into the city?" Starhawk got to her feet. And, when Elia and Teryne looked at one another, she added impatiently "You must have gotten out somehow—*she* must have gotten out. I'd offer to turn over my weapons to you," she went on, annoyed, "except I think we're all going to need them in about—"

The wight flung itself from the darkness.

It had grown. Where Butcher's sword had nearly taken one arm off, another had been grafted in, raising the complement to three: a man's arm, bearing the gouges of the serpentine corpse-worms in its bleeding

flesh and clutching a sword in its hand. Where Battlesow
had hacked its body nearly in two, a head had been
shoved like a plug, eyes staring, mouth leaking blood
as it tried to speak. Elia screamed and Battlesow said,
"Bugger me, it's Lieutenant Egswade!"

Starhawk, nearly borne down by the wight's rush,
slithered out of the thing's way, slashing and cutting—
the whole bulk of the creature seemed greater, swollen
and fleshed out as if it had gorged to replenish itself
after its defeat. With mindless rage it sprang after her,
striking and clawing and grabbing. Battlesow and Elia
intercepted it, halberd and sword flashing in the lantern-
light.

"Bugger this." Butcher caught up the lantern Starhawk
had dropped and made ready to throw.

With a yell Starhawk flung herself at the physician,
wrenching the hot metal from her hand. "Don't do that!"

The wight hurled Battlesow to one side, hurled itself
towards Starhawk and Butcher with a yammering hiss.
Starhawk nearly dislocated her arm, dragging Butcher—
and the lantern—out of the way. "It absorbs what it
touches, dammit! You want to give it fire?"

"Oh." Butcher looked at the little vessel of clay, horn,
metal and oil. "Got any flowers? Or jelly?"

Starhawk fell back again, slashing at the attacking
wight with her sword. The blade-tip caught Lieutenant
Egswade's face across the forehead; the bulging eyes
stared at them and the mouth formed the words "I'll
report that! I'll report you both!" without a sound.

Elia stepped in with a low clean sidelong slash, cutting
the thing's right leg out from under it; it fell, and ran
along the ground at them with its three arms like a
spider's legs. Teryne cried "This way!" and flew back up
the farm-path like a bundle of blown rags, the other
women running for their lives in her wake.

There were tombs along the city wall, doors gaping,
the black charnel-smell flowing forth. Teryne plunged

unerringly up the steps of one, slipped through its half-open grille of iron bars and slammed it shut again as the last of the women bolted through. The lantern flung jolting shadows over low granite walls, niches filled with broken coffin-wood, cobwebs, nasty little messes of hair and cloth and bone.

"This way," the old woman panted. "It's the entry to the catacomb of the House Toth. The other end comes out in the ruin of what used to be their town house. This is how she's been coming and going. Her own tomb's near by."

Starhawk looked around. Every niche was barred with a line of silver spikes, every keystone written with warding-signs that she recognized from Sun Wolf's books, every corpse surrounded by crystals of salt. "I thought so," she panted. "The whole countryside must be infested with wights, the way in some places tapeworms dwell in the water and the earth. You say you knew her?"

"Everyone in the Seven Streets quarter knew her." Teryne sniffed contemptuously. "She was always a soured and bitter woman, ever since Gillimer Cornmonger— Brannis' father—threw her over for someone prettier and with a bigger dowry. I was little more than a child myself in those days. But even after all these years, when Brannis Cornmonger spoke of making a wight, there was only one person so poison-filled and spite-riddled in anyone's memory, that could be its steed. All this . . ." she gestured at the ward-written tombs " . . . is for naught, really. The good need not fear for wights inhabiting their bones."

"Well, there's two schools of thought on that one," said Starhawk, "but I won't argue about it now. Butcher, you go with Teryne. I think the wight'll come after me rather than her, but I don't think anybody should be walking around alone tonight. Those bars look pretty sturdy. . . ." She sheathed her sword, and reached out to grip the iron grillework of the tomb door. "They should hold our girlfriend off for awhile, at least until Elia and Battlesow and I take care of what we need to take care of in town tonight."

As Starhawk feared it would, the wight attacked their party when they emerged from the city again in the dead stillness halfway between midnight and morning, and they were hard put to drive it back. It had increased in size again, having killed, it was clear, another outpost guard—clear because pieces of the man were visible among the bones and rags and threshing, darting worms of its original form. "Holy Three!" whispered Councillor Toth, who had joined Starhawk's party after minimal arguement when she, Elia, and Battlesow had rousted him from his bed. "Is *that* the creature you were proposing to waken, and set upon our enemies?" He turned in outrage and disgust upon Mayor—*Excuse me*, thought Starhawk, *PRESIDENT*—Cornmonger, who had also been persuaded to accompany the expedition, though he had not, as Toth had, been given the option of refusing to come.

"Aren't we being nice in our choices of weapon?" retorted Cornmonger sarcastically. He was a handsome man in his mid-fifties who even in an expensive yellow silk bedgown, tassled red slippers, and a velvet bell-rope tied around his wrists managed to look well-groomed. "Prince Chare will never grant our city the liberties we demand! He will destroy us, if we do not take whatever means we can to turn him away!" He had an orator's carrying voice and a demagogue's habit of speaking to multitudes, even when such multitudes consisted of only two or three. Starhawk suspected he made speeches to his servants and children over breakfast.

"The wight is a weapon of terror, to be used against his men . . ."

"Only it isn't going against his men, is it?" Elia's

motherly face was grim under a mask of slime and blood. "It feeds on both sides of the wall. Mostly in the poorest neighborhoods, which lie closest to the wall and the tombs—I think that was my nephew Dal, whose body now lies out in one of its farm-cellar lairs tonight—but there have been wealthier children who've disappeared, haven't there, Councillor?"

Toth's eyes darkened with understanding, as pieces of things he had heard fit together, and he nodded.

"We all have to be ready to pay the price of freedom," insisted Cornmonger. He glanced around him nervously, for Starhawk had refused to untie his hands when the wight had attacked, and the smell of the thing still hung rank and choking in the air. "It served to turn Chare's mercenaries against him, didn't it?"

"Not a hope, pookie." Battlesow grabbed a handful of the costly fabric of his shirt. "I fight where I sign on. But hoodoo like this wasn't in the bargain." Her piggy black eyes glistened as she moved her head, listening to the deathly, horrible stillness of the dark no man's land of burned farms between camp and wall. "Those faces in that thing's body and chest—I know some of those men. Like I knew the man it killed the night before last. And all I got to say is, you damn well better sign those Articles of Compromise or you're gonna be one sorry man when we *do* break the city wall."

"You'll be sorry even if Chare doesn't," added Starhawk, holding his elbow to steady him over the rough ground. "Once Elia and Toth tell the people about your summoning the wight—*against* the vote of the Council. Once someone sends word to your prospective allies in Kwest Mralwe that you'll use hoodoo against your own people without a second thought." She glanced behind her, around her, in the sicklied wash of late-rising moonlight, her hair prickling at the distant, gutteral growling almost unheard in the sultry blackness.

"And what about you?" Toth hurried to keep up with

Starhawk, for he was a short man, chubby and balding. He was armed with a sword which he handled like a man who'd had only four lessons in its use, and had brought with him three of his servants, also armed. This was fortunate considering the increasing size and ferocity of the wight. "What do you get of this, lady, for going against the man who hired you?"

"Chare didn't hire me." She scraped a gobbet of gore off her neck-spikes, which had barely saved her from having her throat torn open. "I was just called in over this wight business, or my partner was, anyway. And what I get out of it is not seeing my friends slaughtered by a dirty magic against which they have no defense. And the same," she added, "goes for the people within the wall."

They passed the outpost guards along Ari's part of the perimeter, soldiers who knew Starhawk and Battle-sow and accepted their word that the little gang of armed men with them was under their protection. Butcher met them just inside the camp itself. "We built the pyre, like you instructed," said the physician. "The wood's soaked in all the Blue Ruin gin I could find at short notice, and the things you told Teryne to fetch are laid on it. I take it," she added drily, "that they'll keep our agglomerative pal from taking the fire into herself like she takes everything else?"

"Well," said Starhawk, "let's hope so. But you know it's only a matter of time before some idiot pitches a torch at it anyway." She glanced over her shoulder. The smell of the wight had grown as they'd approached the camp, the bubbling, angry mutter of it clearly audible in the darkness all around them. It dogged them through the velvet black among the tents and tent-ropes, the banked watch-fires and the carts: angry, hungry, wanting.

She hoped she'd have time to do what she needed to do. Sun Wolf was a lot more convincing at this kind of thing than she was.

Prince Chare was no happier about being wakened in the smallest hours of the morning than Brannis Cornmonger had been. "Sign the Articles of Compromise?" he blustered. "Nonsense! The city is mine, to do with as I please. Who let you in here? Guards!"

"Your guards are taking a little nap right now." Battlesow touched a taper to the single candle Starhawk had lit at the Prince's bedside and went about the tent lighting lamps. Given the cost of oil and candles—beeswax, not tallow—the Prince was as extravagant about lights as he was about everything else. Gorgeous hangings of the bright-colored silks for which the Middle Kingdoms were famous covered the canvas walls; chairs of expensive inlay and enamel punctuated tufted rugs. Starhawk saw Battlesow pause by the dressing-table and pocket the Prince's emerald neck-chain and several of his rings.

"The city is *not* yours," said Councillor Toth indignantly. "You can't tax us as if we were a trading municipality and govern us as if we were a village of serfs. That recognition is all we ask."

"That's *not* all we ask!" retorted Cornmonger. "We demand—"

"*I* demand," said Starhawk, raising her usually soft voice to a cutting battle edge, "that you sign the Articles of Compromise—both of you—now. You, Cornmonger, summoned a wight, and you, Prince, knew of its existence. According to Butcher you've been covering up the disappearances of outpost guards for days. You don't care whether the people in the city or the soldiers who're fighting for your lands are being slaughtered by this thing, as long as you think you'll each get your way. Now sign the Articles and end the siege, or you will both pay—personally—for the situation you're letting continue."

She fished in the pouch at her belt and held up one of the broken brown fragments she'd dug from the mud: visibly a tooth. In the halo of candleflame her scarred, narrow face was stern and cold, anger and disgust at the waste and violence of war repeated a hundredfold, like the tongues of the wavering fires, in her gray eyes.

"By this I have summoned her," she said, in her best imitation of the Mother at the convent where she'd been raised when she told the girls why they had to be good. In fact it was only the native greediness of wights that would draw the creature, but these men didn't have to know that. "She's going to be here in about a minute and a half. What do you say?"

Prince Chare and the Mayor of Horran stared at one another in blazing defiance, two proud and wealthy men who had never had to pay personally for the consequences of their own actions. Chare opened his mouth to retort, then wrinkled his nose and said, "By the Three, what *is* that smell?"

Outside someone let out a yell, and the side of the tent billowed, sagged, and ripped. Brannis Cornmonger screamed. Battlesow and Starhawk sprang towards the wight—which had increased in size again—but before they reached it the Prince siezed the iron lampstand beside his bed—

"NO!" screamed Starhawk.

—and shoved the blazing ring of candles into the thing's distorted face.

The wight exploded into flame and kept on coming, reaching out five mismatched arms and a writhing mass of snake-heads. Starhawk slashed, stepped back, the oily heat beating against her face. Battlesow caught up the inlaid night-stand next to her and hurled it at the thing, scattering combs and prayer books in all directions but breaking its first rush to let Starhawk spring clear. Chare and Cornmonger fell over one another in their scramble for the door, Chare wearing the shocked expression of one who believed that fire would discourage almost any kind of attack and Cornmonger yelling at him "You mammering dolt!" Elia slashed with her halberd at the burning bones within the whirling fire, then snatched up the Articles of Compromise a moment before the carved table on which they lay caught fire, and fell back, still guarding Starhawk, to the tent door.

Moaning and howling, the wight kept coming, trying to claim its stolen teeth. Warriors came running, half-armed and naked, from their tents, camp slaves rushed to hurl water on the Prince's burning pavilion, and Starhawk fell back, slashing now with her sword, now with a soaked hanging she'd pulled from the tent wall and soused in a horse-trough, fighting to keep the wight off her while she made a retreat. Battlesow and Elia followed her example, fending off the blazing attacker with pole-weapons and dripping rugs while Butcher, with what Starhawk thought astonishing foresight, retreated behind her towards the place where they'd prepared the pyre, clearing her way of tent-ropes, camp debris, cookpots and firewood. The wight was a twenty-foot tower of flame, dry bones, and dripping flesh devoured and absorbed, leaving only an armature of fire, and the fire strode through the camp's darkness howling and crying its rage.

This plan better work, thought Starhawk. She had no idea if it would and wanted to knock together the heads of Prince and Mayor for getting her into this situation. Where the hell was Sun Wolf when you needed him anyway? He was the one who knew about magic, not her.

"We got it!" yelled someone—Dogbreath, she thought—"We got it, Hawk, we'll save you!"

She didn't dare turn her head until the last second, when her mercenary pals Dogbreath and Penpusher crossed the line of her vision hauling one of the wheeled water-butts from which they watered the mules. She yelled "*Don't* . . . !" too late as they levered the thing over, three hundred gallons spewing forth over the wight . . .

. . . which rose in a heaving column of animate liquid and poured over her in a wave.

She sprang sideways, coughing, drowning, water forcing itself into her nose, her mouth. Water surged around her, slowing her steps, dragging her back, water that shrieked in her ears and blinded her eyes and ripped and tore at her hands.

Battlesow yanked her out of the maelstrom by main force and dragged her in the direction of the pyre, a riptide heaving and pulling at their feet, slowing them while the cresting, thrashing waterspout pursued them through the camp. Coughing, Starhawk gasped, *"Don't let anybody else help me!* I know what I'm doing!"

Back at the convent I'd have been doing pennance till Yule for a lie like that.

The pyre lay ahead of them. Teryne and a group of the mercenaries grouped around it, men and women dangerously quiet, muttering. Like Battlesow, they were perfectly willing to face war and weapons but not the vileness of black magic in the dark. Too many had seen the heads and faces of the dead the wight had absorbed, and rumor was running fast. Barely able to breathe and half-blinded by spray, Starhawk saw on the pyre the thing she had sent Teryne to get, a burlap sack containing what appeared to be a collection of rags and sticks. The unfired wood glittered in the orange glare of the flaming brand in Teryne's hand, and the smell of Blue Ruin, the cheap merc gin manufactured by Bron the quartermaster and his wife Opium, almost drowned the charnel stink of the wight. Starhawk wondered what the hell Bron had charged them for the gin. Knowing Bron—or more specifically knowing Opium—she was certain it hadn't been free.

The drag on her feet increased and she felt the spattering of spray on the back of her neck, heard the rattling, metallic roar in her ears. She stumbled, the pressure of the water incredibly strong, dropped her useless sword to yank from her belt the two brown fragments of tooth, closing them tight in her fist against the cold suction. "Torch it!" she yelled, and Teryne thrust the fire into the pyre's wood.

The alcohol-soaked tinder caught in a searing explosion of white heat, and in that second, Starhawk flung the teeth. The waterspout roared over her, throwing her to the soaked mud. A second explosion as the water struck the superhot flame, and billowing steam, scalding, flame-colored itself in the glare. Printed incandescent on her eyes, Starhawk had a vision of the sorry little sack on top of the pyre being consumed.

Then there was only a mush of coals and embers, white scarves of steam floating sullen over the charred jumble of wood.

The sack was gone.

The wight was gone.

Starhawk got to her feet, covered with mud as if she'd been dipped in it and soaked to the skin. Her knees shook and she reached out, holding Butcher's arm for support. Elia, soaked also—all of them were wet as if they'd just been dragged up from the bottom of the sea—started to ask something, but Starhawk caught her eye and shook her head.

On the edge of the crowd of mercenaries, Prince Chare and Mayor Cornmonger stood staring at the steam-wreathed pyre, the sodden ashes in disbelief.

Starhawk wiped the goop from her eyes, and said, "Take a warning, pals." She fished in the pouch at her belt, and brought up the last brown-and-white fragment: a dog's footbone, she guessed it was when she'd found it in the muddy farmyard. But at that distance, in the iron dark and flickering torchlight of pre-dawn, it looked sufficiently like the wight's teeth to pass for one. Her heart hammered so loudly she was sure Cornmonger and Chare must hear it. She turned the bone in her fingers, holding it up, molding her face into the expression of cold and enigmatic arrogance Sun Wolf assumed when he was bluffing, and hoped to hell they bought the story. "Take a warning, and sign those Articles. Because I can bring her out of that pyre, as easy as I sent her in, in a form you don't want to know about."

To her enormous surprise, they both signed. Elia and Councillor Toth made sure they signed all six copies of the Articles, and took them away the moment the sealing-wax was set to send them to various allies, so that neither side could repudiate without severe repercussions. Then Chare went back to what was left of his tent to begin arrangements for paying off the mercenaries and to order his servants to clean up the mess, and Cornmonger headed for to the walls of Horran to let the people know that the siege was over. If they hadn't won all of their independence, at least they wouldn't be sacked, or return to the absolute rule against which they'd rebelled.

Dawn was coming up, gray and thin above the hills.

Starhawk sat down on a wagon-tongue and started to scrape the mud off her face and hair.

"Sorry about the water." Dogbreath brought her a bucket. "You sure that thing's not gonna be back?"

"Pretty sure." Starhawk upended it over her head— she was past any consideration of delicacy. She wondered if the stink would ever come out of her hair. "She got her teeth—that's why she went into the pyre—and once she was there she incorporated what Teryne had brought from the city tombs. That's what she's been wanting all this time."

"What was it?" Butcher came over, wringing out the tail of her shirt. "Teryne dug around the public catacombs for half an hour looking for it."

"The bones of Gillimer Cornmonger," said Starhawk. "Brannis Cornmonger's father—the man who seduced and betrayed her fifty-five years ago. That's what she wanted, all those years. To have him all to herself. And now she does. Once the flesh and the will were at rest, the wight had no more power."

"And you learned that from reading Sun Wolf's magic books?" asked Battlesow wonderingly.

Starhawk looked off across the jumble of burned-out farmhouses and trampled fields, to where the small train of mayor and councillors and their bodyguard had reached the city gates. Cindery light showed the guards coming in from the siege machinery. Somewhere over the camp someone set up a faint cheer, answered, still more faintly, from the cheering in the city behind its walls.

"It was just a guess," she said. "I learned that from the people who live in those cities I used to help destroy." She unbuckled the spiked guards from her arms and neck. "It's not magic, and it's not in books. It's not even logical. It's just what people do and are, and need to make them happy."

"Considering what it takes to make *some* people happy," said Butcher softly, "Brannis Cornmonger was lucky."

Starhawk sighed. "We all were lucky." She flung the chip of dog bone away into the dead ash of the pyre. "And Sun Wolf the luckiest of anybody. This is definitely the last time I open a message addressed to *him*. Now how about some breakfast before I head out?"

A Quiet Knight's Reading

Steven Piziks

Her wounds ached and drops of green blood occasionally spattered the stone floor, but the dragon was determined not to let that ruin her evening. With exquisite care, she licked one claw and turned the page of the thick book on the reading table before her. Her other claws peeled back a nicely blackened suit of armor, making a sound like the foil coming off a chocolate bar, only a great deal louder. The movement made the scratches and gouges on her body cry out and she had to pause until they stopped.

When the pain passed, the dragon took a juicy bite, careful not to let anything drip on the book. She knew very well that it isn't a good idea to eat and read at the same time, but tonight she really deserved the treat.

Besides, everyone needs a vice.

Something this Chaucer person seems to understand completely, she thought, chewing carefully and turning to another page. *So much more compelling than anything that other pompous, puff-headed poet could come up with. Spenserian verse indeed! No wonder he was never admitted at court.*

A pang jolted the dragon's heart and her head automatically snapped around, creating a corresponding jolt of pain. Someone else was in her keep—in the courtyard, to be exact. The dragon could feel stealthy footsteps on her stones, sense ripples wafting through the air as the intruder moved.

Another knight? She looked down at her meal. *I haven't even recovered from this one yet.*

Step step step. The intruder was getting closer, though the pace was cautious. An odd, unfamiliar feeling rose in the dragon's chest.

The dragon set down her dinner, closed the book, and undulated stiffly toward the courtyard of the keep.

The keep itself was blocky and fairly small, with cold, empty corridors and dusty doors. A great hall ran down the center, with human living quarters above and cellars below. Scrubby wind-swept hills surrounded the place, and the nearest human town was almost seven days' human travel away. Unfortunately, almost two hundred years of successful hoarding invariably gives one a certain reputation with treasure-seekers—no matter how far away the closest humans might be.

Step step step. The dragon's odd feeling intensified.

Every idiot who can wave a sword thinks he can conquer the mighty dragon and steal her hoard, she growled to herself. *As if they deserve it—or could even carry it away.*

The dragon slid over a pile of loose rubble and hissed sharply when the stones ground into her still-bloody wounds. She braced herself against the wall until the world stopped spinning.

I can't do this, she thought. *This is the fourth knight in five days. Where are they all coming from?*

Step step step. That odd feeling increased again. The dragon's heart was pounding, her lungs were working like hyperactive bellows, and she was shivering, even though she wasn't cold.

Fear, she realized with a start. *I'm afraid!*

Then anger entered her emotional mix, giving the

world a reddish tinge. How *dare* they? These humans had reduced her to this? To being afraid of tinfoil knights? The anger grew like poison ivy and she bolted forward, intending to rush down to the courtyard with a sky-shattering roar and disembowel the fool with a single swipe of her claws.

The pain stopped her cold. Her sudden movement had torn open partially healed wounds and sent white-hot spasms coursing through the others. The dragon sat in the corridor, concentrating on her breathing until the pain eased.

The roof, she decided. *I'll take a look from the roof.*

The intruder was female. She was clad in the jingling mail so popular with human warriors, and the obligatory sword was out and ready. Her hair was black and bound tightly on the top of her head. She was quite tall by human standards.

The dragon peeked down from the roof of the great hall and shifted restlessly on her perch. She considered incinerating the woman from above, but that last knight's final gouge must have slashed something vital for firemaking—it was difficult to get her flame going. It would be claw-to-hand or nothing, something the dragon didn't at the moment relish.

And then there's the Beowulf factor, she thought fretfully. *"The female of the species is always more fearsome." I can't go through this again. What am I going to do?*

The woman looked cautiously around the courtyard. The dragon's heart began beating faster and she found herself nervously picking at the dry thatching. Fear again. The dragon wanted to scream with frustration. Innis Gorath, the human who had been banished to this prison of a keep, had been dead for almost two hundred years now, and it wasn't as if he needed avenging, for heaven's sake. He'd almost murdered the king's infant son. Gorath and his men had been ripe pickings for a young dragon looking to settle down and start a nice little hoard. So why couldn't the humans leave her alone?

Maybe she should take human shape and pretend to be the dragon's captive. It would be easy to lure the intruder close, and it would be satisfying to see the look on the woman's face when the poor, helpless princess exploded into a roaring dragon.

Then the dragon shook her head and sighed. That wouldn't work. In her current condition, it would take several hours to shift her shape.

What am I going to do?

Impulsively, the dragon leaned over the edge of the rooftop and cleared her throat.

"Go away!" she bellowed.

The woman jumped with a satisfying yelp and spun about, trying to look everywhere at once, sword at the ready.

"Didn't you hear? I said, *go away!*" the dragon shouted. Her voice echoed around the courtyard, impossible to localize.

"Who are you?" the woman yelled back. "Where are you?"

"I own this keep, human," the dragon boomed, "and you aren't going to take it from me. So why don't you just get on that horse you've probably hidden in the hills out there and ride away before you get hurt?"

"Do you give all your victims that warning?" the woman countered, still unable to locate the dragon's voice, "or am I the first?"

"I could fry you where you stand, human!"

The woman cocked her head and lowered her sword. "Then why don't you?"

The dragon didn't know how to answer that, so she remained silent.

"Listen," the woman said, "my name is Lilire and I'm not here to kill you."

Now the dragon cocked her head. This was a new one. "You can't have my hoard, either," she warned.

"Don't want it. Look, can I see you? It feels strange talking to empty air."

It would have been gratifying for the dragon to spread her wings and swoop down on the courtyard, stirring up great gouts of air and letting her scales glitter like liquid emeralds in the sunlight. But any attempt of the kind would certainly end in a bone-jarring splat and leave a liquid emerald pancake.

Maybe she could land on Lilire.

In the end, the dragon simply slithered down the wall, claws anchoring her firmly to the stone. The movement hurt like hell, and the dragon suppressed a grimace. She coiled herself a safe distance away and levelled a hard look at Lilire, who was visibly steeling herself not to run. The dragon found that vaguely mollifying.

"What do you want?" the dragon hissed. "Make it quick."

Lilire swallowed. "I need some scales. Just a few."

"Scales?" The dragon would have blinked if she had eyelids. "What on earth for?"

"The king. He won't promote me to lieutenant unless I 'prove myself' by getting him some dragon scales. You know how it is." Lilire hawked and spat. "Men in charge."

The dragon didn't know, but found herself nodding sympathetically.

"And then there are the men in the army." Lilire spat again. "Military men are pigs, you know? They think any female they see is just dying to bowl over backwards with her legs open for them."

The dragon nodded again. Now that she thought about it, Chaucer seemed to take that attitude. The matter bore exploration. Once this human was gone, at any rate.

"All right then," the dragon said. "If I give you a few scales, will you go away?"

Lilire bared her teeth and the dragon automatically drew back. After a moment she remembered that teeth-baring was a sign of pleasure among humans and she relaxed.

"Happily," Lilire said. She sheathed her sword.

The dragon rubbed her back against the rough stone of the keep, careful to keep her injuries away from the rock. A moment later, she flung a clawful of glittering green scales at Lilire, each one the size of a human hand. They bounced and clattered on the cobblestones. Lilire gathered them up like a child gathering autumn leaves, put them in a large pouch, and thanked the dragon most kindly.

"Before I leave," she said, "may I ask a personal question?"

The dragon narrowed her eyes. She had never talked this much with anyone, let alone a human, but she found it oddly intriguing. "Ask. I won't promise to answer."

"I couldn't help noticing that you're wounded," Lilire said, clutching the fat pouch at her belt as if she feared it would sprout legs and scamper away. "Badly. How did it happen? Other knights?"

"Other knights," the dragon agreed wearily.

"After your treasure?"

"Yes."

"Creeps. Only things on their minds are gold and sex—and they want gold only because it can buy sex."

"Gold?" The dragon cocked her head. "They're after gold? But I don't collect gold."

"Silver, then. Or gems."

"No."

"But all dragons collect treasure, don't they?" Lilire replied, puzzled. "What else could it be?"

The dragon chuckled in spite of herself and some of her pain actually eased. "Dragons collect valuables," she said.

"Like what?"

The dragon looked at Lilire for a long moment. She liked this human woman. This woman knew what it was like to be wanted for only one thing.

"Leave your sword and knife," the dragon instructed, "and I'll show you."

"Incredible," Lilire breathed. "And you have more?"

"Rooms full," the dragon said proudly. "Most of them are in the original author's hand."

Lilire shook her head in amazement and went back to staring into the storeroom. Books were everywhere—stacked in the corners, on tables, upside-down, right side up, *everywhere*. The room smelled sweetly of vellum, parchment, and ink.

"Do you know how much this is worth?" Lilire asked, then caught a look at the dragon's face. "Never mind. Stupid question. And this is why these knights keep coming after you?"

"It is," the dragon grimaced. "And frankly, I don't know how long I can hold out. You're the fourth person to . . . visit in five days, and you know how long it takes your kind to get here. I don't get time to rest and heal between attacks anymore."

"You're getting quite the reputation," Lilire told her. "Bards sing of you all over the country. The mighty dragon and her fantastic hoard."

The dragon winced.

"Most of those pigs can't even read," Lilire said. "They'd probably rip the bindings apart looking for the bars of gold they're sure you've hidden inside."

The dragon's eyes widened in horror.

"Why aren't they on shelves?" Lilire continued, not noticing the dragon's distress.

"I don't know how to build them," the dragon admitted. "I take human shape once in a while so I can write, and until lately I could dry out the rooms with puffs of hot air to keep mold and rot away, but I'm not much good with human carpentry tools."

"My father was a carpenter," Lilire said wistfully. "He liked books, too." She paused for a long moment, lost in thought. "You know, I think we could solve your problem very easily. We could hide you and your hoard where no one would ever think to look. I'll even stay and help, if you like."

The dragon gave her a quizzical glance. "What about becoming a lieutenant?"

Lilire spat again. "I'm really tired of living with pigs."

"That's right," the dragon explained to the man in the long brown robe. "If you ask Lilire, she'll tell you that the dragon and its treasure were just gone when she arrived. Unbelievable, really."

The man nodded appreciatively. "Well, you've both done wonders renovating the keep. And now there's talk of starting a university nearby?"

"Thank you," the dragon said, patting a stray wisp of hair back into the severe bun on the back of her head. "And yes. The distance knights are willing to travel for treasure seems to be nothing compared to the distance scholars will travel for books."

"So true," the man sighed. "So true."

"At any rate," the dragon continued, "the stacks are in the main hall over there. Copy rooms are upstairs, and we're happy to provide parchment, ink, and quills for a modest fee. Ask me or Lilire if you need help finding something."

The man bowed. "Thank you."

"And please remember," the dragon told him severely, "this is not a lending library. Books are never allowed to leave the building under any circumstances." She gave a feral grin almost too wide for a human mouth. "Violators will be eaten."

"I believe you," the man laughed as he headed for the stacks. "I believe you."

The dragon watched him go with a private smile.

Armor Propre

Jan Stirling & S. M. Stirling

Terion bit her lower lip and studied her image in the steel mirror. Sighing, she turned sideways to examine her profile.

"That's gorgeous," her companion, Brunea, growled enviously.

"I know," Teri groaned. She turned, tugged at the waist, "It's sooo beautiful."

"It was made for you madam, and the price . . ."

Both women glared menacingly at the brawny clerk. "If you need me, just call," he excused himself hastily. "I'm Surelle."

"I can't wear this!" Terion exclaimed, tossing her head impatiently. "It's too expensive and too provocative. I'd be making a target of myself." Her eyes filled with regret. "It's magnificent." Longingly, she ran her hands down the sleek sides, "But it's just not me."

"Oooh yes it is." Brunea said firmly. "Surelle's right, much as I hate to admit it. This might've been made to your measure. Besides, it'll be good for your career."

Teri shrugged, then grinned slowly. Her career had endured a disastrous slump after she'd slain a wizard she was supposed to be guarding. Now she'd finally made lieutenant and was looking for something special to mark the occasion.

"Y'know what's making this so hard?" she asked. "I've always dreamed of owning something like this." Teri traced the gold filigree at the neck with a reverent finger. "Ooohhh, I want it!" She laughed.

"Ask your man's opinion," Brunea suggested, jerking a thumb over her shoulder. "Bet he agrees you should have it."

Terion raised her brows over the phrase "your man," knowing that Feric would object to it. But a warm inward glow told her that she approved. She glanced in the mirror at the advancing reflection of her companion—pet wizard—lover, friend. *Mine,* she thought and smiled.

Feric came towards them, his nose leading the rest of his face like the prow of a ship, dark, unruly hair bobbing with his ungainly walk, fine brown eyes dreaming. He carried in his wiry arms their week's allotment of supplies; so loaded that boxes and parcels looked ready to spill in all directions.

"Well!" Brunea demanded in a bark that made Feric jump. "Whaddaya think?"

Terion turned to face him, her blue eyes shining.

"That one over there will do just as well," she said quickly, pointing to a dully gleaming breastplate. She stood straight so that he could get a better look at her. "This one costs a hundred *gis* more." Her face wore a guilty expression, but her hand stroked yearningly down the glossy armor.

Feric examined her, his lips pursed, eyes narrowed in judgement, highly flattered that she'd seek his counsel about something like this. Teri knew he'd no understanding of armor or its quality. He'd told her as much when she expressed the need for a new breastplate before facing the Duke's forces in battle. He appreciated most of all her willingness to let it go, much as she obviously wanted it, if he agreed they couldn't afford it.

And it was too extravagant, well above the limit they'd set.

Teasing her, he stretched out the moment, examining the beautifully made armor she wore. It was enamelled black, with lapped tassets falling to the sides, the whole surface heavily scrolled with exquisite gold tracery.

He liked it. The dramatic color set off her red-gold hair and handsome face.

"Well, my love," he watched her color slightly at the endearment, "if *this* can be had for only a hundred gis more I think you should take it."

Terion laughed and clapped battle scarred hands delightedly.

Brunea leaned over, pinched Feric's cheek and growled, "You're a prize, you are. Even if y'are a wizardling." She winked at Teri. "I'll go hunt up Surelle."

Feric rubbed his cheek.

"Could you ask her to stop doing that?" he whispered. "I'll be able to whistle with my mouth closed if she keeps it up!"

Teri just grinned at him.

"Thank you," she said simply, her eyes glowing with affection. Then with enthusiasm, "Brunea's right, you know. This will help my career. It speaks of confidence and that'll automatically win a bit more respect."

"Because you look so well?" Feric asked, his eyes admiring.

Terion laughed. "Because it says I can hold my own against anybody. Mercenaries make up their kit from armor won on the field, so half the young hot-heads out there will be after me like wasps after honey. The fact I'd dare to wear something like this says I think I'm good enough to keep it." She examined her reflection. "Brunea's right, I'm ready to make that statement."

Terion failed to notice Feric's dawning horror.

"You mean," he asked, appalled, "you'll be in more danger because of this?"

"Love," she said and threw a muscular arm around his slim shoulders, "in this business, more than in any other, timidity doesn't pay. *I* think that what I stand to gain more than outweighs the added risk." She smiled at his worried expression. "Trust me, Feric, I'll profit from this." She looked at herself once more and frowned. "The rest of my kit won't match," she said unhappily. "At the very least I should have black trousers."

"You *have!*" he said.

"But they're so shabby."

"Excuse me, we are talking about going to battle here, aren't we? With the usual blood, dust, and grass-stains, yes? Not a royal tea—am I correct?" Feric thrust his chin out pugnaciously and Teri eyed him in mild surprise.

"If you think we've spent enough," she said mildly, "you've only to say so, dear. There's no need to be sarcastic."

Feric left Terion as quickly as he could and hurried to their spartan quarters.

If I were a cheap, tight-fisted jerk she'd be a great deal safer right now, he thought, miserably, regreting that he lacked such a nature and ignoring the certainty that Teri wouldn't have anything to do with him if he did. *Who could have guessed that a little gilt on her armor would make a difference?*

You could read by the light in their eyes if you even mentioned gold to most mercenaries, let alone showed it to them. The flash of it on Terion's black armor would bring them running like bees to a honeypot. Large, brawny, aggressive, homicidal bees with things that were sharp, or pointed, or heavy—some of them sharp, pointed *and* heavy.

She'd never even think of coming to me and asking, "Sweetheart, would you mind very much if I joined this suicide mission?" So how could she imagine he'd knowingly approve of her making a target of herself for the slings and arrows and knives and spears and swords of outraged fortune hunters? *Well, I won't have it!* he thought.

He dragged his two books of magic out from under the bed and unlocked one with a key he kept around his neck. When he opened the cover the hair on his arms rose from the outflow of power and he shivered slightly.

Feric had been a mere hedge-wizard until Terion stomped into his life and gifted him with these books. With the books for guidance, Feric had discovered that he'd a great deal more power than he'd ever imagined.

His problem was control. Terion had likened Feric's magicking to "using a ten pound battle-hammer to open a soft-boiled egg." After two or three near disasters they'd both agreed he needed a tutor and to put the books away until they found one. Then he'd given his goat to a neighbor and had followed Terion out of his little village into the wide world.

So he shouldn't be doing this. In fact he felt guilty just looking at the books.

But I'm only looking for something small, he rationalized. *A little protection spell to offset her attractive armor.* What could possibly go wrong with that? She'd never know. Besides, it was his agreement that had put her in danger. He was obliged to find a way to protect her. Anyway, he'd no intention of living without her if he'd any say in the matter.

Gritting his teeth, Feric immersed himself in the book's contents.

"Ah-ha!" he exclaimed some time later. "To Render an Object Apparently Invisible."

Thyf spell, he read, *causeth the eye to flee the object*

enchanted, deflecting the gaze as a shield deflectf a blow. Indeed, if it be well cast, thine enemyf entire bodie shall be turned aside.

"Excellent! Just what I was looking for."

The difficult part would lie in getting Teri to leave her beloved breastplate with him to be enchanted.

Two days later, well before dawn on the day of battle, unit commanders, Terion among them for the first time, met for a final briefing with the Prince and his senior staff.

His Highness's brow was clouded this morning. He stood alone, brooding, wrapped in a black cloak.

He probably thinks he looks romantic, Terion thought, not without sympathy, *but what he really resembles is a big-footed puppy someone left out in the rain.* Which was, perhaps, to be expected from a boy of seventeen forced to face his own uncle in battle. Occasionally he looked sulky, as the mercenary officers around him yawned, stretched, drank hot things out of mugs or picked at their teeth with daggerpoints. It was hard to look romantic next to someone finishing a piece of toast and brushing crumbs off their gorget.

The Duke had protested the Prince's right to the throne and had given his young nephew a scant month to surrender his birthright. Then he'd marched immediately upon the royal city of Feval to wrest that concession from the Prince by force. Help was on its way from all quarters, but for now the Duke's army outnumbered them considerably.

A great map hung from the wall slightly to the left of the sulking Prince; the Lady General Ples rose from her place and went to it. With a pointer she began to outline the enemy's positions and their own.

As she described the intended course of the battle to come, Terion leaned towards Brunea.

"Look at that hill anchoring the end of the Prince's

line," she whispered. "They've got *nothing* on it but a few troops! If the Duke gets an inkling of that he'll be over that hill and through our flank like lightning."

"Lady have pity on the poor sod who gets that position," Brunea muttered back. "They're dead, whoever they are."

"Terion of Captain Tesser's company, you'll be here," the General's pointer slapped the hill they'd just been discussing. "I don't need to tell you," Ples said grimly, catching Terion's eye, "how important this position is. At all costs, we are relying on you to hold this hill."

Terion could feel the hair on the back of her neck rise. She knew the eyes of her comrades were on her, so she refused to swallow the lump in her throat until the General had caught their attention again. Then it felt like she was trying to swallow a live cat.

At the conclusion of the briefing the commanders began to file out to muster their troops in the city square. Suddenly, the General was at Terion's side, placing a hand on her arm to stop her. Ples nodded to Brunea, urging her to leave them alone.

"I wanted to emphasize once again the importance of your position," the General said softly. "I doubt you'll see much action way down at the end of the line, but it's still crucial. Thought I'd give you something easy for your first command." Ples smiled at her and squeezed Terion's arm. "Good luck. Carry on," she said and saluted.

Teri returned the salute smartly and walked away. Glancing over her shoulder, she saw Ples cover a smile with her gloved hand. No, she was more than smiling, she was laughing.

What does the Captain think of this easy command? Teri wondered. She glanced around and saw her commander in deep and apparently angry conversation with some of the regular army captains.

Suspicion and dismay roiled within her. Did the

General think she was stupid? *Well, obviously, or she wouldn't have all but suggested that I pack a picnic lunch and something to read.*

But her inexperience at command didn't alter the fact that she was going to be seriously undermanned in a vulnerable position. And the General seemed to find it amusing. Teri frowned.

If she were still a sergeant she would've told her commander that the situation stank and just why she thought so. But as a commander herself . . .

She didn't want to look hysterical, nor like she was afraid of a hard post. *I wish the Prince would stop brooding and start leading,* she thought. She watched General Ples step between Captain Tesser and the Prince. Ples nodded wisely while the Captain expostulated. *Not surprising,* Teri thought reassured by her commander's obvious anger. *This plan looks more like a model for How to Lose a Major Battle in One Easy Step.* Frowning, she went to meet her troops.

In the city's main square the pre-dawn silence was shattered by the clatter of horse's hoofs on cobblestones, the rattle of armor and the barking of dogs and frustrated sergeants trying to get sleepy troopers properly lined up. The scent of animal dung and of sweat, horse and human, added sharpness to the crystalline chill of the morning air.

"Where's Feric?" Brunea asked, tying off her silver shot braid with a thong.

"He's at home," Terion said, her voice clipped, her face pale. "Asleep."

Brunea raised her brows at that.

The whole city was here to cheer the Prince's forces off to battle. And this was Terion's first command. She'd have sworn the scrawny little newt would understand how important this was to Teri. Even if he didn't, this was war, he might not see her again, or not in one piece anyway.

She shrugged her muscled shoulders. Men were hard to figure. Wizards, downright impossible.

Terion stood on the crest of the hill and stared out over the enemy lines. Her heart sank. The Duke's men were lined up awfully deep here and were backed by a rank of cavalry.

Suddenly I feel like the subject of a tragic ballad, she thought. One of those set to an unfortunately bouncy tune. *They slew her then with sword and spear, oh, tra la la and hack-away, aye!*

The air was laden with the scent of crushed grass, horses and massed humanity. The tension was almost palpable, as though you could tear chunks of it out of the air.

She looked down at the enemy and pictured them charging the hill's gentle slope. *They'll barely work up a sweat running up here,* she thought.

The Duke's men were laid out in a gentle arc that half surrounded her position. And they had archers. *But I have no cover.* She flinched inwardly. Teri's eyes flicked left and right as she tried to second guess the enemy commander. She gave that up with a disgusted sound. *Just to see them is to know their plan. They're going to walk up here and use our noses to plow up the grass.*

Her sergeant came and stood just behind her, his hairy face calm, hazel eyes worried.

It's as if they knew *this was our weakest spot,* she mused, then clicked her tongue impatiently. *Irrelevant at this point,* she thought.

Terion wondered if the Prince was aware of this unexpectedly heavy concentration of enemy troops. He might not have noticed how things stood way down here at the end of the line. He certainly seemed to be too busy brooding to be paying attention at the briefing.

So the kid's not a genius. At least he's good hearted. His uncle's head is nothing more than a knot of muscle at the top of his spine and he's as vicious as a drunken wolverine.

And there was something to be said about fighting on the side of the light. But at the moment, staring at the thick shouldered mass of her enemies, she couldn't remember what.

"Sergeant," she said, "send my respects to his Highness. Tell him the Duke has enough men here to push us back at the first go 'round. Tell him they have archers and they're backed by cavalry."

"Yessir," the sergeant said. He turned and called out a name, spoke briefly and sent a long-legged girl running for the center of the line.

A herald bearing a silken banner with the Duke's device came forth from the enemy lines and approached the Prince's position. He read a long and, no doubt, eloquent speech that Terion couldn't hear, but which almost certainly demanded the Prince's surrender.

She heard his Highness's ringing response of "Never!" from her hilltop, though. And all of the Prince's troops called out "Never!" after him in a roar that rolled after the retreating herald like thunder.

All the feeling in her body seemed to coalesce in her stomach, making her breath come short. Now, in a moment, the battle would begin. She lowered her visor and breathed a prayer to the Lady.

No word had come from the Prince, not even her messenger had returned. She decided to send another. Things would be no worse here for the loss of two soldiers, and it might just help. She reminded herself that her status as a commander entitled her to the Prince's attention.

She'd known at this morning's briefing that she was in trouble. The General's insistence that she and her troops "stand" had been her first inkling. Experience had taught her that rhetoric like that meant "so long, sucker."

Terion needed archers here and she had pikemen,

and not nearly enough of them. She rubbed her gaunt-leted hands together and tried to think of some new way to deploy her troops that would lessen the enemy's advantage in numbers.

Fine, cold sweat misted over her body, and a shiver ratcheted up her spine, making her gasp. Someone stepping on your grave her mother had said, or maybe that was Feric.

Thinking of Feric got her dander up, which was just what she needed right now. She welcomed the spurt of anger. He'd been asleep when she'd gotten home last night and she hadn't been able to wake him this morning.

Who does he think he is? she demanded of herself. *How dare he ignore me at a time like this!*

She wondered, and worried, on a deeper level about just what he'd been doing to make him so tired. Jealousy popped its head up briefly, wondered what it was doing here and vanished without really making an impression. *Nah. Whatever he's up to it doesn't involve another woman.*

The enemy troops began to march, massed spear points glittering in the sun like the surface of a wind ruffled pond. There was a tremendous clanking of armor and the sound of a ringing battle hymn as they moved inexorably forward, picking up speed as they came.

She watched the archers take stance and draw their bows.

"We're going to charge," Terion suddenly said to her second. "On my signal."

"*What?*" he roared.

"If we stand," she said, "they'll shoot us to shit and then ride right through the gaps. If we charge it might break their line in confusion. Our third option of course, is to simply desert. But the archers will still skewer us and whoever wins here, the Captain will hunt us down and kill us for cowardice. So I'd say charging is really our only course. If that's all right with you, sergeant."

"Yessir," he said, eyes round.

Terion waited until the advancing troops were halfway up the gentle slope of the hill before she gave the signal and charged screaming down upon them at the front of her pikemen.

She waved her sword over her head and tried to keep her balance as she ran on the slippery grass. Now she was committed to action she needed to neither feel nor think beyond the killing of the foe.

The Duke's men stumbled to a confused halt and started to brace for the impact of Terion's troops.

But as the black-clad virago leading them came closer, they saw in horror that she had no body. Legs pumped furiously as she rushed towards them, her unadorned helmet glinted in the morning sun and gauntleted hands brandished sword and dagger, but there was no body.

The more they stared, the greater the compulsion they felt to look away. Terrified, they felt their bodies forced to follow their eyes' example. Then, as one, they spun 'round and fled shrieking.

The cavalry horses, already alarmed by the rout, suddenly rolled their eyes in terror as Terion came near. They took the bit between their teeth and fled the field squealing, their riders needlessly, but frantically, trying to whip greater speed from them.

Terion stopped flat-footed and lifted her visor as the last of the enemy turned tail. She and the sergeant eyed each other, then stared, open-mouthed, after the retreating forces.

"But I bathed just last Lugsday," the sergeant muttered.

Then—all in a moment—everything was clear to her. Terion stood torn between a scream of rage and a sigh of resignation. She whirled her sword through a complicated arc, then furiously paced back and forth, wondering what to do.

She turned to her sergeant.

"Get the troops back into position and hold this hill. I'll be back. Probably."

Then she charged towards the Duke's lines where they'd already engaged with the Prince's.

Wherever she went chaos reigned, the heat of battle cooled in cowardly rout, and the Prince's men poured in joyous pursuit of the enemy. In two hours the battle was over, the Duke defeated and kneeling in humiliation before the Prince.

"FERIC!"

Startled from a sound sleep he sat up with a gasp. At the horrific sight of a bodiless warrior charging towards him he scrambled backward. Trying to get out of bed he tangled himself in the bedclothes, falling to the floor with a crash.

"Ow," he groaned.

Terion tore off her helmet and threw it on the bed.

"How dare you?" she bellowed. "What were you thinking of? Are you trying to get me hanged?"

All she could see of him from where she stood was the top of his curly head and his terrified eyes.

"Well?" she screamed.

Fighting down his fear, Feric stammered, "P-p-please c-c-calm d-down. Or, or I-I'll have to r-r-run away."

She turned her back with a snarl and stomped over to the window. Taking a few deep breaths of fresh air, Terion deliberately squashed her anger. Then, desperately calm, she turned to confront him.

"What did you do to me?" she asked quietly.

"Nothing," he said.

Her eyes blazed and he flinched.

Terion calmed herself once more with a heroic effort and said, calmly, "I'm not stupid, you know. You did *something*!"

"Yes," he admitted, with a sheepish smile, his eyes

frantic. "But not to you directly. I, uh, I enchanted your new armor."

"Oh! We-el." She threw up her hands as though all she'd needed was an explanation. "Of course! That's just fine. Yes, lovely. And do you happen to know the penalty for using magical swords or armor in battle?" she asked sweetly.

"No," he said in a tiny voice.

"Death!" she hissed. She glared at him and then turned her back. "If you had left well enough alone I'd still be dead, but at least I'd have my self-respect."

That wouldn't matter if you were dead, he thought, but, wisely, did not say.

"No one needs to know," he said. "I can remove the enchantment."

She threw him a look. "Well, that's not exactly honorable either. Now is it?"

Feric stood up and walked over to face her.

"Terion," he said firmly, taking her hands in his. She made to pull them away but he held them with surprising strength. "I love you. And I don't want you to die. Not for money, not so someone can steal your armor, not for honor. I've waited for you too long, I've had you for too little time and I need you too much to watch you put your life at risk and do nothing about it."

"I'm a soldier," she said defensively. But she was cooling down, fighting a smile in fact. "Risking my life is what I do."

Feric's lips thinned to a grim line and he nodded sullenly.

Terion yanked him into a sudden embrace and he made an "Unh!" sound as she pressed him to her unyielding armor. Putting her hands on his shoulders she gently pushed him to arm's length.

"Now," she said. "What did you do?"

"I found a spell that was designed to give objects the

effect of being invisible. The idea is that your eyes just slide away from an object, it can still be seen, but you can't look at it, so it has the effect of being invisible. D'you see?"

She nodded.

"I adjusted it so that you and those you're friendly to could see your breastplate, but your enemies couldn't," he finished proudly.

"Feric," she said, "the enemy ran away from me. *All* of them. This was a little more than not being able to see me, I was an object of terror. Wherever I went, they fled in panic."

"Oh." His face flushed puce with embarrassment. "I suppose . . . I must have put . . . too much emphasis into the spell. Like last time," he mumbled.

"Like when you meant to create a puff of smoke and you made your cottage explode?"

He sighed, "Yes. Too much emphasis."

"We've got to get you a teacher," she said. "You're dangerous."

Some hours later Terion found herself facing the Lady General. She stood to attention and fixed her gaze on a spot just over Ples's head. Still, she was quite aware of the dagger-like stare being directed at her.

"I find myself in a most peculiar situation with you, Lieutenant." Ples pronounced the rank with utter scorn. "On the one hand you're a hero, having won the battle virtually single-handed. On the other, you obviously broke the law to do it. You see my position." She held her hands palms up as though weighing something in each. "The Prince wants to see you rewarded, the law demands your death. Reward, death, reward," she sighed. "And then I saw the solution. I give you your life, but you must leave the city tonight. Also, you must leave that breastplate behind." Ples smiled slyly and rubbed her palms together. "I'm assuming that therein lies the enchantment. You've always been known as a good soldier, but never as a terrifying one. I mean, people have never wet their drawers at the sight of you before. Now have they? Hmmm?" Her affable smile turned into a smoldering glare. "So take it off and get out."

Terion blinked. Her armor? One hand went protectively to her chest. This was unexpected, but she supposed it shouldn't be.

"What of my pay?" Teri asked.

"Your pay is your life."

Terion began to remove her breastplate.

"It was very expensive," she said regretfully.

"I'm sure it was. Let that be a lesson to you."

"I didn't know it was enchanted," Terion muttered, lifting the armor over her head. "It was a reputable shop."

"A likely story," Ples said in disgust, "with your lover being a wizard. If I cared to spend the gelt, we'd hire a full-fleged mage to sniff out the enchanter." She gazed steadily at Terion. "I think we both know where the trail would lead." Ples pursed her lips and looked down at a report for a moment. "I doubt you'd want to," she said, raising her eyes again, "but if I hear of you boasting of this escapade I'll have you hunted down and dragged back here to be hanged. Is that understood?"

"Yes." Teri laid the armor on her desk and stroked the glossy surface, reluctant to part with it.

"Go!" the General snarled.

Terion turned without saluting and walked quickly away. This was bad. The breastplate had taken most of their savings, making the loss of her pay a serious handicap. She barked a sour little laugh. *I can't even sell my dress armor, since the General has it.*

Terion turned to spit in the direction of the Lady General's tent and to her surprise saw Ples rush out, dragging two, obviously heavy, saddle bags. And the General was wearing *Terion's* armor!

Flinging the bags over the back of a very flash horse,

Ples mounted. Then, with a laden pack horse in tow, she galloped off to be swallowed in the darkness.

Teri closed her mouth slowly as, for the first time, she noticed the absence of guards around the General's tent. *Now why,* she asked herself, *would such a trusted member of the Prince's inner circle feel the need to do a midnight flit?*

Without thinking, Teri loosed one of the horses picketed nearby and hoisted herself onto its bare back. Then she galloped in pursuit of the runaway general.

As she neared the camps perimeter she slowed, but Ples charged onward into the darkness.

"Who goes there?" a startled voice demanded.

"Your worst nightmare!" the General bellowed. "Run awaaayyy!"

There was the *thuwk!* of a crossbow bolt being released, an "Unh!" and the distinctive sound of an armored body hitting the dirt.

Terion could have sworn that she heard a strangled and rather plaintive, "But . . . ?" from that fallen form.

Slowly, she grinned and then, just as Ples had before sending her out to die, Terion began to laugh.

Terion and Feric were plodding down the wide and dusty high-road when the sound of hoofbeats and a familiar voice made them pause and turn.

Brunea pulled up gasping.

"I've been yelling at you forever," she declared.

"What's the matter?" Teri asked warily.

"I've got your pay," Brunea said and tossed it over.

Terion caught the little sack in surprise, pleased by its comforting weight.

"But the General said I wasn't to be paid!"

"She gave no such orders," Brunea said, grinning. "Too busy trying to save her backside, I suppose."

"Why?" Feric asked, puzzled. "Did the Duke's army rally and try to rescue him?"

"Ha! Lady bless you, lad." Brunea leaned over and pinched Feric's cheek.

Briefly he considered trying to turn her into a rabbit. But a mental image of himself trying to deal with a Brunea-sized rabbit discouraged him.

"The Lady General," Brunea sneered, "tried to slip through the lines last night. When the watch challenged her— she just charged 'em. Naturally they killed the fool. Oh! Were those worried lads!"

"I know," Teri said smugly, "I saw."

Brunea raised her brows.

"You didn't tell me," Feric said indignantly. "Why was the Lady General running away?"

"She was running from the Prince's men," Teri said. "I believe she was selling our battle plans to the Duke."

"And the Duke, like the traitor he is," Brunea paused to spit, "was happy to name her a spy. So she was to die anyway. Not so soon a'course," Brunea said regretfully. "Ples had your armor on, the gretch, so I filched it back for you." She slapped a meaty hand against a flattish package tied behind her. "It's got a hole in it, but I'm thinkin' maybe your wizardling can fix that." She stuck her tongue in her cheek, then said off-handedly, "So long as he doesn't put that enchantment back on."

Teri and Feric glanced at each other, then looked at Brunea, their faces carefully bland.

"Well," Teri said, "I'm just glad to be paid."

"Yes," Feric agreed. "Money, always useful."

"There's work up north," Brunea said. "Mind if I travel with you?"

"You're welcome to join us," Teri said. "But we're looking for a wizard willing to teach Feric."

"What wizard is going to take on an apprentice his age?" Brunea demanded scornfully.

"We'll know when we find one," Terion told her and rode placidly on.

A Big Hand for the Little Lady

Esther M. Friesner

It was just another night in Hrothgar's hall, high Heorot, and the bloodstains on the plank floors hardly showed at all. Men sat at the long boards, drinking and swapping lies. Mead, beer, and wine flowed freely, most of it down the gullets of those warriors who'd stayed in noble Hrothgar's service long enough to have seen too many of their comrades die at the hands—if they *were* hands—of the fen-dwelling fiend the scops named Grendel. (How the scops ever got close enough to the hellspawned monster to learn his name without being themselves devoured remained a mystery.)

While the doughty Danish warriors sopped up enough liquor to float a longship, serving wenches passed between the feasting boards, refilling cups and drinking horns while at the same time slapping down or encouraging the attentions of the men, as they pleased. Among this lot there was one young woman who stood out from the rest, though not even the most nimble-tongued harper could ever say that she stood above them.

"Well, woodja looka that, Hengest," said one of Hrothgar's men, staring across the hall through booze-bleared eyes. "They got kids serving in here now?"

His seatmate gave him a comradely thwack in the

head. "Thass no kid, Wulfstan, you beetle-brain. Thass m' sister, Maethild."

"Uh." Wulfstan squinted at the doll-like woman threading her way through the maze of tables. The other wenches towered over her, as did some of Hrothgar's boarhounds. It wasn't that she was a dwarf, although Hengest could have told Wulfstan that the girl had borne more than a few crude gibes from would-be wits who wanted to know where she kept her hammer or asked to see her treasure hoard. (In the latter cases, Maethild generally contrived to lay hold of a something heavy and hammer home a few free lessons in manners.) She was as sweetly formed a woman as the Lady Frey had ever blessed: hair of gold, eyes like a windswept summer sea, trim waist, and thighs that could crush a full keg of autumn ale between them. She was simply . . . short. She balanced a heavy jug of beer on her shoulder as effortlessly as if it were made of cloud instead of clay, sometimes using it to beat aside too-familiar hands.

"You washed 'er wrong," Wulfstan said at last. "She shrunk."

Hengest bellowed with laughter and thumped Wulfstan on the back. "I like you, Woofspam," he slurred. "I don' got a lotta friends here yet 'cos I jus' come south to get into Hrothgar's service. See, I'm hopin' I'll be the one to killa monster that's been makin' all you Ring-Danes slink outa this fine hall ev'ry night so's he won' eatcha. Ol' Hrothgar, he'll pile a ton o' treasure on the man does that, and that man's gonna be me. But I *like* you. I like you a *lot*. Tell ya what: If you don' get eat up an' I killa monster, you marry Maethild. Deal?"

Wulfstan gave the diminutive maiden another long stare. "Well, she *looks* cheap to feed. 'Kay. Deal." The two men shook on it, and both of them fell off the bench backwards in the process. Hengest was the first back on his feet. He bawled out his sister's name.

One of the serving women reached down to tap Maethild on the shoulder. "You're wanted."

"I know." Maethild gave her brother a look of disgust which the other wench misinterpreted.

"Look, if you don't want him bothering you, drop that jug where it matters. I've been watching you; you don't have any trouble handling these trolls."

"That's no troll; that's my brother."

"He is?" The wench looked from tiny Maethild to titanic Hengest, mystified. "Are you *sure*?"

"Different fathers," Maethild replied. "Mine was a swordsman, his was a scop."

"A swordsman? *Your* father was the swordsman?" The wench was even more baffled by this sliver of family history.

"A short swordsman," Maethild replied tersely, and stomped across the hall, thumped the jug down on the board, gave her brother a killing look and snapped, "What?"

"Now, Maethild, be nice," Hengest soothed. "We don' wan' 'nother thing like wha' happen' in Healfdan's hall."

"Huh?" Wulfstan blinked. "Wuzza hoppen Healfdan's hall, hey?"

"Nuthin'." Hengest was suddenly embarrassed.

"I'll tell you what happened in Healfdan's hall," Maethild replied pertly. "Healfdan was my brother's former lord, a windbellied braggart. His way of telling a woman to hold her tongue was to give her a couple of healthy slaps. He heard me speaking my mind to my brother and he didn't care for my tone of voice, so he tried teaching me my place." She showed her teeth. "Once. They call him Healfdan of the Seven Fingers now."

Wulfstan's lower jaw dropped. Hengest writhed with the shame of having so unsuitable a sister. " 'S why we come here," he mumbled into his beard. "After what she did to Healfdan, we hadda run. I couldn't fight all of his men myself."

"Who asked you to?" Maethild demanded. "If you'd only have given me a sword—"

Hengest slammed his knuckles onto the table and rose from his place in a rage. "No woman of *my* blood is gonna use a sword, an' *spesh'ly* not one that's dangerous 'nuff 'thout one!" he hollered, and then slumped across the board, dead to the world.

"Beautiful," Maethild sneered over her brother's snores. She shot Wulfstan a hard look. "Well? Are you just going to sit there gaping like a *lutefisk* or are you going to leave the big lumpbrain here for Grendel to eat tonight?"

"Uh . . ." Wulfstan rubbed his temples as if his hangover had arrived ahead of schedule. "I guess I could haul 'im outa here. Leas' I c'n do for fam'ly." He was young and brawny, like Hengest, whom he soon had draped over his shoulders like a lamb's carcase. He started for the great door of Heorot, but a small hand clamped itself to the back of his belt and held him firmly.

"'Family'?" Maethild inquired. Her smile was too sweet. A sober man wouldn't have believed it for an instant.

"Uh-huh. I'm gonna marry you after your brother kills the monster." Drunk as he was, Wulfstan caught the warning light in Maethild's eyes, swallowed hard, and added, "Your brother *said*. An' we shook on it." He hauled Hengest out of Heorot's high hall hastily.

He *tried*. He just managed to clear the doorway and make it out into the chill night air when Maethild laid hold of his belt again. For the first time, a glimmer of realization sparked feebly inside Wulfstan's brainbin: This wee wench was holding *him* immobile. Not only that, a backward glance revealed she was doing it one-handed. What was even more frightening, she was smiling at him *that* way again. "You . . . want something?" he asked nervously.

"The question is, what do *you* want, noble warrior?" Maethild asked, dainty and demure. "Do you *really* want to marry me or was it just the mead talking?"

Wulfstan didn't answer. Right then, what he most wanted was to escape this strange young maiden and live to see another dawn. He had the feeling that these two distinct desires were intimately connected.

"Don't be shy," Maethild coaxed. "I swear to you, I won't be offended if you say that you'd rather not be my husband."

"You won't?" Wulfstan cheered up visibly. This lasted all of two breaths. His smile crumbled along with his hopes. "We shook on it," he repeated. "It's sealed in honor. If I try to back out, your brother'll kill me." He was speaking as distinctly as though he'd drunk nothing but goat's milk all evening. The cold night air and Maethild combined to have a radically sobering effect on him.

"I can handle Hengest," the little woman assured him.

Wulfstan had no doubts on that score. He had the feeling that Maethild could handle Grendel itself, if she had a mind to. Unfortunately, it wasn't that simple. "No good," he said gloomily. "It'd be all right if we'd done it in private, but we struck our bargain under Hrothgar's roof, with plenty of folk there to witness the terms."

"Huh!" Maethild snorted, then spat dead center between Wulfstan's feet. "Any who saw you two at your stupid games were just as mead-muddled as you! They won't remember a thing."

"The women will." Wulfstan's face thinned with misery. "I don't know what got into me, promising to marry anyone, let alone you. I've been in Hrothgar's service for years and I've managed to avoid getting shackled to a wife. Any one of those wenches who heard me give my word to your brother will run tattling to Hrothgar if I break it. Hrothgar's big on honor. He'll force your brother to fight me if I back out of the bargain, no matter what any of *us* want."

Maethild considered this information, head bent, chin in hand. After due deliberation she looked up at Wulfstan, and if her earlier smiles had been disquieting things, the grin now bunching her cheeks would have sent a lesser man screaming straight down Grendel's gorge as the lesser of two evils. "I know how we can fix everything. Come with me." She led him away from Heorot's moonshadow, far from any of the buildings comprising Hrothgar's hold, almost to the edge of the wild lands whence Grendel roved and rampaged.

At last, in a place of utmost privacy and desolation she said, "Now we'll settle things between us once and for all." And she took off her dress.

Wulfstan whistled long and low. "Loki's left nut, I swear I've never seen a sweeter little piece of—"

"This old thing? I've had it forever." Maethild dimpled as she fingered the cuff of the fine mail shirt that until this moment had remained hidden beneath her dress. "It was Daddy's, and it fits me slick as an eel's skin. Now if you can get me a sword, we'll have this whole ugly mess settled by morning."

"Er?" Wulfstan shifted Hengest's body to a more comfortable perch on his shoulders. "Howzat?"

Maethild clucked her tongue, impatient with the big warrior's failure to grasp the beauty of her scheme immediately. It seemed perfectly obvious to *her*. "You promised to marry me after my brother killed the monster. If my brother doesn't kill Grendel, the deal's off."

Wulfstan goggled at her in horror. "You're going to give poor Hengest to the monster! Hel's tits, woman, if that's your plan, you can do it without me!" He emphasized his refusal to participate in fratricide by dropping Hengest headfirst to the ground. Maethild's brother groaned but didn't wake.

Maethild folded her arms across her chest. She'd lied about the fit of her father's mail: It was more than a trifle tight at the bosom, forcing her breasts *up* and perilously close to *out* at the neckline. "You're a fine, strapping, handsome man, Wulfstan. I might not mind marrying you, if it came to that, but you're *stupid*. If I wanted Hengest dead, I've had more than my share of chances. He's my brother, you big twit, and I love him, even if he's more of a chunkskull than you."

"Thank you?" Wulfstan replied doubtfully.

"If anything's getting killed tonight, it's Grendel. Now give me that sword."

"Give 'er that sword an' *die*," Hengest announced from the ground. He clambered to his feet, but only made it as far as hands and knees. "I said no woman of my blood uses a sword an' I *mennit*. 'S a marrera honor. So *there*." He underscored the last word by flopping facedown on the earth.

The look that Maethild and Wulfstan exchanged was the first thing the two of them had ever had in common. "Don't tell me," the little woman said, her voice dull. "He said the H-word so now you'd rather die than go against his wishes."

"Well, I wouldn't rather *die*," Wulfstan admitted. "But I will if I must. A warrior's honor is a matter beyond question, more precious than many gold arm-rings, brighter than the hunting hawk's eye, all that marks his place in the world when Hel's dark doorway closes on his spirit and forth he fares upon the wide whale-road, flames setting sharp teeth to timbers of the swan-winged ship that bears him—"

"Yatta, yatta, yatta," Maethild concluded. "In other words, I don't get any help from you about that sword."

"Er . . . no." Wulfstan gave his own blade a nervous sideways glance. Though the mail shirt was all the amrory Maethild seemed to possess, he vividly remembered the wench's iron grip. If she took it into her head to wrest his sword from him, he dreaded the outcome.

"Oh, relax." Maethild waved away his troubling

thoughts as if he'd laid them out like runestones for her to read. "I won't even try taking yours. If I failed, I'd be dead, and if I succeeded, you would. That was never part of my plan. I'm a woman, so I haven't got any of your precious honor to uphold by racking up a corpse-tally. You take care of Hengest; I'll look after the rest." She turned on her heel and strode off into the dark.

"Wait!" Wulfstan cried after her. "What do you mean? Where are you going? What're you gonna do?"

From already a long way away, Maethild called back over one shoulder, "I don't have to marry you if Hengest doesn't slay Grendel, and Hengest can't slay a monster that's already dead. Bye!" The night devoured her, a slip of silvery mail that vanished like a dream.

Wulfstan heard what she said, but it took him awhile to believe his ears. He started after her, a cry of protest on his lips, then looked back at Hengest's sprawled body. He couldn't just leave a comrade lying out here, so near the dark borders where monsters dwelled. This, too, was a matter of honor. Reluctantly he hoisted the snoring man back onto his shoulders and bore him to safety, but his heart had run off into the night with Maethild.

When Hengest woke from his stupor next morning, he was less than grateful to Wulfstan. "You gristle-head!" He drove the heel of his hand into his comrade's chest. "What'd you let her do that for? Go off unarmed, a helpless woman—"

Breathless, Wulfstan was beginning to wonder whether there was any such thing as a "helpless" woman, but his personal doubts took second place to defending his actions in the teeth of Hengest's accusations. "Hey! *You're* the one wouldn't let her have a sword," he pointed out.

"Well—well, you should've done *something*!" Hengest bellowed with the force of anyone, man or woman, caught in the wrong but desperate to shout down the truth. He gave Wulfstan another wallop.

The two men had been sleeping in a corner of one of Hrothgar's lesser houses until dawnlight roused them both. Though Hengest had been dead-drunk for most of the last night's doings, when he woke he recalled enough to rile him and he pummelled the rest of the details out of Wulfstan's hide. Wulfstan did little to stop him, feeling a little responsible for Maethild's fate. However, enough was enough. When Hengest next raised his fist, Wulfstan intercepted it and clamped his own beefy hand around it.

"If you want *something* done, let's do it now," he gritted. "Let's follow her trail. Maybe we're not too late to save her."

"Too late?" Hengest's snort was almost as derisive as his sister's. "She set forth after dark and it's now past dawn. What do you hope to save? Grendel's leftovers? But all right. She was my sister: Least I can do is pick up the pieces."

The two men set out as silently as possible, treading on tip-toe and speaking in whispers. They needn't have bothered: The rest of Hrothgar's men slept the deep sleep of the totally sozzled. Outside the hall, daylight hit them between the eyes like Thor's hammer. They stumbled out of the Ring-Dane settlement, moaning and squinting, headed in the fenward direction Maethild had taken the previous night.

"Poor li'l Maethild," Hengest sniveled, wiping his nose on the back of one hairy hand. "Soon as we find her body—what there is of it—I'm gonna give her the best funeral Hrothgar's money can buy. And I'll make up a fine death-song for her, too. I've got me some talent in that line," he said proudly. "My dad was a scop."

"I know. Maethild told me." Wulfstan's feet dragged. He missed the girl. He was scared spunkless of her, but he missed her all the same. The thought that he'd never see her again—that the fair, proud, headstrong wench was now just another lump of meat in Grendel's gut—

pierced him to the marrow. He wished he were back in the hall letting Hengest pound the carp out of him. Physical pain might help to dull the pangs of regret ripping him apart inside.

"It'll be a good death-song, you'll see," Hengest vowed, marching onward. "I thought I'd start it something like: 'Beauty and boldness both dwell in the damsel's doings. Manliest of maidens, Maethild, swordless sought the mangler of men, grim Grendel, gruesome in gore.' Well? How do you like it so far?"

"Mnyeh." Wulfstan really wasn't in any mood to play the appreciative audience, although his friend's fine grasp of the scop's art of alliteration left nothing to be desired. Eyes on the ground, he trudged behind Hengest indifferent to everything. The only way he knew that they'd entered the fen country which was Grendel's haunt was when his shoes stopped stamping on earth and started squelching through mud.

Hengest didn't like having his versifying brushed aside like that. He renewed his assault on literature, determined to gain Wulfstan's admiration. "That's not all there is," he insisted. "I haven't even given it a good start yet." He turned around and walked backwards, the better to simultaneously cover ground and make sure Wulfstan was giving his poetry the attention it merited. " 'Small in stature, sizeable in spirit, sibling of scop's-son Hengest, took she to task the tall warrior Wulfstan, wight unwilling to ward her well, worthless, witless—' *waaaugh!*"

Hengest tumbled heels over head, putting an abrupt end to his volley of verbal barbs against Wulfstan. Wulfstan himself hardly noticed Hengest's impromptu somersault any more than he'd heeded the man's reproachful poesy. What did grab his attention was the small, shrill voice that came from under the big man's body, filling the air with a stream of curses that lacked alliteration but packed plenty of vim.

"Frey's frickin' cat-cart, can't a girl sit down to catch

her breath without one of you lunks falling on top of her?" Maethild railed. "Why in Hel's name don't you look where you're going?"

Shortly later, Hengest stood staring down at his sister—blood-smeared and bruised, but very much alive—and the little souvenir she'd been dragging cross country. "Shaft me with a holly bough, we're buggered," he declared.

"*Now* what's wrong?" Maethild snarled. "Wulfstan and I didn't want to be forced into marriage by some stupid promise you two made while you were boiled as a pair of owls, so I found the way to get us out of it without besmirching anyone's precious honor. And when you insisted that it was *another* matter of honor that I couldn't have a sword, I worked around it."

"Obviously," Wulfstan said, eying the item she sat on. It was the size of a goodly log, but there were no trees of that girth in the area. This was another sort of limb altogether.

Black-clawed at one end, bloody and raw at the other, Grendel's arm now served Maethild for perch and pulpit as she declaimed, "The monster is dead, I didn't use a sword to kill it, Hrothgar's going to piss treasure all over us, so *why* are we buggered, brother dear?"

"Because, my darling, dimwitted sister, *you're* the one who killed the monster!" Hengest yelled. "With your bare hands, no less. Oh, Hrothgar's going to *love* this. He'll piss, all right, but it won't be treasure."

"He wanted the monster dead," Maethild said sulkily. "It couldn't be much deader. It bled like a stuck pig when I tore its arm off, and when the fiend fell I beat its head in with the shoulder end—it's meatier—just to make sure. I don't see the problem."

Hengest struck a scop's dramatic hark-and-attend pose and launched into spontaneous song: "Hear ye of Hrothgar, holder of high Heorot, besieged by the bothersome beast, gruesome Grendel, fen-walking fiend, he whose nightly nourishment was the doughty Danes. And yet when Hrothgar's highest heroes fell as fiend-fodder, the marsh monster's loathsome limb was lopped, his death devised by a damsel, dainty, delicate, and demure. Gone, gone is Grendel, girl-slain! Saved are the skins of warriors by a wee woman! Say now, ye scops, were there ever in Middle Earth as Hrothgar's hench-men such sappy sissies?" He finished with a scowl and said, "*Now* do you get it, stupid?"

Maethild said nothing, matching Hengest scowl for scowl, but Wulfstan spoke up: "He's right, Maethild," he said reluctantly. "Hrothgar would rather throw himself down Grendel's gullet than have his men rescued by a woman. He'll kill you for this."

"Let him try." Maethild was hunkering down for a battle.

Her brother rolled his eyes.

"This is *exactly* what happened in Healfdan's hall. Damn. I guess this means we've for the swan-road again. And I liked it here." He sighed heavily.

Maethild's face softened to see her brother's sor-row. "I'm sorry, Hengest. This is all my fault; I'm too impetuous. I've got my father's temper, his armor, and his strength, but I keep forgetting that I don't have his—"

"Nah, nah, don't fret yourself." Hengest put his arm around his sister fondly. "When it all comes down to the bone, I'm that proud to have you for my kin. Remember those bandits we met on the Jutland road? The ones you . . . surprised?"

Maethild grinned; she remembered. "Never thought a man's jaw could drop so wide."

"Never thought a man's jaw could shatter into so many pieces, either." Hengest patted her on the back with only a little less force than he used on his male companions. "The trouble is, sister, the world's just not ready for women like you, and that's the world's loss, if you ask me. I say that if lords like Hrothgar find any shame in taking help at your hands, then we oughta let the pride-blind buggers fight their own fen-fiends."

"Does this mean you're going to get me a sword?" the maiden asked eagerly.

"Let's not get carried away. Tearing monsters limb from limb's handwork, sort of like embroidery and tapestry weaving and such, but using a sword—! That's not ladylike." He shook his head. "No woman of my blood is gonna—"

"All right, all right," Maethild said. "Never mind that now. First you'd better help me dump this into the nearest bog before word gets back to Hrothgar and he sends all his men after us." She bent to grab Grendel's severed arm.

"Not *all* his men." Wulfstan laid one hand on Maethild's shoulder. "You're not going anywhere." Seeing her glare at him, he swiftly added, "Not unless you decide that's what you *really* want, Maethild."

The roar of rejoicing rocked the rafters of high Heorot, Hrothgar's hall. Men muddled in their mead called out their incredulity, but doubt itself was dimmed and done for when Hengest Scop's-son sang his song again, to the approving thunder of thanes' drinking vessels banging on the long boards.

"Beo-*who*?" asked one man, a trifle less sunk in wine than his table-mates. "Never heard o' him."

"*Sure* you did," his friend assured him. "We all did. Can'tcha hear what Hengest's singing? How Beowulf the Geat showed up here an' killed Grendel and then he went' back an' he killed Grendel's mama too, jus' t' make sure there'd be no more o' that kinda goin's-on in Hrothgar's holdings?"

"Uh?" The warrior blinked in bewilderment. "But— but— but if there was this Beo-thingie come here with a whole buncha men li' Hengest says, how come I don'

remember any o' 'em? An'— an' Grendel's *mama*? I don'
'member the beast havin' no mama."

"*Ever'body's* got a mama, dung-for-brains. Stan's to
reason. An' Tiu's titties, half the time you're so drunk
you don' even 'member— 'member—" The second Ring-
Dane paused, his face the blank wide-open space of
freshly made parchment. "Well, I forget what it is that
you don' 'member, but anyway, you don'. 'Sides, if
Beoleopard the Geat didn' show up here with alla his
men li' Hengest's singin', then how'n Hel you 'splain we
got *that* hangin' up there onna wall? *Elves*?" And he
pointed triumphantly at the grisly trophy nailed to the
wall. Grendel's severed arm added its unique aesthetic
note to the interior decor of Heorot, to say nothing of
its unique aroma.

"Oh." The first man studied the monstrous relic
awhile, then said, "Well, seein's believin', even if it's not
rememberin' . . . I think."

"Right," his friend confirmed. "There's the arm, there's
Hengest singin' all about it, what more d'you want? If
you can't trust a scop, who can you trust? To Beowoof!"

"To Beowhoosh!" The two men clanked tankards and
their toast was soon taken up by every male throat under
Heorot's broad roofbeams. Their continuing tribute to
the mysterious hero of the hour soon drained every
liquor-bearing vessel in the hall. A roar went up for the
serving wenches to fetch more drink.

As they awaited their turn at the mead casks, one
woman turned to another and said, "Beowulf this and
Beowulf that; I think the men have finally gone loony
as a pack of lemmings. I don't remember anyone named
Beowulf the Geat coming to visit, do you?"

"Why, of course *I* do, Gytha dear," Maethild purred.
"Hrothgar himself sent me to warm the hero's bed after
he slew Grendel."

"You?" Gytha's eyebrows rose.

"If you don't believe me, you can come see the lovely

mail shirt he gave me as a morning gift before he and all his men went back home again," Maethild said sweetly.

Gytha's skepticism went up a notch. "What on earth could *you* do with a mail shirt?"

"Oh . . . give it to a hero's son." Maethild set her jug aside, folded her hands coyly over her belly, and looked modest. "If my brother's song and the monster's arm aren't enough to make you remember the mighty Beowulf, maybe when I bear the hero's babe it'll jog your memory."

"Bear a hero's babe? *You?*" Gytha scrutinized Maethild closely.

"Mmmm." Maethild smiled and cast her eyes sidelong to where Wulfstan sat drinking with his fellows. She was well aware that she and Hengest both owed the young warrior a deep debt for having showed them the way to remain under Hrothgar's roof despite her rash behavior in the matter of Grendel's dismemberment. Gratitude was a more stimulating emotion than Maethild had ever suspected. Now that she didn't *have* to marry the man, he looked very attractive indeed. If, as her brother said, the world wasn't yet ready for a woman like her, perhaps it would be ready in her daughter's day, or her daughters' daughters'.

First things first.

"A hero," Gytha muttered. "A hero that not one single, solitary, sober person in all Hrothgar's holdings remembers. And you say *you'll* bear this once-upon-a-maybe hero's babe? Hmph! I'll believe *that* when I see it."

"You will, Gytha," Maethild said softly, taking up her jug and sashaying over to Wulfstan's table. "You will."

Blade Runner

K. D. Wentworth

I, Hallah Iron-Thighs, eldest daughter of Marulla Big-Fist, hereby proclaim I will take no more contracts with professional blades. Everything about the breed sets my teeth on edge, the way they're always mooning around the One-Handed Virgin, posturing and making calf's eyes at the serving lad just to keep in practice, running their best lines with one another, and generally making a nuisance of themselves. In my opinion, they ought to be driven out of the kingdom altogether, but the eight unmarried princesses currently in residence are fond of the breed, and so they hang about, hoping to one day get past the portcullis and ply their trade. Even their designation, *blade*, is an offense, sounding as though they have trained, as have I and my sisters-in-arms, to sell the services of their swords, a time-honored profession, when nothing is further from the truth.

My partner, Gerta, and I had just made it back from a tough run across the mountains to the Kingdom of Damery, which lies adjacent to our own Alowey, fair land of really exceptional milk goats and beautifully tooled salt cellars. We'd had a profitable, though difficult trip, delivering a choice brace of priests to a rundown monastery just beyond Damery's principal castle. They

237

have a chronic shortage of priests there, something to do with the king blaming God when the crops fail and, of course, the weather is always just dreadful in Damery.

As usual, Gerta and I had been attacked by bandits when we crossed the pass. Bandits, being such awful sods, are always worried about the state of their immortal souls and simply desperate to unburden themselves with a priest. Gerta, who hails from across the channel, is inclined to cut a truly repentant bandit a bit of slack and give him a word with one of our boys, gratis. Me, I say if the little bleeders want a priest so bad, they should buy one of their own just like everyone else. This go-round my sword, Esmeralda, left three of them lying gutted at the bottom of the nearest chasm whilst the other two scampered up the nearest granite cliff and headed for the peaks.

I'd broken three nails defending our profits and the priests' integrity, and lost one of my best greaves into the bargain, the one with the magical inscription that protects me from crow's-feet, so by the time we reached the One-Handed Virgin, I was in a really foul mood. The serving lad, Barth, had enough sense to bring me a foaming tankard without being asked and then top it off at regular intervals. I like that in a boy.

I was just sizing him up—those limpid eyes, blue as a mountain lake, that abundance of crinkly black hair, and all the other fine ways in which the little rascal had really filled out in the last year, thinking he might be capable of warming a girl's pillow now—when someone plunked down several more brimming tankards in front of Gerta and me, then slid into the opposite chair.

He was slim, but well built, dark in the way the princesses favored, but reeked of crushed violets, a cheap scent and therefore not a promising sign. Also he was a bit long in the tooth for our discriminating young ladies, but several of them are just kinky enough to want to get it on with a bloke old enough to be their father, so I supposed he might still have a chance at wooing them. Gerta took in the fancy clothes, then grinned broadly, the ale blurring her already not very discriminating palate. I crossed my arms and leaned back in my chair, propping one mud-encrusted boot up on the table. My mail clinked merrily. "Yeah?"

The blade cleared his throat and tugged an elaborately embroidered red and green sleeve just a fraction straighter. His mouth was wide and generous, the sort our girls down at the castle might even call voluptuous. "I've been asking a few questions of the other patrons of this fine establishment, and everyone says you two ladies really know your way around."

"You bet your little pink toes we do!" Gerta slapped the table and cackled heartily.

He gave her a pained smile, then met my gaze with guileless brown eyes. "I need to get into the castle."

"You and every other blade for a hundred miles, sonny boy," I said.

He blushed, which was a nice trick. Even seasoned philanderers can rarely manage that. "No, no, you have it all wrong," he said and leaned closer across the table, his face sincere. "This is a truly noble cause, one well worth fighting for."

I laced my fingers across my sword belt. "Yeah, that's what they all say."

"Show us the color of your gold!" Gerta said too loudly. The noise level in the One-Handed Virgin dropped precipitously as everyone turned to stare.

"Shut—up!" I said to her under my breath, then shot out my hand to stop the blade from untying his purse. I gripped his wrist with my sword hand hard enough to hurt. "Not here, you idiot!"

His skin was warm beneath my fingers, the black body hairs nice and springy, and for a moment I forgot to let go. He looked away, blushing again, and I found myself charmed. I released his wrist. "Sorry."

Gerta shoved back her chair and it fell over with a crack. "Out—side!" she said merrily and staggered toward the door. I retrieved Esmeralda, and threw a handful of coppers down for our drinks.

Barth scooped them up and gave me a smoldering, regretful look. I pinched his downy cheek with my free hand. "Later, you little devil."

Outside, the sun was just setting and the air was cool enough to help clear my head. Our potential client was glancing nervously back at the One-Handed Virgin, his dark brows knitted together in a most appealing way. Wondering if he had to practice that, or it just came naturally, I took his arm and hustled him down the street. "So where's the fire, sweetcakes?"

He looked up at me and cleared his throat. "My name is Reginaldo and I am an old—well, *acquaintance* of the queen."

Gerta, who was in the process of buckling on her scabbard, stopped to poke him in the ribs with her elbow. "Did you and her Royal Highness get it on in Damery before she married our Good King Bentley? I hear she was a real speed-ball in her younger days!"

He raised his chin. "Do not speak of her so. She is the most beautiful woman in all the world, and I revere that brief time we spent together."

Gerta snorted. "Better not let our eight young unmarrieds hear you say that. They're not much into nostalgia."

He struck a noble pose. "I am not here to see the crown princesses, lovely though they must be. My business is with Her Majesty, the Queen."

My hand flew to the pommel of my sword and curled around the comforting cold steel. I smelled a rat. "Are you crazy? Everyone knows girls will be girls, but queens are supposed to settle down, and our king takes his husbandly duties very seriously."

He dropped to his knees in the street before me and raised folded hands in supplication. "Please, name

your price! I have to see the queen, and I'll pay
anything!"

I grabbed a handful of his shirt and hauled him to
his feet. "Stop that!"

He threw his arms around my armored chest. "I'll
die if I don't get into the palace before noon tomorrow.
I'll do anything, even—" He pressed his cheek to my
hauberk so that his voice was muffled. "—marry you!"

"*Marry* me?" I shoved him away so hard, he stumbled
and fell on his backside. "That's disgusting, you little
sewer rat. Nobody marries a blade!"

"I can cook," he said abjectly from the ground, "at
least I think I could learn, and I could massage your
feet and soap your back." He looked up with tears
in his tragic brown eyes. "You'd like that, wouldn't
you?"

"You stay away from my back, you little weasel!" I
kicked dirt in his face and went for my sword, but Gerta
caught my arm.

Her mouth was twisted in a grim smile. "Don't waste
your anger on this trash." She thumped me on the
shoulder. "Come on, I'll buy you another drink."

We left him scrambling to his knees, beating the thick
road dust from his beautifully tailored breeches.

Early the next morning, I became foggily aware that
someone was singing "A Blade Went A-Courtin' " in my
ear. Despite the polished quality of the performance,
the sound stabbed deep into my brain. I had apparently
imbibed far too freely the night before and had a dim
memory of pulling the serving lad Barth down on my
lap, fondling him quite thoroughly, ordering drinks for
everyone, then drawing Esmeralda for the sighs of
admiration she always invoked.

The singer reached the chorus and lifted his voice.
Pain threatened to split my head in two, and I flailed
out. "Stop that, you little turd!"

The song never flagged. "—went a-courtin' and he did ride, oh, yes!"

I cracked my eyes open. Gerta's pale blond head was pillowed upon her arms on an ale-soaked table, and she was snoring in a way that indicated waking would not occur for some time yet. Beyond her, the blade, Reginaldo, was perched on a stool, watching me while he sang. I gritted my teeth. "If you don't stop that caterwauling, I'll rip your lips off!"

He smiled. "I bet you say that to all the boys."

I buried my head in my arms and groaned.

"We have unfinished business," he said crisply, "and little time. I have received a desperate communique from the queen, bidding me appear discreetly at the castle to address an unresolved personal matter."

I snorted. "Dream on, buster."

"And, as I now hold your note for a considerable amount of gold, while you, on the other hand, are quite without funds, it does seem as though we should come to some sort of accommodation."

I groped for my purse and found it flatter than a ten year old virgin's bosom. The receipts of our last venture, and therefore the source for the purchase of our supplies for the next, were gone. Another groan escaped me. I had an exceedingly hazy memory of wagering the lot on how long I could kiss the serving lad without coming up for air. He had proved disappointingly uncooperative.

I pinched the bridge of my nose. "You cheated!"

He waved a deprecating hand. "Well, young Barth has no wish to remain a poor serving lad forever, giving it away free when he could have royalty, adventure, and glamour, and I did offer to give him a few pointers—"

"Yeah, yeah." I buried my face in my hands.

Reginaldo slid off his stool. "As to our bargain."

"We have no bargain!" The words escaped me with a force that made my head pound. I squeezed my eyes shut.

"Oh, but we do," and I could hear the slimy smile in his voice. "You owe me a large sum, and if you cannot satisfy your debt in some fashion, I shall foreclose upon your assets."

I opened my eyes. "I don't have any—" My gaze followed his to the gleaming sword and scabbard hanging over the back of my chair. "Not Esmeralda! You wouldn't dare!"

"Wouldn't I?" His smile was poisonously charming. "Now, as to getting inside the castle—I don't want to hear any of the usual bilge about climbing up through the necessary facilities. I know how you muscle-bound types think . . ."

Since the latrine tower had been ruled out, Gerta and I sobered ourselves up with a liberal sousing of cold water, and then resorted to our next-best tactic for running blades into castles—subterfuge. It's quite one thing to fight your way in, hacking guards to bits and losing essential bits of yourself along the way. It's quite another to dress appropriately and saunter in with the rest of the lackeys. Castles require a fearful amount of goods and services throughout a normal day, and clever runners use their heads, instead of their swords, whenever possible.

Reginaldo crossed his arms and scowled. "But I don't see why I should herd this filthy, stinking pig!"

"Her name is Betina," I said crossly. "It's obvious that, as the shortest in our party, you will appear the youngest, who in most families does all the—" I elbowed Gerta in the ribs. "—*grunt* work!" We dissolved into fits of helpless giggles.

Reginaldo jerked on his newly acquired peasant girl smock and turned away, his cheeks a smoldering red. Clean-shaven and with a smudged kerchief tied jauntily about his head, he could pass for a maiden, if one didn't look too closely at that telltale professionally seductive pout.

Then Gerta and I strapped our swords to our backs
and tugged on loose homespun shirts over our mail.
With the addition of a bit of healthy grime, we made
hulking swineherds. I turned to Reginaldo. "Mind you
take care of that pig; it belongs to my second cousin's
mother-in-law and she's very attached to it."

"I can just imagine." Reginaldo flexed the hazel switch
that had been provided along with the winsome Betina.

We headed for the castle's town gate and joined the
stream of peasants carrying barrels of grain and salted
fish and tallow and the hundred other commodities
destined for the castle's larders. The guard, picking his
teeth, nodded at the pig. "For His Majesty's cooking
class?"

Reginaldo ducked his head in apparent agreement.

"Then you'd better step lively there, dearie." The
guard scratched his left armpit and looked thoughtful.
"King Bentley don't brook no tardiness with His ingre-
dients." He threw back his head and guffawed.

Reginaldo, in reply, only switched the pig, which
squealed and darted through the gate into the first
courtyard. Gerta and I sprinted after them, barely able
to keep the two in sight. The fair Betina, unaccustomed
to brutality, was having none of it, and had availed
herself of the first escape route available, a winding alley
that led down and back into the lower kitchens.

"Hell's bells!" Gerta threw me a worried, bloodshot
glance over her shoulder. I just gritted my teeth and
followed, mail links jingling like a whole legion of
soldiers. We rounded the next corner, frightening a flock
of pigeons, then skidded to a halt.

"Oh, *there* you are," said a petulant voice. "But I
thought I ordered mutton." Our revered sovereign, King
Bentley the Culinary, stood behind a butcher's block,
hatchet in hand, where he had evidently just decapitated
a startled looking lamb. A whole swarm of noticeably
pale courtiers and ladies-in-waiting were spread out

before him, pressing perfumed handkerchiefs to their noses and taking half-hearted notes.

Reginaldo's mouth worked, but no sound emerged. Betina eyed him nervously, so I snatched the switch out of his hand and shoved him aside. "That you did, Your Majesty. This here pig's for tomorrow's demonstration, something about Braised Ham Ratatouille, the head chef said."

"Gracious!" His Majesty threw up his bejeweled hands. "Never touch the stuff! Who's been mucking about with the class curriculum again?" He tapped his toe on the cobblestones. "Come now, out with it. Confess!"

A shamefaced dandy clad in crimson velvet raised his hand, then sank abjectly to his knees.

"I thought so!" The King crossed his arms, still holding the hatchet, which dripped gore down the front of his royal robes. "Bread and water for you the rest of the week, Lord Duningham, and not a single bite of candied eel for dessert!" He waved his hand. "Guards, take him away!"

A brief look of relief shot across Lord Duningham's pinched visage and he fairly threw his wretchedly skinny person into the arms of the guards.

"As for you three disgusting, grubby peasants," the King continued, "take that unfortunate beast to the slaughterhouse. I suppose we can make use of it next week, once we reach the chapter on cinnamon-mustard chitlings." Someone whimpered in the audience and King Bentley's eyes narrowed.

"Yes, Your Majesty." I hastily touched my cap and nudged Gerta to do the same. "We'll just be on our way then."

"See that you are." The King sniffed and turned back to what seemed to be his class. "Now, as I was saying, the lamb must be marinated for twenty minutes in sour milk and rosemary and—"

Reginaldo reached for the hazel stick. Betina, the poor porker, uttered a tremendous squeal and thundered off in the opposite direction. I broke the damned stick over my knee and followed.

Betina led us a merry chase through a series of courtyards and gardens, both kitchen and formal. Reginaldo lost his kerchief somewhere along the way and I was developing an impressive bruise where Esmeralda was thumping into my chain-mailed back at every step. We lost Gerta at one particularly tight turn by the chapel, and so finally it was just the panting blade and myself who cornered our borrowed porker in the happy confluence of the castle alehouse and chaplain's quarters.

Panting, I waved Reginaldo back. "If you stampede that pig again, I'll return *you* to the swineherd in her place. I doubt she'd notice the difference!"

Reginaldo leaned weakly against the warped boards of the alehouse. "Quit making excuses! I have to get to the Queen."

"You!" a female voice said frostily from the entrance to the courtyard. "We thought so! We had word that a person of your description had been seen scampering through His Majesty's cooking class."

Reginaldo and I whirled to face Her Majesty, Queen Anna Conda II, former Princess of Damery, and notorious connoisseur of blades in her wild youth. "Beloved!" he exclaimed.

I fell to one knee on the cobblestones and bowed my head. "Your Majesty."

"We had expected better of you, Hallah." Her tone was crisp. "While it's no secret that you've run a blade or two in for the princesses from time to time, you've always shown a fair amount of taste, for someone who spends all her time in apparel that must positively chafe the skin off your—" She rolled her eyes. "You *know*."

Indeed I did and had to resist the urge to rub that

nagging rawness just behind my breastplate. "This little rat insists he has business with your Majesty." I glanced up sideways at Reginaldo who was now doing an uncomfortable little prance. "If he's lying, just say the word and I'll be glad to run him through with Esmeralda."

Reginaldo darted forward. "Now, Annie—"

"Don't you 'now, Annie' me, you little snake!" She pulled off a slipper and shagged it at him, hitting him dead square in the middle of the forehead. He staggered back, the imprint of her heel clearly visible. "I've waited for years, *years*, do you hear me, for you to come and take this misbegotten thing back!" She fished in the pocket of her voluminous gown, then held up an ornate silver spoon.

He had the grace to look discomfited. "I always meant to come back and check in on you, really I did, but I've been ever so busy. If it wasn't riding with the Princess of Feldenstein one day, it was peeling grapes for the little sister of the King of Makberg, or being absolutely forced to take tea and crumpets with Her Majesty of Nunpoor, you know how she is about being neglected—"

"Excuses, excuses!" Queen Anna Conda wrenched at her remaining shoe and stood barefoot, her head thrown back, ready to let the second slipper fly. "Do you know what it's been like all these years, bearing princess after princess, with never a single prince to soothe the old ball-and-chain's itch for a son, and having to watch poor Bentley turn into cooking maniac? The entire kingdom is in disarray because he cares more about sauces and meringue than he does about borders!"

A single tear trickled down her still handsome cheek. "And he has no taste, not so much as a smidgen." She turned away. "Do you know he invented a strawberry-lemon Yorkshire pudding last week? It was—" Her shoulders heaved. "—ghastly."

Reginaldo edged forward and examined the spoon in

her trembling hand. "I did tell you to use it sparingly, my love." His voice was gently reproachful.

"But I thought if using it a bit was helpful, using it a bit more would be even better." Her words were strained. "At first, right after we were married, I only laid it out once a week, no more, just as you said, but then—" She broke off and stared down at her clenched hands. "He began to notice me, when he came to my bed, began to really like me, and it was so nice, I thought a bit more couldn't hurt."

Reginaldo traced the spoon with one finger. "And now?"

"And now, he won't eat without it, says everything tastes flat unless he has his one, his very special spoon." She glanced at the courtyard door. "He'll be calling for it soon, you know, it's almost time for luncheon."

"Then I must take my leave," Reginaldo said simply.

"Wait!" She dabbed at her eyes. "I think I understand about the obsessive cooking; you said the spoon's magic would enhance all his natural passions, but why so many daughters? Why have we never once had a son?"

Reginaldo caught her hand and pressed his lips to it, his dark eyes twinkling. "Ah, but that was your passion, was it not, my love, producing all those dulcet little doves through whom you could relive the wild and wonderful days of your own youth?"

She snatched her hand away. "Certainly not!"

"My mistake," he said smoothly, then held his own hand out. "The Sacred Spoon of Nunpoor, your Majesty?"

With a sob, she thrust the gleaming implement at him and turned away.

"I say, sir, unhand that spoon!" A voice rang out through the enclosed space, followed closely by the portly bulk of King Bentley the Culinary. The spoon slipped through Reginaldo's startled fingers and clattered upon the cobblestones.

"Bentie, darling!" The Queen reached out to him.

"What a pleasant surprise! I take it the Sour Lamb Supreme is safely in the oven then?"

"I should say not! Who can cook with all this commotion going on?" The King swooped down and plucked up the spoon, then thrust it inside his robes. He turned to his wife, his mustache trembling with fury. "I won't have it, do you hear? It's not bad enough that we have blades skulking about here day and night, when the princesses ought to be thinking about improving their custard recipes and honing their white sauces." He whirled upon Reginaldo. "But now, you're giving one of the wretched creatures my spoon, the one that whispers special recipes in my ear round the clock so I may braise what no man has ever braised before!"

I stepped forward and set myself between Reginaldo and the King, for no reason I could name, except the habits of a lifetime die exceedingly hard. "Shouldn't that be 'no *one*'?"

The King bristled. "And what business is it of yours, swineherd?"

"None at all, Your Royal Highness." I held up my empty hands and backed away, still shielding Reginaldo. "Hey, you want to eat out of one of the Thousand Cursed Spoons of Nunpoor, that's no business of mine."

He lifted an eyebrow. "Cursed?"

I shook my head, then gazed around. "You haven't seen my pig, have you, your Worship? I could swear I heard it squealing nearby."

"Never mind the blasted pig!" He sidled closer. "What's this about a curse?"

"Nothing, really." I motioned to Reginaldo to stay behind me. "It's just that I used to deliver hogs to Nunpoor, and I saw these cursed spoons lying all over the place. The way I hear it, you use one long enough and it makes your privates shrivel up and fall off. No one with any sense will even pick one up. That's why everyone in Nunpoor eats with their fingers." I cupped my hands to my mouth and called, "Pig, pig, pig, pig, sooooo-ey!"

"Stop that!" His face went fish-belly pale as he groped beneath his robes for the offending implement, then stared at it as though it were a viper about to strike.

"Bentie, dear," the Queen began, "I swear I was just thinking of your welfare."

"I—see." He thrust the spoon at me. "Here, peasant, get rid of the vile thing! I never want to see it again!"

I edged away, hands behind my back. "Not me! I'm too fond of my private parts."

"Then you!" he cried and slapped it into Reginaldo's limp hand. "Take it away at once!" The blade stared at it mutely. "Look lively, now! I want that thing out of the castle!"

Reginaldo gazed up at the Queen, whose eyes were bright with unshed tears. "It was a glorious spoon," she said, "but now its day is past. We must think of the future."

The blade bowed his head. "By your command," he said simply, then swept out of the courtyard.

"You, swineherd!" The King pointed after the blade. "See that he leaves the castle, or I'll have your head!"

"My goodness, Bentie," the Queen purred, "you are feeling forceful this morning."

"As a matter of fact," he said, sweeping his arm around her waist and pulling her against his chest, "I feel quite frisky."

"But what about the Sour Lamb Supreme?" she asked. "Shouldn't we check on it—you know, before?"

"Damn the lamb!" He buried his face in her neck.

I caught up with Reginaldo and we hurried back out past the blacksmith's shed and the chandlery, the fleece storehouse and the cattle pens. There was no sign of Gerta and I was getting worried.

Reginaldo gave the spoon a final glance, then thrust

it into his purse. His lips were quirked into a most knowing smile.

"How did you come by that thing anyway?" I shook my head. "And why did you give it to the Queen? Aren't Sacred Spoons worth quite a bit of gold?"

He threw back his head and laughed out loud as we passed through the town gate out into the sunshine, and then leaned back against the stone wall beside the moat, giggling and snorting until the tears ran down his face and he had to beat upon his thigh with his fist.

I stared at him angrily. "I don't understand."

He shook his head, almost too weak with hilarity to speak. "There is—no such thing as—the Sacred Spoon—of Nunpoor."

I narrowed my eyes. "What?"

He pulled the spoon out of his purse, then buffed it on his breeches. "I made the whole thing up to impress her."

I picked Reginaldo up by his collar and hefted him out into the middle of moat, where he hit the scummy green water with a most satisfying splash and sank, spoon and all.

Gerta didn't emerge from the castle for five days, and ever after displayed a distressing yen for strawberry-garlic crumpets, extremely difficult to satisfy out on the trail. Despite repeated inquiries, we never recovered the poor pig, Betina, who reputedly ended up as the following Wednesday's lesson, Ham Dumplings Ala Mode.

The blade, Reginaldo, eventually floundered to the opposite bank of the moat, where a passing milkmaid reportedly took pity upon him and fetched him home to nurse. The last I heard, they were married, had three sly-eyed brats, and he wasn't so pretty anymore, having put on forty pounds around the middle, the result of good plain food and toting about all those shovels of manure. Couldn't have happened to a nicer bloke, as they say.

As for me and Esmeralda, we've given up blade-running altogether. I know they say there's no real harm in it, just a bit of fun to amuse princesses and upper class daughters, who will all settle down eventually and raise families of their own, but I just don't have the stomach for it anymore.

I mean, what's the world coming to when you can't even trust a damned spoon?

Keeping Up Appearances

Lawrence Watt-Evans

Maribelle stared at the little black-iron cage in dismay. She had known when she returned from visiting her family and found the room deserted, with a note from Armus dated the day before yesterday directing her to look for him here if he wasn't home yet, that there was trouble.

But she hadn't expected *this*.

The hamster in the iron cage stared back at her. It was small and round and golden and looked totally harmless.

And rather stupid, but that didn't surprise Maribelle at all. "That's really Armus?" she asked.

"So the wizard's messenger said," Derdiamus Luc replied.

The hamster squeaked and nodded.

"Oh, dear," Maribelle sighed. "*What* will I tell his mother?"

"I'm sure I don't know," Luc said with an uneasy smile.

"Speaking of things you do or don't know," Maribelle said, "would you know how to turn him back? I mean, is this permanent? Is there some way to break the curse?"

"I'm afraid I have no idea," Luc said. "The messenger didn't tell me much of anything."

"Did the messenger tell you *why* the wizard Esotissimus turned Armus into this little furball?"

"Well . . ." Luc coughed.

Maribelle tore her gaze away from the hamster and looked at Luc. It wasn't hard to see that the merchant was hiding something.

And it wasn't hard to guess what it was, either. When she got Armus home she intended to have a few words with him, whether he was hamster or human at the time.

For now, though, she stared at Luc in wide-eyed innocence, pretending she hadn't a clue as to why the wizard would have been irked with Armus.

"I'm afraid it's partly my fault," Luc admitted. "Esotissimus has been telling my customers the most terrible lies about some of the goods I sell, and I hired the young man to deliver a strong complaint about this practice." He glanced at the hamster. "It appears the wizard didn't appreciate it. I *am* sorry."

Maribelle sighed again.

Actually, she supposed the wizard had been merciful, since the "strong complaint" Armus was supposed to deliver had almost certainly been a dagger between the ribs. And the "terrible lies" were probably accurate assessments of the value of some of the charms and potions Luc sold; Maribelle was fairly certain that Luc's so-called "irresistible love spells" were just civet and musk, and the "miraculous medicines" nothing but willow bark in distilled wine, with no magical content at all.

But what had Armus thought he was doing, going after a wizard alone?

"Well, I'm sure you meant well," she said, picking up the cage. She turned to go, then paused and turned back to Luc. "Um . . . while I can see that the response wasn't what you might have hoped, Armus apparently *did* deliver your message. Shall I send a bill, or would you like to pay now?"

Luc's jaw dropped, then snapped shut.

"Pay?" he said, sounding a bit strangled.

"Well, yes," Maribelle said. "I'm afraid that the Assassins' Guild would insist. Armus is a member, after all, so even though you merely hired him as a messenger, Guild rules would apply. Wouldn't they, Armus?"

The hamster made a noise that was clearly meant as agreement.

"Assassins' Guild? You mean there really *is* . . . " Luc stopped in mid-sentence. He looked at Maribelle's wide-eyed innocent gaze, and at the hamster's beady little eyes, both fixed on him.

"Of course," he said through clenched teeth. "I believe we had agreed upon a price of fifty royals . . ."

Armus cheebled angrily.

"How foolish of me," Luc said, forcing a laugh. "I mean *one hundred* and fifty. I'll just write you a chit . . ."

"Sire Luc, I'm afraid I may be traveling soon, on short notice," Maribelle said, her voice oozing regret. "I'll need to have cash."

"Well, I don't see how I . . ." Luc began.

Maribelle interrupted him, her tone still regretful but a little harder than before. "I wouldn't want to tell my friends in the Guild you were *uncooperative*, after you got the man I love turned into a *hamster* . . ."

Luc winced. "Of course," he said quickly.

Maribelle waited patiently as Luc counted out the coins. So far as she knew there *was* no Assassins' Guild, here in Verengard or anywhere else, but Luc wouldn't know that. Merchants heard all the rumors, and never knew which to believe. And Luc certainly knew what Armus did for a living. What's more, the amount of money involved confirmed that Luc hadn't hired Armus the Assassin just to deliver a message. He could have hired any urchin off the street for two royals—or maybe it would have taken as much as five, since a wizard was involved.

A hundred and fifty meant something more than a message, something a bit more pointed.

Twenty minutes later, back in the rented room two streets over, Maribelle opened the cage and pointed to the sheet of parchment and the little pan of ink she had set out.

"Now," she said, "would you mind telling me what you thought you were doing, contracting for an assassination without me? And agreeing to kill a *wizard*, without properly researching the job? I was only gone for eleven days! You couldn't wait that long?"

The hamster cheebled angrily at her.

"I can't understand anything you say," Maribelle told it. "Just dip a claw in the ink; I know you can't hold a pen."

The hamster glared at her for a moment, then scurried to the ink.

The result was smeared and messy, but legible.

I WAS BORED. LOOKED EASY. PAID WELL.

"A hundred and fifty royals?" Maribelle protested.

The hamster let out an offended squawk, and scrawled 600. 150 ADVANCE, 150 MORE EVEN IF WIZARD LIVED.

"And the rest if you actually pulled it off."

Armus nodded.

"And did you *really* think you could kill a wizard single-handed?"

The hamster shook his head, and reached for the ink.

SCOUTING, he wrote. THEN WAIT FOR YOU, FINISH THE JOB TOGETHER.

"But you got caught."

The hamster looked sheepish—which was an impressive accomplishment for a hamster, but Armus had always been a talented, charming individual.

Not all that *bright*, but talented and charming.

"All right," Maribelle said. "Tell me all about it, step by step. Then we'll see about getting you turned back."

She didn't say it aloud, but mentally added, if you *can* be turned back. She knew perfectly well that transformations were tricky stuff. Some could only be reversed by the wizard who initiated them. Others could only be ended by the wizard's death—she didn't think she would very much mind arranging that in this case.

And some transformations couldn't be undone at all.

She shivered at the thought as she watched the hamster scratching ink onto the parchment, leaving smudgy little footprints everywhere. She and Armus had been working together for a little over four years now, and she had hoped they would stay together for the rest of their lives. She'd put aside almost half the money they had earned as assassins, with the intention of someday retiring on it and settling down somewhere—after all, they couldn't keep killing people forever. She wouldn't always be sufficiently young and pretty and innocent-looking to use their preferred methods, where Armus would threaten the intended target, drawing all the attention while poor helpless-looking little Maribelle put a knife in the victim's back.

Settling down with a hamster, rather than a man, hadn't been at all what she had in mind.

The wizard Esotissimus was clearly a traditionalist. His establishment was built of wrought iron, smoke-blackened oak, and equally smoke-blackened granite, lavishly trimmed with spikes and gargoyles. Maribelle paused on the street and looked up at it before entering.

Maribelle usually liked traditionalists; they tended to be easy targets, never ready for the unexpected. They either ignored her completely or tried to seduce her, and both options provided plentiful opportunities for poison or a quick stroke of the blade.

She wasn't here to kill this particular wizard, though, but to coax a favor out of him, and traditionalism might work against her there. Wizards had a traditional dislike for reversing their spells.

And Esotissimus was not merely a traditionalist, but a very powerful wizard. That was why Maribelle had chosen the direct approach. Armus swore he hadn't even seen the wizard's hands move when the transformation spell was cast. He hadn't even realized the wizard was really angry with him until he started shrinking and growing fur.

Armus had attempted a ruse; he had pretended to be a prospective customer, hoping to study the layout of the wizard's home and learn a bit of his capabilities. He still, he said, didn't know what had gone wrong, or how the wizard had known he was lying.

Maribelle lifted the immense iron knocker and let it fall; a muffled boom echoed, and with a creak of bending metal the two black iron gargoyle faces on either side of the door turned to look at her.

She looked back, quickly putting on her dumb-and-demure working expression and smiling at first one, then the other. Just because the iron faces could move that didn't mean they could see her, but there was no reason to take unnecessary chances.

And it was very obvious that this was *real* magic here, not the cheap imitations offered by Derdiamus Luc and his ilk.

The oaken door opened a crack, and a heart-shaped female face framed in lustrous black curls peered out at her.

"Hello there," Maribelle said. There was no point in turning the charm on full for a woman, but she smiled brightly. "I'd like to see Esotissimus, please."

"You don't have an appointment," the black-haired woman said accusingly.

"I didn't know how to make one," Maribelle explained. "Please, it's *very* important." She adjusted the strap of the bag slung over her shoulder.

"What's it about?" the woman demanded.

Maribelle looked at her, trying to judge whether to admit the truth or insist on seeing the wizard. The woman was short, shorter than Maribelle—she would scarcely have reached Armus' shoulder if Armus were still himself. She wore a low-cut, tight-fitting gown of black velvet that combined with her lush mop of hair to frame and accentuate her pale skin and fine features. She had made herself up expertly, but Maribelle could see that she was past the first bloom of youth—perhaps thirty, or even thirty-five. If she were a slave-girl kept entirely for her decorative appearance she could expect to be cast aside any day now, whenever her master might trouble himself to really look at her and see past the cosmetics.

If she had other talents, Maribelle couldn't see them.

She was likely to be balky, then—she would be insecure in her position, and reluctant to risk any disturbance should she admit the wrong person. Better, then, to tell her the truth.

"It's about my husband," Maribelle said.

The woman's eyes darkened. "Oh?"

"Yes," Maribelle said. "The wizard turned him into a hamster. I'd like him turned back."

Enlightenment struck; the woman's eyes widened with sudden understanding.

"Oh, the *hamster!*" she said. "I hadn't . . . well, come in; I'll tell the great Esotissimus you're here." She swung the door wide, and ushered Maribelle inside, down a corridor to a small, windowless, sparsely-furnished room lit by a dozen fat candles.

"Wait here," the attendant said.

Maribelle settled onto an oaken chair and waited. She opened the bag so that Armus could have a little light and air—though the air was sufficiently thick with candle-smoke that it probably wasn't much of an improvement over the inside of the pouch.

"Was that woman here before?" Maribelle asked.

Armus nodded and gave an affirmative cheeble—the two of them had worked out a few simple codes to aid communication.

"She let you in?"

Again, Armus nodded.

"Did you see any other servants?"

That drew a negative hiss. Of course, that didn't mean there *were* no other servants. The place might be full of spying apprentices, for all she or Armus knew, peering through invisible eyeholes in every wall, or watching them with scrying spells.

Armus was looking up at her expectantly, as if he had more to say, but she couldn't think what it would be. They hadn't brought paper and ink; it hadn't seemed practical.

"Did Esotissimus keep you waiting—"

She didn't have a chance to finish the question, as the door opened just then. The dark-haired woman stood in the corridor, beckoning. Apparently Esotissimus did not keep visitors waiting long.

Maribelle gave Armus a second or two to settle securely back into the pouch, then rose and followed the woman down the passageway and through an imposing set of double doors.

The room beyond was large, dim, and mostly empty. At the far end a dais held a throne, and seated on the throne was a robed figure; all the light in the room came from some hidden source behind the throne, so that the figure's face was completely hidden in shadows.

Maribelle knew she was supposed to be impressed—in fact, she *was* impressed—so she dropped her jaw and said, "Ooooh!" in her best little-girl voice.

Behind her, the dark-haired woman slammed the great doors shut. Maribelle blinked foolishly, then turned to look—she always wanted to know whether anyone was in a position to stab her in the back.

The serving woman, or whoever she was, was leaning

casually on the closed doors. Maribelle suppressed a frown. It was probably silly to worry about such things when she was facing a powerful wizard, but she really hated having anyone behind her during a negotiation.

At least she could put some distance between them. She put on a scared-but-attempting-bravery expression and marched forward, toward the throne.

"Greetings, mighty wizard!" she said, letting her voice squeak a bit.

The figure on the throne raised one hand and said, "Come no closer!" The wizard's voice was deep and rich and echoed from the stone walls.

Maribelle stopped and looked puzzled. "All right," she said. "I didn't want to shout, that's all."

"I will hear you well enough where you are," the seated shape announced. "What would you have of me?"

"Well," Maribelle said, holding up the pouch, "you turned my husband into a hamster. I'm sure you had your reasons—I know he can be *very* annoying at times—but could you please turn him back now? I promise he's learned his lesson, and we won't bother you again."

"You say that the assassin who intruded upon me was your husband?" the wizard boomed.

She hesitated before replying as she debated whether she should object to hearing Armus called an assassin. If she were truly the naive innocent she was pretending to be, she should at least express some surprise.

Generally speaking, though, arguing with wizards wasn't a good idea.

"Well, we never got around to a formal marriage ceremony, but we've been together for a few years," she said.

Then, abruptly, she turned—she wasn't consciously aware what had alerted her, whether she had heard breathing or felt the air moving, but she knew someone was coming up behind her, and she whirled to find the black-haired woman had come forward from the door and was now just a few feet away.

Maribelle let out a yip.

"You *startled* me!" she said, backing away—but carefully not even beginning to reach for any of her hidden weaponry.

"Pay no attention to my servant!" the wizard thundered.

"Oh, *excuse* me, sir!" Maribelle said, turning back toward the throne. She bowed, and then stepped aside, farther off the line between the woman and the throne, so that neither the woman nor the wizard would be directly behind her when she spoke to the other.

The woman frowned at her, and drummed her fingers on the black velvet covering her thigh. Maribelle noticed that the servant did not glance at the wizard for direction before retreating to one of the side walls. There she leaned back against the stone and stared at Maribelle.

"Does she have to be in here?" Maribelle asked the wizard, jerking a thumb at the woman. "She makes me nervous."

For a moment the wizard sat silently—Maribelle couldn't see his face, couldn't guess at his thoughts. Finally he spoke.

"*She* makes you nervous?"

"Well, I mean, of course *you* make me nervous, too, but you're *supposed* to. You're a wizard, after all."

"She makes you nervous."

"Yes, she does. Could you send her away?"

"No."

That didn't leave much room for argument. Maribelle shrugged. At least the woman was at the side now, rather than behind her, and Maribelle had had plenty of practice watching people out of the corner of her eye.

"Whatever you say," she said. "But could you please change Armus back to a man?" She held up the pouch, displaying the hamster.

"Why should I?" the wizard asked. "He came here

to slay me. The two of you are fortunate that I permit him to live in *any* form!"

"Oh, absolutely," Maribelle agreed, "it was very kind of you to let him live. But you know, he didn't come to kill you at all, he *swore* to me that he didn't!"

"And you believe him?"

"Of course I do! He's my husband."

"And why did he come to me, then?"

Maribelle glanced at the servant, still leaning against the wall; she couldn't make out the wizard's expression at all, but the woman's face was interestingly blank.

The time had come, Maribelle thought, to surprise Esotissimus and tell the truth.

"Oh, he came to decide whether or not to take the job of killing you. But he hadn't agreed yet, and he wouldn't have, once he saw you."

Maribelle thought she saw the woman's mouth twitch, as if she were suppressing a smile.

"And you think I should forgive him for even *considering* an attempt to slay me?"

"Well, yes," Maribelle said. "It was stupid, and he should have known better, definitely—but everyone does stupid things once in awhile."

"And when they do, they must pay the price!" Esotissimus roared.

"But no harm was done," Maribelle insisted. "Won't you please forgive him? Isn't there *anything* I can offer you to change him back? We have money—we could pay you."

"What use do I have for earthly wealth?"

Maribelle blinked foolishly. "The same uses as anyone else," she said. "I know you charge people for the magic you do for them."

"If I did not, they would never cease to trouble me," the wizard said. "I need no gold."

"Maybe we have information you could use?" Maribelle suggested. "After all, Armus knows who hired him."

"Derdiamus Luc," Esotissimus said.

"Oh," Maribelle said, crestfallen. "You knew."

"Of course. My servant knew where to take the hamster, did she not?"

Maribelle glanced at the woman leaning against the wall—*she* was the messenger who had delivered Armus to Luc?

"Well, if you like, Armus could kill Luc for you," Maribelle said.

"I could dispose of him myself, should I choose to do so," the wizard replied.

That was probably true enough. Maribelle was running out of suggestions, but there was always one possibility. Her voice suddenly dropped the better part of an octave and turned husky. "Surely there must be *something* I can do for you?"

"Are you offering to betray your husband?"

"I'm trying to *save* my husband," Maribelle protested, holding up the pouch.

"I have no interest in you," the wizard said coldly. "I am above such worldly concerns."

"But you must be lonely . . ." Maribelle began. Then somewhere in her head something fell into place, and instead of finishing the sentence she turned to look at the dark-haired woman.

A mighty wizard who claimed to be above any sort of earthly matters, but who still had one servant—and *only* one—who he insisted must be present during this audience. A woman who was not quite the young beauty she tried to appear. Armus hadn't seen the wizard even move when he was transformed. And Armus tended to fiddle with weapons behind his back when he was nervous.

Maribelle looked down at the hamster. "She was behind you when it happened, wasn't she?" she asked.

Armus cheebled, and Maribelle looked up in time to see the dark-haired woman's hands raised, fingers arranged to cast a spell. Maribelle flung herself sideways, out of the line of fire, ignoring Armus' tiny shriek of terror as he flew out of his pouch; she landed rolling on the floor, and rose to her knees as she pulled one of the concealed daggers from her sleeve.

She didn't want to use the knife; for one thing, it probably wouldn't work. Even as she prepared to throw it she groped for alternatives, and one came to her.

If her guess was right, then the black-haired woman might well want something Maribelle was uniquely equipped to provide.

"Wait!" she shouted, as she readied the knife. "Please, wait!"

The black-haired woman turned, hands raised to enchant.

"*Aren't* you lonely?" Maribelle called.

The woman paused, fingers poised and ready but unmoving. Clearly she had expected Maribelle to beg for her life, or offer some sort of bribe, not repeat the question she had asked the wizard. "What?" she said.

"Aren't you lonely?" Maribelle repeated, lowering her dagger. "I mean, living here all alone with just him— is he even real? Wouldn't you like someone to, you know, just *talk* to?"

The woman looked at the dagger, and belated realization dawned—a realization very much like the one that had struck Maribelle. "You aren't just an assassin's *wife*, are you?" she asked.

Maribelle risked a faint smile. "And you aren't just a wizard's servant."

The woman lowered her hands. "Go on," she said. "What did you want to say?"

"Armus wasn't going to kill you," Maribelle said. "If we'd taken the job, I would have. Armus is a sweet boy, but he isn't much of an assassin—I'm the brains, he's the decoy. And you're the wizard, and that thing on the throne is just for show." She pointed to where the wizard sat, unmoving and completely uninvolved in the rather intense discussion going on a few yards away. "You're the brains, it's the decoy."

"So now I really *should* kill you," the woman said, raising her hands again. "Not only are you an admitted assassin, but you know my secret."

"And you know mine," Maribelle said. "You can kill me any time—but wouldn't you rather have someone you can talk to? Someone you can trust? Someone who's used to keeping secrets? Aren't there times it would be handy to have a trusted friend who's trained at theft, deception, and assassination? Someone you can talk shop with?"

"It *would* be nice," the wizard said hesitantly. "It *is* lonely. But can I really trust you? Both of you?"

"Why not?" Maribelle said. "I'll vouch for Armus— he can be foolish, but he can keep his mouth shut, and I'm sure he doesn't want to be a hamster. We've kept *our* secret well enough—why not yours?" She put the dagger on the floor and displayed her empty hands. "My name's Maribelle, by the way."

For a moment the dark-haired woman still hesitated, but then she gave in. "I'm Essi," she said, reaching out a hand to help Maribelle to her feet.

"I'm pleased to meet you," Maribelle said. "I've never met a female wizard before."

"I don't think there are any others," Essi said. "My father trained me in wizardry, but after he and my mother died no one would ever take me seriously—it's not just that I'm female, but I'm so short, and not ugly enough for a witch. Besides, I don't know witchcraft, just wizardry. I could have changed my appearance, but that's so uncomfortable and hard to maintain! So I made Esotissimus over there—he's a homunculus, sort of half-alive—and played the part of a servant."

"Nobody would hire a woman to fight openly," Maribelle said, dusting off her skirt. "So I tried to hire out as an assassin, but even that wasn't working until I teamed up with Armus." She looked around, and spotted the hamster trying to scramble up onto the dais. "Could you *please* change him back?"

"Of course," Essi said. A moment later Armus, restored to human form, sat on the corner of the dais, looking dazed.

"Mari?" he said.

"I'm fine," Maribelle answered. "Now shut up and let us talk."

Armus blinked. "All right," he said. He turned and began poking experimentally at the homunculus' unresponsive legs.

"You really *are* the brains, aren't you?" Essi asked, staring at Armus.

"Of course," Maribelle replied.

Essi smiled.

"Mari," she said, "this could be the start of a beautiful friendship."

La Différence

Harry Turtledove

First, Jupiter. In Io's black sky, nothing rivals it—certainly not the sun, whose distance-shrunken disk blazes brilliant but cold, cold. Jupiter's great orb sprawls across almost twenty degrees of sky, forty times as wide as Luna from Terra and nearly four hundred times as bright.

And when you have seen Luna once through her phases, you have seen all she has to offer. Jupiter is an ever-changing spectacle, banded clouds always swirling into new shapes, white or orange spots—cyclones that could swallow continents—bubbling up from the interior only to fade away in hours, weeks, years (or, like the Great Red Spot, not at all).

Renée Messier never tired of the show. The crawler pilot resented the attention she had to give her vehicle as she zigzagged northwards through the lava-and-sulfur uplands south of Loki toward the United European seismic station beyond the volcano.

Even more, she resented the two Japanese crawlers on her trail. The men in them would kill her if they could.

They likely could.

She used the intercom to talk to Alec Hall, who was

in the seat to her right. They both wore their space armor. The Japanese invaders might hole the crawler without wrecking it. In suits they could keep going, at least until they were hit again. "Give Loki Station another call," she said.

Hall was a geochemist by training, but all Io personnel could handle crawler equipment when they had to. She fiddled with the shortwave. Renée did not think the Japanese could pick up its signal; not many people used amplitude modulation any more. But on a world without comm satellites and with an ionosphere—even a tenuous one—the old-fashioned system made sense.

The call went out. Through her face plate, Renée saw Hall listening intently, trying to pick up the reply; even with the best static filters, Jupiter put out a lot of background noise.

His face fell. "We're on our own," he said bleakly. His French, the official tongue of United Europe, had a soft British accent. "They're just starting to weld missile rails onto one of their crawlers; it won't be ready for hours yet. By then we'll either be there or—" He spread his gauntleted hands.

"At least they can mount weapons," Renée growled. Her crawler was an unarmed research vehicle. No one had expected the longstanding dispute over mining rights in the asteroid belt to become a shooting war. When it did, hardly anyone thought it would spill over into the Jovian system. She shook her head. "To think I was one of the people who laughed at the waste when they mounted their missile batteries around Loki Station."

"We were all laughing," Alec said. "I was glad to be down at Sengen Base, where they didn't bother with such barbarisms." He pronounced the name of the base—which was only rubble now—with a hard "g," English-style, instead of the proper French "j" sound.

Hoping to take his mind, and her own, off their predicament, Renée teased, "You still have trouble talking straight, eh? Such a pity, for you look much more French than I do." No one could argue that. Alec was small, slim, dark, and sharp-featured, while her broad-shouldered frame, square craggy face, and flaxen hair might have belonged to a Dane. *Vikings in the woodpile*, she thought.

He turned to glare. "*Merde*," he said. "How's that?"

"Clear enough, anyhow." She tried to smile, but her chuckle came out hollow. Being the only two people alive from a seventy-person base was too big to joke at. Had she and Alec not been out taking soil specimens from the slopes of Sengen Patera, forty kilometers away, they would have gone with everyone else when the Japanese attacked.

Typically thorough, though, the enemy had landed crawlers to finish off stragglers. They must have been fetched from the Japanese Luna Farside base, Renée thought. Only the lead she'd started with had kept them from overhauling her till now.

Not that she could hope to lose them for good. The tracks her wide, wire-wound tires were leaving would stay visible for years, until the sulfur dust raining down from Io's volcanic eruptions finally covered them over. That dust blanketed Io's surface, painting the moon in brilliant shades of red, orange, and yellow.

Renée yanked at the tiller, swung the crawler to the right to avoid a boulder. The dust the tires kicked up rose and fell in neat parabolic arcs. It slid off the titanium chevrons mounted on the tires' sides for extra surface area. The design went back over a hundred years to the first lunar rover, maybe the high point of the ill-fated American space program. Engineers were natural conservatives; if something worked, they stuck with it.

"We've been climbing the last few kilometers," Alec said. "Next chance we get, we ought to look back to see if we can spot the Japanese crawlers."

"Good idea." Renée pulled behind the first outcrop

of stone large enough to shield the crawler from view
from behind: if the enemy was close, no use presenting
a stationary target. She cautiously raised the outside
video camera on its motorized boom until it could peek
over his shelter. A radar pulse, of course, would have
fingered the Japanese at once, but also would have
screamed "Here we are!" to their detectors.

She panned the camera back and forth, peering at the
screen to pick up motion against the colorful landscape.
A flash of light made her gasp, but it was only the sun
reflecting from a patch of sulfur dioxide snow.

"There!" Alec said suddenly. "No, go back, you lost
it." Renée reversed the camera control, stabbing at the
STOP button. Then she also saw the two moving insectile
specks. They traveled side by side, tiny as midges in the
distance.

"How far away are they, do you think?" Alec asked.

"We passed that very red patch there, hmm, what
would you say, fifteen minutes ago? So they're ten
kilometers behind us, possibly twelve."

"They've gained a lot of ground," Alec said, his voice
low and troubled.

Messier shrugged, a Gallic gesture that did not suit
her. "Why shouldn't they? They only have to follow a
trail, not make one."

"They'll catch us long before we get to Loki Station."

"I know. But we're not caught yet. As long as they're
not shooting at us, I refuse to worry." *Out loud, at any
rate*, she amended to herself.

She lowered the camera and started traveling again.
A few minutes later, she began cursing in earnest, for
the crawler came up against a long scarp lying square
across the path. Such cliffs were common on Io, where
the sulfurous crust often fractured under pressure. This
one was a good two hundred meters high, and much
too steep to climb. Getting around it wasted half an hour
and took her farther from Loki Station.

"Hot spot ahead," Alec warned, his eyes on the infrared sensor. "Temp is up around twenty Celsius."

"Thank you." Messier drove around it. Most of Io's surface was as cold as one would expect for a world more than three quarters of a billion kilometers from the sun, down around -145° C. But, especially in the volcanic equatorial regions, black sulfur from the lower part of the mantle could force its way to the surface. It soon got covered by sulfur dust like the rest of Io, and was hard to spot visually.

Alec went aft to put a fresh canister of lithium hydroxide in the air recycler. Renée hardly noticed him getting up; she was intent on putting kilometers behind them to make up the delay from the scarp.

She jumped when the incoming signal lamp lighted. It was not a call from Loki station, but on the ordinary deep-space band. She accepted the signal. A voice sounded in his headphones—badly accented French: "Stop in place and we will accept your surrender. Otherwise you will be destroyed."

"Thank you, no." Renée did not bother transmitting the reply. When the Japanese remilitarized in the early years of the twenty-first century, they went back all too closely to the traditions of *bushido*. Dying at once was usually better than falling into their hands, even for a man. Giving up did not bear thinking about, not for her.

A missile slammed into the ground about ten meters to the crawler's right. Rocks and chunks of sulfur rained down. The only thing that saved the crawler from worse damage was that Io's atmosphere was too thin to transmit the blast from the explosion.

Fear knotting her guts, Renée fed emergency power to the electric motors in each wheel hub. She slewed the crawler leftwards, dashing for the shelter of a ridge of rock. She got there just in time; the missile from the pursuer, which had been homing on her, blew itself up against the suddenly interposed barrier.

"*Cochons!*" she cried, shaking her fist at the Japanese. Then reaction set in. Sweat oozed over her skin, the clammy, clinging sensation made worse by its lazy flow in Io's .18g. If they'd been in the open when that second missile struck—

With an almost physical effort, she forced herself to optimism. "We've gained some time, at any rate," he said. "They'll have to suit up and EVA to reload their missile racks."

"You're right." Alec came forward to strap himself in again. He rubbed at his hip through the space armor; Renée's desperate maneuver must have thrown him head over heels. But he still sounded as calm and practical as if the discussion were about the best place to dig a sample trench. "The eclipse will slow them, too."

"Eclipse?" Renée echoed foolishly; she hadn't consciously noticed how narrow Jupiter's crescent had become. The planet, of course, hung unmoving in the sky; from Loki, it stood about forty degrees above the horizon, slightly south of west. But the sun was within a few degrees of it, and would soon vanish behind its bulk.

Elation filled Renée for a moment, but gloom quickly replaced it. "Eclipse matters less to them than it would to us. We have light from the sun, Jupiter, or both for all but a couple of hours out of every forty-two, but on Luna Farside they're in dark phase two weeks of four."

Alec frowned. "Unfair for men from a different world to be better prepared for this one than we are after we've spent so much time on it."

"If ever two worlds were similar, they're Luna and Io," Renée said with a sigh. "Io's radius is only about eighty kilometers greater, and they they have about the same density, too—like as two peas in a pod, as far as worlds go."

"That's superficial," Alec said. "Luna is dead, but Io still has a molten core. And our sulfur-based geology is different from anything else in the solar system."

"That's nice," Renée said politely, "but it doesn't help us, and the Japanese will take advantage of the similarities."

She drove on in gloomy silence. The sun slipped behind Jupiter's disk. Even in eclipse, Jupiter did not vanish altogether. Coldly gleaming aurorae and crackles of lightning from titanic storms still showed its place in the heaven. A sudden bright streak marked the incineration of a meteor.

None of that, however, was enough to drive by, nor was the pale light from the outer satellites. Before she switched on her headlamps, Renée turned the crawler around to see if she could spot the Japanese. She did not expect to be able to; the halt to put on fresh missiles should have made them fall below the horizon.

She gasped in dismay. She needed no TV pickup to spot them; their driving lights glowed in the darkness like fireflies. "They didn't reload!" she said indignantly, as if some rule had required them to. "They'll just catch up with us and do us in with gunfire, the dirty *salauds*."

Alec seized her arm hard enough to hurt, even through the metal and fabric of her suit. "Maybe not, if we have just a little luck," he said. "Listen—"

She listened. When he was done, she said, "If it fails, we're dead—but then, we're dead anyway, right? Let's try; what do we have to lose?"

Following the crawler track, Sublieutenant Mitsuo Onishi was more bored than anything else. He wished the missiles had taken out the United European vehicle. Then he could have gone back to base. Instead, every minute took him almost a kilometer farther away.

Well, it wouldn't be long. He'd been gaining since the eclipse began. The United European wasn't much of a night driver, he thought with faint contempt. Radar showed the other crawler only seven kilometers ahead now. Because it was on higher ground, Onishi could see the pools of light its headlamps cast before it.

He jammed a fresh thirty-round magazine into his rifle and hung several more on the belt of his spacesuit. This time, no misses.

His driver gave a surprised grunt. At the same time, Ensign Mochifumi Nango's voice, high-pitched with excitement, came over the crawler-to-crawler circuit: "We must have damaged them after all, sir! Their steering's failing!"

"*Hai!*" Onishi said, grinning. The United European vehicle was making small, helpless circles dead ahead. "Let's go do our job. Nothing to it now."

Both Japanese machines sped forward. Onishi imagined the consternation of whoever was inside the crawler. He smiled.

"Sir," the driver said, "ground temperature is rising ahead. "Up to ten degrees Celsius, now twenty, now twenty-five—"

"What of it?" Onishi snorted. "Lunar day is over 100 Celsius, and we're rated safe past 150. Move, damn you; I want this over with."

"Aye, sir."

The radio crackled to life again. Nango asked, "Why does the trail stop short up there, sir?"

Onishi clapped a hand to his forehead in exasperation; was he the only person on this mission capable of rational thought? "The dust peters out, *bakatare*. There has to be one clear, flat patch on this miserable moon, *neh*? What do we care about the trail now? There's the enemy waiting for us. Do you want him to wait longer while you have the vapors?"

Nango could say only one thing, and he said it: "No, sir."

"All right, then." Onishi broke the circuit. He watched with satisfaction as the other crawler came abreast of his. Nango was all right. No one could call him a shirker.

They sped past the place where the tire tracks of the United European crawler stopped short. Onishi admitted to himself that they did end rather abruptly, but he was damned if he'd say so out loud. It was of no consequence, anyway.

He gave Nango credit. The ensign was even trying to get ahead now; sulfur powder flew from his wheels as he accelerated.

Onishi watched for several seconds before that registered. If there was still dust here, then the crawler they were after *hadn't* come this way—and probably had a reason for it.

"Reverse!" the sublieutenant said urgently. "It's a—"

Before he could finish, the ground buckled beneath his crawler. It happened with eerie slowness, as most things do on a low-gravity world, but no less inevitably on account of that. Slabs of yellow sulfur gave way like thin ice.

The crawler tipped with that same sense of nightmare leisure. Through the window, Onishi, who was cursing and praying in the same breath, saw Ensign Nango's crawler go down nose first.

One after another, alarm bells began to ring.

From their hiding place behind a boulder close by the circling crawler, Renée and Alec watched fearfully as the lights from the Japanese vehicles stabbed toward it. When those lights suddenly slewed wildly, Renée let out a whoop that almost deafened her inside her helmet.

She hugged Alec. It wasn't much of an embrace; the thick suit material saw to that. The crawler pilot did not care.

Alec pressed his helmet to hers. "We did it! We did it!" he shouted over and over. He was yelling in English, but Renée did not care about that, either. She knew what he had to be saying.

They danced round and round in glee, holding each other's hands. At last, panting, Renée thumbed her portable transmitter. The crawler obediently broke off its circuit and came over to the boulder. With a deep bow, Renée waved Alec into the airlock ahead of her.

Once they were both inside the crawler, they shed spacesuits with cries of relief. No one would be shooting at them now. And neither of them seemed surprised when the shedding did not stop there; tunics and shorts quickly followed. The latter were not made for modesty in any case, having openings here and there for the suits' sanitary arrangements.

The crawler's bunk was narrow, and covered only by a thin foam pad. In .18g, that didn't matter.

"Very glad to see the two of you. To be honest, I didn't think I would," said Jacques Guizot, commandant of Loki Station. The office in which he received the newcomers was small and cramped, like all the chambers in the station's tunnel system. The domes above were abandoned, though thus far the batteries around them had knocked down all incoming missiles.

"To be honest, we didn't expect to get here," Renée said.

Beside her, Alec nodded. "We were very lucky."

"No," Renée said, giving him credit. "It was your cleverness. If you hadn't thought of how the Japanese were unfamiliar with Io, we'd have been done for."

"It never would have occurred to me without you," he insisted, "and I'm not a good enough driver to have brought it off by myself."

Guizot raised a bushy gray eyebrow at this mutual admiration society. "What exactly did you do?" he asked at last.

"We lured them into a hot patch," they said together.

The commandant's other eyebrow shot up. His

thundered laughter was positively Jovian. "Magnificent! How did you manage that?"

"I drove up to the very edge of the patch," Renée answered, "Then I reversed, backing up in my own tracks till I could turn and skirt the patch. Once I was on the other side, I set the crawler to circle, as if it were disabled."

Alec took up the story: "Then we both EVA'd and hurried back to sweep away the tracks that showed where we'd turned. Luckily, we were in eclipse—we just had to get rid of a few meters of the trail, what the Japanese headlights would pick up. After that, it was hide and wait and hope."

"And they fell into the trap," Renée said. "Literally."

"Why not?" Alec said. "They were used to driving on Luna, which has been dead for billions of years. But hot patches are places where molten black sulfur reaches the surface. Once it gets up there, it starts to freeze again, and gets covered over by yellow sulfur dust, but underneath—"

"Underneath, it's still black sulfur," Messier interrupted with a savage grin, "and a lot like hot black tar. Only the thin crust on top keeps it from showing its true temperature—"

"—which is around 200 Celsius," Alec finished. "And the crust is *very* thin. When a crawler tries to cross it . . ."

"Magnificent!" Guizot said again. "Using the enemy's ignorance against him is a first principle of warfare."

"My own ignorance, too," Renée confessed. "I said Luna and Io were much alike. You can imagine, sir, how glad I was to be proved wrong. And, as is more often said in another context" —she looked fondly at Alec— "*vive la différence!*"

Tales from the Slushpile

Margaret Ball

Halfway through the SalamanderCon panel *On Thud and Blunder*, the stuffy hotel air was likely to put me to sleep before my demo came up. Right now Brian Spooner was droning on about how the sociology of most sword-and-sorcery novels was completely off base, they didn't begin to understand how many peasants it took to support one fighting man (*man*, naturally; this was one of the Spooner-Upshaw Gang talking). He had all kinds of numbers and charts to support his contention. He was also way off base, not having actually lived in a society where personal combat was a way of life. One thing he hadn't taken into account was how many swordspersons (to be non-sexist about it, Paper-Pushers style) it took to protect a string of farms in border territory. Another thing he didn't consider was the effect of motivation on productivity. Those tests about how long it took English students to build a replica of an early Norman castle were completely irrelevant. I've supervised quick fortifications out on the boundaries of Duke Zolkir's territory, and I can promise you those kids would've worked a lot faster given the encouragement of a swordswoman behind them and Baron Rodo's roughs just over the hill, raring to skewer them for brunch.

279

But I wasn't here to argue with Brian Spooner's book-based theories of how agrarian societies actually worked, or even to enjoy Susan Crescent's wickedly funny comments on writers who thought a horse was a kind of four-legged sports car requiring no daily maintenance. I was *supposedly* here to demonstrate my military expertise to D. McConnell. Who had still not put in an appearance.

"But now," the moderator interrupted Brian, as the audience's coughs and shuffles threatened to overwhelm his reedy voice, "before we run out of time, let's hear from our martial arts expert! Riva Konneva, author of several delightful stories in the Sword and Sorcery genre and a recent SFWA member, has kindly consented to give us a demonstration of just what's wrong with the fighting passages in some of the books we've been discussing."

Sigh. Even if D. McConnell wasn't here, I had a responsibility to do my part of the Thud and Blunder panel. I stood up and laid out some of my demo props on the table, around the stack of books my fellow panelists had been tearing to shreds. The thirty-pound sword had been a real pain to put together, but I'd found an SCA blacksmith who reluctantly agreed to subvert his craft long enough to add an inconspicuous line of lead weighting along the blade of one of his failed swords. The morningstar had been easier; all that had cost me was a quick Call Trans-Forwarding to a wizard in my home reality of Dazau and an exorbitant Inter-Universal Express fee for sending some standard Bronze Bra Guild equipment to me here on the Planet of the Paper-Pushers. And Sasulau, my own personal sword, hadn't cost me anything at all . . . yet. The barely perceptible humming as I drew her from the scabbard warned me that she would expect to taste blood before she was sheathed again. "Not this time, Sasulau," I muttered to her. This was a peaceful talkfest of science

fiction writers and fans, a place where the only blood
shed was psychic as writers' dearest creations were
ripped apart by self-appointed editors and critics.

Like me.

"Could you talk into the mike, Riva?" the moderator
asked. "We couldn't quite hear that."

I waved the mike away. The audience and other
panelists hadn't been meant to hear my comment to
Sasulau; and what I did want them to hear I could
convey without the aid of one of those squawking Paper-
Pushers toys. After whipping a troop of Bronze Bra
recruits into shape, making my voice heard across this
medium-sized hotel room full of fans was child's play.

"Let's start with weapons," I said. "Brian, have you
noticed how many of these books have their barbarian
hero wielding a twenty-kilo mace or a fifty-pound sword
or something equally impressive?" I knew he hadn't, but
I needed to get around the fact that I hadn't actually gone
through the stack of assigned reading and made the notes
I'd meant to make. I just couldn't get through all the
pages of *Cant the Conqueror, Blunt the Barbarian, Warrior Priests of Guck*, and the other colorful paperbacks
we were supposed to be discussing. The only book I'd
actually read was a slim volume published by some local house nobody here had ever heard of. Because the
cover was plain yellow paper instead of a painting of
somebody with thews like Vordokaunneviko the Great,
I'd thought it wouldn't be as silly as the other books; and
because it was only half an inch thick, I'd thought it would
be easier to skim through.

Wrong on both counts. Dwight Mihlhauser's opus was
so dumb I didn't really want to make fun of it here;
seemed unsporting, like spearing a sleeping wizard.

Brian didn't let me down, though. I knew I could
count on a guy not to admit ignorance. "Oh, yeah, sure,"
he said, nodding wisely. "That bothered me, too, but I
thought I would let you speak to that point, Riva."

Susan Crescent, bless the lady, flipped through *Cant the Conqueror*. "You mean like this? *With one slash of his mighty sword, weighing as much as a tub of butter, Cant hewed through his adversary's armor-plated shoulder and clove him to the waist.*"

"Exactly! A tub of butter—well, you know how small one of those one-pound blocks of butter you get at the supermarket is? You got to figure at least twenty of those to make a decent-sized tub," I said, "and then this is a preindustrial society, the tub is wood and adds another five pounds minimum. So old Cant is swinging around a twenty-five pound sword. I had this one made up for demo purposes. Who wants to heft it?"

I stepped down from the small dais on which the table sat and offered the sword to a volunteer in the front row of the audience who obligingly made my point by dropping it, staggering under the weight, and even tottering around the front of the room trying to swish the blade back and forth.

"If the weight's evenly distributed, as in this model," I said, taking it back, "the blade is way too heavy for you to move it quickly; I could get under your guard and disembowel you with a ballpoint pen while you're fighting off incipient bursitis." I demonstrated on the guy who was tottering around with the sword and he obliged me by falling to the floor and writhing in dramatic but unconvincing death throes. "If that thirty pounds is mostly in the hilt," I went on, returning the sword to the table, "the balance is so far off you won't get a single slash in. And in any case, carrying that weight at the end of your arm is going to exhaust you before the fight's even started."

"Yeah, but don't you need something heavy to get through the armor?" somebody asked.

"Glad you asked that question." I picked up the borrowed morningstar and smiled, remembering how one just like this had smashed through the front rank of Rodo's Rowdies and spattered the second line with red and grey brain porridge, back in the Battle of Zolkir's Ford. Several people in the front row pushed their chairs back, away from me. I don't know why smiling makes Paper-Pushers so nervous.

I went into a demonstration of how the morningstar got its punching force not from an overweighted business end but from the velocity of the swing. This I could do on automatic; I'd given exactly the same talk to years of fresh-faced Bronze Bra Guild recruits doing Weapons Training 101. While I talked, I scanned the audience one last time and concluded that no, D.McConnell really hadn't showed up. So much for Norah's brilliant plan!

Better back up a little. I don't know if you noticed, but the moderator introduced me as "author of several stories," *not* as author of a wonderful, brilliant, funny, authentic book about a woman warrior's adventures on the Planet of the Piss-Pot Paper-Pushers. I'd finished that book last winter, shortly after the adventures it described, and had been trying without success to sell it ever since. A few short stories based on various little episodes from my Bronze Bra days had made it into the fantasy magazines, enough to earn my SFWA membership, but the book manuscript bounced back from major sf publishers so rapidly I was beginning to wonder if I'd accidentally printed it out on rubber. The last straw had been the prissy, self-righteous rejection letter I'd received from a new editor at Chimera. This D. McConnell had the gall to turn down my book because "it is well known to current feminist psychological theorists that women are naturally nonviolent and nurturing and hence could not have the true intuitive feeling for swordfighting and the joy in mindless violence displayed by this heroine. The style, however, is not entirely unappealing, and I would be willing to look at another book by Riva Konneva when she chooses to write about something she knows about from personal experience."

Believe me, this is *not* a letter to send to somebody who did twelve years' hard service in Duke Zolkir's Bronze Bra Guild. My first impulse was to fly to New York and demonstrate my expertise in swordfighting to D. McConnell in person, ending with a virtuoso demonstration of *fybilka*, or the art of executing an opponent by chopping inch-sized cubes of flesh off his bones. My second was to send him a letter (preferably printed on asbestos paper) detailing my military experience and possibly challenging him to single combat.

Norah Tibbs, a single-mother friend of mine who writes science fiction when she's not cranking out romance novels to pay the mortgage, said she had a better idea.

"Editors who've been chopped into stew meat can't buy books," she pointed out, "and as for the resume, he wouldn't believe it. Remember, most people here don't know that Dazau is real. You're trying to sell the book as *fantasy*, not autobiography. What you need to do is demonstrate your skills to him—"

"That," I fumed, "is what I said first, only you told me I shouldn't prepare him for an entry in the SalamanderCon Chili Cookoff."

"—in a non-destructive way," Norah went on firmly. "Look, this McConnell guy is new, nobody knows anything about him. He was probably brought in from one of the other branches after Singleday bought Chimera and Arbor bought Singleday. But he's coming to SalamanderCon, and they just sent out the preliminary schedule. You're on this panel." She pointed to a line that read, *"On Thud and Blunder: Homage to Poul Anderson. Tibbs*, Konneva, Crescent, Spooner."

"The italics mean I'm the moderator," she explained before I could ask, "which means I can do just about anything I want with the panel format. At least that's how I'm interpreting it. And—"

"Who's Poul Anderson? I didn't know you people had

the custom of homage, but I'm not about to put my hands between the hands of some baron I don't even know."

"It doesn't meant that kind of homage," Norah said. "Poul Anderson is a great science fiction writer—you really should read the literature in your own field, Riva— and he wrote an absolutely marvelous essay called, 'On Thud and Blunder,' about the stupid unrealistic things writers of sword-and-sorcery novels do. At least read the essay before SalamanderCon, okay? I'll lend you my copy."

"All right," I promised, "but I don't see . . ."

"Look at the schedule, stupid! Our panel's at one. McConnell's on the next panel in that same room, at two o'clock. And my friend Lee Justin just called from Oklahoma City, she's coming to SalamanderCon and she's having lunch with McConnell at noon that day. She's one of Chimera's biggest writers," Norah explained in a sort of footnote, "naturally the new editor wants to make her happy. He'll have an hour to kill between lunch and his panel, it'll be real easy for Lee to steer him into our panel to fill the time. And what will he see when he gets there?"

"A bunch of geeks sitting around a table talking about science fiction?" I suggested, just to show that I wasn't totally ignorant.

Norah gave me one of those you've-missed-the-point-again looks that make me feel a bit younger than my middle-school-age daughter Salla.

"He will see," she said, slowly and emphasizing every word, "Riva Konneva, in full battle gear, giving a stand-up demonstration of what's wrong with the fight scenes in most sword-and-sorcery novels, and how an experienced swordswoman would really do it. And if you in your padded chain mail, with Sasulau singing through the air, can't convince him you know what you're doing, then I give up."

"*Then* can I chop him into little pieces?"

"Only," Norah said firmly, "if he doesn't agree that you're an expert and that Arbor SingledayChimera should buy your book."

Then she'd gone off on a tangent about how Lee had missed SalamanderCon last year because she was busy having a baby and how much she was looking forward to seeing little Miles, and we'd sort of quit discussing the great plan.

Which was fine with me, because it actually sounded like a pretty good idea. It had gone on sounding like a good idea right up to thirty seconds before one o'clock today, when Norah admitted that she was looking flustered because Lee and McConnell hadn't shown up yet.

"His plane's late," she whispered. "Look, I'll do what I can. I'll put you last on the speakers list, okay? Give him time to get here."

She'd done that. But now it was a quarter till two, and although the fans seemed to be enjoying my part of the talk, it wasn't doing me any good at all with an editor who didn't even have the decency to show up for his part in the plan.

The door opened, Norah gasped, and I swung round to look at her. The morningstar, at the apex of its swing when I turned, thudded down on the table and turned it into two splintered halves under the shreds of the white linen cloth, which sagged down like a hammock into which the pile of paperbacks gently thudded, one by one.

The audience applauded wildly. I didn't have the heart to tell them it wasn't part of the planned show.

"Lee's here," Norah whispered.

I looked back at the opening door. A tall, slim woman with long black braids was trying to sidle into the room, but she was hampered by a large baby in a sling. Behind her came a couple of men I didn't know. The tall lean one was wearing an Army fatigue jacket two sizes too

big for his shoulders and covered with insignia that had
a home-brewed look; the short square one had acne,
bulging tattooed arms, and a shiny bald head. They
weren't exactly my idea of sophisticated representatives
of the New York publishing industry, but I recognized
Lee Justin from her book-jacket pictures and by squinting I could just make out the letters D—M—on the
tall weirdo's name tag. Great! Norah's friend had produced McConnell just in time!

I decided to use my best prop after all. I'd gotten
the idea from that Poul Anderson essay Norah insisted
I read, and a perfect example had come up on page ten
of Mihlhauser's *Spears of Thunfungoria*. My com-
punctions about using such an abysmally crummy book
as panel-fodder vanished. So it was like spearing a
sleeping wizard; so what? That's actually the best time
to impale them, if you don't want to risk spending the
rest of your life in the Reptiles and Amphibians section
of Baron Rodograunnizo's private menagerie. And I
didn't have much time left in which to make an impression on McConnell.

All the best advice to public speakers recommends
that you fix your attention on one member of the
audience to establish that sense of personal connection,
and that's just what I did. My eyes never left McConnell
as I stepped back behind the shattered table, dropped
the morningstar, and pulled the ten-pound rib roast out
of its supermarket bag.

"One of the books I read in preparation for this
panel," I said, holding up *Spears of Thunfungoria*,
"actually has the hero cutting off an enemy's head with
a single stroke. This sounds good, but has anybody here
actually tried it?"

"I bet you could do it with one of those Japanese
samurai swords," somebody else opined, "you know, the
ones that they make them with several thousand folds
of steel . . ."

"The ones that they cost several hundred thousand bucks?" Susan Crescent interrupted. "Hey, I was in the Marines, buddy, and let me tell you, even the U.S. Army's defense budget doesn't provide the average grunt with that class of equipment."

"Susan's absolutely right," I said, "and certainly your average self-employed mercenary can't afford it, much less a . . ." I thumbed through *Spears of Thunfungoria* in search of the first description of the hero, " . . . *a half-naked barbarian tribal warrior from the frigid north, mounted on a hirsute Arctic stallion, clad only in a kilt made from the hide of his first saber-toothed tiger kill and flaunting the crude weapons of his fatherland*. That's on page eight," I added, "and this head-lopping occurs on page ten. He doesn't exactly have time to get high-technology weapons."

"And if he's riding a stallion in a kilt and no underwear, he's gotta have saddle sores like you wouldn't believe," Susan interjected.

McConnell shifted in his seat and crossed and uncrossed his legs. One foot beat out a nervous tattoo against the carpeted floor. His eyes twitched in their sockets, showing whites laced with red veins. All that espresso coffee they drink in New York must be pretty hard on the system.

"Now Sasulau, here, is worth a dozen of your average mercenary's swords," I said, whisking the blade back and forth so that everybody could admire Sasulau's finely honed edge and perfect balance. "Brian, if you'll just hold this rib roast up by the attached string, I'll show you what happens when you swing at a big piece of meat that's not supported by a chopping block."

"Hey," McConnell interrupted in a voice that wavered between squeaky and gravelly, "we're talking human beings here, lady. Gort killed *people*, not rib roasts. This book is about real fighting and real men, not about some kind of word game for Jews and queers." He leaned forward and emphasized his point with a stabbing finger while the musclebound hulk beside him nodded approval.

Somehow I'd expected a New York editor to have smoother manners and sound less like an escapee from an Aryan Power survivalist camp. But I was unwillingly impressed that he'd done so much reading in the field that he'd already worked his way down to *Spears of Thunfungoria*. On the other hand—depressing thought— maybe that was what he thought good sword and sorcery novels ought to be like.

Well, I'd just have to show him how wrong he was.

"Human beings," I said, smiling sweetly in his direction, "*are* just big pieces of meat unsupported by a chopping block, if you think about it from a swordswoman's point of view. Part of the art of swordfighting is to deal with what's actually in front of you, not what might be convenient for your purple prose. Brian?"

Looking just a tad green around the gills, Brian stuck both arms out and tried to hold the rib roast as far away from his body as possible, dangling at the end of the string I'd wrapped around it. He must not have much confidence in my aim. I'd better move fast; his arms were already trembling with the effort.

I backed up, swished Sasulau through the air a few times, put the full power of my right shoulder and a good full-body follow-through into my swing . . . and got Sasulau stuck in the middle of the rib roast. Brian staggered but managed to remain upright.

"That," I said, eyes on McConnell, "is what happens if you try the kind of slash-and-thud fighting described in *Spears of Thunfungoria*."

His mouth moved and his fingers twitched, but he didn't say anything this time. "And what would really happen next would not be that my enemy would topple over decapitated, but that Brian here would eviscerate me while my sword was stuck in this piece of meat."

Brian looked a bit doubtful about this plan, but I didn't give him time to voice any objections. "Now, Brian, just put the rib roast down on the table—no, not the broken one, the other one—and I'll show you how easily Sasulau can go through this with proper support, just in case any of you suspected I wasn't using a real sword for that demonstration."

All it took this time was a flick of the wrist; Sasulau was sharp and thirsty. She sliced through the meat and bones as if they were molded of lard, stopping a hairsbreadth short of the tabletop to protect her edge.

There was another round of applause from the audience, noticeably excluding McConnell. His hands were working as if he wanted to put them around my neck. So much for the plan. He was obviously too pissed off at being contradicted to be impressed by my experience. And there wasn't time to mend matters; a con gofer stuck his head through the door making cut-throat signs, and Norah announced that we were almost out of time, had to clear out for the next panel, and Riva could take maybe one question before we left.

To my short-lived joy, McConnell was the first one with his hand up. "You might not realize this," he began with a nasty sneer, "but Gort is a member of a superior Aryan race that hasn't been weakened by mongelization and crossbreeding with Jews and Blacks and Spics. Naturally you don't understand the difference this makes, just like anybody else in the publishing industry, it's so full of Jews a decent white man doesn't stand a chance. . . ."

Lee Justin moved as far away from him as the close-packed seating would allow. She patted her baby's head and concentrated fiercely on counting his fingers, probably to keep herself from telling her new editor that he made her sick at her stomach. Having given up hope of making a favorable impression, I didn't feel any need for such restraint. But I was confused about why he was trashing his own industry.

"Surely, Mr. McConnell, as an editor yourself, you realize—"

"I am *not* an editor!" he interrupted me in turn. "Editors are blood-sucking ghouls who eat their young, haven't you figured that out yet?"

Actually I had begun to suspect something of the sort, but I hadn't expected to hear it from the guy I had been working so hard at impressing.

"But . . . aren't you the D. McConnell who's with ArborSingledayChimera?"

Beside him, Norah's friend Lee was shaking her head and making the same sort of cut-your-throat-and-shut-up gestures the timekeeper at the door had made. Susan Crescent grabbed her briefcase and said something about another appointment. Most of the audience was leaving too, and I couldn't blame them. This exchange could hardly be of gripping interest to anybody except me.

"I certainly am not," the guy I'd been thinking of as McConnell said. "And you know it. It was all a plot, wasn't it?"

"Well . . ." Okay, there had been a little scheming and plotting going on, but if he wasn't D. McConnell, what did it have to do with him?

"A plot to humiliate me!" Little flecks of saliva sprayed from his narrow mouth.

"Huh?"

The bald man next to him, the one with the bulging steroid muscles, acne, and tattoos, said, "This here is Dwight Mihlhauser, lady. He's the guy who wrote *Spears of Thunfungoria*. And it wasn't real nice of you to make fun of his book when he was right here in the audience, was it now? Little darkie girlies oughta learn better manners than that." He leered in a way that made me want to swing the morningstar into his yellowing teeth. It made Brian Spooner decide that it was time to get to his next panel. Quite a number of people shared that opinion; there were only about six of us left in the room now, and one of those was a dark-haired girl who had just come in. She gave Lee a little wave and seated herself in the front row, probably waiting for the next panel to start.

"Editors never really read manuscripts by an unknown," Mihlhauser announced. "It's impossible for a newcomer to get a fair chance. I know if anybody from a major publishing house would read *Spears of Thunfungoria* all the way through—if anybody would—they'd recognize my genius and I wouldn't be reduced to self-publishing."

That explained why I'd never heard of the publisher. "MiDPublications," was just a fancy name for "Vanity Press."

"I read it all the way through," I pointed out.

At that moment Brian finally made it out the door, hot on the heels of most of the panel audience. He let the door slam behind him when he left, which wasn't such a great idea. Dwight Mihlhauser looked around and realized that his audience had dwindled alarmingly. "Nobody else leave this room!" he shouted, and leapt to his feet.

Lee Justin leapt with him. They seemed to be tangled together in some way that involved Lee's baby sling. After a moment's confused wrestling, Dwight had the baby, Lee had the sling, and she was going for his eyes with all ten fingernails. His bald buddy grabbed her by the wrists long enough for Dwight to hit her on the chin, hard, with his free hand. She slumped down between the chairs where I couldn't see her. Norah started for her, but Dwight squeezed the baby so hard that little Miles let out a squawk of fright. "Nobody move or the kid gets it!" he shouted.

We all stood absolutely still.

He jerked his head at me. "Okay. You, little lady, down among the audience. You too, fat broad," he told

Norah. "The guys are running this show now." We followed his directions, taking seats in the front row next to the newcomer. Norah looked furious. I tried to look cowed. He'd made me leave Sasulau on the table, but I wasn't completely out of options yet.

Mihlhauser strutted to the stage, holding the baby under his arm like a football, and grabbed the plain-paper edition of *Spears of Thunfungoria*. "I'm gonna have a fair reading now," he told us, "and nobody's gonna interrupt. Got that?"

"The next panel—" the girl beside me started to say.

"Skull, I want you to secure the exits," Mihlhauser snapped. "Now!" He lifted the book reverently in one hand and rather awkwardly opened it to the first page. I was grateful that the baby seemed too stunned to struggle; no telling what would happen if he gave Mihlhauser a problem. We had to get that kid out of his arms, but how?

Skull swaggered back from the barred doors and sat down beside the dark-haired girl, arms folded. She shrank a little from him, which brought our heads close enough together that we could, carefully, murmur to each other without attracting Mihlhauser's attention.

"*Nebulous clouds of crepuscular twilight gleamed green in the thunderous sky as Gort the Barbarian wended his way down from the northern mountains,*" Mihlhauser began.

The girl beside me shuddered. "Does it all go on like that?"

"Nope," I said. "It gets worse."

Mihlhauser raised his voice a little. "*In the decadent metropolis of Thunfungoria, the lasciviously apathetic minions of corruption's own queen, Agagaba the Diabolically Decadent, hustled and bustled in the marketplace with odious greed.* I hope you all appreciate that poetic alliteration," he adddd, "*hustled* and *bustled*? Pretty good, huh? I've got a real way with words."

"Yeah, and Torquemada had a real way with suspected heretics," the girl beside me murmured. "He doesn't even know the difference between alliteration and rhyme!"

" 'Terminate your nefarious transactions,' Gort bellowed baldly, 'for Gort the Grand and Illustrious has shown up out of the north to requite the misdoings perpetrated upon your inculpable prey!' He spurred his stallion over the prostrate bodies of the apprehensive priest-traders and with the tip of his sword sliced the shackles from an undraped slave girl whose bosom quiverered with ecstasy at the scrutiny of this puissant hero. Both her bosoms, actually."

The girl beside me sighed. "Somebody has to stop this. Out of respect for the English language, if nothing else. Mr. Mihlhauser!" she called out.

Mihlhauser stopped in the middle of a leering description of the slave-girl's navel. "Do I have to warn you again? Want to see me play baby-toss with this kid and the costume lady's prop sword?"

Sasulau gave an ominous hum as he reached for her, and I shuddered. She was angry; she wanted blood. And she might take the baby as her sacrifice. I was never entirely sure about Sasulau's ethics.

"Mr. Mihlhauser," the girl went on calmly, "I'm an editor with Arbor SingledayChimera, and what I've heard of your work so far has made a very strong impression on me."

Mihlhauser absentmindedly rested the baby on his shoulder. Miles gurgled happily and drooled down the writer's shirt collar. "It has?"

"An unforgettable impression," she said with a barely concealed wince. "I might go so far as to say I've never before heard prose with the rhythms and cadences you bring to it."

Mihlhauser squinted down at her name tag. "Hey. You're shitting me. Chimera already turned this book down."

"That," the girl said, "was before Singleday bought Chimera and Arbor bought Singleday and they brought *me* in. If you'll send your manuscript back to us, Mr. Mihlhauser, marked Attn.: Dacia McConnell, I can promise you that your work will get the attention it deserves."

"Nauzu's Blood! *You're* D. McConnell?" I exclaimed. "Why weren't you here half an hour earlier?"

"My plane was late. Don't distract me. If that jerk hurts Miles, one of my best writers will be too upset to produce for months. We can't afford to lose Lee Justin." She turned back to the front of the room. "How about it, Mr. Mihlhauser? Or—" She snapped her fingers. "Say! I've got an even better idea! Why don't I just take that copy of your book now? I can read it tonight and we can talk contract terms tomorrow. I happen to know there's an opening on our spring list."

Mihlhauser teetered back and forth from the balls of his toes to his heels in an agonized semi-dance of decision. Miles seemed to enjoy the movement; he grabbed the collar he'd been dribbling on and began gumming it like a puppy going after a large soup bone.

"Naah," Mihlhauser decided finally. "Why tie myself down to one house? You can listen to the reading like everybody else, then you can join the bidding. Hey, Skull, you tell those geeks outside I want this room's mikes patched into the sound system for the whole hotel. Let's give everybody a fair chance!"

While Skull negotiated through the locked doors, Mihlhauser hefted the baby up higher on his shoulder, reopened the yellow paperback and resumed his reading. Dacia McConnell slumped down in her chair and sighed in frustration. On my other side, Norah alternated between rubbing her aching head, craning her neck to see if Lee had sat up yet, and staring hungrily at the baby in Mihlhauser's arms.

We were well into the first dumb fight scene, where

Gort skewers a couple of city guards through the heart, when a glimmering of an idea came to me. "Mr. Mihlhauser, that's not such a great technique. You know, the heart is an awfully small target. Also you've got to get through the rib cage. Me, I prefer to take them in the abdomen. It's a nice big soft target, and any fighter knows how much a gut wound hurts, so even if you don't get them the first time they're running scared and they'll probably forget to protect their throats. Slash the throat and you've got them. Or if your employer wants them brought back alive, go after the legs and try to cripple them." That point was engraved on my memory; I'd once had a *very* embarrassing discussion with Duke Zolkir after a call Trans-Forwarded from the PTA had distracted me in the middle of a swordfight so that I forgot to keep any of the thieves I was after alive long enough to stand trial.

Mihlhauser gave me a cold, reptilian glance. "Gort," he said, "is the world's greatest swordsman. For him to pierce an opponent through the heart is child's play."

"Oh, yeah? You just don't know how hard it is. I bet you've never tried."

"I've done my research!" he snapped.

"And I've *lived* mine."

Dacia McConnel grabbed my leather wrist-guard. "Are you crazy? Don't make him mad. He might hurt the baby."

"Trust me," I whispered, "I know what I'm doing."

Mihlhauser had resumed reading, but I knew I'd get another chance to badger him in a minute. Dacia seemed smart and cool; she could help me here. "Look," I said, barely moving my lips, "this is what I'm trying to get him to do. And then this is what'll happen next . . ."

"How do you know?"

"Because," I said smugly, "those who can, do . . . and I *can*. Then when *this* happens, you'll be in a perfect place to . . ."

I barely had time to outline the plan to her before Mihlhauser had reached the next stupid fight scene.

"Uh, Mr. Mihlhauser? Excuse me, but it's not that easy to pierce chain mail. Sure, you can bruise your opponent pretty badly, especially if you keep hacking away at the same spot, but actually getting a blade through is another matter."

"Lady, will you *stop interrupting*? I've studied the matter in great detail, and . . ."

"Let's have a demonstration, then." I stood up, wriggling slightly so as to get maximum jingle from my chain-mail corselet and divided skirt. "I'm willing to come up on stage and let you try and skewer me."

"Well . . ."

"You can even use that big heavy sword," I suggested, pointing at the specially weighted prop sword, "just like the one Gort would have had." I took two steps up to the dais on which the tables sat while I was talking. "And all I ask for to defend myself is this skinny little thing." As soon as my hand touched Sasulau, her joyous hum transmitted itself through my body. She knew, now, that she'd drink blood. And she was thirsty; it had been too long since she'd been drawn for anything but practice bouts.

"Or are you scared to fight a girrrl?" I added with a teasing pout and another strategic wriggle.

"What's in it for me?" Mihlhauser demanded. "You're not an editor; what can you do for me after I win?"

"*If* you win," I said, winking, "you can name your own reward, sweetie."

That decided him. He thrust baby Miles down from the dais for his buddy Skull to hold and assumed a fighting pose, holding up the weighted prop sword in both hands. Even that way, his muscles quivered with the strain. "Here I am, baby," he called, "come and get me!"

I sidled around him, trying to look scared. "No, that's

not the way it works. Aren't you supposed to try and poke me?"

Skull guffawed. "Oh, he'll do that later, little lady!"

Mihlhauser raised the sword over his head, preparing for a downward swipe. I'd counted on that; there wasn't much else you could do with something that heavy. If this had been a real fight, I'd have had Sasulau in and out of his skinny gut before he knew what happened to him. But I really didn't want to disembowel somebody in the middle of SalamanderCon. It might make a bad impression on my editor. I sliced into one of his thighs instead.

It wasn't that much of a cut; the best I'd been hoping for was that blood loss would slow him down so that I'd be able to take him out without doing too much more damage. But he yowled, dropped the sword and clapped one hand to his bleeding leg.

"Tell your buddy to give the baby back," I said, "and we're even."

"That *hurt!*" Mihlhauser complained.

I guess he hadn't done all that much research.

"Well? It'll hurt more if I have to do it again, I promise you." I waggled Sasulau close enough for him to hear her thirsty song.

Mihlhauser's left eyelid developed a fast nervous tic. "Put that damn thing down and we've got a deal."

I laid Sasulau back on the table—I wasn't going to sheathe her again until I'd cleaned her—and reached out as if to shake hands on our "deal."

"Look out, Riva!" Norah cried as his hand came up again from his hip, holding something small and black. "He's cheating!"

My half-opened hand met his and opened a slash of red across the wrist where my secondary blade, razor-sharp and small enough to fit in the palm of one hand, just touched him. The black thing fell to the floor and exploded in a burst of sound that temporarily deafened me. I could see Norah's lips moving again; then something solid and heavy fell on my back.

Perfect.

A glance to my right showed me Dacia McConnell with Miles in her arms, backing slowly down the aisle away from the fight. Good girl.

I twisted slightly to one side, grabbed a massive wrist and used Skull's own weight and momentum to flip him around and over. A crunching sound as he hit the floor suggested that the move might have dislocated his shoulder. Certainly he didn't appear to be in any hurry to get up again. As for Mihlhauser, he was crouched under the shattered table, moaning and nursing his two superficial cuts and crying for someone to get the medics.

I wiped Sasulau's blade on the tablecloth and sheathed her just as Dacia reached and opened the double doors at the far end of the room.

We had a bit of confusion there, what with cops, EMT's, and con organizers all pouring in at once. With a couple of competent women directing things, though, it didn't take long to get priorities straight. A groggy Lee was reunited with Miles, the cops decided to accompany Mihlhauser and Skull to Seton Emergency, and the captive audience departed in all directions to unload the story of their ordeal on the nearest willing ear. It seemed the panel Dacia was to've appeared on had been postponed "due to unavailability of meeting room," which I thought was an excellent example of the Paper-Pushers' art of telling the truth in a totally misleading way. So after Norah hugged me and dashed off to look after Lee and Miles, Dacia McConnell and I were left grinning at each other in a messy but momentarily empty room.

"That was a good idea after all," Dacia allowed. "How did you know Skull would leap in to help his buddy?"

"They always do," I said.

"How did you know Mihlhauser was going to cheat?"

"I didn't . . . but *I* always do. Fighting isn't a game;

it's about winning. And sometimes," I added, thinking of a drooling baby, "it's really important to win."

"And you knew Skull would hand the baby to me?"

"I figured in the excitement of the moment, he'd naturally expect a woman to hold the baby, and you were the closest one. After all," I quoted from her letter, "most people think women are . . . how did it go . . . 'naturally nonviolent and nurturing.' "

Dacia frowned slightly, as though she knew she'd heard those words before and couldn't think where. "Anyway," she said crisply, shaking off her momentary confusion, "I think we made a great team."

"I think so too," I agreed, "and I hope we can go on doing it."

"You want to go through something like this *again*?"

"No, I want to sell you a book. Remember the manuscript you rejected because you didn't believe women knew anything about fighting?"

Dacia's eyes traveled to my name tag. "Riva Konneva . . . Uh-oh."

"I think uh-oh," I agreed, letting one hand rest on Sasulau's hilt. "Do you believe I know something about fighting now?"

Dacia nodded slowly.

"And you did say you had an opening on your spring list."

"That was a bargaining point in a hostage situation," she protested.

"Well," I said, moving slightly so that I stood between her and the door, "I'd hate to think that a writer's best chance of being published is to take hostages rather than to negotiate in a civilized manner."

"I'm sure we can work something out," Dacia said quickly.

The hotel staff showed up then to clean out the room for the banquet, so she was never in any danger, not really. But we did establish a mutually agreeable deal.

I had to use some stupid pen name because she thought "Riva Konneva" was too hard for most Americans to pronounce, but they bought the book and published it. It's out in the stores right now, in fact.

You *are* going to buy a copy, aren't you? I'd hate to have to argue with you about it. Surely we can work something out.

EPILOGUE
Yes! We Did Say Chicks!

Adam-Troy Castro

On the fourth day of his Quest, beset by a raging storm, the brave Sir Rodney sought refuge in a humble barn.

He slept on a bed of straw, woke early the next morning, donned his battle armor, and resumed his treacherous journey.

But even before he climbed the next ridge, he began to fidget uncomfortably.

He frowned. Twitched. Looked first startled and then embarrassed.

Whereupon he returned to the barn, laboriously removed his armor, and coaxed out six recent hatchlings, who had fallen asleep in his tunic during the night.

This was not a very promising start to the day.

But he was not the first brave knight forced to contend with . . . Chicks in Chainmail.

302

About the Authors

WALTER VANCE AWSTEN is a retired high school teacher and sometime essayist who took up writing fantasy stories because in his opinion it beats the heck out of golf or soap operas as a way to pass the time. His work has previously appeared in *Adventures into the Twilight Zone*, and like everyone else, he's working on a novel; he took time off from it to collaborate with his former student Christina Briley. He lives in a decaying farmhouse in rural New Jersey, alone except for his three cats—Adolf, Hermann, and Josef.

MARGARET BALL lives in Austin, Texas with her husband, two children, three cats, one dog, and a constantly changing assortment of ferrets, turtles, and other small animals. She has a B.A. in mathematics and a Ph.D. in linguistics from the University of Texas. After graduation she taught at UCLA and then spent several years honing her science fiction and fantasy writing skills by designing computer software and making inflated promises about its capacities. When not writing she plays the flute, makes strange beaded and quilted objects, and feeds the pets.

MARK BOURNE has sold fiction to *Asimov's Science Fiction, Fantasy & Science Fiction*, and anthologies such as *Full Spectrum 5, Sherlock Holmes in Orbit, Alternate Tyrants*, and of course the original *Chicks in Chainmail*. Novels are coming—honest. Wielding a barbarian passion for astronomy, Mark has provided nonfiction articles for magazines and scripts for videos, TV, science museum exhibits, and planetarium shows nationwide. He's merrily married to artist Elizabeth Lawhead Bourne, who—like Xora—looks *great* in leather. You can find him online at http://www.sff.net/people/MBourne.

CHRISTINA BRILEY was born, raised, and still resides in the Greater Boston area. The third of four daughters, she grew up in a large, old house full of books and cats. After a brief, unfinished college stint as a clothing and textiles major, and a long, decidedly finished stint as a wife, she now lives, with her three children and two cats, in an even older, larger house where she makes wedding gowns for a living. New to the writing business, she tends to write what she knows, which, in addition to cats, wedding gowns, parenting, and old houses, includes dancing, vintage stuff, obnoxious husbands, and, at long last, really wonderful love affairs.

ADAM-TROY CASTRO's list of short story credits is considerably longer than his contribution to this anthology, which by itself isn't saying much, but still. He is currently hard at work on a Spider-Man trilogy scheduled to see the light of day in 1999.

KEITH R. A. DECANDIDO left home at the age of sixteen to pursue a career in fisheries, but came back home an hour later when he realized he forgot to pack a lunch. He left home again at the age of twenty-one to pursue a career in publishing, where he's had a bit more success. His editorial accomplishments range from the anthologies *OtherWere* and *Urban Nightmares* to editing a highly successful line of super hero novels to helping bring Alfred Bester back into print. With José R. Nieto he was written a Spider-Man novel called *Venom's Wrath,* which will be unleashed on a panting reading public in the fall of 1998.

DORANNA DURGIN spent her childhood filling notebooks first with stories and art, and then with novels. After obtaining a degree in wildlife illustration and environmental education, she spent a number of years deep in the Appalachian Mountains. When she emerged, it was as a writer who found herself irrevocably tied to the natural world and its creatures. *Dun Lady's Jess*, Doranna's first published fantasy novel, received the 1995 Compton Crook/Stephen Tall award for the best first book in the fantasy, science fiction, and horror genres. The novel *Touched by Magic* followed, and *Jess's* sequel, *Changespell*, came out in February 1997. Doranna lives in upstate New York with an old hound and his irrepressible Cardigan companion, and a young Lipizzan gelding who thinks too much.

LAURA FRANKOS has published a mystery novel, *St. Oswald's Niche* (Ivy Books), and has had science-fiction and fantasy short fiction appear in *Analog*, *Chicks in Chainmail*, *Alien Pregnant by Elvis*, and elsewhere. She is married to writer Harry Turtledove. They have collaborated on three daughters.

MARINA FRANTS was born in the Soviet Union back when there was one, but left in a huff when she realized that no Soviet publisher had a decent fantasy line. Emigrating to the U.S., she went on to achieve a Master's in Electrical Engineering from MIT. A former book reviewer for *Publishers Weekly*, she has also written for *The Journal of Irreproducible Results*, *Wilson Library Bulletin*, and *Horror*. Her short fiction has appeared in the magazines *Pulphouse* and *Dreams of Decadence* and in the anthology *OtherWere: Stories of Transformation*. In her copious spare time (hah!) she is working on a fantasy novel and also scuba dives and is an underwater photographer. She always wanted to write a Baba Yaga story, and is grateful to Esther for giving her and Keith the chance to write one.

ESTHER FRIESNER is still at large.

LAURA ANNE GILMAN has been described as "the kind of person you see on a made-for-tv movie, the sweet co-ed who turns out to be a psycho killer." She denies this completely, of course, and on the advice of her lawyer. Her short fiction has appeared in the magazines *Amazing Stories* and *Dreams of Decadence*, and the anthologies *Lammas Night, Highwaymen: Robbers and Rogues,* and *Urban Nightmares*, among others. Her story "Exposure" for the anthology *Blood Muse* was reprinted in Oxford University Press's *Blood Thirst: 100 Years of Vampire Fiction* in 1997, and another story, "Clean Up Your Room" from *Don't Forget Your Space Suit, Dear*, was reprinted in a high school text book, where she can corrupt the young at will. She also co-edited the anthology *OtherWere: Stories of Transformation.*

ELIZABETH MOON is a native Texan who did not grow up on a ranch (she wishes), never owned an oil well (ditto), and wasn't a cheerleader with big hair (ditto, NOT.) To compensate for these fundamental gaps in a Texas girlhood, she joined the Marines, programmed computers, got elected to public office, worked on a rural ambulance crew, and finally started finishing the stories she wrote. Her novel *Remnant Population* was a Hugo Nominee in 1997. Her most recent novel is *Once a Hero*; a collection of short works, *Phases*, is forthcoming.

JODY LYNN NYE lists her main career as "spoiling cats." She lives northwest of Chicago with two of the above and her husband, SF author Bill Fawcett. Jody is a graduate of Loyola University of Chicago. Before going on to writing full time, she worked in a variety of jobs, including as a technical operator/manager at a TV station, and wrote mystery games. Among the novels Jody has written are: *Mythology 101, Mythology Abroad,* and *Higher Mythology, Taylor's Ark and Medicine Show.* Jody also wrote *The Dragonlover's*

Guide to Pern and has collaborated with Anne McCaffrey on *The Death of Sleep*, and three other novels. Her newest works include a humorous contemporary fantasy, *The Magic Touch* and *The Ship Errant* (Baen Books), a solo sequel to *The Ship Who Won*.

When not occupied in petting cats or writing fiction, Jody reads, travels, does calligraphy, or gardens.

STEVEN PIZIKS is an English teacher in southern Michigan, where he lives with his wife and son. His short stories have appeared in *Marion Zimmer Bradley's Fantasy Magazine* and *Sword and Sorceress*. He just sold his first novel to Baen Books. When not writing, he plays the folk harp, dabbles in professional oral storytelling, and spends more time on-line than is probably good for him. This story is a sort of prequel to "Hoard" (*Sword and Sorceress IX*), the first story he ever sold. "I always rather wondered exactly how one convinces a dragon to change vocations. Now I know."

Former Chick ELIZABETH ANN SCARBOROUGH does not wear chainmail, but does like both mail and jewelry, some of which has chains. She is a former Army Nurse and served in Vietnam. Her novel, *The Healer's War*, was based on this experience and won the 1989 Nebula. She is the author of 21 novels, including the collaborative *Powers* trilogy with Anne McCaffrey, and numerous short stories. She lives in a log cabin in a Victorian seaport on the Washington coast, and is ably assisted in all of her endeavors by four feline associates.

JAN STIRLING writes, "When I was thirty-eight they came out with a statistic that women my age were more likely to be killed by terrorists than married for the first time. Along came Steve, who proposed, rescuing me from those hypothetical terrorists. We married, I changed my name and moved to another country (Canada), thus beginning a whole new life.

Within two years I tried writing for the very first time (this happens to a lot of SF&F spousal units, must be something in the air) and two years later made my first sale to *Chicks in Chainmail.*"

S. M. STIRLING. Stephen Michael Stirling: Born September 30, 1953 in Metz, Alsace, France. (Or Germany, depending on who you ask.) Father born and raised in Newfoundland of Anglo-Scottish background; mother born in Lancashire, England, and raised in Lima, Peru and Halifax, Nova Scotia. Residence: France, England, Canada, U.S.A., Kenya, several years each. Temporary residence in Italy, Israel, Tanzania, South Africa, Spain, Mexico. Education: Honors BA in History/English, Carleton University; LL.B., Osgoode Hall. Employment: farm, secretarial, bouncer (very temporarily). Have never practiced law due to moral scruples. Currently full-time novelist and husband of Janet Catherine Stirling (since 1988 for both). Hobbies: History, literature, anthropology. Brown belt, second dan, Tao Zen Chuan karate.

HARRY TURTLEDOVE writes science fiction and fantasy, much of it alternate history and historical fantasy. He has won a Hugo Award for Best Novella and has been a Nebula finalist. Recent books include *Fox and Empire* (Baen), *How Few Remain* (Del Rey), and, with Richard Dreyfuss, *The Two Georges* (Tor). He is married to author Laura Frankos.

LAWRENCE WATT-EVANS taught himself to read at age five in order to read a comic book story called "Last of the Tree People," and began writing his own stories a couple of years later. Eventually a fantasy novel actually sold, and since then several more novels and dozens of stories have made it into print, covering a wide range of fantasy, science fiction, and horror. His short story, "Why I Left Harry's All-Night Hamburgers," won the Hugo award in 1988; he served two years as president of the Horror Writers Association. His most recent novel is entitled *Touched by the Gods*, and his funniest, written in collaboration with Esther Friesner, is *Split Heirs*. He lives in the Maryland suburbs of Washington, D.C., with his wife, a son, a daughter, a cat, and a gecko.

K. D. WENTWORTH lives in Tulsa and teaches 4th grade at a local elementary school, but is considering giving up teaching to raise chinchillas because they have better tempers and have been known to clean up after themselves occasionally. In her secret life as a writer, she has sold over thirty short stories to such publications as *F&SF, Alfred Hitchcock's, Return to the Twilight Zone*, and *Realms of Fantasy*. She also has three novels out from Del Rey—*The Imperium Game, Moonspeaker*, and *House of Moons*.

SARAH ZETTEL figures most of her quirks can be explained by the fact that she's a genetic Californian and a third-generation SF fan. She has, to date, committed fifteen short stories in three genre flavors: SF, fantasy, and horror. She has also completed two SF novels, *Reclamation* and *Fool's War*, and is hard at work (really, really hard, honest) on her third.